The End of the Beginning

Tulloch at War
Book 3

Malcolm Archibald

For Cathy

"CUIMHNICHIBH   NA   SUINN   NACH   MAIREANN MAIRIDH AN CLIU BEO GU BRATH"

"Remember the heroes who are no more: their renown will live for ever."

Taken from the memorial to the Cameron Highlanders, Scottish National War Memorial, Edinburgh Castle.

"Now this is not the end. It is not even the beginning of the end. But it is, perhaps, the end of the beginning."

Winston Churchill

Glossary

Alex: Alexandria, Egypt
Blighty: Great Britain
Blue, the: The desert
Bundook: Rifle
Conchie: Conscientious Objectors: men who refused to fight on religious or
    conscientious grounds.
Decko: Look
Doover: Dugout
Duffy: Fight, skirmish
Get tae: Go away!
Get to Freuchie: Go away!
Gin ye daur: If you dare.
Glasshouse: Military prison
Gorgie Road: Street in Edinburgh near Heart of Midlothian's football ground
HE: High Explosive
Hibees: Hibernian, an Edinburgh football team.
Jildi: Quickly
Jock: Scottish soldier
Just the Job: Very good
Kip: Sleep
L.P: Listening Post
LRDG: Long Range Desert Group
NCO: Non-Commissioned Officer: men above the rank of private but below
    officer rank.
O.P: Observation Post
On the trot: Deserting
PBI: Poor Bloody Infantry
Pongo: Royal naval term for a soldier.
Portee: Truck with six-pounder gun mounted on the back. The gun can also be
    dismounted for ground fire.
Quad: Vehicle used to tow artillery
RHA: Royal Horse Artillery
RSM: Regimental Sergeant Major
Rummel them up: Shake them up; disturb them
Saint Barbara: Patron saint of artillerymen
Scrappy: Scrap metal merchant
Sangar: Simple fortification built of loose stones.

Glossary

Stonk: Artillery barrage
Stour: Dust, dirt.
Wallahs: People

Chapter One

our Platoon rose, some crouching, others moving quickly as Tulloch ran, zig-zagging, for the Italian position. The hill steepened further as he advanced, so he leaned forward for purchase on the slope. To his right, Hardie was leading a dozen men, with Atkins fifty yards to his left. Tulloch heard the insane chatter of another Italian machine gun, saw a man stagger and felt something smash against his shoe.

They've hit me.

Tulloch looked down and felt another thump as if somebody had punched him in the ribs. He glanced down, grunted in surprise, and collapsed.

"Sir!"

Lieutenant Douglas Tulloch of the Lothian Rifles shook himself awake, escaping from the recurrent nightmare that haunted his dreams. "I'm awake," he said.

"You're duty officer, sir," Private Hood reminded, standing at attention beside the cot. Middle-sized and slight, Hood was a veteran soldier who tried to be an efficient batman.

"Thank you, Hood." Tulloch swung himself off his cot and buckled on his belt. He checked his revolver was loaded and turned his boots upside down to ensure no scorpions were lurking inside. Although Hood had cleaned and polished the boots the previous evening, a trickle of sand emerged. Sand was everywhere, on every surface, every bite of food, in everybody's hair, ears and in the air, carried by the ever-present wind.

Tulloch slipped outside the tent, with the desert sky scattered with stars and a scimitar moon low on the horizon. Most of the battalion was resting, with only the sentries on duty. Tulloch saw the outline of their steel helmets against the sky and heard their muttered comments as they huddled into greatcoats against the cold of the night. The old sweats were accustomed to the plunging temperatures that marked the dark hours, but the difference between night and day always surprised the replacements, men who had not yet got their knees brown.

Tulloch saw a flare rise far to the north and heard a brief stutter of artillery, quickly stilled. Silence returned, save for the soft hiss of wind and sand.

Captain Muirhead, a hard-bitten veteran who commanded C Company, nodded briefly on his walk to his dugout. "It's all yours, Tulloch. Nothing to report."

Tulloch watched Muirhead slide under the sandbagged entrance of his dugout and stepped to the duty sergeant.

"Anything happening, Paterson?"

Sergeant Paterson, a relative newcomer from Easthouses in Midlothian, saluted. "All quiet, sir. We had some shooting to the north, but nothing serious."

"Thank you, Paterson," Tulloch replied. He dismissed the recurring nightmare of his final day at the Battle of Keren and began his rounds. The Lothian Rifles were twenty miles behind the lines, acting as a mobile reserve in case the Axis powers broke through the Allied position at Gazala.

Lieutenant Kennedy, another relatively new addition to the Lothians, stiffened to attention as Tulloch approached.

"There's no need for that, Kennedy," Tulloch told him. "We're the same rank, dammit. Anything to report?"

"Nothing at all, sir," Kennedy said.

"I'll take over now," Tulloch said. "You grab some kip while you can." He watched as Kennedy marched away, his boots crunching across the sand.

Tulloch sighed, wondering if this damned war would ever end. It was May 1942, and they had been fighting since September 1939, nearly three years. Britain and her allies had campaigned in North and East Africa for the best part of two of these years. The Allies had cleared the Italians from Eritrea, Somaliland and Abyssinia but had less success with the Western Desert, where supply lines mattered as much as the quality of the men and their equipment.

After pushing the Italians back from Egypt and deep into Libya, the Allies split their forces to cope with the Axis invasion of Greece. The result had been a disaster on both sides of the Mediterranean. The Axis forces pushed the understrength Allies from Greece and Crete and forced them out of Libya. However, there was some brightness in the gloom as the Allied defence of Crete decimated the German airborne forces, and the Australians held Tobruk for months against fierce Axis attacks. An Allied counterattack combined with a breakout had relieved the town and regained the initiative.

The balance swung to the Allies as they pushed the Axis forces westward across the desert. When their supply lines were at full stretch, the Axis, under the *de facto* command of Erwin Rommel, held the Allies and successfully counter-attacked. Now, both armies faced each other across an arid stretch of sand. The Allies, now under Lieutenant General Ritchie, prepared to meet Rommel's next attack.

Tulloch mounted a small ridge, lifted his binoculars and peered west. He knew the defended Gazala Line lay between him and the Axis forces, but there was always the possibility of a raiding force striking an unwary camp or the *Luftwaffe* or

Regia Aeronautica – the Italian Air Force – coming to bomb and strafe.

"Empty," Tulloch murmured. "There are no aircraft engines and no sound of vehicles."

"What was that, sir?" Paterson asked.

"Nothing," Tulloch said. "Nothing is happening here. We are all alone." He smiled, still fighting his tiredness. "What did Keats say?

O Solitude! if I must with thee dwell,
Let it not be among the jumbled heap
Of murky buildings; climb with me the steep,
Nature's observatory—whence the dell
Its flowery slopes,
Its river's crystal swell."

"Yes, sir," Paterson replied doubtfully. "We could do with a river here."

"We could," Tulloch agreed and continued his slow patrol of the battalion's perimeter.

Ritchie had opted for a linear defence from the town of Gazala southwards, some thirty miles west of Tobruk. The outermost defences were tens of thousands of mines stretching from Gazala inland to Bir Hacheim, about fifty miles to the south. Behind the mines, the Allies waited in defensive Boxes, the old redcoat squares of Waterloo on a massive scale, replete with barbed wire, machine guns, and anti-tank artillery.

Behind the defensive Boxes, the British armour waited in reserve. Undergunned compared to their Axis opponents, they would pounce on any enemy breakthrough.

The Lothian Rifles' camp was twenty miles further to the east. After enduring the campaign in France that ended at Dunkirk, fighting with O'Connor's early offensive in Libya, and facing the Italians at Keren, the battalion had remained in reserve to retrain and replace its casualties.

"Lieutenant Tulloch!" Colonel Hume emerged from the gloom. Tall, supremely fit, and with a neat moustache, he was fully dressed with a pipe in his mouth.

"Yes, sir?"

"I'm holding a conference in my tent at ten hundred hours." Hume looked wide awake despite the hour. "We're also expecting a new draft of officers and men tomorrow."

"Yes, sir," Tulloch said.

Hume walked away, intent on inspecting the battalion's defences. Tulloch checked the sentries, recognising most by name. The Lothians had been re-equipped since the battle of Keren with two six-pounder anti-tank guns, one three-inch and three two-inch mortars, and a Vickers machine gun on one of its six universal – Bren gun – carriers. Some old faces had gone, and many new men who trickled in had yet to settle, but the officers and NCOs strove to maintain the old regimental spirit.

Tulloch eyed the two anti-tank guns as they sat under their camouflage netting with their crews nearby and a single bombardier as sentry. The Lothians had trained the gunners to respond to any tank attack on the battalion. Each six-pounder had a Bedford QLT three-ton lorry as portee, with the driver ready to rush to the point of danger, but they could also be dismounted and fired from the ground. Three men operated each gun, with one loader, one layer, and one firing. The portee also carried a Bren gunner for self-defence. Tulloch had observed the six-pounder on the range, watching it rear up when it fired, digging the spades at the end of the trail deep into the ground.

"They're more powerful than the old two-pounders," Captain Muirhead had noticed Tulloch's interest. "With the Germans using Mark IV Panzers now, the two-pounders are largely ineffective."

"I'm glad to have the six-pounders in the battalion," Tulloch said.

"Me too," Muirhead agreed. "We'll be facing the Germans again soon."

"Yes, sir," Tulloch nodded.

After the British defeat in France, a few high-placed staff officers doubted the Lothians' fighting ability, but they had proved themselves in General O'Connor's campaign in late 1940 and again in Eritrea. Now, with Rommel gathering strength for a forward surge, the Lothians would face the Axis army of Germans and Italians. Tulloch hoped he was ready for the challenge.

Tulloch raised his binoculars and peered to the west as dawn lightened the sky at his back. The desert night had been cold, but already he fancied he felt the first of the furnace heat that would torment the day and bring sweat to every man in the regiment.

A solitary aircraft hummed overhead, heading westwards, and Tulloch wondered if it was a British plane flying to bomb the enemy or an Axis plane returning from a similar mission over Egypt. He did not care, provided it left the Lothians alone.

The battalion's perimeter was secure, with standing and mobile patrols, and the men were alert at the anti-aircraft Bren guns. Tulloch was satisfied that most replacements had bedded into the Lothians and were ready to return to the war.

"Sir?" Hood was waiting when Tulloch returned to his billet. "The colonel has a meeting at ten, sir."

"Thank you, Hood," Tulloch said. Most privates would welcome the post of officer's batman as it relieved them from attending many of the most tedious parades, but Hood seemed slightly resentful.

"Your number one uniform is ready, sir," Hood said.

"I don't think I'll need it," Tulloch said, not wanting to wear his best uniform for a mere colonel's gathering. He grabbed something to eat, used some of his meagre allowance of water to shave and sluice some of the desert dust from his face, and marched to the meeting.

Colonel Hume looked over his officers, smiling grimly. They stood outside, with Hume balancing in the body of a universal carrier to slightly elevate him above the others. Tulloch surveyed his fellow officers. Captain Muirhead, commanding C Company, was experienced and approachable. Major Brownlow, the second-in-command of the battalion, commanded HQ Company with quiet authority. Lieutenant Hardie had a history in the King's African Rifles before he joined the Lothians. Erskine was an unarmed combat expert, and Captain Kilner of B Company was a greying veteran of the First World War. At the back, justifying their lowly status, were the subalterns, including the slightly nervous Lieutenant Kennedy and the quiet Lieutenant McGill of the Motor Pool.

Tulloch realised that the colonel was talking and gave him all his attention.

"Well, gentlemen, you all know the situation. Rommel is knocking on Egypt's door, and we don't want him to enter."

The officers nodded.

"General Ritchie has formed a defensive line southwards from Gazala, and this time we will be part of it. The general has attached us to Fifty Div, the Northumbrians, one of the finest fighting divisions in the army, so we're in good company."

"I remember them from France in 1940," Tulloch said. "They fought the Germans to a standstill and sent them packing at Arras."

"Good lads, the Geordies," Kilner agreed.

"We leave at oh two hundred hours tomorrow," Hume said. "Most of us will use the battalion's transport, and the brigadier will supply trucks for the remainder. Have your men ready, gentlemen." The colonel began to fill his pipe. "We also have the last of the new drafts arriving today. Ensure they feel welcome, Tulloch."

"Yes, sir," Tulloch said.

Hume struck a match and lit his pipe. "Dismissed."

"Here we go again," Captain Muirhead murmured as they strolled away. "Once more unto the breach, dear friends, once more."

7

"Let's hope we don't have to close up the wall with our Scottish dead," Tulloch continued the Shakespearian theme.

"Let's hope not," Muirhead agreed with a wry smile and a sidelong glance.

Tulloch spent an hour writing a long letter to Amanda, the girl he had barely met but with whom he corresponded regularly. He told her they were moving up the line without adding any details that the censor would block out. Tulloch knew that Amanda would understand. He was unsure how he felt about Amanda or if their relationship would outlast the war. At present, peace seemed too distant for Tulloch to contemplate, yet writing to Amanda was therapeutic and always left him smiling.

Tulloch knew Britain would never surrender, yet the Axis powers were advancing on all fronts, from Russia to Egypt and Burma to the Pacific. Singapore had fallen, the Japanese were completing their conquest of Burma and threatened India, yet Malta held out, and Britain clung on defiantly to Egypt, the Middle Eastern oilfields, and the lifeline of Suez. The United States and the USSR had joined the Allies, and although both were reeling under powerful blows, they had tremendous potential. The outlook was bleak rather than hopeless.

Tulloch finished his letter and hesitated over the signature. *Damn it all, this may be the last letter I ever write her,* he thought, and put "With my love, Douglas." Supremely daring, he added two Xs, folded it quickly, and slid it into an envelope. As he was unsure where Amanda was based, he addressed the letter to her home address in Meigle, Perthshire, and handed it to Hood to put in the post bag.

I can't allow myself to think of Amanda. I must concentrate on the war.

"Sir!" Hood stood at attention. "The new draft has arrived, sir."

Tulloch nodded and stood. "Sergeant Drysdale!" he shouted to his platoon sergeant. "You're with me!"

Ten men stood in the centre of the Lothians' camp, looking around them at the confusion as the battalion prepared to move to the front. A tall officer wearing the insignia of a lieutenant stood with them.

"Welcome to the Lothian Rifles," Tulloch said, nodding to the lieutenant. "I am Lieutenant Tulloch. Sergeant Drysdale will take you men to Captain Erskine's D Company. You," he addressed the lieutenant, "will come with me."

The men looked raw, some with sunburned faces, except for a lean, tanned corporal who inspected Drysdale and Tulloch through musing eyes.

While Drysdale marched the men away, Tulloch shook the lieutenant's hand.

"I am Lieutenant Rutlane," the new officer introduced himself. Taller than Tulloch, he had darting grey eyes and the bearing of a guardsman.

"You've arrived at the right time," Tulloch told him. "We're short of officers and going up the line tonight."

"I heard that," Rutlane said. He looked westwards. "We'll be facing Rommel, then."

"Probably," Tulloch agreed. "If Rommel attacks."

Rutlane nodded. "Rommel will attack. Nothing is more sure."

"Then we'll push him back," Tulloch said.

"I hope so," Rutlane replied.

Tulloch escorted Rutlane to the colonel, who greeted him with a firm handshake. "Welcome to the Lothians, Rutlane. I'm putting you in Captain Erskine's D Company. I'm sorry we're a bit rushed just now; blame that nasty wee man, Hitler."

"I will, sir," Rutlane said. "Where is D Company?"

"Over to the left. Come on; I'll take you. Lieutenant Tulloch has his men to organise. You can tell me all about yourself as we walk. Carry on, Tulloch."

Having delivered the replacements to D Company, Sergeant Drysdale was busy with Tulloch's Four Platoon. He ensured each man had his quota of kit and weapons, every water bottle was full, and Corporal Borthwick did not clash with the volatile Private Hogg.

"Everything all right, Sergeant?" Tulloch asked.

"Yes, sir," Drysdale replied. "The lads are ready."

Is anybody ever ready for war? Tulloch wondered.

Chapter Two

They moved out in the dark of night, a long convoy of fifteen-hundredweight and three-ton trucks packed with silent, sleepy men. The veterans knew what lay ahead, while the replacements were apprehensive, wanting to ask but nervous about the replies.

After only a few minutes, the dust made it impossible for anybody to talk, as sand seeped into every opening. It entered ears and noses, eyes and mouths. The veterans protected their rifle barrels and mechanisms with old socks or any other handy piece of cloth, but still, the sand penetrated. The men sat with bowed heads as the trucks rolled and banged across the desert in a long, monotonous convoy. Everybody hoped wordlessly that enemy aircraft would not find them.

Tulloch sat beside Townsend, the driver, a taciturn man with a cigarette seemingly permanently attached to his lower lip. The convoy moved slowly, with Townsend keeping his gaze on the vehicle in front and sand billowing and coating everything. Townsend used the wipers to clear the sand from the windscreen, so he peered forward through an arc of nearly clear glass fringed by thick, browny-yellow.

Outside the narrow beam of the shaded headlights, the desert was dark and mysterious. Tulloch stared out the side window, wondering what the future would hold. He had not been in action since he had been wounded at Keren the previous year, and his convalescence had been longer than he expected.

Every mile brought the Lothians closer to the enemy and the real possibility of death or hideous wounds. Of the two, Tulloch preferred the former. The idea of lying in agony for hours or days and remaining crippled and dependent on others was worse than death.

Tulloch started as the truck hit a bump in the road. The men in the back voiced their disapproval with a chorus of dissent, mixed with some choice obscenities aimed at the driver.

"Sorry, sir," Townsend apologised. "I didn't see that hole."

"I am sure there is worse ahead," Tulloch replied. "Keep one eye on the road and the other on the vehicle in front."

"Yes, sir," Townsend replied.

The convoy trundled on, with the road progressively rougher and more traffic gathering around them. Tulloch heard the rattle-clank of tanks in the distance and prayed they were friendly, not some of Rommel's Afrika Korps. He glanced at the now-lightening sky and hoped the RAF provided air cover, for the *Luftwaffe* and *Regia Aeronautica* would lap up a column of soft-skinned vehicles on a desert road.

The convoy halted as a red band of dawn stretched across the eastern horizon. The drivers cut their engines, and silence fell, oppressive after the internal combustion growl. When the dust settled softly around them, Tulloch heard the men talking in the back of the truck.

"Wait here," Tulloch ordered. "I'll see what's happening ahead."

Sliding from his seat, Tulloch found himself stiff after hours in the same position. Movement was a relief as he strode forward up the interminable convoy, where concerned men, officers and NCOs were engaged in the same business. Other men took the opportunity to ease cramped limbs or empty complaining bladders, so Tulloch pushed through a crowd of khaki-clad soldiers.

"What's happening?"

Young Lieutenant Kennedy, his face peeling and sun-raw, shrugged. "I don't know, sir. The truck in front stopped."

Tulloch pushed on to the head of the convoy. "What's happening?"

Captain Muirhead stood beside the leading truck, scanning the western horizon through his binoculars. "We heard a rumour there were German tanks ahead," he said calmly. "The colonel sent Erskine and a couple of carriers to check."

Erskine was an ex-Royal Scot with experience in the Holy Land before the war.

"God help the Germans if Erskine finds them, sir," Tulloch said. "He'd tear off their tracks with his bare fists."

Muirhead smiled without humour. "We don't know how long Erskine will be with us, Tulloch. He's a bit derring-do for ordinary infantry."

Tulloch peered across the dark and seemingly limitless desert. "It would be a shame to lose him."

"It would," Muirhead agreed, "but he was talking about joining one of these irregular formations, the SAS, Commandos or the Long Range Desert Group."

Tulloch nodded. "He would certainly fit in with these lads," he agreed. "I hope we keep him for a while yet."

"So do I," Muirhead lowered his binoculars. "Each intake gets younger and less experienced than the last. We need all the quality officers and men we can get." He nodded to the southwest. "That dust cloud is approaching fast, Tulloch; that will be Erskine now."

Erskine pulled up in the leading carrier. "There's nothing out there," he said. Sun-browned and athletic, he looked more like a film star than a typical Scottish soldier with his Clark Gable attitude and moustache. However, Tulloch knew the carefree attitude concealed a ruthless streak.

Colonel Hume appeared from behind a truck, pipe in mouth. "Very good, Erskine. We'll move on. Get the men back aboard."

"Back on the buses, lads!" Tulloch ordered Four Platoon. "All aboard for Princes Street or Gorgie Road for Hogg!"

When Four Platoon responded with dark humour, obscenity, and complaints, Tulloch knew all was right with his men. He would start to worry when British soldiers failed to grouse.

The convoy restarted five minutes later, driving with the rising sun behind them and the enemy somewhere in front. They passed a formation of British armour, light Crusaders armed with two-pounder popguns. The crews had spread camouflage netting over each tank, and sentries stared at the sky for enemy aircraft. The Lothians greeted them with cheerful jeers, to which the cavalry responded with pointed insults.

Tulloch felt his stomach tighten. He was going back into action. His now-healed wounds began to ache as if he needed a reminder of what was ahead.

"Trouble over there, sir," Townsend said quietly, nodding to the north-west.

Tulloch saw the flashes briefly lighting the horizon, indicating explosions, although he could not tell whether they were bombs or shell bursts. Above the engine's growl, he heard a Bren gun's steady, controlled rat-a-tat-tat. "Two miles away," he estimated.

"Yes, sir," Townsend agreed laconically.

The convoy slowed, heading more south than west, and came to a gradual halt. Sand and dust rose around them to slowly dissipate. The distant gunfire ended, and when the drivers turned off their engines, the silence pressed down on them.

"Debus, lads!" Muirhead's calm voice sounded from ahead. "We're on foot from here!"

The Lothians jumped from their trucks, looking about them at the flat, featureless terrain.

"We're in the middle of bugger-all," Hogg's harsh voice sounded. "Why the hell do we want to fight for this?"

"It's better fighting here than in a civilised country," Innes, one of the platoon's two Bren gunners, replied. "There are no civilians to get in the way."

"There are no pubs either," Private Elliot said. "And no women."

"You and your bloody women," Smith said. "How is it that it's always the ugly men who hunt for skirts."

"The good-looking ones don't have to hunt," Corporal Borthwick replied. "Do we, Cattanach?"

Cattanach, one of the quietest men in Four Platoon, smiled without replying.

"This way, lads," a tanned subaltern from the Durham Light Infantry marched up to the Lothians. "Keep to the taped path, please. There are minefields on either side."

The Lothians passed the information from man to man, with the NCOs giving ferocious warnings of the fate of any man who strayed.

"If you step on a mine," Sergeant Drysdale snarled, "you'd better pray that it kills you clean because otherwise, I'll have you parading around the desert in full kit until you die of old age!"

Tulloch marched his platoon forward, with the sun already hot and the dust rising from the feet of seven hundred men. Some stumbled and swore; others marched silently or spoke to their neighbours. They kept to the taped path, with the newer men watching the surrounding minefield, half expecting to see metallic horns or other signs of the horrors below the sand.

A shell exploded a hundred yards away, raising a tall column of yellow sand. The veterans marched on; the replacements ducked and looked around, trying to hide their embarrassment. Nobody commented on the replacements' behaviour. Everybody had once been a recruit and knew the struggle to fit in. Every experience helped the recent civilians become soldiers fit to fight the forces of evil.

"You're here, Lothians," the Durham subaltern stopped at a series of slit trenches and sandbagged dugouts. "The engineers did a good job, and we've left the trenches nice and tidy for you." He gave a tired grin. "You Jocks will no doubt want to add a few touches of your own, maybe tartan wallpaper or portraits of Robert Burns."

"No doubt," Captain Muirhead replied dryly. "We'll have to take down your pictures of slag heaps and rows of back-to-back brick houses."

"*Touché*," the Durham man replied. "Well, sir, the best of luck to you."

"And to you," Muirhead replied.

Colonel Hume ordered each company to its position, with Muirhead's C Company, of which Tulloch's Four Platoon was part, on the left flank and regimental headquarters a quarter of a mile further back. Major Brownlow accepted his near-administrative role without complaint.

"The enemy is out there, somewhere," Muirhead said. "Thirty-odd miles away. There is probably some Italian officer or German tank commander peering towards us right at this minute, wondering who they'll face in their next attack."

"Probably, sir," Tulloch agreed.

Muirhead allocated positions to his platoons, with Four Platoon on the left and Five on the right. The officers had a dugout in the centre, and Muirhead placed his Brens on the flanks to give crossfire if the enemy should attack.

"Sir!" Second Lieutenant Thompson, new to the battalion, hurried to Muirhead. "Colonel Hume's compliments, sir, and could all the officers join him at 10.00 hours."

Muirhead eyed the subaltern gravely. "Thank you, Thompson. Please tell the colonel that we will be there."

As the NCOs arranged the men, Colonel Hume addressed the officers.

"Here are the dispositions of the Gazala Line. Pay attention so we know who our neighbours are. The 1st South African Division is on our right flank, gentlemen. They did well in East Africa but are short of equipment. We're attached to the 50th Northumbrian Div, holding the Boxes here, with the 150th Brigade of the 50th holding the Sidi Muftah Box. The 2nd South African Division is in Tobruk, and Lieutenant General Strafer Gott is in overall command of our section of the line."

Tulloch nodded; it was important to know who guarded the flanks. He knew little about the South Africans but was happy to be brigaded with the Northumbrians, sturdy men and stubborn fighters.

Hume continued. "On the extreme left, the Free French Brigade holds Bir Hacheim. We don't know how they will fight, but I suspect they will be keen to prove themselves against the Germans. There is also a second line of manned Boxes behind us, and our armour is waiting to pounce on any enemy who slides between the Boxes."

The officers nodded approval, with a few taking notes. Overall, Tulloch thought the defensive arrangements were sound.

"Return to your companies and dig in," Hume ordered.

When Tulloch returned, Sergeant Drysdale had Four Platoon well in hand, with the slit trenches manned and Bren guns ready. The battalion's six-pounders were dug in, with the crews adding sandbags and calculating ranges ahead of them.

Tulloch toured his platoon, with his feet making no noise on the soft sand, and he heard the men talking to one another.

"What's that bastard doing here?" Private Hogg's grating voice rang out clearly through the background noise.

"What's who doing here?" Innes asked.

"That corporal, the new one in D Company. What's he doing here?" Hogg pointed towards D Company's position with a broad, stubby finger.

"That's Corporal Russell," Innes said as he cleaned his Bren gun. "He was wounded in Crete and transferred to us from the Argylls. Do you know him?"

"Aye, I know him," Hogg said. "He's trouble, Innie, major trouble on two legs. You keep well clear of Corporal Rab, bloody Russell."

Innes shook his head. "You don't like corporals, do you, Hoggie? You don't get on with Corporal Borthwick either."

Tulloch moved on before he heard Hogg's opinion of Corporal Borthwick. He wondered how Hogg could have met an Argyll corporal, for the Lothians and the Argylls had never been brigaded together. He shrugged and dismissed the incident from his mind. Such grievances were the small change of any battalion, and it was unlikely that Hogg would have many dealings with a corporal in a different company.

When Tulloch entered his dugout, Hood had his living quarters ready and produced a meal on his Benghazi Cooker, a contraption made from half a fuel can filled with petrol-soaked sand.

"Welcome home, sir," Hood said.

"Thank you, Hood." Tulloch saw his equipment and possessions arranged neatly beside the sandbags, while the corrugated iron roof also had a protective three-deep layer of sandbags. In an uncertain world, his new home was as safe as anywhere along the line.

At noon, the men ate bully beef and drank tea without milk, while Tulloch accompanied Sergeant Drysdale as they checked and strengthened the platoon's defensive barbed wire. The Durhams had left him a chart of the local minefields, showing their extent and the safe passages through.

"The Durhams know their stuff," Sergeant Drysdale commented. "The safe passages are all doglegs, with Brens covering them. Unless the enemy also has a plan of our minefields, they'll take casualties."

"We'll patrol tonight, Sergeant, and get to know the area better."

"Yes, sir," Drysdale agreed. "Do you think Rommel will attack?"

"Yes," Tulloch said. "It's not a matter of if, Sergeant, and more of when."

"Aye," Drysdale said. "He's made himself a reputation, has our Rommel."

Tulloch glanced at his sergeant. "He's certainly made himself a talking point, Drysdale."

"All the boys know his name," Drysdale agreed, "maybe more than we know our own generals."

"He's only one more man to fight," Tulloch said.

"Aye, that's all he is, sir," Drysdale agreed.

They toured the perimeter and learned about their surroundings, stopping to look around them every few moments.

The defensive Box held three British battalions, the Lothians and two from the 50th Division, plus Royal Artillery, Royal Engineers, and a small hospital, well-marked with a red cross. Each dugout had a corrugated iron roof covered with sandbags for protection against anything other than a direct hit.

Wires connected each dugout, with rattling tin cans at the end. If the enemy attacked one dugout, the occupants pulled the wire to alert the next in line.

"It's a bit primitive, sir," Drysdale said, "but effective unless the enemy cut the wire."

In front of the Lothians' positions, the engineers had laid a three-hundred-yard-deep perimeter of mattress wire—flattened barbed wire—within an extensive minefield. The engineers had marked every zig-zag gap in the mattress wire with white tape and had gap-covering parties ready for outgoing British patrols.

"What's the system here, lads?" Tulloch asked a group of engineers working under the direction of a serious-faced sergeant.

"You tell us when you're taking a patrol out, sir," the sergeant replied. "We lift the mines along the taped path and cover the gap with a Bren and rifles until the patrol returns, and then we replace the mines."

"I see; thank you, Sergeant," Tulloch said. He knew that engineers seldom received the praise they deserved. They were often in the most dangerous areas, unheralded, working under fire as they handled explosives, built bridges, and ensured the infantry and armour could do their work.

"I hope there are anti-tank mines as well as anti-personnel in that field, sir," Sergeant Drysdale said. "If Rommel decides to come through here with his Afrika Korps, our two wee six-pounders won't hold them for long."

Tulloch nodded. "The Royal Artillery is also here, and their twenty-five pounders are effective, and we have British armour in reserve."

"Yes, sir," Drysdale said. "Our tanks are too light, and most are undergunned. Their shells bounce off the German armour, and Rommel's Panzers knock us out like ducks at a shooting gallery."

"Not like the days when we advanced with O'Connor," Tulloch replied.

"If we had kept going, sir, Rommel would never have got a foothold in Africa," Drysdale said. "We'd have been hammering at Sicily's door rather than waiting to repel the Afrika Korps."

"Maybe so," Tulloch agreed. "But our intervention in Greece delayed the German attack on Russia, so they did not reach Moscow before winter." He stopped. "However, our job is to deal with the situation we have rather than what might have been."

"Yes, sir," Drysdale said.

"Sir!" Second Lieutenant Thompson ran up and nearly skidded to a stop. "Colonel Hume wants you, sir!"

Tulloch raised his eyebrows. "Was that the message, Thompson?"

"Yes, sir." Thompson pulled himself to attention. "Colonel Hume requests that you attend him at your earliest convenience, sir."

"That's better, Thompson," Tulloch said. "Always be accurate when delivering messages. It was a slovenly message that led to the Light Brigade's charge at Balaclava and cost us hundreds of lives."

"Yes, sir," Thompson said, making Tulloch feel like a middle-aged schoolmaster rather than a junior officer in his twenties.

"Tulloch," Colonel Hume was studying a plan of the battalion's defensive perimeter. "Take Four Platoon on outpost duty tonight. The Durhams tell me they have two proper outposts half a mile into the desert. I want our OP surveyed and manned twenty-four hours a day. Ensure it is fit for us."

"I'll soon find out, sir."

Hume gave his wry smile. "I'm sure you will, Tulloch."

Chapter Three

GAZALA LINE, WESTERN DESERT, LIBYA, MAY 1942

The engineers gave Tulloch a reassuring nod as he arrived at the gap in the minefield. "Keep to the marked path, Lieutenant, and remember the password when you return."

"The challenge is Gin, and the reply is Whisky," Tulloch replied.

"That's right," the engineer said. "Don't get it wrong. My boys can get a little jittery at night and tend to fire if they're in doubt."

"I'll remind my sergeant," Tulloch said.

Four Platoon followed Tulloch through the gap, with the men careful not to walk at the edge beside the minefield. Sergeant Drysdale acted as rearguard, wordlessly shepherding the men, watching the horizon for tell-tale flashes of artillery and listening for enemy aircraft.

Once through the minefield, Tulloch used a compass to navigate across the desert, hoping Drysdale could keep the replacements with the main body. He had trained them in night patrolling, but crossing an empty and relatively safe desert was far different from patrolling when the enemy could be waiting in ambush. He glanced over his shoulder, saw his men in an extended formation with nobody missing, and moved on.

After a quarter of a mile, Tulloch heard the rattle of a Vickers machine gun further north and saw explosions light up the sky.

"Somebody's hit trouble," Private Oldham, one of the replacements, murmured.

"As long as they keep it over there," Private Weeks, another new man, replied.

"Keep the noise down," Sergeant Drysdale grunted. "Sound carries at night."

Tulloch saw the outpost's squat shape under the glimmer of the stars and sighed with relief. He had a nightmare vision of wandering about all night until he blundered into the enemy lines and led his men into captivity.

"Here we are, lads," Tulloch whispered. The OP consisted of deeply dug trenches, with sandbag emplacements for all-round defence. "I want a Bren at each corner, ready to have crossfire on every angle. Put the three-inch mortar in the centre, with Smith and the Boys anti-tank rifle facing west." The Boys was a clumsy weapon and virtually useless against modern tanks, but, properly used, could disable a German halftrack or an Italian armoured car. "The rest of you, distribute yourselves evenly around the perimeter except Corporal Borthwick and two men. I want you in the listening post two hundred and fifty yards further out."

"Yes, sir," Borthwick was a crusty veteran who knew his job. He chose two men from his section. "Hogg, Cattanach; you're with me."

Tulloch agreed with Borthwick's choice. Hogg was the best soldier in C Company to have on one's side if there was a duffy, while Cattanach was a steady, quiet man. Tulloch knew that Borthwick did not like Hogg, but the corporal would choose him for his military skills rather than his friendship.

"There's a landline from the listening post to the telephone here," Tulloch said. "Keep your voice down and report anything you hear."

"I will, sir," Borthwick said expressionlessly.

"Off you go, then," Tulloch said. He disliked sending men into danger, but manning a listening post was a corporal's job.

Four Platoon settled down. Tulloch reminded them to only talk in whispers and not to smoke, for a man's voice travelled hundreds of yards in the brittle air of the desert, and the smell of tobacco would alert any enemy patrol.

The desert was quiet, lit by the stars above and the occasional flash and crump of a distant shell. Tulloch toured his men, ensured they were in position, and returned to his dugout. Waiting was part of a soldier's task. For every hour in action, he knew he would spend hundreds of hours waiting, yet it was the action people remembered. The intense, adrenaline-fuelled moments when life and limb hung on a slender thread, fear battled with courage, and duty competed with sense and self-preservation.

The machine gun chatter started again up north, brief and disturbing. The insane clatter of an Italian Breda 37 joined the heavy thudding of a Vickers. Some of the platoon's novices looked up, grabbed their rifles, and peered north. The veterans either ignored the sound or opened a lazy eye, checked to see if they were involved, and returned to sleep. They knew that sleep was a precious commodity to snatch whenever possible. Only the sentries remained alert.

"I'll try to sleep," Tulloch told Hood. "Wake me if anything happens."

"Yes, sir," Hood replied. He was in his early twenties but displayed a row of medal ribbons.

Although Tulloch closed his eyes, he could not sleep. Returning to the front brought back a host of memories of past events. He tried to look composed and relaxed but was glad when the buzz of the telephone from the listening post demanded his attention.

"What is it, Corporal?"

"There's lots of movement out here, sir. I can hear engines passing out to the west."

"Which direction?" Tulloch asked.

"They're from the north and heading south, sir."

"I'll come out." Ordering Sergeant Drysdale to take command, Tulloch crawled to the listening post. The position was little more than a saucer scraped in the ground, with a single deep slit trench under a sandbag-covered corrugated-iron roof.

"Can you hear them, sir?" Borthwick asked when Tulloch slid into the trench.

Tulloch nodded. The distant grumble of engines was distinct, although he was unsure which direction the vehicles were travelling. "I'll go closer," he said. "Hold the fort for me."

"Yes, sir," Corporal Borthwick said. "Should you not take somebody with you?"

"I'm quieter alone," Tulloch said, sliding out of the listening post.

The sand was harsh under his hands as Tulloch crawled forward, compass in hand. When a betraying gust of wind shifted the clouds to allow the moonlight to come through, Tulloch felt very exposed and vulnerable, like a black beetle crawling up a white-painted door. He froze for a moment and moved slowly across the arid surface. He remembered the geography books he had perused as a schoolboy, which portrayed the desert as endless sand dunes with strategically placed oases complete with palm trees and the ubiquitous Arabs on camels. The featureless, drab reality was nothing like the romantic image.

Tulloch checked his watch. He had been crawling for ten minutes, and the engine sounds were slightly louder. Tulloch stopped and scanned the west through his binoculars. He saw a faint gleam on the horizon, not in sufficient clarity for him to be sure, but he suspected it was the reflection of shaded headlights on the shifting cloud.

Another five minutes, Tulloch decided and began crawling again. He stopped as something scampered across the ground before him—a small creature, perhaps a mouse or a jerboa. He waited until the animal was clear and moved on, less cautious as his confidence grew.

As long as I don't meet a snake or a scorpion.

Tulloch stopped again and peered ahead. He heard the high purr of an aircraft above the growling traffic.

That's far enough. I don't know if the enemy has patrols out.

Tulloch counted the number of muted headlights that passed in a five-minute period and crawled back faster than he had on the outward journey. After ten minutes, he looked up, hoping to see the listening post. The wind had shifted the cloud back over the moon, so the desert was darker. Tulloch saw only the level plain, shifting slightly as the wind ruffled the top layer of dust and sand.

I followed the compass bearing out. If I follow the opposite bearing back, I must find the L.P.

Tulloch slowed, inspecting the ground ahead. He knew the dangers. He might crawl around the desert for hours until the daytime sun burned him or a German or Italian patrol captured him. At the worst, a jumpy British sentry could mistake him for an enemy and shoot him.

The ground was slightly disturbed ahead, with a darker patch blocking the lowest stars. Tulloch realised with sudden relief that he had come across his outward track. He silently prayed thanks and crawled towards the listening post, hoping he remembered the correct password.

"Gin!" he whispered.

"Whisky," Corporal Borthwick replied, and Tulloch slid into the trench. He saw a scowling Hogg lowering his rifle and wondered how close he had come to being shot.

"You're right, Corporal," Tulloch said. "There is definitely movement out there. I'll report that to the colonel. You stay here for another half hour, and I'll send out your relief."

The journey back to the outpost was equally nerve-wracking. Tulloch knew that the Lothians' sentries would be tiring as the night eased towards dawn when the Germans usually launched raids or attacks. The Germans seldom fought at night, giving the Allies more freedom to roam around no-man's land.

Tulloch passed the message to Major Brownlow at battalion HQ, keeping his voice down. When he replaced the telephone receiver, he felt he had done a good night's work, and Four Platoon had done their duty.

"Heading south, were they?" Colonel Hume asked when Five Platoon relieved Tulloch's men in the outpost.

"That's what I estimated, sir," Tulloch replied.

"How many?" Hume asked.

"It's hard to say, sir. I only heard the engines and saw what I thought were the reflections of lights on the clouds. My estimate was twenty vehicles every five minutes, so I'd guess quite a lot, sir. At least a brigade and maybe more."

Hume tapped his fingers on the travelling desk. "All the same engines or different types?"

Tulloch pondered for a moment. "Different types. Some were heavier than others."

"I've already alerted the brigadier," Hume said. "No doubt he'll advise the RAF to have a look, but I'll send out a couple of patrols as well. Hardie will take the morning's patrol and you the afternoon. Grab some sleep, Tulloch, and leave at 13.00 hours with two carriers."

"Yes, sir."

"Patrol to the west and see what you can find."

"I will, sir," Tulloch said.

"It's an observation patrol," the colonel reminded. "Don't contact the enemy unless they see you first. Information is more important than a few German corpses." He paused for a moment, "Or ours."

"I understand, sir," Tulloch said.

Tulloch ensured his men ate before they left on patrol. In the

Lothians, every officer and man ate the same hard tack—solid and tasteless biscuits—and bully beef, which slopped out of the tin in a semi-liquid state to be immediately furred by flies. Colonel Hume did not believe in favouritism when the battalion was at the front, in the Blue, as the men called the desert.

Water was rationed to half a gallon daily, with two pints for drinking and the remainder for washing and shaving. In the Lothians, every section cooked for itself, and on the very odd occasions when tinned pineapples came onto the menu, the men acted as though it was Christmas.

At quarter past twelve, Tulloch toured Four Platoon, placed an ascorbic acid tablet on every man's tongue, waited until they swallowed it, and moved on to the next in line. The officers could trust most men to swallow the vitamin C tablet, but every unit had a proportion of the stupid or the plain bloody-minded who would refuse purely because it was an order from above.

"You'd better down that pill, Elliot," Sergeant Drysdale growled. "I don't want you catching scurvy to get sent home to Blighty. You swallow it like a good lad, or I'll have you running around the desert in full kit with your rifle held aloft until you've worn a hole so deep the kangaroos will be popping up to see you!"

Knowing Drysdale was not joking, Elliot swallowed.

"That's my lad," Drysdale said with a smile. "Always willing to do your duty for King and Country."

Tulloch checked his two Bren gun carriers, ensured they had ammunition and water, and loaded maps on each.

"Come on, lads," he said. "Watch out for enemy aircraft and patrols." He had Hood as his driver and Innes with his Bren. The second carrier held Smith with his Boys anti-tank rifle and the truculent Hogg, with Corporal Borthwick in command.

"Best of luck, sir," the engineer sergeant shouted and stepped aside as Hood negotiated the barbed wire and the minefield before heading into the Blue.

Travelling in the daytime was even more risky than patrolling at night, Tulloch thought as he headed west. He kept his carriers a hundred yards apart and drove slowly to raise as little dust as possible. Dust plumes could be seen for miles, attracting unwelcome attention from enemy patrols or aircraft. An open universal carrier had little protection against an enemy plane.

With the carrier's crews ready behind their guns, Tulloch watched the surrounding desert for tell-tale dust. After ten minutes, he glanced behind him. Except for the glint of sunlight on barbed wire, there was no sign of the defensive Box. The desert could be empty.

"What's that, sir?" Innes gestured to the north. "It looks like a tank."

"Stop the carrier!" Tulloch signalled for the second carrier to halt and keep watch while he examined the vehicle through his binoculars. "It's a Panzer Mark Three," he said, "but I think it's dead."

The tank sat hull down in the sand, with its gun pointing directly at the oncoming British patrol. Tulloch saw the black smudge of fire damage on its side. "Take us closer, Hood."

"Yes, sir," Hood said and drove slowly towards the Panzer, with Innes sitting behind the Bren. Although he knew the bullets would only bounce from a Mark Three's thick armour, Tulloch knew that Smith would have his Boys rifle pointed toward the tank.

"It's empty, sir," Hood said.

The tank had not moved, and the fire damage was more evident as they crept closer.

"We'll check it anyway," Tulloch told him. "Stop here." He left the carrier and ran towards the tank, weaving to disrupt the aim of any prospective enemy. Hood was nearly correct. The tank was damaged from a previous battle but not quite empty, as charred pieces of men filled the cramped interior. A host of flies lifted, furiously buzzing as Tulloch glanced inside. Screwing up his face against the sights and stench, he looked for any useful documents, but the explosion and subsequent fire that had killed the crew had also destroyed anything flammable.

"Drive on," Tulloch ordered, and the patrol ground across the desert. They saw remnants of the earlier fighting, with British, Italian, and German vehicles damaged or destroyed, left to the mercy of the desert sands. Some still contained the charred remnants of their crews, men who had died for their country, their beliefs, or because their government had ordered them into a war in which they had no interest.

"If I were a scrappy, I'd make a fortune here," Hogg murmured when they stopped at a slight ridge to survey the land to the west.

"You could come here after the war," Hood said. "Charter a ship from Leith, load it with all these dead tanks and bring them home. You'd have enough steel to last a lifetime."

"I could start my own business," Hogg said. "Gorgie scrap metal merchant; top-quality steel for the discerning buyer."

"Enough, lads," Tulloch said. "Concentrate on today. Back in the buses, and on we go." He felt lost in this arid immensity.

The men relapsed into silence as they crawled across the desert.

"Sir," Innes pointed to the south. "Something is moving towards us. Over there, sir."

Tulloch swivelled his binoculars to look south. "Dust," he said flatly. "Are you ready on the Bren, Innes?"

"Ready, sir," Innes replied.

"Stop the carriers," Tulloch ordered. "Pull camouflage netting over them, and let's see what's coming our way." He felt the tension rise inside him. He could be in serious trouble if the dust concealed anything heavier than a half-track.

The carrier crews prepared the vehicles and waited. The sound of engines drifted across the desert, and then the dust cloud increased, rolling towards them. Tulloch nudged Innes and pointed to the dust. Innes nodded, wordless. Tulloch knew that Corporal Borthwick would be ready in the second carrier. He raised his hand as the vehicles appeared through the dust, sand-smeared and nearly impossible to distinguish.

"Hold your fire!" Tulloch shouted. "They're friendly!"

Lieutenant Hardie stood in the first of two carriers and pulled up beside Tulloch. "There's no need for you to go any further, Tulloch. We've found out what's happening."

"What's happening?" Tulloch asked. He felt his men's interest.

"Rommel's moving hundreds of supply trucks round the south of our defences," Hardie told him. "He must be building up a supply depot for his offensive."

"He won't try and batter through the Boxes then," Tulloch said. "You'd better tell the colonel so he can alert the brigadier."

Both patrols returned together, with the weary engineers replacing the mines in the cleared path and reconnecting the barbed wire after they passed.

"It never ends," the engineer sergeant sighed. "Lift mines, wait as the blasted infantry play silly buggers out in the desert, then plant mines again."

"It's all the infantry is good for, sergeant," an equally tired corporal said. "It lets them justify their existence while we do the real work."

Colonel Hume listened to Hardie's report with an expression of grim satisfaction.

"Supply convoys," Hume nodded. "We'll have a smack at them. Well done, Hardie. It's time the battalion did a little commerce raiding. Are you sure you saw no armour?"

"None, sir," Hardie replied with equal satisfaction. "I only saw soft-skinned vehicles."

Hume glanced at his watch. "We'll leave at oh-two hundred hours tomorrow," he ordered. "Four carriers, four truckloads of infantry, two anti-tank guns and a Vickers machine gun. That should be enough to frighten any convoy." Hume grinned. "We're not going to wait here for Rommel to come to us, gentlemen; we'll take the war to him."

Tulloch remembered the last time the Lothians faced the German army, which had ended in the retreat to Dunkirk. Many men had died since then, and the battalion had experienced action in Egypt, Libya, and Eritrea. Now, he wondered if the men were hoping for revenge or if they felt Rommel's Germans were superior soldiers.

I'll ask my platoon, Tulloch decided.

Chapter Four

"We'll soon be fighting the Germans again," Tulloch said.

Sergeant Drysdale nodded without expression. "Yes, sir."

"How do you feel about that, Sergeant?"

"Fine, sir," Drysdale looked slightly puzzled at the question.

They stood outside the Lothians' tent, with the mechanics working on the vehicles on one side and the men checking their weapons on the other. Someone was singing *Lily Marlene* with a broad Midlothian accent, and Innes was looking down the barrel of a Bren gun before cleaning it with a pull-through.

"The men might welcome the chance to avenge Dunkirk," Tulloch suggested.

"Maybe, sir," Drysdale said. "It could wipe something off the slate, as Kipling said about the Boer War. But I don't know if many think like that."

"How do they think?" Tulloch asked.

"The Germans are just another enemy, sir," Drysdale replied after a moment's thought. "The older men, the old sweats, are

33

professional soldiers. They've fought the Paythans, the Italians and the Germans. They know war has its ups and downs and accept that."

"How about the younger men, Sergeant? Those who have not seen action yet?"

"They're more likely to talk tough, sir," Drysdale replied. "Yet they're also nervous, which is natural. They'll be OK once they've fired a couple of rounds."

"Thank you, Sergeant," Tulloch said. "Let's get the men ready."

When the vehicles were fuelled and armed with spare ammunition and water, Tulloch ordered the men to get some sleep. He knew the average British veteran could sleep through a thunderstorm or an air raid but knew the replacements would be nervous about the coming patrol. He was unsure if he should speak to them and decided to leave them with their mates.

The Lothians gave a good account of themselves in France and against the Italians. I am sure the old soldiers will look after the replacements, and I'll watch over the platoon.

Colonel Hume's commerce raiders left the Box under a cold glitter of starlight. Tulloch rode in a Bren gun carrier, with Four and Five Platoon travelling in the trucks, followed by the six-pounders on portees. Captain Erskine travelled in another carrier as a rearguard. The colonel travelled in a fifteen hundred-weight truck with a number 19 wireless set and a three-inch mortar on sandbags in the back.

Sergeant Drysdale commanded one truck and Corporal Borthwick the second.

"Let's go, men," Colonel Hume shouted, adding the Lothians' motto. "Gin ye daur!"

"Gin ye daur," some men replied while others sat silently, staring at the surrounding darkness.

They moved out in the dark, with Lieutenant Kennedy, now the battalion intelligence officer, navigating alongside Hardie. The men were silent as they wondered what lay before them.

The Lothians travelled in desert formation, well spread out, with the carriers on the outside and the soft-skinned vehicles in the centre.

Tulloch had taken Hood as his driver, with Innes on the Bren and Hogg as the loader. As always, they moved in a curtain of dust, with the stars glittering above, but this time, the half-moon was clear and cold, gazing down on them. Tulloch cursed the moon, preferring a darker night to hide their movements. Although he knew the Germans disliked night operations, there was always the possibility of a stray enemy aircraft spotting their progress and reporting back to Rommel's headquarters.

They headed west, then southwest, with Hardie in the leading carrier and the others following until they halted at a small escarpment overlooking a rough track. The men placed camouflage netting over the vehicles, spread them out as a precaution against aerial attack and searched for shade in a shadeless environment. They knew that, however sharp the night, dawn would bring rising heat.

"Wait in the lee of the escarpment," Colonel Hume ordered. "Get the guns ready and wait for movement."

Dawn glorified the horizon, and the sun rose rapidly, a white globe in the blue sky. By mid-morning, the sun had warmed the carrier's armour and touching the bare metal without getting burned was almost impossible.

"Maybe no more vehicles are coming," Lieutenant Kennedy, sunburned and doubtful, said. "Maybe we're wasting our time."

"Wait!" Captain Muirhead ordered sharply.

The Lothians waited silently, with the men dozing or checking their weapons and the officers on the lip of the escarpment scanning the desert. They saw a flash of light to the northwest as the sun reflected on glass or metal, and a few minutes later, they heard the grumble of engines. When Colonel Hume gave the gunners marks to aim at and ordered the men to debus, Tulloch felt the tension rise.

It was over a year since he fired a shot at the enemy, and now his war was beginning again. He glanced over his platoon. They lay in the lee of the ridge, holding their weapons, waiting for orders, and all keyed up, except for Innes, who was as calm as if he sprawled on a bench in Dalkeith's King's Park.

"Fifteen, no sixteen vehicles," Muirhead reported. "Italian trucks with a single armoured car for escort."

Hume nodded and gave brief orders: "The gunners will target the armoured car, and then the infantry will rake the trucks. Hardie, take your carrier to the front of the enemy and stop them from progressing. Tulloch, block their retreat."

The Lothians moved into position, using the escarpment as cover and hoping the noise of the Italians' vehicles blanketed their engine sounds. Tulloch moved five hundred yards to the north and waited with the engine off to save petrol. The dust settled; the sun peeped from the east, and a hundred flies continued their persistent explorations.

Innes checked the Bren for the tenth time and settled down as Hogg counted his ammunition, and Tulloch scanned the track through his binoculars. The sky above was achingly blue, stretching to infinity, thankfully unmarred by the unwelcome specks of enemy aircraft. The Italian convoy grumbled on, throwing up dust like ships sending spray in choppy seas. The armoured car drove two hundred yards in front. They passed Tulloch's carrier and drove on, leaving dust in their wake.

Hume stood on the bonnet of his truck, glanced at his men, lifted a hand, and dropped it.

"Fire!" Hume's voice sounded across the desert, a call to action.

The two six-pounders fired immediately. One shot exploded in front of the armoured car and the other at its side. The gun crews hastily reloaded while the enemy vehicle rocked, swerved, and sought these unexpected attackers.

The gunners fired again, with one shot smashing right into the body of the armoured car, blowing the turret off. Nobody emerged. The Italian lorries scattered as Colonel Hume ordered the men to fire. They had been waiting impatiently and opened up, with the Vickers hammering at the trucks as the men fired Brens and rifles, sending the trucks running, with one veering to the side. The Italians inside jumped out, falling under the Lothians' musketry. Some of the Italians returned fire, with bullets crashing into Hume's fifteen hundredweight truck. He remained on the bonnet to direct his men. Two Italian trucks accelerated forward, where Hardie's carrier was waiting. Three trucks tried to return and ran into Tulloch.

"Short bursts with the Bren!" Tulloch ordered.

"Yes, sir," Innes replied and put half a dozen bullets into the engine of the leading truck. The vehicle stopped, the crew baled out, yelling, and Innes concentrated on the next in line. His bullets hammered the truck, which slewed to one side. A brave man jumped out of the passenger door and fired a rifle towards the carrier until Innes chopped him down. The crew of the third truck did not wait to be hit but abandoned their vehicle. One man raised his hands in surrender, and the others ran into the desert.

"Let them go," Tulloch ordered. He did not want to fire at fleeing men.

The other Italian trucks had scattered, some escaping into the desert and two already bogged down in soft sand. The Lothians were firing at them, setting a further three alight so flames and smoke coiled upwards. Italian soldiers lay on the sand, silent and still or writhing in pain. Others tried to run or stood with their hands raised in surrender, while a few returned the Lothians' fire.

"Sir!" Hogg pointed to the west. "Aircraft, sir!"

Tulloch saw the three dots in the sky gradually increase in size. Coming from the west, they were more likely to be Axis than Allied. The rising smoke would attract their attention, whoever they were.

"Drive to the colonel, Hood," Tulloch ordered. "We'd better warn him."

Of the sixteen Italian vehicles, seven were on fire or damaged beyond repair, three had bogged in soft sand, and the rest scattered into the desert. It had been a relatively successful ambush unless the aircraft inflicted casualties on the raiding party.

When Hume saw the approaching aircraft, he ordered his convoy to scatter and spread camouflage netting over themselves. The Bren gunners mounted their guns on tripods and aimed upwards, aware the enemy aircraft would vastly outgun them but keen to return fire. They waited, hoping their dust dissipated quickly, hoping the aircraft flew on without deviating, licking dry, dust-covered lips.

Tulloch checked his platoon, ensuring the camouflage netting was secure and the men in hastily dug slit trenches sufficiently far from the vehicles to be safe if they caught fire. The aircraft arrived a moment later, circled the scene of the recent ambush, and then zoomed closer to view the combatants.

"Messerschmitt 109s," Drysdale commented.

"Don't fire unless they do!" Tulloch ordered. "They won't know who we are and might leave us alone."

The aircraft passed low overhead, evidently examining the burning trucks. Tulloch could plainly see the large black crosses on the underside of their wings.

Innes swung the muzzle of his Bren skyward, his hand eager on the trigger. Ignoring the questing flies, he followed the track of the closest aircraft.

"Keep still!" Tulloch snarled. "They don't know who we are!" With so many vehicles captured, both sides used the enemy's equipment, so there was no positive identification by vehicle type.

Three Messerschmitt 109s came so close that Tulloch could see the pilots in their cockpits. He waved as if to a friend, and the aircraft waggled its wings and flew away.

"That's a relief," Innes said, lowering the barrel of the Bren. His face relaxed, the tight lines around his eyes and mouth softening.

"I wouldnae worry about the planes," Hogg jerked a thumb over his shoulder. "I'd worry about that dust there and listen to the sounds."

Tulloch saw the cloud of dust rising in the northwest and heard heavy engines.

"Tanks," Hogg said. "I'd know a tank anywhere. Not the wee toy Italian tankettes either."

Others had also heard the engines, and Colonel Hume ordered Hardie and Kennedy to probe towards the approaching dust cloud. They returned at great speed within twenty minutes.

"German tanks," Kennedy reported breathlessly. "Hundreds of them. Half the German army is on the move."

"Move out!" Hume ordered immediately. "Take the Italian officers prisoner, leave the rest here and head back to the Box."

The Lothians did not hesitate, freeing most of the prisoners, giving them water, and keeping in formation as they drove eastward across the desert.

Tulloch was no longer worried about making too much dust. Gaining distance was more critical as the Lothians changed from commerce-raiding predators to possible prey as they scurried away from the oncoming Germans. Carriers had limited range, and the convoy stopped to refuel after half an hour, with Hume ordering the anti-tank guns as rearguard.

"You remember the drill, lads?" Tulloch reminded the gunners. "If a tank is moving sideways before you, aim for the tracks. If it's coming towards you, it will move up and down. However flat the ground looks, there are hidden undulations. When the tank moves up, aim for the belly. If you can't manage that, try for the top of the gun, which should knock off the turret. It all sounds so simple, doesn't it?"

"Yes, sir," a long-faced corporal replied.

"On the gun's telescope, you'll see a cross. When the tank's nose reaches the cross, you fire."

"Yes, sir," the corporal repeated. "We know the drill."

"Do you remember how Dr Johnston said that the prospect

of being hanged concentrates the mind?" Muirhead asked. "Having heavy German armour in the vicinity has the same effect on me."

Tulloch nodded. "And on me," he said. He watched Hogg pour petrol into the carrier's fuel tank.

"These tins leak like the Hibs defence," Hogg said. "The Jerry cans are far better."

"We'll ask Rommel to lend us some," Innes told him as Hood cleaned sand from the engine.

"Get moving!" Hume ordered as Hogg discarded a five-gallon petrol can and jumped into the carrier. The Lothians' commerce raiding patrol had ended in a frantic withdrawal.

"Hardie!" Hume shouted. "Get behind us and see if the Germans are following!"

"Rather him than me," Innes said as Hardie motored in the direction they had come.

The six-pounder portees led the way, and the rest of the raiding party moved on, every man feeling an uncomfortable tingling at the base of their scalp at the thought of German Panzers following them.

"Keep an eye open behind us, Hogg," Tulloch ordered.

"I am, sir," Hogg replied. "I'm watching for Rommel and Lieutenant Hardie."

After an hour, Tulloch saw a thread of rising dust and ordered Innes onto the Bren. The dust was too thin for more than a single vehicle, but Tulloch was uncertain if it was Hardie returning or a probing German tank.

"It's ours, sir," Hogg said after an anxious minute, "Lieutenant Hardie."

"Stand down, Innes," Tulloch tried to keep the relief from his voice.

Hardie's report eased the tension. "The Germans are heading steadily south by east and not bothering with us. I've never seen so many enemy tanks. Rommel must have begun his offensive on the Gazala Line."

"He's caught our intelligence wallahs napping then," Hume said. "We'll report that to the brigadier when we return to the Box." He gestured to his wireless. "An Italian bullet smashed our set."

The Lothians were glad to thread through the minefield and the barbed wire to their now-familiar dugouts and slit trenches. The engineers waved them through and returned to their dangerous task of replacing the mines.

"These sapper lads must hate us," Hogg said.

"They'll hate it worse if the Germans come," Innes replied.

While Hume contacted the brigadier with news of the German troop movements, Tulloch ensured his men were fed and watered and looked up as Muirhead wandered across.

"Evening, Tulloch," Muirhead glanced over Four Platoon's defences. "I see you've put a couple of booby traps in your wire."

"Yes, sir," Tulloch replied. "Anything to deter a raiding party."

"Good show," Muirhead said. "Although if Rommel is heading south, that may be the focus of his main attack rather than a direct thrust at the Boxes." Muirhead produced his pipe and began to stuff tobacco into the bowl. "Our intelligence wallahs tell us he is planning a push with the Italian Ariete Division. Maybe he'll hit the Free French at Bir Hacheim and roll us up with flank attacks."

"Maybe," Tulloch said. "But the Boxes have all-round defences. He'll meet resistance wherever he attacks."

"Rommel will find a way," Muirhead said, lighting his pipe. "He's not called the Desert Fox for nothing. That man is a genius at war, far better than anybody we have."

"O'Connor would have matched him," Tulloch said.

"The Italians have O'Connor in the bag," Muirhead reminded. "Now we have Neil Ritchie and Auchinleck, the Auck."

Tulloch nodded uncomfortably, unwilling to openly criticise senior officers. He had never seen, let alone met, Ritchie or Auchinleck and hoped they knew their job. The entire army knew Rommel's reputation as the best general the enemy possessed, a man who made lightning decisions and always outmanoeuvred his opposition. The Germans and Italians were said to idolise him as he cared for his men and fought within the rules of German chivalry. There were no incidents of maltreatment of prisoners when Rommel was in command, so even British soldiers admired the German general.

"We'll beat him," Tulloch said.

"I hope you're right, Tulloch," Muirhead replied. "The colonel wants our esteemed company at 17:00 hours. He'll probably give us more details then." He stood up, puffing smoke. "Keep adding booby traps; I have a feeling we might need them."

Tulloch nodded. His traps were simple trip wires attached to grenades, but every device might reduce the number of the enemy.

"Rommel has moved right around our front-line Boxes," Colonel Hume told the officers. "He's attacking the Free French at Bir Hacheim."

"How are the French holding out?" the usually quiet Major Brownlow asked.

"Very well," Hume said. "But they can't hold on forever. We'll have to try and take some of the pressure off them."

"What can we do, sir?" Tulloch asked.

"We'll take out patrols and attack his supply lines," Hume replied. "Even Rommel needs ammunition, food and water, and his convoys will have to pass us to get south." He grinned. "We hit them, gentlemen. We hit them hard, and we continue to hit them. The Durhams have the same idea, so between us, we can starve Rommel of supplies and weaken his assault on the Free French."

Hardie and Kennedy commanded the first patrol, ambushing an Italian convoy and capturing a couple of water tankers while setting a food truck on fire. They returned without incurring a single casualty and with the men in high spirits.

Colonel Hume looked moderately satisfied. "Captain Kilner, you and Erskine go next. Pick your section of road and create mayhem."

Erskine grinned. "We will, sir," he promised.

Tulloch watched as Kilner led the three-vehicle patrol into the desert. Two hours later, the Lothians saw a flash on the horizon and a rising column of black smoke.

"Kilner's patrol has hit something," Muirhead said quietly.

"It looks like a fuel tanker," Tulloch focused his binoculars, but the smoke was well beyond the horizon. The Lothians waited expectantly until Kilner led his three carriers back. Erskine was grinning as they dismounted. "Did you see that explosion? It must have shaken Hitler in his bunker!"

"We saw it," Tulloch replied. "What did you blow up?"

"An ammunition convoy," Erskine replied. "The first truck exploded, the flames hit the second, and the whole clamjammery blew to hell." He lit a cigarette, smiling. "Best fun I've had for ages."

"Was there an escort?" Tulloch asked.

"An armoured car," Erskine replied. "It got caught between two of the trucks. The poor buggers inside must have roasted to death." Although Erskine still smiled, Tulloch saw the strained lines around his eyes.

Muirhead nodded. "You did well, but the enemy will be wary now. They'll increase their escorts."

The first air raid came an hour later, with half a dozen Italian fighters arriving over the Box. They circled for five minutes before diving low to strafe the defences.

"Down, lads!" Tulloch shouted. The Fiat Freccias passed across the Lothians, firing their twin machine guns, zoomed up, and attacked the neighbouring Durhams. British anti-aircraft fire followed them, with Bren and Bofors guns trying to down the aircraft.

The Freccias flew away, mission complete, with no casualties on either side.

"That's the start of it," Muirhead emerged from the trench where he had thrown himself. "We can expect a lot more."

"If the French can hold out, so can we," Tulloch said.

"Rommel will push the French aside," Rutlane commented. "Then he'll come for us."

Muirhead grunted. "We'll be ready for him," he said.

Rutlane shrugged. "I doubt that will be enough."

Muirhead glanced at Tulloch, raised his eyebrows, and said nothing.

Chapter Five

"Lieutenant Tulloch," Colonel Hume said. "Lieutenant Rutlane has no experience of desert navigation."

Rutlane stood at the colonel's side, looking slightly sheepish.

"Take him out and teach him," Hume ordered. "Don't run into trouble."

"Yes, sir," Tulloch said. "Come on, Rutlane. We'll take a fifteen hundredweight and a section." Tulloch knew the men would complain about carrying a raw officer in a pointless patrol, but everybody had to learn, and an officer who could not navigate out in the Blue was only a liability.

"You'll enjoy desert navigation," Tulloch said once they cleared the British minefields.

"Will I?" Rutlane looked at the flat, arid terrain with an expression of distaste.

"Have you heard of Ralph Bagnold?" Tulloch asked.

"No," Rutlane shook his head.

"Bagnold was a British army officer who swanned around the Sahara about ten years ago and invented the technique of desert

45

driving and navigation. If you find his book, *Libyan Sands,* grab it. It's an invaluable guide."

Rutlane nodded. "What did he say?"

"As you see," Tulloch swept his hand across the horizon, "there are no landmarks here, which means we must pretend we are sailors and our trucks are ships of the desert." When Rutlane did not respond, Tulloch explained further. "We navigate by the compass, the sun, and the stars."

Rutlane nodded. "Right," he said.

"When a company or a battalion moves in the desert," Tulloch explained, "we travel widely dispersed as a protection from air attack. We drive in parallel lanes and follow the directions of the navigator's vehicle. At night, we laager—form a circle and dig in the trucks. We do that after dark and move away before first light."

Rutlane nodded again. "How does the navigator work during the day?"

"With a sun compass," Tulloch stopped the truck to demonstrate. The sun's heat hit him as soon as he left the vehicle, and the flies descended in a hungry buzz.

"A sun compass is a simple device," Tulloch said. "It's like a reversed sundial. In the Lothians, we carry the Cole sun compass," he showed the sun compass to Rutlane. "It's a six-inch metal plate with a needle in the centre and the hours written around the perimeter. As you know, we point a sundial to the north, and the shadow tells us the time. With the Cole sun compass, we set it for the correct bearing, and the needle's shadow falls onto the correct time."

"That seems simple enough," Rutlane said.

"Simple in flat terrain," Tulloch agreed. "Less simple when a sandstorm hits us, or we divert for a wadi, or any of a hundred things creates a course alteration. Here, you take us two miles out and back."

Rutlane shrugged and navigated them competently in the flat terrain. "That was easy," he said.

When they returned, Captain Erskine approached. "How was it, Rutlane?"

"Simple," Rutlane replied.

"That's the way," Erskine said and walked away, smiling.

"Lieutenant Tulloch," Colonel Hume said quietly. "You take the next patrol. The enemy might be prepared, so be careful."

Tulloch had guessed it was his turn next. "I will, sir," he replied.

Tulloch took three carriers, a fifteen hundredweight truck fitted with a three-inch mortar, and two six-pounder anti-tank guns on portees.

"If Rommel wants a fight, I'll give him one," he said.

"That's the spirit," Erskine approved. "Good luck, Tulloch."

Four Platoon was accustomed to desert patrols and studied the surroundings and the sky as they headed west. A lone aircraft droned overhead, heading westward. Tulloch watched it for a while, decided it was harmless, and continued with the patrol. He kept his vehicles spread out in case of an aerial attack, moved slowly to minimise the inevitable dust, and scanned ahead through his binoculars.

"They'll be waiting for us," Innes said quietly.

"We'll be looking for them," Hogg replied.

They growled across the nearly featureless terrain, with the men engaged in only desultory conversation. Innes tested the Bren's mechanism, staring at the sky for enemy aircraft.

"Dust cloud to the west," Hood reported laconically. "A big one. Maybe a convoy."

Tulloch halted the patrol. "Bed down," he ordered. "Camouflage netting! Prepare the mortar and the guns!"

The six-pounders found a stance behind a knee-high ridge, and the gunners loaded with quick, professional movements. The mortar truck circled to face the British lines, so the mortar in the back pointed towards the oncoming enemy convoy. The riflemen lay on the ground, with some scraping indentations to allow themselves a modicum of cover. There was a murmur of conversation, quickly stilled, and the men waited.

Tulloch climbed to the roof of the mortar truck, lifted his binoculars, and scanned the land to the west and north. "Lots of dust," he reported. "We have a fat, juicy target approaching, men."

The dust rose hundreds of feet, a grey-yellow curtain that concealed everything beneath. Tulloch remained standing, hoping to see details. He saw a single vehicle emerge from the flanks of the cloud, followed quickly by a second. He focused his binoculars until the details became clear.

"Mark IV Panzers!" Tulloch shouted and swore as more tanks emerged from the dust. The Mark IV Panzers had 50-mm armour and a long 75-mm gun. They were formidable vehicles, especially when opposed to thinly armoured carriers and soft-skinned trucks.

"They're heading this way, sir," Sergeant Drysdale reported. "That plane must have reported us to their higher command."

"It looks like it," Tulloch agreed.

"What do we do, sir?" Drysdale asked as a dozen German tanks headed towards the Lothians' patrol, still a few miles away but approaching fast.

"We get out of here, fast," Tulloch said. "We can't fight heavy armour." He shouted orders that saw the men scrambling to roll up the camouflage netting and board the trucks. Tulloch knew his anti-tank gunners would fight and probably account for several tanks, but inevitably, the enemy would outflank and destroy them. When the six-pounders were out of action, the Panzers would massacre the Lothians' patrol.

"Move out!" Tulloch ordered, and the patrol headed back over the desert with the tanks in pursuit.

"We're faster than they are," Tulloch assured Hood. "They won't catch us."

"We're not faster than their aircraft, sir," Hogg reminded,

scanning the skies. He held his rifle firmly as if a bolt-action Lee-Enfield was a match for a Messerschmitt 109.

"Their aircraft are not following us, Hogg," Tulloch said.

"That one might be, sir," Hogg nodded upwards and to the west, where a single black bob rapidly grew larger.

Tulloch swore silently. "Let's hope it has other occupations," he said.

Innes swivelled the Bren, pointing it skyward as Hood concentrated on his driving. Tulloch's hopes proved false as the aircraft flew directly towards them, circling overhead.

"It's a Junkers 88," Innes said.

The twin-engined aircraft circled the patrol twice, then came lower.

Tulloch surveyed his patrol. They were already in extended formation. If they scattered further, the slower vehicles would lag, becoming prey to the pursuing tanks. On the other hand, if he concentrated them in a tighter formation against the Panzers, the aircraft would have an easy target for a bombing run.

"Weave a little, Hood," Tulloch said.

"Yes, sir," Hood replied. "We'll lose speed if we do, sir."

"I'm aware of that," Tulloch said.

As the carrier weaved, it threw up more dust, which acted as a makeshift smokescreen against the Junkers.

The aircraft circled again and flew closer, firing its machine guns into the dust. Innes returned fire, emptying his magazine at the Junkers. The other carriers did the same, so three Brens fired upwards.

The aircraft zoomed upwards, avoiding the Brens' fire, circled, and returned.

"This bugger's not giving up," Innes said as Hogg handed him a new magazine. He clicked it in place and waited until the aircraft returned.

"Here it comes again!" Hogg warned.

The Junkers dropped two bombs, one of which exploded fifty yards away from Tulloch's carrier, and the other landed beside a fifteen hundredweight truck. The truck slewed to one side, with steam gushing from the engine, the front offside tyre burst, and the wheel buckled.

"Drive to that truck, Hood!" Tulloch ordered. He saw the men spilling from the rear and hoped there were no casualties.

"Anybody hurt?" Tulloch halted the carrier ten yards from the stricken vehicle.

"One man wounded, sir," Corporal Borthwick reported. "A splinter in his hip but nothing serious."

"Load the men onto any other vehicle," Tulloch looked upwards, but the Junkers was a fast-retreating speck in the distance. He waved down the mortar truck and the other fifteen hundredweight. "Get on board, lads! Quickly, now!"

The men scrambled aboard the other vehicles, with Sergeant Drysdale and Corporal Borthwick counting them onboard.

"That's everybody, sir," Borthwick reported.

"Right, off you go," Tulloch ordered. He glanced over his shoulder, for the delay had enabled the German tanks to close the gap. He saw two Panzers racing towards them, both running ahead of the dust storm they created.

"Get moving, Hood!" Tulloch ordered.

The leading tank fired a speculative shot, which landed well short of the Lothians, raising a fountain of sand.

"We've still got the legs of them, sir," Hood said. He gunned the engine as the second tank fired, with the shell again landing behind the patrol.

"Keep moving," Tulloch ordered. He checked the other vehicles of his patrol. They retained their loose formation, although the fifteen hundredweight truck was labouring under the weight of its extra passengers.

We've no time to redistribute the load. The driver will have to do his best.

The tanks fired again, with the explosions a hundred yards behind the rearmost British vehicle.

"I think we're safe enough now, sir," Hood said.

"Aye, maybe," Hogg grunted. "They Germans aren't giving up."

Tulloch raised his binoculars. The German tanks continued to pursue them, although no longer firing. He saw a smaller vehicle join the chase and then another.

"Light Italian tanks," Tulloch said. "Faster than the Germans and still with more powerful guns than us."

"Can they catch us, sir?" Innes asked.

"I don't know," Tulloch replied. "We're not far from the Box now, so we should keep ahead of them."

"They're coming pretty fast, sir," Innes reported.

"We'll just have to go faster," Tulloch said. "How's the fuel, Hood?"

"Under a quarter of a tank, sir," Hood replied. "She's not meant to move at this speed for long periods."

One of the six-pounders opened fire from its portee, with the shell exploding sixty yards from the leading enemy tank, a warning to stay clear.

"That's for you!" Hogg shouted.

The armoured cars opened fire with their Breda machine guns, the bullets raking the ground two hundred yards behind the patrol.

"Shall I return fire, sir?" Innes asked.

"Yes. You won't damage them, but it might be a distraction," Tulloch said. He glanced ahead, hoping for sight of the British Box. All he saw was a featureless desert with a few bland humps.

Three explosions rocked Tulloch's carrier and sent tall columns of sand and smoke into the air.

"Bugger this for a game of soldiers!" Hogg said.

"The Germans are getting closer," Hood remarked as small stones rattled from the carrier's armour and sand showered them.

"Those were British shells," Hogg said. "Our gunners are firing at us."

"Weave, Hood," Tulloch ordered. "The artillery must think we're the enemy. They won't make us out through the dust."

"Aye, they German tanks behind us have confused the gunners," Hogg said.

The patrol began to zig-zag, with British shells falling amongst them and fragments of shrapnel clattering from the sides of the carriers. As Tulloch watched, the second fifteen-hundredweight truck swayed to one side and came to a dead stop.

"Damn! Go and help them, Hood!"

"Sir." Hood eased into a circle back to the crippled vehicle, still weaving to confuse the British gunners. Sergeant Drysdale was on the other side of the truck, with the driver and co-driver baling out. One of the mortar crew was dead, the top of his head sheared clean off, and the others were shaken but unhurt.

"Can we rescue the mortar?" Tulloch asked, ducking as another British shell exploded nearby.

"Yes, sir!" Drysdale said and helped the mortar crew. Another shell landed, scattering shrapnel, and Tulloch waved his carrier on. "Get back to the Box, Hood! Tell the artillery to stop firing!"

"What's today's password, sir?" Hood asked.

"The challenge is Tyne," Tulloch said, "and the counter is Tees!"

"Yes, sir." Hood momentarily hesitated until Tulloch pointed to the east.

"Go!" Tulloch ordered and watched as the carrier drove away. He counted the men and distributed them among the remaining vehicles. "Get moving!" he ordered and ducked as another shell exploded.

Drysdale gasped as a fragment of red-hot shrapnel slammed into his shoulder. He swore, clutched at the wound and carried on, bleeding profusely.

With the three-inch mortar on the second carrier and the men boarding whatever they could, the overloaded vehicles drove back towards the defensive Box.

The delay had allowed the pursuing German tanks and Italian armoured cars the opportunity to close, and they opened fire.

"Now everybody is trying to kill us," Corporal Borthwick said as the vehicles dodged between British and German explosions.

At that point, the British shelling ceased as the gunners lifted their sights to hit the pursuing tanks.

"Hood must have got through," Tulloch said as the explosions erupted behind them.

"Thank God for small mercies," Sergeant Drysdale replied.

The Italians turned away immediately, but the German tanks followed for another three minutes before halting their pursuit. The British twenty-five-pounders followed the enemy armour until they were out of range, and then the gunfire ended. Tulloch led the patrol to the minefield and barbed wire.

"Welcome back, Lothians," the weary engineers said. They frowned at the overloaded carriers as they negotiated the minefield and the barbed wire, then painstakingly began to replace the anti-tank and anti-personnel mines.

"Does the infantry think we've nothing better to do than dig up and dig in mines all day long?" a grousing private asked.

The sergeant shook his head. "Slaves we are boy, slaves to the infantry's desires. Now shut up moaning and get these mines back before Rommel comes a-calling."

———

"THE GERMANS WILL LIKELY ATTACK TOMORROW," HUME SAID.

Tulloch nodded. Some of his men were depressed with the failure of Four Platoon's patrol and the loss of their companion, but Hogg and others were kicking a ball around with loud shouts and more skill than Tulloch had ever possessed. A few sang *Lili Marlene*, with Oldham revealing a surprisingly fine baritone.

"Underneath the lantern,
By the barrack gate
Darling, I remember
The way you used to wait
T'was there that you whispered tenderly,
That you loved me,
You'd always be,
My Lilli of the Lamplight,
My own Lilli Marlene."

Oldham laughed. "You might have captured hundreds of miles of useless desert, Fritz, but we've captured your song, and you're not getting it back!"

Tulloch agreed there was something very satisfactory about stealing the enemy's song, and he listened as the soft sounds of singing drifted across the desert. He saw Sergeant Drysdale sporting a bandage on his shoulder as he checked the platoon's defences, snarling at a loose tripwire and adding a couple of grenades to a booby trap

A few men tried to push thoughts of the morrow away by playing cards for pennies and cigarettes. Others boiled what water they had over a Benghazi cooker to brew a handful of much-used tea leaves into a welcome mug of char without sugar or milk. Never defeated, British soldiers used NAAFI-issue boiled sweets as sweeteners. All around the perimeter, the anti-aircraft gunners constantly searched the blue abyss of the skies. In the distance, far to the south, a low thunder reminded that the Free French were still heavily engaged with the enemy.

"How is your platoon, Tulloch?" Colonel Hume sauntered, seemingly casual, to Tulloch's side.

"The men are as ready as they'll ever be," Tulloch said.

"Are they? I wonder," Hume gestured for Erskine and Muirhead to join them. "We have a few malingerers," he said quietly. "It's a problem the Lothians have never had, but Captain

Macquarie informs me we have some men reporting sick who are fit enough to fight."

Captain Murdo Macquarie was the battalion's medical officer, a dedicated doctor who did not suffer fools gladly but would do anything when somebody genuinely needed help.

Hume glared over the assembled officers. "I won't have that in the Lothians, gentlemen. Tell your men not to report sick until they think they are dying. If a man can stand and hold a rifle, he is fit to fight."

The officers nodded.

"I've told Macquarie to send any malingerer to his platoon commander," Hume said. "I expect you to deal rigorously with them. Put any repeat offenders on report, and I'll deal with them."

Tulloch remembered the men he had seen queuing at the hospital tent.

Colonel Hume nodded. "Carry on, gentlemen," he replied, thrusting his pipe between his teeth and continuing his inspection of the battalion.

With Four Platoon's defences as secure as he could make them, Tulloch returned to the perennial problem of water. In this desert war, water was as much a precious commodity as petrol or ammunition. Whenever one side pushed the other back, the retreating army salted the water wells to deny it to the advancing force, which caused problems for the resident population as well as both armies. Tulloch knew the Axis forces would have similar, or worse, difficulties as they were at the end of a long supply line, but that knowledge did not alleviate his concerns.

In addition to the water problem, the ever-present flies brought sand fly fever and desert sores. Tulloch was bothered by the latter, with leg ulcers caused by the flies' maggots. Macquarie cured the sores by dusting them with sulphanilamide, but the scars remained. Most of the men had suffered Gyppy Tummy, an upset stomach, with the newcomers always worst affected. The most severe cases resulted in dysentery, with men sent to the brigade hospital or even back to Alexandria.

"The battalion seems to be losing a lot of men to sickness," Muirhead said.

"I noticed that," Tulloch agreed. "C Company is not too bad at present."

Muirhead nodded. "D Company is worst hit. Keep an eye on your platoon, will you, Tulloch? Ensure they take all the precautions."

"I will, sir," Tulloch promised. "Sergeant Drysdale's a good man. He knows the score."

The bugles called the stand-to just before sunset, and the football, card playing, and tea brewing ended. Men occupied their sandbagged posts, with gunners at the artillery and infantrymen waiting with Brens, Lee-Enfields, Vickers machine guns, and mortars. Tulloch peered westward, where the sun reflected from acres of barbed wire, and Rommel's army waited. He shifted his attention to the south, wondering how long the stubborn Free French could hold out against the Axis attack. The distant grumbling continued, carried by the fluctuating wind.

"Those poor Frenchies are getting it rough," Muirhead said.

"Let's hope they're giving as good as they get," Tulloch replied. "The longer they hold Rommel, the better it will be for the rest of us."

Behind the Lothians were the medical and stores sections, with the most vulnerable units in the centre of the Box. As Tulloch watched, a medical orderly escorted a suffering man to the hospital tent.

Four Platoon waited in their slit trenches, rifles ready as the sun set and darkness spread over the Box. Tulloch organised the sentries and sent the remainder to rest. His soldier's instinct told him that Rommel would attack the following morning, and he would be fighting crack German troops for the first time since France in 1940.

Are we ready to face Rommel's Afrika Korps? We'll find out tomorrow.

Chapter Six

At one the following morning, Tulloch saw a dozen coloured flares rising from the enemy side of the minefield. He was used to flares at night as patrols marked their positions and listening posts indicated activity, but never so many.

"Rommel's building up to something," he said quietly.

Muirhead nodded. "He'll hit us tomorrow without a doubt." He pulled the scarf closer around his throat, for the desert nights were cold.

Tulloch sighed. "This war is bleeding us dry. Three years now, and apart from O'Connor's advance and our relief of Tobruk, all the army has done is retreat."

"The men are all right," Muirhead replied. "And the junior officers have plenty of fight in them, but the top brass don't seem to know what they're doing. I don't like sitting in these defensive Boxes. We're too rigid, and the Boxes are too far apart to lend each other a hand if Rommel attacks. Ritchie has ignored the basic principle of warfare: concentrate one's forces on the enemy's weakest section. Ritchie has spread our strength all along the line with no individual Box capable of defeating a concentration of force."

"That's a pessimistic viewpoint," Tulloch said, surprised to hear an officer of Muirhead's experience repeatedly criticising higher command.

"It's a realistic one," Muirhead replied. "We don't have a Rommel or anything like." He glanced around to ensure none of the men were within earshot. "I have lost all confidence in our generals, Tulloch. They don't seem to have a grip on things."

Tulloch was unsure how to reply. "We'll keep fighting," he said.

"It's all we can do," Muirhead agreed. "Let's hope it's enough." He turned away, stopped to square his shoulders, and marched to his dugout.

If Muirhead is losing confidence, things must be grim, Tulloch thought.

The tension prickled as the bugles sounded stand-to at 05:30, and the Lothians manned their defences. The morning was still as the world and the veterans waited for the expected onslaught, with even the artillery in the south quiet. Tulloch saw his men checking the bolts of their rifles or ensuring they had spare magazines for the Brens. The replacements tried to act like old sweats, staring into the pre-dawn darkness as the perennial wind whipped dust into their anxious faces.

"Will the Germans come today?" Private Weeks, a recent replacement, asked.

"Maybe," Elliot, an old sweat, replied. "Rommel normally sends us a postcard to say he's coming, but he didnae bother last time."

"Nae manners, that man, Rommel," Innes said. "My auld granny would skelp his lug for him."

"I wish your auld granny were here now," Elliot said.

"So do I," Innes replied. "She'd sort Rommel out and his Afrika Korps."

Tulloch waited in his dugout, peering over the sandbags

towards the barbed wire and minefield, half listening to the banter of his men until he heard a distant growl.

"Silence, lads! Can you hear anything?"

Four Platoon stopped talking. Sergeant Drysdale lifted his head. "Aye, sir," he said. "I can hear vehicles out to the west."

Many of Four Platoon nodded agreement as the sound of engines became more distinct through the still-dark early morning. Tulloch saw a series of distant flashes to the southwest and knew they were the muzzle flares of enemy artillery.

"Heads down, lads! Rommel's saying hello!"

Four Platoon dived or ducked into cover as the scream of incoming fire sounded. A salvo of shells exploded amongst the wire, the explosions bright against the darkness. After the shell bursts, smoke and dust clouds rose and spread across the British positions.

The Lothians sat tight, with the veterans keeping the replacements calm as the slow barrage began. The enemy did not hurry; they knew the British were not going anywhere. The next salvo landed in the minefield, detonating two mines, and the third landed behind the Lothians and among the Royal Artillery.

"They've bracketed us," Drysdale rubbed at his wound.

"Aye," Tulloch agreed as a shower of small stones pattered onto the dugout roof. "Hopefully, they are just probing."

The Royal Horse Artillery's twenty-five pounders returned the enemy fire, so shells screamed in both directions above the Lothians. The men sat tight, feeling like pawns in this industrial war in which the minions of Saint Barbara contested for mastery.

"The Panzers will be next," Muirhead predicted.

"Probably." Tulloch was unsure which was worse: the hell of an artillery barrage or the grinding horror of enemy tanks. He heard somebody screaming from an adjacent platoon and wondered if a shell had wounded him or if his mind had gone under the strain. Tulloch knew that every man had his breaking point; it was not cowardice, merely the natural reaction of a man who had been tested beyond his ability to endure.

The steady shelling continued for an hour, with most shells landing short or over, but the occasional salvo struck the Lothians' position. Tulloch heard the cry of "Stretcher-bearers!" from Kennedy's Five Platoon and the rumble-clank of tanks ahead. He looked up from the dugout and lifted his binoculars to see vague shapes through the dust and smoke as German armour probed around the edge of the minefield. The RHA had also seen them and fired at the intruders, raising columns of dust around the tanks. The enemy pulled away, with only one firing towards the Lothians' position. They vanished into the dust.

"That was a bit weak," Sergeant Drysdale lifted his head. "Not like the Germans at all."

"They'll be back," Tulloch replied as the artillery duel continued. "They were just probing our defences."

"According to our Intelligence wallahs," Muirhead said, "Rommel's still hammering at the French in Bir Hacheim, but he's sent some units round the rear of our main Gazala line. The Durhams have done wonders against the Ariete Division, and one Durham carrier captured an entire undamaged tank."

"Well done, the Durhams," Tulloch replied.

"They couldn't take the tank in," Muirhead said, "but they got the crew." He peered out of the dugout. "Has Rommel run out of shells? The Germans have stopped firing."

"It's a ploy," Tulloch said, scanning the landscape through his binoculars.

Ten minutes later, the shelling recommenced with greater intensity. Explosions erupted around the Lothians' and Durhams' positions, and Italian infantry advanced into the minefield.

"Here they come!" Drysdale shouted, with others echoing his call.

Hume ordered the Vickers to fire, and the machine gun sliced into the slowly advancing Italians. They pressed on, with their engineers searching for a safe passage through the minefield, until their casualties became too heavy, and they withdrew, leaving dead and wounded men on the ground.

Macquarie and a party of stretcher-bearers moved into the minefield to help the casualties, ignoring the danger.

"Some of these medical lads are conshies," Muirhead mused. "The bravest men I have ever met."

Tulloch agreed. He had heard that some civilians abused conscientious objectors, but many joined the medical teams and braved shellfire and mines to help the wounded. Tulloch had never heard a serving soldier treating them with anything but respect and often with admiration.

The artillery fire continued, with airbursts above the Lothians and the Durhams and heavy machine guns raking the forward positions. Casualties mounted, with one dugout taking a direct hit and eight men killed or wounded. Captain Macquarie raced to the spot to help.

"Come on, you bastards," Hogg shouted. "The Gorgie boys are waiting."

Another flurry of artillery hit the Lothians, and then the armour returned, with German and Italian tanks pushing to the edge of the minefield without venturing inside. The Lothians' anti-tank gunners joined the RHA in firing, leaving two Italian M14 tanks smoking wrecks and blowing the tracks from a German Panzer Mark III.

"We're holding them back," Lieutenant Kennedy said.

"They haven't mounted a serious attack yet," Tulloch said. "They are only gauging our strength or keeping us occupied."

The shelling increased in the afternoon. The enemy targeted the Royal Artillery position behind the Lothians, with the 25-pounders returning fire. Tulloch saw the RHA hammer an enemy convoy, setting most on fire, while to the south, British and enemy tanks engaged each other in murderous gun battles around El Harment.

When the enemy barrage died away, the Lothians took the opportunity to escape the confinement of dugouts and trenches.

They eased cramped limbs, stared at the shell craters and looked for casualties.

Erskine lit an Egyptian cigarette and wandered across from D Company with Rutlane at his side.

"Rommel's outflanked us," Rutlane said. "He's going to attack the Boxes one at a time and wipe us out."

"The brass designed these Boxes for all-round defence," Tulloch reminded. "And the enemy hasn't put in a determined attack yet."

"He will," Rutlane said. "Rommel always knows how to defeat us."

"He's never faced the Lothians before," Muirhead reminded. "And the Durhams know how to fight."

Rutlane opened his mouth to reply and closed it as Colonel Hume arrived, pipe in mouth and steel helmet pushed to the back of his head. "This attack is only beginning, gentlemen," he said. "Ensure you keep the men fed and rested."

The shelling started again, intensified towards evening, and died away around ten. Smoke drifted across the Lothians' position. Tulloch looked around, with burning vehicles illuminating the night. Four Platoon had escaped with one man slightly wounded.

"Get some sleep if you can," Tulloch ordered. "Tomorrow might be a busy day." He doubled the sentries, retired to his dugout, dismissed Hood and lay fully dressed on his bed. Tulloch closed his eyes and tried to blanket the thought of tomorrow, and within half an hour, he heard shouted orders from the RHA to their rear.

"What's happening?" Tulloch struggled to his feet, groggy with weariness.

"The RHA is moving away," Muirhead reported.

The enemy must have heard the engine sounds and began to shell the Horse Artillery, with the flash of each explosion allowing a tiny vignette of movement. Tulloch saw the gunners loading their quads and carrying stores, ammunition, and equipment across the desert. He saw shouting NCOs and swearing drivers, men hitching up guns, and others ducking from the shells. Tulloch also heard the occasional scream as enemy shells found their mark.

Although the RHA shifted further back, dawn found the Lothians in the same position, with the wire and minefield intact before them and enemy tanks patrolling outside. The Lothians' anti-tank gunners quietly readied their six-pounders.

"They'll come in force today," Colonel Hume said. "Remember, we're the Lothians."

Some men grunted; others made quiet comments, some favourable, others humorous or obscene. Tulloch toured Four Platoon and ensured the men ate something and their water bottles were full. When the enemy artillery altered their targets, with more shells landing among the Lothians' positions, Tulloch ducked into his dugout. He lay there as the barrage continued, listening to the crash of exploding shells, the growl of distant engines and the patter of sand and small stones landing on his dugout roof. The RHA responded from their new positions, with the bark of their 25-pounders adding to the general mayhem.

"Here they come!" Captain Muirhead shouted. "Take your posts!"

Tulloch swore and forced himself to stand, holding a Lee-Enfield as he faced westward.

"Up you get, lads!" Tulloch shouted.

The Lothians rose from the bottom of the slit trenches, raised their weapons and cursed the enemy.

"Fire as soon as they're in range," Tulloch ordered. "The more we drop, the fewer there are to drop us!"

Italian infantry supported the German tanks as they crashed into the minefield. The RHA was busy firing at the tanks, leaving the Lothians to deal with the infantry. The Vickers fired first, hammering at the advancing infantry, and then the Brens joined in. The Italians threw themselves to the ground, with one unfortunate man landing on a mine and blowing himself up.

"Six-pounders!" Hume shouted, and the Lothians' two anti-tank guns opened fire. Within minutes, the sound was deafening, so Tulloch knew Four Platoon would not hear his orders. Aiming his rifle, he fired and saw an Italian NCO spin and fall. He felt nothing, for during action, the enemy soldiers were less than human. To think anything else was to invite weakness and lessen his professionalism as a soldier. He could allow sympathy for the fallen when the fighting was over.

"Get that Bren firing, Innes!" Sergeant Drysdale ordered.

"Changing magazines, Sergeant!" Innes replied.

A moment later, Tulloch heard the reassuring regular thump of the Bren, so different from the crazed rattle of the enemy machine guns. The German tanks pushed forward, firing as they came, with their shells exploding amongst the barbed wire before the Lothians, whose two anti-tank gunners fired back. Brass shell casings piled up beside the six-pounders as the gunners sweated, bare-chested in the heat.

One Italian M14 swung away, momentarily exposing its flank as a shell exploded in front. The Lothians' six-pounders took full advantage and fired an anti-tank round at the tank's broadside. Tulloch distinctly heard the clang as the heavy shell smashed right through the hull, and the tank came to a sudden halt. The hatch opened, and one man scrambled out, yelling. He lay beside the tank as the Lothian gunners searched for the next victim.

Enemy shells burst above the Lothians' positions, sending showers of sharp shrapnel downward as the Italians cautiously picked their way across the minefield. Tulloch heard a yell and saw Private Weeks rise from his trench, holding his face. A burst of machine-gun fire caught him, tearing off half his head. Tulloch looked away, knowing Weeks was beyond help.

The riflemen were firing, working their bolts and firing again, with the Italian infantry's advance slowing as they took casualties from the mines and the Lothians' bullets. Two tanks pushed through the Italians to roll directly onto the barbed wire, creating a path for the infantry until both the Lothians' six-pounders fired in unison. The nearest tank slewed sideways, gushing out smoke and with its turret at a crazy angle. One man emerged, burning, and another tried to follow, only to collapse back inside the now-blazing vehicle. The second tank slowed and began a quick return, with six- and twenty-five-pounder shells searching for it.

"Shoot the buggers!" Hogg roared, firing, working the bolt and firing like a man possessed. His lips were pulled back, revealing misshapen but surprisingly white teeth.

"They're losing interest," Muirhead shouted as the Italian advance slowed.

"Push them back," Tulloch ordered.

The Lothians increased their rate of fire, encouraging the Italians' retreat. One British private rose from his trench to improve his aim, only to die as a tank's machine gun targeted him. The Italians withdrew in good order, still losing men to the Lothians and the mines. The British artillery concentrated on the tanks until they also retired, leaving five of their number on the ground. The enemy artillery increased and then died away, leaving the contested ground to the smoke, the dead and the wounded. Captain Macquarie sent his stretcher-bearers out to help the suffering men.

"Sergeant Drysdale!" Tulloch shouted. "Give me a casualty report!"

"Sir!" Drysdale responded immediately. "Private Weeks is dead, sir, and Lance-Corporal Burnham wounded."

Tulloch nodded. Four Platoon had escaped lightly. He looked at the sky, always surprised at how quickly time passed in action. He would have said an hour had passed since the enemy attack, but it was nearer four hours. "The day is wearing on," he said. "They won't be back today."

"We've beaten them back," Kennedy remarked.

"We have," Tulloch said. "Yet they don't seem to have

launched a powerful attack yet. A push of one Italian battalion and a dozen tanks is hardly worth mentioning."

"What do you think, Tulloch?" Kennedy asked.

"I still think Rommel is operating a holding action with us and putting in his main attack elsewhere," Tulloch replied. "Come on, Kennedy, best check our defences and ensure the men have water and ammunition."

Kennedy nodded. Tulloch did not mention the tear stains on his cheeks; he had seen scores of men cry in battle.

When the Axis' attack faltered, the artillery stopped for an hour, and then the barrage restarted, hammering the Lothian and Durham positions.

"They're softening us up," Rutlane shouted.

"Keep your heads down!" Tulloch gave unnecessary orders as he dived into the bottom of his dugout. The bombardment continued until dark, after which only a few shells landed to keep the men from sleep.

Tulloch checked the sentries, ducking whenever a shell landed close. He sent two lightly wounded men to the regimental field dressing station where Murdo Macquarie worked by torchlight. The Axis respected the red cross flags that flapped in the breeze, and Macquarie operated on British, Italian and German wounded with equal care.

Another shell landed, throwing Private Maxwell into the air and landing him outside his trench, face up and mouth open in shock. Tulloch hurried across, saw the great tear across Maxwell's chest and wondered if he would live. He called for stretcher-bearers and pressed a field dressing over the wound.

"We'll see you back soon, Peter," Tulloch said, placing a cigarette between Maxwell's lips.

"Yes, sir," Maxwell said, too dazed to realise how badly wounded he was. "Thank you for the fag, sir."

Tulloch wondered where the British Army would be without their daily ration of Victory V cigarettes. Smoking calmed the nerves of battle-battered men and soothed the worries of the rest. In Tulloch's opinion, the smokers were less likely to suffer battle fatigue and could cope better with the stress and horror of battle.

A man in the hospital tent screamed again and again and then sobbed into silence. The sound seemed to echo across the Box, a reminder, if one was needed, of the true nature of war.

"All right, Tulloch?" Colonel Hume appeared from the dark, pipe in mouth, with his eyes surveying Tulloch from scratched steel helmet to sand-coated boots.

"Yes, sir," Tulloch replied.

"You know, in thirty- or forty years, when we are old doddering men, we'll bore our grandchildren with stories of our days in the desert and how grand it was and how we enjoyed the experience." Hume stopped to refill his pipe. "Utter nonsense, of course. Only a psychopath or a fool could enjoy war in the desert or anywhere else. War is a disgusting business, always was and always will be. But we are doing our bit for freedom and democracy, and it's an experience that will live with us the remainder of our lives."

"Yes, sir," Tulloch agreed. They stopped to watch a flare rise to the north, blaze briefly, and slowly sink to the earth.

"Get some sleep, Tulloch," Colonel Hume ordered. "This battle isn't over yet."

Tulloch nodded. He could hear tanks rattling and creaking beyond the minefields. "Tomorrow is another day, sir."

Chapter Seven

The half-past-five stand-to brought an intense barrage that sent the Lothians into their dugouts and saw the supporting Royal Horse Artillery fire to the west, south, and east.

"They're all around us, sir!" Sergeant Drysdale re ported.

"I noticed," Tulloch agreed. He slipped from his dugout as the barrage eased and checked Four Platoon. One man, Donaldson from Dalkeith, was dead, and two others were wounded. *The enemy is slowly whittling us down.* Tulloch sent the injured to the Regimental Aid Post and looked upward as he heard aircraft engines.

"Stukas!" Innes yelled a warning.

The British anti-aircraft guns opened up, followed by the Lothians' Brens. Tulloch counted a dozen German dive bombers peeling off, one after another, with the sinister black crosses prominent on their wings and tail. Tulloch threw himself into the nearest slit trench, holding his helmet with both hands. He remembered the hellish scream of the Stuka from the campaign in France two years previously and tried to burrow his way deep into the sand at the bottom of the trench.

The sound enveloped him, seeming to tear at his sanity so it replaced all rational thought. There was only the sound of the Stukas, that hideous scream that preceded the bomb, that noise that filled his head to the exclusion of all else.

"Come on, you Nazi bastard!" Hogg's snarling voice broke through Tulloch's fear, and he realised his fists gripped the sand, and he had pressed his face into the bottom of the trench.

Dear God, am I near my breaking point after being wounded at Keren?

Tulloch forced himself to crouch and then stand. Innes had lifted his Bren and pointed it to the sky, with Hogg at his side, aiming his rifle in a defiant, if near-futile, gesture.

"Now, Innie!" Hogg shouted and fired his Lee-Enfield.

The Stukas dropped their bombs in their near-vertical dives, then rose away. That was when they were at their most vulnerable, and the British anti-aircraft gunners took full advantage, hitting them as they climbed. Tulloch could only admire the courage of the men who stood at their posts under that terrible scream as he heard the steady stutter of the Bren guns. Innes was among them, firing at the exposed underbelly of the dive-bombers.

When Tulloch emerged from the slit trench, he saw eleven Stukas flying away, one with smoke streaming from its left wing and another with its engine stuttering. The remaining aircraft was burning on the ground as a section from D Company's Six Platoon approached it with fixed bayonets.

"What's the odds that Adamson sticks his bayonet in that Nazi pilot?" Innes asked calmly.

"About evens," Hogg replied. "They Stukas are more noise than anything else. They're fine at dropping bombs when nobody's fighting back but rubbish when fired at."

As the smoke cleared and men emerged from their slit trenches, Tulloch heard another roar of aircraft, and half a dozen

Italian fighters appeared, strafing the ground with machine guns. The Brens retaliated as the Lothians dived for cover again.

"Welcome to another happy day inside the Gazala Box." Captain Muirhead skidded beside Tulloch, with one hand holding his helmet in place and the other grabbing at the trench wall.

Tulloch edged aside to make room. "It's a bit busy," he shouted.

"Busier than you think!" Muirhead shouted. "The Germans are still pushing hard at the southern edge of the Box with tanks and infantry. We don't know how long the boys down there can hold out."

"How about our armoured reserve?" Tulloch asked, trying to think amongst the bedlam of battle.

"I hope Ritchie uses them soon," Muirhead replied, ducking as a shell exploded twenty yards away, showering them with sand and stones. "But even so, Valentines and Honeys against Mark Four Panzers! The German armour far outmatches ours. I say the tankies are heroes."

"We have Grants as well," Tulloch reminded.

"Grants are little more than armed and tracked petrol tanks," Muirhead said. "The lads in them sit on gallons of fuel and explosives. If the enemy hit them with a shell, the poor buggers haven't got a hope in hell. Organise your platoon to face south, Tulloch."

"Yes, sir!"

Fortunately, the trenches were arranged for all-round defence, so Four Platoon could fight an enemy from the south without significant movement. Tulloch ignored the expected grumbles as the men shifted their alignment, with the Bren gunners moving sandbags to give them a better field of fire if the enemy attacked from a different direction.

At eight that morning, Tulloch heard the first gunfire from the south and saw the orange-red flowers of explosions.

"Here we go again," Smith said.

"Here's spare ammunition, sir," Hood appeared at Tulloch's side. "And a biscuit."

"Thank you, Hood," Tulloch replied automatically, pocketing the biscuit as he glanced around Four Platoon's position.

Innes and Gordon guarded the flanks with the Brens while Corporal Borthwick commanded the three-inch mortar team.

The Lothians' anti-tank gunners crouched behind their six-pounders as the RHA artillery swung into action, firing to the west and south.

"Tanks!" Hood warned as three ominous shapes crawled out of the smoke and dust to the south. "The Germans have broken through the defences."

Hogg swore foully and aimed his rifle. "Nae infantry yet, lads! Come on, gunners, do your stuff!"

"They might be friendly!" Elliot warned.

"Friendly, my arse!" Hogg replied crudely.

The Lothians' six-pounders held their fire until they were confident the tanks were enemy, then both fired simultaneously. The leading tank slewed to the side with one track blown off, and the Bren gunners and Hogg mowed down the crew as they escaped.

"That's done for you, you murdering Nazi bastards!" Hogg shouted.

The second tank turned and withdrew, but within a few moments, more tanks arrived, British and German together. They engaged in a vicious fight that spread across the south of the Box, with their guns firing as they shifted across the sand. The heavier German tanks held the advantage, and Tulloch saw three British Valentine tanks on fire with their crews running for cover as the Germans machine-gunned them. Men fell, one burning and another diving into the meagre cover afforded by the sand ridge a turning tank had created.

The RHA joined in, firing at German tanks approaching from the west and south, with their twenty-five pounders firing nearly non-stop and empty shell cases piling up beside the guns.

"Gunners!" Hume shouted to the Lothians' anti-tank guns. "We have limited ammunition. Only fire if the tanks threaten our position."

A corporal raised his hand in acknowledgement as a squadron of Stuart tanks occupied the slight ridge behind the Lothians' position.

"That's bad news," Kennedy said. "They'll draw the German fire right onto us."

"Or protect us from the enemy," Tulloch responded.

A battery of German 88-millimetre guns opened up, hammering the infantry positions and the ridge.

"Where the hell did they come from?" Tulloch asked. "Our south flank must be wide open."

"They've got our number," Muirhead shouted as two shells landed close by, sending shrapnel and small stones over their dugout.

Tulloch heard a pitiful scream, wondered who was wounded and hoped it was not one of his platoon. "Where's our artillery?"

"Mostly knocked out," Muirhead replied. "That first salvo landed right among the RHA." He ducked as another shell landed close. "The 88s are firing a mixture of HE and shrapnel. Maybe they're softening us up for an infantry assault."

"I prefer facing infantry to being shelled with no possibility of replying," Tulloch said, his eyes constantly roving around his platoon. "What happened to our tanks?"

"Here they come now!" Muirhead said. "They must have been forming up."

Tulloch glanced over his shoulder at the ridge. The noise of the artillery had shielded the tank engines, but now he was aware of the squealing, grinding sound they made. He saw a squadron of American-built M3 tanks, officially known as Stuarts but more often known affectionately as Honeys.

"Who are these tankies anyway?" Tulloch asked.

Muirhead glanced over. "They're the County of London

Yeomanry," he replied. "I know nothing about them but their name."

Tulloch watched as the Yeomanry's colonel spoke to an officer of the Royal Horse Artillery. The artilleryman shook his head in violent disagreement, but the colonel smiled and raised his hand to his troop.

"What the hell is that man doing?" Muirhead asked as another shell exploded nearby.

"Watch and see," Tulloch advised.

"He's charging them!" Muirhead said. "The bloody idiot is charging the 88s!"

Tulloch saw the colonel lift a red flag and heard him shout in a lull between shell bursts. "Charge! Tally ho! Tally ho!"

"It's not a game!" Muirhead said, shaking his head. "That idiot acts like he's still hunting foxes!"

With the colonel in the lead, the London Yeomanry charged forward against the dug-in battery of German 88s.

"The brave, suicidal fools!" Muirhead said.

"He's getting his men killed," Tulloch replied as many of the Lothians stopped to watch the Yeomanry charge the German artillery.

Presented with the dream target of a regiment of light tanks advancing against them in the open, the German 88 gunners took full advantage. They fired on the hunting colonel's tank first, blowing off the turret and leaving only a smoking wreck. Others soon followed, with destroyed or disabled Honeys quickly littering the killing zone. When they realised the suicidal nature of their attack, most of the remaining tanks halted or turned away, while a few continued, firing blindly into the smoke and dust that concealed the German position.

Tulloch saw one tank reverse out of the battle as if the steering gear was jammed. Others tried to fire at the Germans until it was apparent they were outgunned and fighting a hopeless battle. The survivors withdrew, having achieved nothing except giving the enemy target practice and sacrificing brave men on the altar of Mars.

"What a bloody waste," Muirhead said, shaking his head. "What a bloody, futile waste."

"As a Frenchman said when he watched the Charge of the Light Brigade," Tulloch said, "It's magnificent, but it's not war."

Muirhead sighed, lifted his binoculars and scanned the battlefield, now littered with disabled and burning British tanks. "Until we learn how to use our tanks properly," he said soberly, "we'll never win this bloody war. We're too profligate in human lives and material, and we don't have a sufficiently deep reservoir of either to squander men forever."

"We need a decent general and better training," Tulloch said. "Or we're destined to repeat the same mistakes until we run out of soldiers."

The German tanks seemed to be everywhere, firing, manoeuvring and returning to the smoke, only for another to take its place. Tulloch watched through his binoculars as the Germans destroyed more British tanks and overran the RHA positions. The British tanks and gunners fought, firing until the German armour overpowered them, and Tulloch saw a thin trickle of khaki-clad men led away as hapless prisoners.

"Rommel's defeated us again," Rutlane said.

"We're not beat yet," Tulloch replied. He aimed and fired his rifle, aware it was useless against German armour but determined to resist.

"Gin ye daur!" Sergeant Drysdale shouted. He had borrowed Smith's Boys anti-tank rifle and fired at the closest German tank, swearing when the shot made no impression.

Tulloch saw Corporal Dawson dash from his trench to rescue a badly wounded man. Then a tank fired, and Dawson vanished. When the smoke cleared, Dawson lay on the ground with his lower half shredded. He lifted a hand and died without saying another word.

Mixed with the bite of acrid smoke was the sickening stench

of human flesh roasting inside the tanks. Tulloch saw three Valentines emerge from the smoke and charge towards two Mark IV Panzers. The Valentines' shots bounced off the Panzers' armour, and then both German tanks fired. The first two British tanks stopped, with one burning, and the third continued its attack, trying to ram the nearest Mark IV until another German shell blew its turret off.

"Brave, brave men," Kennedy said.

"What a waste of lives," Tulloch replied, repeating Muirhead's earlier phrase.

The remaining RHA guns targeted the Mark IVs, hitting one and forcing the other to retreat inside the smoke.

"Thank God for the artillery," Muirhead said. "Tulloch, get over to HQ and tell the Colonel we're holding out, but we need more artillery support."

"Yes, sir," Tulloch said.

Negotiating a hundred yards of open desert to Colonel Hume's dugout was nerve-wracking, and Tulloch was glad to dive through the sandbagged entrance and deliver his message.

Hume nodded. With his pipe a fixture between his teeth, he seemed to be a symbol of security in the frantic world of the Gazala Line.

The Listening Post telephone rang, and Colonel Hume lifted it. Tulloch heard the voice at the other end of the line: a sergeant from Lieutenant Kennedy's Three Platoon.

"The Germans are right in front of us!" the sergeant said, his voice rising at the end of the sentence.

"Get out of there!" Hume ordered. "Leave the post and get back inside the Box!"

"It's impossible, sir! They're too close." The sergeant shouted something incoherent.

Tulloch heard the crackle of musketry, followed by shouting, a long scream and a German voice, then silence.

"That's the LP gone," Colonel Hume said as he replaced the telephone receiver. "The opposition is pressing us hard now!"

The shelling began again, a salvo of a dozen shells around the Lothians and RHA positions.

"The Germans will attack from the west now," Hume said, blowing three blasts of his whistle—his signal for the Lothians to man the defences.

When the Lothians emerged from their slit trenches, the enemy infantry and tanks had advanced past the OP.

"They're at the western wire!" Lieutenant Hardie of E Company shouted as the Lothians opened rapid fire to the west.

German engineers led German infantry in halftracks through the minefield the Italians had probed the previous day, while half a dozen armoured cars growled in the rear. The Lothians greeted them with small arms fire supported by the Vickers machine guns and the steady thump-thump of the three-inch mortar. The Germans pushed on in short rushes, accepting casualties from anti-personnel mines and Lothians' bullets. One halftrack rose and fell with a heavy thump as it ran over a mine, spilling out its cargo of infantry, and others followed the path the Italian and German engineers cleared.

The Lothians fired on the infantry, with the enemy tanks and armoured cars trying to quell the British fire.

"They're advancing on two sides, sir," Captain Muirhead reported.

Colonel Hume nodded and ordered B and D Company to face the threat from the south.

With the Lothians well dug in, the men remained static, firing at everything that resembled an enemy soldier. Shells screamed overhead, targeting the surviving Royal Horse Artillery, whose guns were causing havoc on the enemy vehicles.

"Six-pounders! Hit those halftracks!" Colonel Hume ordered, and the Lothians' anti-tank guns altered their targets. A German shell landed between the guns, with the shrapnel scattering onto both emplacements. Most of the six-man crew of one gun fell, dead or wounded, while the second gun remained unscathed.

The men redistributed themselves and continued to fire both six-pounders, albeit at a slower rate.

The German infantry had negotiated the minefield, and their engineers and halftracks were clearing a way through the barbed wire. Tulloch saw two German quick-firing guns mounted on portees ease through the smoke in the south, with squads of infantry on either side. They moved quickly, worryingly professional, as they approached the Lothians' positions.

The Lothians' six-pounders split, with one concentrating on the advancing portees and the other on the halftracks. The German artillery continued to pound the RHA, with only one British twenty-five-pounder still firing, and the remainder dismounted, surrounded by dead and wounded men. Tulloch saw one gunner lying screaming, with the splintered bone of his thigh showing through. A gun quad lay on its side, and a three-ton lorry blazed, spouting black smoke. A bombardier ran through the shell fire to rescue another wounded man, who lay with his clothes burning and one arm hanging loose.

A shell landed beside the two Lothian six-pounders, dismounting one and killing half the already reduced crew of the other. The remaining men, dazed from the explosion, recovered and continued to work their surviving gun. The Germans in front rolled up the shattered remnants of the RHA, capturing those men who could not escape. A squadron of Panzers followed, heading straight for the Lothians' position.

"Mark IIIs and Mark IVs," Sergeant Drysdale grunted, "and we have one workable anti-tank gun and half a crew."

The six-pounder fired, with the shot crashing into a Mark III and damaging the left track. The tank skidded to a halt, its gun swivelling to point directly at Tulloch's dugout. It fired, missed, and the crew baled out when a ribbon of smoke rose from the inside.

"Thank God for that," Tulloch said.

"Message from the brigadier, sir!" A panting runner shouted, ducking as an exploding shell showered him with sand and stones. "The Germans have broken through in the south and west. We're withdrawing to the next Box to the north."

Hume cursed. "Move out!" he ordered. "We've lost our armour and artillery. Keep together, men, and shoot anything that looks German or Italian."

Tulloch remembered the chaos of the retreat to Dunkirk. "Four Platoon! Stay with me! Sergeant Drysdale, take the rearguard."

"The Germans are too close," Rutlane said. "They'll overrun us."

"Only if we allow them," Muirhead replied. "Tulloch, Four Platoon is rearguard. Do what you can."

"Get the Boys Rifle!" Tulloch ordered, looking around for Smith, his specialist in the anti-tank rifle. "Sergeant Drysdale fired it last!"

"We may as well throw stones at the tanks than fire that thing!" Kennedy said.

"It's a damn sight better than nothing!" Tulloch snarled as Smith lugged the unwieldy weapon to the front and balanced it between two sandbags.

"My elephant gun can do wonders," Smith said defiantly. "Wait until the bastards get close, and I'll have a go at them!"

"Save it for the Mark III or portees," Tulloch ordered. "Don't waste it on the Mark IVs."

"Yes, sir," Smith replied.

Heavy machine-gun fire sprayed the dugouts, puncturing the sandbags and sending a fine spray of dust into the air. The men ducked low, bobbed up, and returned fire with their rifles. Hogg was snarling his hatred, and Tulloch briefly wondered if he wanted to attack the German tanks with his bayonet.

"They're getting closer!" Private Kelly shouted, firing three rounds rapid and working the bolt frantically.

"Are you ready with the Boys, Smith?" Tulloch asked as the first German tank clanked closer, half-hidden by the smoke gushing from the blazing British Matildas.

"Ready, sir!" Smith confirmed. "It's not close enough yet! We must wait until it's within three hundred yards."

The Mark III clanked closer and fired its 50-mm gun. The shell passed over the Lothian's forward trenches and exploded in the rear, causing only minor damage and incurring no casualties.

"Fire the bloody thing, Smith!" Gordon shouted.

"Another minute, Gordae!" Smith insisted.

Tulloch swore quietly as the tank fired again, with its machine gun rattling at Five Platoon's dugouts, raising clouds of dust and sand. The platoon replied with futile musketry.

"Fire the thing!" Tulloch ordered.

Smith pulled the trigger, and the Boys recoiled, jerking him backwards. The projectile clattered against the tank's flank and bounced off harmlessly. Smith swore. "It doesn't have enough penetration, sir!"

"Down, boys!" Tulloch said as the tank rumbled to within two hundred yards and swivelled its machine gun towards them.

"Aircraft, sir!" Hood shouted as the Bren gunners swung their weapons to face the sky.

"Friendlies!" Hardie screamed as four RAF Blenheims roared down. One by one, they dropped bombs on the Germans and reformed for another run. Their first run destroyed the leading Panzer and forced the others to withdraw.

In the resulting temporary vacuum, Colonel Hume withdrew the Lothians.

"On the buses, boys!" Hume shouted. Only the fortunate boarded what remained of the battalion transport, while the majority marched, shouldering their personal weapons and heading northward while the Germans recovered.

"Captain Muirhead!" Hume ordered. "C Company is the rearguard! The anti-tank gun will remain with you."

Tulloch nodded; as C Company was in the most southerly position, he expected nothing else.

"Keep down, boys," Muirhead ordered. "Smith, take the

Boys, but only for armoured cars or half-tracks. Move out on my word!"

Tulloch saw that one of the Lothians' six-pounders was still useable, and sufficient gunners were alive to form a skeleton crew. The Bedford three-tonner was battered but workable, able to tow the gun, and the mechanics spent a few frantic minutes attaching the weapon before joining Tulloch's Four Platoon at the very tail of the rearguard.

The Lothians headed north, with the Germans consolidating their position except for a few probing tanks. A squadron of British Grants contested the German advance but were outgunned and outnumbered. They stood their ground until the Panzers reduced them to blazing wrecks, buying the retreating infantry precious time at the expense of their lives.

The Lothians marched north through an array of wrecked and burning tanks and lorries. Most of the casualties were British, although the Axis had also lost heavily. Smashed British guns lay amid the sand, with dead bodies from both armies lying side by side. A shifting blanket of flies furred the dead in an obscene parody of life as the sweet smell of death merged with acrid smoke and raw blood as the Lothians passed through.

"What a bloody shambles," Sergeant Drysdale grunted.

"All we do is fight and run," an anonymous voice from Six Platoon commented. "We may as well wait for Rommel as lose more men fighting him."

"Minefield ahead!" somebody shouted, and the battalion halted. Tulloch could see men in the distance, khaki-clad soldiers heading eastward towards Egypt in a general retreat. Burning vehicles added to the black smoke pall above, with an occasional attack from the Luftwaffe. Tulloch did not see any British aircraft, with the Axis powers having near-complete command of the air.

At the rear of the battalion, Tulloch was unsure what was happening ahead. He heard the crackle of small-arms fire and the crump of exploding shells.

"We'll have to hold the line here," Muirhead said, "until the colonel can find a way through the minefield."

Tulloch thought again of the retreat in France, except here, there were no allies to blame for the British Army's failings.

The men fought as best they could. We are facing a military genius in Rommel.

"Dig in!" Tulloch ordered, and Four Platoon hacked at the ground with whatever tools they had, creating shallow trenches which seemed little enough protection against German tanks.

"Keep digging, boys," Drysdale ordered. "Cattanach, you need more depth."

"I've hit solid rock, Sergeant," Cattanach replied quietly.

"Then pile sand in front," Drysdale said. "It won't stop a tank but might slow a bullet."

"Message from the colonel, sir!" Second Lieutenant Thompson panted up to Muirhead. "The tanks and engineers have made a route through the minefield. Wait for further orders, and then follow the white markers!"

"We will do," Muirhead said. "Tell the colonel we're right behind him."

"Yes, sir," Thompson looked strained, with rivulets of sweat down his sand-caked face. He had aged in the past few days. He turned away and ran back, slithering on the loose sand.

Everybody ducked as a flight of Messerschmitt 110s strafed C Company, sending men diving for cover. Tulloch threw himself into the bottom of the shallow trench he had scraped in the rocky sand and lay there as machine-gun bullets raked the ground. The aircraft made three passes and flew on, and when Tulloch emerged, Thompson was dead, with his blood soaking into the sand. A rising wind whipped up the surface sand, obscuring visibility. Their last six-pounder was also gone, blown to twisted fragments along with its crew.

"We'll miss these lads," Muirhead said, "and the firepower."

"I can't see the rest of the battalion," Tulloch said, peering into the stinging sand.

"We'll remain here until the wind drops and then follow," Muirhead told him. "We won't find the gap in the minefield with all this muck flying about."

The sandstorm lasted longer than Tulloch expected, and it was nearly dark when the wind finally dropped. They heard the rumble-clatter-squeak of tanks as the light faded and then relative silence, broken by intermittent shooting. Tulloch saw the slow rising lights of tracer fire, followed by the rapid descent, and then saw the bright flash of exploding shells, although he could not tell whether they were British or German.

"We'll move at first light," Muirhead amended his previous instructions. "The Germans are quiet at present, but we won't see the cleared passage through the minefield in the dark."

"Keep alert!" Tulloch posted sentries to watch the platoon's front. "The Germans don't attack at night but might send out patrols."

Innes lay beside his Bren, staring into the fire-punctuated dark. "We'll be ready for them, sir."

Muirhead toured the perimeter, stopping to talk to each sentry. He stood beside Tulloch, staring into the dark.

"This situation is very familiar, Douglas."

"Too familiar, sir," Tulloch replied. "I thought we had finished with defeats by now." He thrust his pipe between his teeth. "I thought O'Connor's victories had turned the tide, but we've not had much luck on land since the Italians captured him."

"We need a general like Rommel," Muirhead said. "The men are becoming disheartened with constant defeats and reverses. So am I."

"I've heard the men talking," Tulloch agreed. "They see Rommel as unbeatable. The Jocks always grumble, but the officers are as bad now."

"Let's hope we can turn the tide," Muirhead lifted his binoculars and scanned the night.

"It's not only here," Tulloch said. "We're doing badly in the

83

Far East as well. We've lost Malaya, North Borneo, Singapore and Burma, and the Japs are pushing at India as well."

Muirhead nodded. "If Rommel takes Egypt, he'll advance to the oil wells in Iraq and Persia; we'll have lost the Mediterranean and the Middle East. Things are even grimmer than they were in 1940."

"If Hitler controls the oil fields, he'll have won the war," Tulloch said. "He'll push his armies through Persia to attack India in the west while the Japs attack the east. Either that, or he'll strike at Russia from the south. We've quietened the pro-Nazi groups in Persia and Iraq, but if Rommel arrives, they'll rise again, and we don't have the manpower to stop them."

Both officers looked up when firing broke out to the east.

"I'd better see what's happening," Muirhead said. "You hold on here, Douglas. Grab some sleep if you can."

Tulloch knew he needed sleep, yet he could not settle with Four Platoon in danger. He compromised by dozing in his trench, relying on Hood to wake him if necessary. The intermittent crackle of small arms and crunch of artillery punctuated the night with flares and the occasional rumble of vehicles.

"Sir," Hood spoke quietly. "It's nearly five." By some miracle, Hood had produced a mug of hot coffee sweetened with a mint humbug. Tulloch drank it gratefully, shivering in the cold desert dark. He checked Four Platoon and got them ready for the day.

Muirhead withdrew the rearguard at five, with the sound of desultory gunfire to the south, west and east.

"We'll find the marked passage through the minefield," Muirhead said. "And move the ribbons when we're through. No sense in helping Rommel."

C Company moved platoon by platoon, inching to the north and east, leapfrogging each other as they searched for the tape-marked passage through the minefield.

"There's no sign of the battalion," Kennedy reported.

"Shades of Dunkirk," Tulloch said, forgetting Kennedy had joined the Lothians long after the campaign in France.

The light was growing when they found the white tape in the minefield, half-buried by the recent sandstorm. Muirhead was first to enter, ensuring the passage was safe, with the rest of C Company following on.

"That's the first stage complete," Tulloch said. He was the last man to leave the box and shifted the white tape so it led directly into the mines. After a hundred yards, Tulloch snipped the tape and rolled it up.

"Stay within the ribbons, lads," he ordered, looking behind him.

That's the end of the Gazala battle. Now, where do we go?

Chapter Eight

"Tanks!" Hood warned.

"Down, men!" Muirhead ordered.

C Company froze, lying on the bare surface and feeling very exposed as the officers studied the tanks.

"Italian," Muirhead said. "They're in the Box."

"Nobody's firing," Tulloch remarked. "The garrison has either packed it on or left."

"Either way can't help us," Muirhead said. He glanced over his company. "It looks like Rommel has broken Ritchie's line."

"We're buggered then," Kennedy said.

They scanned the surroundings, seeing smoke rising from a dozen different places. Tulloch heard artillery fire to the north.

"Somebody's fighting, at least."

"Where do we go, sir?" Kennedy asked.

"Tobruk," Muirhead said. "If anywhere holds out, Tobruk will."

"Tobruk held out before," Tulloch agreed. "It will hold out again. The South Africans hold it, so I hope they're as good as the Aussies."

Kennedy nodded. "Tobruk," he repeated as if he was hailing the Gates of Heaven.

"We're cut off here," Muirhead informed them. "Rommel must have pushed Ritchie well to the east if we have Axis forces all around us."

"Rommel's scattered us," Kennedy said. "He's ripped us apart. Our only chance is Tobruk."

"Let's hope Colonel Hume had the same idea," Muirhead said. He pulled a map from his fifteen-hundredweight truck.

"Gather round, men." He pointed to Tobruk. "With luck, we can make it by nightfall."

They moved on, less concerned about concealment now and more with covering the miles. They passed burned-out and abandoned vehicles, shell craters and the occasional dead body—British, Italian or German.

"We've lost a lot of men, sir," Hood said.

"Too many," Tulloch agreed.

The company motored on, stopping to refuel in a waste of gravel. The wind was rising, and men nervously watched the sky for enemy aircraft.

"The petrol cans are leaking, sir," Hood reported. "We've lost more than half the fuel. I wish we had jerrycans rather than this useless British rubbish."

"We'll ask Rommel to lend us some," Tulloch replied. "How much is in the tank?"

"Between a quarter and a half, sir," Hood said. "And that's the last can."

"Dump the cans," Tulloch ordered. "Maybe Rommel will pick them up and run out of fuel."

C Company moved on, grinding over the gravel waste for an hour without seeing another vehicle, enemy or friend. The gravel ended gradually, easing into an undulating sandy plain that slowed their progress to a crawl.

"This soft sand is eating our fuel, sir," Hood said. "We're already down to a quarter of a tank."

"It will be the same for everybody," Tulloch said.

"Yes, sir," Hood agreed. "We'll end up walking to Tobruk." He glanced out the side window. "The wind's picking up again."

Tulloch nodded. "We'll have to navigate by compass," he said.

The convoy jolted on, losing speed with every mile as the wind whipped up surface sand. Hood tried the windscreen wipers, swearing when they only caused a yellow smear across the glass.

"I can hardly see the vehicle in front, sir."

"Put your lights on," Tulloch replied. "Ensure the truck behind can see us."

"I have, sir," Hood replied.

"Sound your horn," Tulloch ordered. "Let the truck in front know we can't see him."

"Yes, sir!" Hood had to shout above the whine of the wind. He blew the horn without any response from the vehicle in front.

"We'll have to rely on faith, luck and prayer," Tulloch yelled.

The wind buffeted the truck, blasting sand against the windscreen and the canvas cover. Hood drove on, struggling with the steering wheel.

"It's hard to control her, sir. I can't see a thing in front!"

Tulloch tried to look in the side mirrors, but the sand had coated them, denying him any view behind.

"We'll have to stop or lose the rest of the platoon!"

"Yes, sir!" Hood pumped his foot on the brake, flashing the brake light to warn the following truck. He stopped, and Tulloch dismounted. The truck with the remainder of the platoon was ten yards behind, with its lights hardly visible through the flying sand.

"Debus, lads," Tulloch ordered. "We're going nowhere until this storm blows itself out."

Four Platoon filed outside, sheltering their faces from the stinging sand.

"Find some shelter," Tulloch ordered. "Lieutenant Kennedy and I will stand watch."

"The Germans won't operate in a sandstorm," Kennedy said.

"Did they tell you that?" Tulloch asked. "Take the north and west. I'll take the south and east."

"Yes, sir," Kennedy replied.

The storm lasted for two hours, scouring and building up sand on the windward side of the trucks. After a last flurry, it eased away, leaving a yellow-brown landscape seemingly empty of life.

"I can't see the rest of the company, sir," Sergeant Drysdale said. "We're alone."

"We'll move faster alone," Tulloch said. "We'll try to get to Tobruk before Captain Muirhead."

"He'll be well ahead, sir," Kennedy said.

"We'd better get moving then," Tulloch told him.

"We'll have to drive the trucks out of the sand," Kennedy said.

"Driving will only dig them in deeper," Tulloch said. "We'll need the sand channels. Have you used them before?"

"No, sir," Kennedy said. "I've never heard of a sand channel."

"All our vehicles carry them," Tulloch explained. "They're straightforward and very effective devices." He looked up as Hood produced a pair of sand channels from the rear of the truck.

"You see, Lieutenant? It's a steel sheet a foot wide and the same length as the truck's wheelbase. All we have to do is dig out the sand from the rear wheels, insert the channels under the wheels and drive."

"Why the rear wheels, sir?" Kennedy asked.

"The trucks are rear-wheel drive," Tulloch replied.

The men worked in shifts, hacking at the sand with shovels, sweating and swearing as flies clustered around them. The sand trickled back, so the men repeated their efforts twice or thrice to clear the same material.

"If I wanted to dig holes, I'd have been a bloody navvie!" Hogg growled.

"Think yourself lucky," Connington, an ex-coal miner, told him, digging with short, economical strokes. "When we were down the pit, we shovelled three times this weight lying on our side eight hours a shift in an eighteen-inch space."

Hogg snarled back, and they continued digging.

"Right, lads," Tulloch ordered. "That might do. Let's try the sand channels." He watched as two men slid the devices under the wheels and the drivers started the vehicles.

"Hurry up, for God's sake," Elliot murmured. "I heard a plane a minute ago."

The drivers drove along the channels, hoping to create sufficient momentum to overcome the soft sand. The men watched, some openly praying, others cursing, and the majority silent. Both trucks continued, kicking up thick clouds of sand.

"Throw the channels on the trucks!" Tulloch ordered urgently. "Then board yourselves!" He knew the extra weight of the platoon would put more strain on the vehicles and watched anxiously as the men clambered inside, one by one. He was last on, opening the passenger door of the cab and climbing in beside Hood.

"Off you go, Hood!"

"Yes, sir," Hood said and slowly depressed the accelerator.

The platoon gave an involuntary cheer as the trucks moved forward, sliding in the soft sand yet moving approximately northeast, towards sanctuary, towards the fortress town of Tobruk that had already defied everything Rommel could throw at it.

Tulloch allowed Hood to concentrate on driving with the compass on the dashboard and the needle wavering only slightly. They hit an area of hard, stony ground and powered on, increasing speed to a steady twenty-five miles per hour. Tulloch began to relax as his mind drifted to Amanda. He wondered where she was, what she was doing, and if she ever thought of him out here in the Blue.

Would he still see her after the war? Tulloch wrestled with the question for only a minute. Yes, he decided. Their desultory relationship was not a mere wartime romance but the real thing. He smiled at the prospect, pictured Amanda in a white wedding dress at the door of St Cuthbert's Church in Edinburgh's New Town and then realised he had not asked her yet.

The truck slammed to a sudden stop, throwing him forward against the dashboard and causing shouts and curses from the men.

"What the hell's happening?"

"Hey, driver! What are you playing at?"

"I want my fare back! The driver cannae drive!"

"Sorry, sir," Hood apologised. "We've hit soft sand again."

"Debus, men!" Tulloch ordered. "Is anybody hurt?"

Apart from a few bumps and bruises, nobody was injured, and the men disembarked and started the whole process with the sand channels again.

By the time the truck was again moving, daylight was fading. Tulloch ordered them to stop for the night.

"If we toodle up to Tobruk in the dark," he explained, "the sentries are more likely to shoot than ask for our visiting card. We'll arrive when they can see us coming."

The stars were brilliant that night, making the desert seem peaceful in defiance of the tens of thousands of men dedicated to killing each other. Tulloch ordered camouflage nets spread over the trucks, posted sentries, and hoped the water and fuel would last. Both trucks were well under a quarter full, with the soft sand rapidly draining the tanks for minimum mileage covered.

Flashes to the south and west disturbed the peace with the sound of distant gunfire, although nothing came close to Tulloch's Four Platoon. They spent an uneasy night, and Tulloch had them moving an hour before dawn, watching for enemy movement as they drove towards Tobruk.

Hood looked around as the engine coughed, recovered and coughed again.

"She's nearly out of fuel, sir."

"Push her as long as you can, Hood."

"Yes, sir."

Hood managed to squeeze another mile from the truck before it stopped, with the dawn glorious in the east and the second truck pulling up at their side.

"Trouble, sir?" Sergeant Drysdale asked.

"Out of fuel," Tulloch replied. "How are you?"

"About the same, sir," Townsend, the second driver, replied. "We're scraping the paint from the fuel tank now."

"Drive on," Tulloch ordered. "My men will march at your side."

Townsend's petrol lasted another half mile, and then Four Platoon was foot slogging over the desert with the sun burning down on them.

"Sergeant Drysdale," Tulloch ordered. "Take three men and scout ahead. We should be near Tobruk's outlying minefield now."

"Yes, sir," Drysdale said. "Innes, Hogg and Cattenach, you're with me."

Tulloch waited until the patrol was a hundred yards ahead before following with the main body. He moved slowly, ready for a challenge from Tobruk's outposts or a warning shout from Drysdale.

"Dust, sir," Hood warned, and Tulloch motioned for the men to lie down. Prone sand-smeared men in khaki were less visible than upright soldiers. They heard heavy engines and the sudden blast of artillery, and then the rising dust altered direction.

"The defenders are awake, then," Tulloch said.

"Indeed," Kennedy replied.

"Here comes Sergeant Drysdale," Corporal Borthwick said. "He looks a bit agitated."

"Sir!" Drysdale said. "We reached the old minefield, but the sappers have lifted the mines, sir."

Tulloch narrowed his eyes. "Are you sure?"

"As sure as I can be, sir. I know a minefield when I see one, and we probed for a hundred yards square and found nothing except a few holes where mines used to be."

"Very good, Sergeant," Tulloch said.

Four Platoon moved on, keeping in Drysdale's footsteps as they reached the margin of the old minefield. Tulloch saw the gouges where the sappers had moved the large anti-tank mines.

"We'll take this slowly," he decided, "and probe for mines as we advance."

The platoon advanced slowly, with their confidence increasing when they found no mines. Tulloch saw low, white buildings in the far distance, with smoke above them.

"That must be Tobruk, sir," Drysdale said.

"Halt!" The command came from ahead.

"That sounded like a German to me," Kennedy said.

"Who are you?" The voice was guttural and strongly accented.

"Down, lads," Tulloch ordered, "they might be hostile."

Four Platoon needed no second command and threw themselves down. Innes readied the Bren, with Gordon at his side with spare magazines. Tulloch remained standing.

"Who are you? Tell me, or we fire!" The unseen man repeated his demand in German and another language Tulloch did not recognise.

"Four Platoon, C Company, Lothian Rifles," Tulloch replied. He braced himself, waiting for the blast of machine gun fire that would cut him in half.

"Come forward slowly," the voice sounded again.

"Who are you?" Tulloch asked.

"Second South African Infantry," the voice responded.

Of course! That explains the accent.

"Right, lads, extended formation, move slowly and be prepared for an ambush," Tulloch ordered.

As Four Platoon walked forward, Tulloch heard heavy artillery to their right, and the sharper crack of small arms.

Men in khaki uniforms waited behind low sandbagged walls, with a Bren gun and a dozen rifles pointing. Knowing how nervous men in OPs could be, Tulloch ordered Four Platoon to halt thirty yards from the South African position.

"In you come," the subaltern in charge ordered. "I am Lieutenant Johannes Van Collier."

"Lieutenant Douglas Tulloch and Four Platoon."

"I've notified the battalion commander of your arrival," Van Collier said.

"Thank you, Lieutenant," Tulloch said.

"We made it!" Kennedy said. "We're safe now! The Germans will never take Tobruk!"

Chapter Nine

TOBRUK, SUMMER 1942

Tulloch had expected to see gun emplacements, barbed wire and heavy machine guns defending Tobruk's perimeter, especially with the absence of a minefield. He was surprised to see only a handful of six-pounders and some bemused Durhams.

"What's happening?" Tulloch asked a Durham subaltern with his arm in a sling and blood and sand caking one side of his face.

"No idea," the Durham looked dazed. He forced a weak smile. "I think there is a rallying point somewhere within the Tobruk defences."

"Are you all right?" Tulloch asked.

The Durham nodded. "A bit shook up."

"Do you want to join us?" Tulloch gestured to his platoon.

"No, thank you. I'm sure there will be other Durhams along shortly." The subaltern glanced at the half dozen men who stood, smoking and talking quietly behind him. "This is all that's left of my platoon."

"Here! You!" A beefy South African major bustled up. Tall, blonde and erect, he halted close to Tulloch.

"Who are you?"

"Lieutenant Douglas Tulloch, Lothian Rifles," Tulloch replied evenly. "Who are you?"

The major's eyebrows drew together in a frown. "I am Major Bosman." He looked Tulloch up and down.

"You are under my orders now, Lieutenant," he said.

"Yes, sir," Tulloch agreed. He felt his men bristle behind him.

"If you leave my unit or disobey my orders, I will charge you with desertion." Bosman glanced over Four Platoon. "Your men are a disgrace."

"My men have been moving and fighting for weeks, Major," Tulloch felt his anger rising.

"They are neither moving nor fighting now," Bosman said. "Get them tidied up."

"Yes, sir," Tulloch replied. "As soon as I find them water, food and ammunition." He saw Major Bosman's frown deepen.

"I'll remember you, Lieutenant, and report you to your commanding officer."

"His name is Colonel Hume, sir," Tulloch called helpfully as Bosman marched away.

"Was that wise?" Kennedy asked. "We're under his command."

Tulloch grunted. "I am not sure about that," he said.

"He's a superior officer," Kennedy reminded.

"He's not in the Lothians," Tulloch replied. He saw Sergeant Drysdale standing a few yards away.

"I'll tell you a couple of stories later, Kennedy. Sergeant Drysdale!"

"Sir!" Drysdale said.

"Can you find us water, food and ammunition? If anybody objects, use my name. If they press, use Major Bosman's."

Although Drysdale's expression did not change, his eyes warmed. "I'll do that, sir."

Tulloch found a vacant area and settled Four Platoon down behind a sandbagged sangar, which provided some protection against enemy air or artillery attacks. He called Kennedy to him.

"Now, Kennedy, in a previous war, a notable commander named Pakenham commanded a small British army fighting in the War of 1812. The Lothians had survived five years of fighting in the Peninsula and were weary. Two veterans were on sentry duty at a mansion during a ball when Pakenham stormed in. Neither of the sentries came to attention or saluted, which annoyed Pakenham. He demanded to know why they refrained from showing him the respect due to his rank."

"What did they say, sir?" Kennedy asked.

"They said they only obeyed officers from the Lothians," Tulloch replied. "Of course, Pakenham went through the roof. He cursed them and the regiment for everything under the sun and swore he'd never have the Lothians under his command again. That is why we were not at his famous battle of New Orleans."

"We lost that one, didn't we, sir?" Kennedy asked.

"We did. Pakenham was an atrociously bad general, and New Orleans was another shockingly mismanaged battle in an unnecessary conflict, a by-blow of the Napoleonic Wars." Tulloch was quiet as he watched Sergeant Drysdale feed and water Four Platoon.

"I have another regimental story for you, Kennedy."

"What is that, sir?"

"Go back another century and more to the Glorious Revolution of 1690," Tulloch said.

"I remember it well," Kennedy said solemnly. "That was when William of Orange became king and deposed King James the Somethingth."

"That's correct. William landed in England with his army of Dutch and Scottish soldiers, and James fled. Most of the Royal regiments switched allegiance without a qualm, presumably because William was Protestant and James was Roman Catholic."

Kennedy nodded. "I think I knew that," he said.

"The Lothians refused to follow the trend," Tulloch held Kennedy's gaze. "Nearly alone of the King's regiments, they remained true to their salt. They marched back to Scotland, and it was some time before the Scottish parliament persuaded them to swear allegiance to William."

"Were the Lothians a Catholic regiment?" Kennedy asked.

"Roman Catholics were not permitted to join the army," Tulloch replied. "They were honourable men. The Lothians have always been different from other regiments. We do what we think is right, and if a senior officer gives us an order we believe dishonourable, we disobey."

"I see, sir," Kennedy said. "What are you trying to say?"

"I am saying that I won't follow orders from an unknown officer if it means sacrificing my men."

Kennedy looked startled. "You can't disobey orders, Tulloch."

"I hope I don't have to," Tulloch said.

Four Platoon made their new home as secure as possible, replacing the sandbags to create deeper dugouts and placing their Brens to provide crossfire. Major Bosman visited, grunted as he saw them dig in, and stalked away with a frowning lieutenant at his back.

"See who our neighbours are, Sergeant," Tulloch ordered.

"I have, sir," Drysdale replied. "We don't have many. The South Africans have only a thin defence and not much artillery."

Tulloch nodded. "Thank you, Sergeant." He glanced around Four Platoon's position. The South Africans on either flank looked nervous, with camouflaged transport parked a few hundred yards behind and men already looking over their shoulders.

Let's hope the Auck has something up his sleeve. I don't like the atmosphere here.

The Luftwaffe appeared shortly after dawn the following morning. The first wave consisted of thirty Ju87s, the dreaded Stukas, backed by fifteen twin-engine Ju88s. Simultaneously, the

Germans launched their infantry at the town's meagre outer defences.

"Here come the Luftwaffe!" Drysdale warned as most of Four Platoon crouched deep into their trenches. Only Innes and Hogg retaliated, with Innes firing short bursts with his Bren and Hogg mixing invective with Lee-Enfield bullets. Tulloch saw a few of the South Africans also firing.

The German aircraft dropped a mixture of smoke and thousand-kilogram bombs, with the smoke mixing with rising dust. Tulloch heard the clatter of small arms to his right, mingled with hoarse shouting and a high-pitched scream.

"That doesn't sound good, sir," Innes said as the Luftwaffe roared away and the defenders cautiously emerged from their dugouts.

"Hold the line," Tulloch replied, peering into the confusion of smoke, fire and dust ahead. The screaming continued, high-pitched, as if a youngster was severely wounded.

"Fire if you see the enemy."

Four Platoon manned their defences, rifles ready, eyes narrowed and hard in faces already coated in sand. They heard firing ahead, the steady thump of Bren guns mixed with the staccato crackle of rifles and rapid chatter of Italian and German machine guns.

"They're pushing at the South Africans," Kennedy said.

Nobody replied. Tulloch saw Bosman and his satellite lieutenant on their left, scanning their front through binoculars. A column of smoke rose vertically, smudged as a gust of wind whipped it, and resumed its climb.

"Where's the enemy infantry?" Kennedy asked.

"Waiting," Tulloch replied. Smoke covered the ground, thicker in the old shell holes that disfigured the ground, visibly shredding above twelve feet.

"They're in the smoke, either crawling closer or gathering for a rush."

"Can we fire, sir?" Hogg asked.

"No," Tulloch replied. "Let them come close, and we'll destroy them."

Hogg nodded. His thin lips twisted into a parody of a grin. "Yes, sir."

"Here come the Luftwaffe again, sir," Innes said, nodding to the sky in the west.

"That will be to precede the assault," Drysdale said quietly.

"Get down, boys; the Germans won't send their men forward into an aerial bombardment."

The Luftwaffe arrived three minutes later, half a dozen Me110s that circled, ignoring the Bofors anti-aircraft fire until they lined up their target. They came over one after the other, dropping sticks of bombs behind the Lothians and South Africans' positions, with a couple falling astray. The Lothians remained in the slit trenches, face down, praying, cursing and hoping to survive the next day, the next hour or the next few minutes. The bombs exploded in a series of crashes, throwing up sand and smoke, spreading shards of deadly metal, and tearing holes in the ground.

Innes swore, stood and fired his Bren at the rapidly disappearing aircraft.

"You're wasting ammunition, Innes. They're out of range."

The Me110s flew serenely away without damage despite the Bofors shells that exploded around them.

Tulloch heard a South African voice shout, "They've hit the Regimental HQ!"

Smoke rose behind them from the new bomb craters as men rushed to repair the damage, and stretcher-bearers ran to attend to the wounded.

The explosions began again in spurts of six and then ten, landing around the Lothians and South African trenches.

"Mortars!" Tulloch shouted.

Mortar bombs rained down on the front-line positions, landing in groups of ten and probing from one section of the line to another. Tulloch disliked mortars because there was no warning and no defence. They came silently and landed vertically so that slit trenches gave little or no protection from a direct hit. Four Platoon crouched inside, cursing the bombs that lifted the sand and rained dust on their helmets and uniforms.

"German infantry approaching!" Sergeant Drysdale shouted.

"Stand to, lads!"

"Where are minefields when we need them?" Innes asked, lying beside the Bren gun.

Drysdale shook his head. "The Engineers lifted most of the mines to use on the Gazala line."

"Bugger this for a game of soldiers!" Hogg gave his habitual response.

Tulloch saw the German infantry moving with professional skill, covering each other as they moved quickly in small groups. He had taken a rifle from a dead man, worked the bolt, aimed and fired as Four Platoon tried to repel the German attack. Innes fired short bursts with the Bren, grunting with satisfaction whenever he brought down his man.

"We're holding them, boys!" Drysdale shouted.

Tulloch flinched as a bullet passed within an inch of his head, and another raised a fountain of dirt at his left shoulder. He heard Hogg speaking in a constant monotone that mixed obscenity with blood-curdling threats as he fired, worked the bolt and fired again.

"We've got bolt-action rifles," Kelly said, "and they have machine guns. It's hardly a fair contest." He unhooked a grenade from his webbing, dragged out the pin and threw it forward. As he recovered, a bullet smashed into his face, tearing his lower jaw away. He stiffened, lifting his hand to his face, and a burst of machine gun fire ripped into his chest.

"That's Kelly gone," Hogg said, firing with unconcealed venom.

"The Germans have penetrated the line!" Drysdale shouted.

"They're behind us!"

Tulloch glanced over his shoulder and saw German infantry

two hundred yards to Four Platoon's left, heading in their direction.

"Number Three Section, veer left and hold them!"

A German Spandau opened up on the right flank, raking the front of Four Platoon's position with rapid fire and sending men diving for cover.

"They're on both flanks, sir," Hood shouted.

"They've broken through the South Africans."

"Time to retire, lads," Tulloch ordered, "or the Germans will cut us off."

"They're no' putting me in the bag," Hogg said, savagely squeezing the trigger.

Tulloch pulled the platoon out section by section, with Drysdale taking the leading section as he remained with the rearguard, firing whenever he saw an enemy soldier.

"Ammo!" Innes shouted. "Ammo!"

Hogg passed over his two spare Bren gun magazines and shouted to see who had a spare magazine.

"Come on, lads! Don't be shy! Help out Innie!"

"They're all around us!" Smith said, staggering under the weight of the Boys.

Tulloch saw two German machine gun teams set up MG42s on either flank of Four Platoon.

"Get down!" he ordered.

The men threw themselves into the bottom of the slit trenches or behind sandbags as the German machine guns raked their position. One man stiffened and rolled over as the others clung to the sand, trying to make themselves as small as possible.

When the German machine gun fire moved to other targets, Drysdale checked the casualty.

"McDonald's dead, sir."

Tulloch nodded. McDonald was one of the latest to join the platoon, a tall, dark-haired Portobello man with an air of superiority and little else.

"The Germans will take care of him."

In the desert campaigns, each side looked after their opponents' dead and wounded. The atrocities committed by the SS in France or by the Japanese in the Far East were unknown. In that respect, the North African campaign was as civilised as war could be.

Four Platoon continued the withdrawal, moving section by section across the battered desert, halting whenever they found somewhere defensive and moving on when they heard German or Italian voices between them and the town of Tobruk. Twice, they thought they reached a secure position, only to find enemy troops surrounding them.

"The South Africans have collapsed," Kennedy panted.

"Maybe," Tulloch said. "They might have a defensive line further back."

"Armoured cars, sir," Drysdale warned. "Italian Fiat 611s!"

Two of the Italian armoured cars moved forward with their machine guns poking forward, seeking a target.

"Do you still have your elephant gun, Smith?" Tulloch asked.

"Yes, sir," Smith showed the clumsy Boys.

"Take out the leading car," Tulloch ordered and raised his voice.

"Find some cover, men, and defend Smith!"

Chapter Ten

TOBRUK, SUMMER 1942

Four Platoon lay down, some scraping at the harsh sand, others prone behind the sandbags the previous defenders had left. Cattanach rolled over to Smith, carrying spare ammunition for the Boys.

The Fiats moved slowly, twenty yards apart. One drove directly for the Lothians' position.

"He's seen us!" Kennedy said.

"I've got him, sir," Smith aimed the Boys, blinking sweat away from his eyes. "Wait until he comes closer."

The second Fiat fired to the right of Four Platoon, spraying a slight undulation and raising a cloud of dust.

"Another ten yards," Smith said. "Come on, my friend." He took a deep breath, released it slowly and fired.

The shot rocked the Fiat sideways and knocked a hole in its side. The hatch opened, and a man scrambled out, yelling.

"Leave them," Tulloch ordered. "They're no threat to us."

Smith reloaded hastily as the second Fiat turned towards Four Platoon, with its machine gun hammering. Drysdale threw a grenade, which bounced from the Fiat's armour and exploded in the air, scattering fragments. The Fiat continued its advance, still firing.

"Brave man," Tulloch commented.

"Shoot it, Smith! Kill it!" Kennedy yelled.

Smith swore. "The gun's jammed, sir!"

"Clear the jam!" Kennedy yelled, looking over his shoulder.

The armoured car reared closer, firing its machine gun in short bursts. Innes replied with his Bren, knowing his bullets could not penetrate the Fiat's armour.

The Fiat came closer, kicking up dust.

Tulloch did not see the South African artillery until a salvo exploded around the Fiat. The armoured car slewed to the side, and another salvo followed. A direct hit smashed the front of the vehicle, sending smoke and fire high into the air.

"Thank you, Lord," Tulloch said.

"Over here!" A South African voice called. "A hundred yards behind you!"

Four Platoon thankfully ran back to join the South Africans in a line of sandbagged entrenchments, well camouflaged.

"I know you. Who are you?" Major Bosman demanded. He peered towards the burning Fiats.

"Lieutenant Tulloch, Lothian Rifles," Tulloch said.

"Oh yes, I remember you people. You came from Gazala." Bosman was about forty, with a broad face and bright blue eyes.

"That's right, sir," Tulloch agreed. "The enemy is pressing hard here."

Bosman nodded. "I don't think we'll be able to hold them," he said.

"We'll do our damnedest!" Tulloch replied.

"It won't be good enough," Bosman said simply. "We've lost Tobruk."

"What?" Tulloch frowned. Tobruk had been a symbol of endurance when the Australian infantry and Royal Artillery held it during a seven-month siege the previous year. Losing Tobruk was unthinkable.

"We'll keep fighting, sir."

"It's no use," Bosman said. "Rommel is too good for us. We've lost Tobruk, and we'll lose Egypt as well."

Tulloch saw Hogg staring at the major in disbelief while Kennedy nodded in agreement.

"With all due respect, sir, we haven't lost Tobruk, and we won't lose Egypt either," Tulloch said.

"Don't argue with me, Lieutenant!" Bosman snapped. "You don't understand the gravity of the situation! Don't you understand? We're finished. Rommel has won! The sooner we surrender, the fewer lives we'll lose."

"Bugger that for a game of soldiers," Hogg grunted. He glared at the major.

"We'll keep fighting," Tulloch dropped the sir. "We'll keep fighting until we win."

"Here they come, sir!" Innes shouted. "Elliot! You're my number two on the Bren!"

"Take positions, men," Drysdale shouted. "Give the Springboks a hand!"

German infantry advanced through the smoke, with the South Africans greeting them with desultory small arms.

"Let them have it, Lothians!" Tulloch shouted.

"Gin ye daur, you bastards!" Sergeant Drysdale roared the Lothians' motto.

"Gin ye daur!"

"Aye, gin ye bloody daur!" Hogg glanced at the South African major and yelled a slogan from his pre-war gang fighting days.

"No surrender!"

Four Platoon fired like the veteran soldiers they were, with Tulloch thinking that Hogg's venom was directed as much at the South African major as the enemy infantry. Tulloch aimed at a tall German NCO, fired, saw his man spin, worked the bolt of his rifle and aimed again. Innes's Bren hammered, clearing a space in front of the left flank, and then a halftrack loomed through the smoke, crammed with men.

"Smith!" Tulloch shouted.

"Have you cleared the Boys yet?"

"Yes, sir," Smith replied.

"Then hit that thing!"

"Yes, sir!"

Smith aimed the Boys, waited for a moment and fired when the halftrack rounded one of the burning armoured cars. The vehicle leapt up, its nearside track broken and unravelling. The infantry spilt out, led by a shouting NCO. The Lothian riflemen and Innes picked them off with professional callousness.

"Gin ye daur!" Drysdale shouted. He tossed a grenade, grunted at the resulting carnage and glanced around.

"Keep your line, boys. Fritz is sending more men."

"Ammo!" Innes shouted. "I need magazines for the Bren."

"I'm down to two bullets for the Boys," Smith said.

"Sir!" Hood yelled. "The South Africans are packing in!"

"What?" Tulloch looked to his left, where the neighbouring unit had raised the white flag.

"What the devil is that all about?" He saw a group of South Africans stand up with their hands raised.

"No surrender!" Hogg sounded incensed.

"We're no' fucking surrendering!"

Major Bosman approached Tulloch.

"The town of Tobruk has surrendered," he announced. "You are ordered to lay down your arms and walk to the nearest German soldier to give yourself up."

"I am damned if I will," Tulloch told him.

"Not a chance!" Hogg supplemented his words with a powerful string of obscenities.

"You are under South African command," Bosman reminded them. "If you fail to surrender, you are disobeying orders, and if you leave Tobruk after our lawful orders, you are guilty of desertion."

"Aye, get to Freuchie!" Tulloch snarled.

"We're not surrendering." He raised his voice.

"With me, Four Platoon!"

"Maybe we'd better do as the major says," Kennedy said. "We're under South African command here."

"Remember what I told you about the Lothians," Tulloch reminded. "We only obey orders from our own commanders." He grunted.

"And as for surrendering, talk to Private Hogg."

As the South Africans walked towards the Germans with their hands raised in surrender, Tulloch led Four Platoon in the opposite direction, with Hogg glaring over his shoulder at Major Bosman.

"Where are we going, sir?" Drysdale asked.

"To the harbour," Tulloch said. "If we can escape from the Germans in France at Dunkirk, we can escape from them in Libya. We'll find something that floats and head east along the coast to Egypt."

"What if there isn't a boat?" Kennedy asked.

"We'll bloody swim," Tulloch roared and then moderated his tone."We'll cross that bridge if we come to it."

Four Platoon withdrew at speed, with the Germans either not concerned with a few escapees or too busy rounding up prisoners to notice their departure.

"Don't stop," Tulloch ordered, "ignore everybody unless they fire at us." He led them at a fast trot, passing burning vehicles and shattered houses, with dozens of shell and bomb craters and many dead bodies. Looking dazed and confused, South African and British troops waited in small groups, some hoping for a superior officer to give them orders, others angry or frustrated.

An occasional German or Italian aircraft flew over, but the anti-aircraft guns were silent, and their crews waited listlessly in the streets.

"We've surrendered," one man shouted as Tulloch led Four Platoon past.

"We havenae," Hogg responded.

"The garrison has to give up!" the man replied.

"Aye? Get tae!"

Tulloch smiled grimly at Hogg's comment. Four Platoon marched on, breaking into a trot when they passed open ground, heading northwards towards the docks. A few other men, stragglers, individuals and small groups moved in the same direction. Some attached themselves to the Lothians.

"Are you men surrendering?" a Royal Artillery bombardier asked.

"Nae chance," Hogg replied.

"We'll join you, then," the bombardier said, whistling up a couple of gunners.

"Come on, lads, we're not dead yet!"

When they reached Tobruk, half the town seemed to be on fire, with palls of smoke coiling upward or wafting through the narrow streets. The inhabitants mingled with soldiers, staring at the Lothians as they marched past.

"Is this Tobruk?" Elliot asked. "It's no' worth defending. It's worse than Gala, and that's a dump."

Tulloch felt himself grin. Trust a Borderer to bring up local rivalries in the middle of a World War.

"Keep moving, boys," Sergeant Drysdale encouraged.

They passed more bewildered soldiers, South African and British, and heard outbreaks of firing from behind them.

"Some people are still resisting, sir," Drysdale said.

"Maybe we should join them."

"If we do, we'll end up in the bag," Tulloch told him. "I mean to rejoin the battalion and defeat Rommel."

"I can smell the sea, sir," Corporal Borthwick said.

The town opened up quickly to the harbour, where black smoke smudged the water, and the dead crew lay around a bombed Bofors gun.

Wrecks littered the harbour, memorials to the previous year's epic siege, but Tulloch looked in vain for anything like a seaworthy boat. Two jetties thrust into the water, which seemed invitingly cool compared to the oppressive heat on land. A litter of bodies lay on the quay, with one khaki-clad and wounded infantryman apathetically watching the Lothians. Smoke rose from the gun positions that should have defended the harbour entrance, and Tulloch saw a desolate gun barrel pointing skyward.

"What now?" Kennedy asked. "There aren't any boats."

"See that wreckage in the water?" Tulloch grated.

"Gather it together. We'll make a raft!"

Kennedy opened his mouth to object, saw the determination in Tulloch's eyes and nodded.

"Very good."

A litter of rubbish lapped the sides of the harbour, from hatch covers to lengths of timber and all the tragic paraphernalia of sunken ships.

"A raft, sir?" Drysdale asked.

"A raft," Tulloch repeated. "We'll paddle out of here if we must. Get the lead out, Sergeant, before Rommel comes knocking at the door."

"Yes, sir," Drysdale replied.

Four Platoon had barely started pulling together a collection of planks when a German voice sounded from behind them.

"Here comes Uncle Rommel now," Innes said, reaching for his Bren.

Tulloch looked around to see a section of enemy soldiers marching towards them, with an athletic-looking NCO in charge.

Chapter Eleven

Hogg aimed his rifle as the German infantry marched into the harbour.

"Wait!" Tulloch ordered. "They don't know who we are. Don't make any aggressive moves. Keep working." He watched the Germans as they marched towards Four Platoon.

When the German NCO barked something that sounded like a command, Tulloch looked up.

"What do you want now?" he asked. "Your officer ordered us to clear the harbour of wreckage."

The German NCO looked confused. He pointed to the Lothians' rifles and asked something else. About half the patrol levelled their weapons at Four Platoon.

The heavy machine gun clattered from the harbour, and a motor launch eased from behind one of the wrecked ships, with the white ensign flapping astern. It came close inshore, with its twin Oerlikon hammering the German patrol, and eased to a halt as the Germans fell, scattered or leapt for cover.

"Come out!" a fruity English voice ordered. "Swim out and join us! Hurry!"

"I cannae swim!" Hogg shouted.

"Grab a plank, Hogg!" Tulloch ordered. "Keep afloat, and we'll push you out." He saw Hogg hesitate at the water's edge and nearly pushed him into the water.

"I'll get you, Hoggy!" Innes shouted.

"Sir," Smith held up his Boys rifle. "What about the elephant gun? I can't swim with it."

"Ditch it!" Tulloch ordered. "We'll get you another." With millions of pounds' worth of equipment burning or abandoned between Tobruk and Gazala, Tulloch was not concerned about a weapon that was fast becoming obsolete.

"Sir," Smith complained until Tulloch grabbed the Boys and threw it into the sea.

"Move!" he shoved Smith in behind the floundering Hogg. "Get in the water before the Germans summon reinforcements."

Four Platoon and the men who had joined them swam towards the motor launch. Hogg clung tightly to a plank of wood and kicked gamely as Innes and Cattanach helped push him forward. The launch stopped firing as the crew threw ropes into the water to help the struggling soldiers.

"Hurry up!" a petty officer urged. "We can't hang about for long. We're a sitting duck here."

A young petty officer stretched a hand to help Hogg on board.

"Up you come, Pongo." He grinned at Hogg's snarling response.

"A simple thank you would suffice."

With Four Platoon and the others on board, the 115-foot-long Fairmile Motor Launch was grossly overcrowded, with every inch of deck space occupied. Once again, Tulloch was reminded of Dunkirk as the launch eased out of the harbour. Another section of German infantry arrived, with the NCO in charge immediately ordering them to fire at the Royal Navy vessel.

"Dry your weapons!" Tulloch ordered.

"What with?" Elliot asked.

"Anything you can find," Tulloch replied. "Use your imagination. When they're dry, return fire."

The German bullets splashed around the launch and smashed through the thin hull. Private Grainger grunted and stared at the neat hole in his chest.

"They got me," he said in surprise. "It's a Blighty wound." He died with a faint smile on his face.

With their weapons cleaned, Four Platoon added their firepower to the launch's twin Oerlikon and machine guns.

"Anybody got a spare bundook?" Smith pleaded. "I havenae got my elephant gun!"

"Take mine," Tulloch passed over his rifle. "It's dry."

"Thank you, sir!" Smith replied. "Anybody got any dry ammo?"

The German NCO was a brave man, ordering his section to continue firing even as the Oerlikon sought him out. Tulloch saw the heavy 20-millimetre bullets cut the man in half, and then the launch eased through the harbour entrance in a flurry of shots and spray.

"Keep your eyes open for stray mines," the petty officer warned as the launch's guns ceased fire. "We keep a channel swept clear, but any wild weather can free some mines, and enemy submarines can lay their eggs between our minesweepers' visits." He grinned without humour.

"If we hit a mine, you'll know all about it, or you'll know nothing at all."

Tulloch passed the advice to his men.

"Watch for floating mines, boys! Big round things with horns."

Four Platoon nodded and obediently scanned the water. With the waves breaking in silver-white surf along the pristine beaches on their right, it was hard to imagine danger, yet Tulloch knew life along this coast was as dangerous as any North Atlantic convoy.

Despite Tobruk's surrender, Tulloch heard continued firing

from the town, the stutter of small arms and an occasional deeper boom from a tank or artillery piece.

Maybe we should have remained behind. Tulloch shook his head.

No. Capture was inevitable with the enemy surrounding the town. I was right to get my platoon out.

"You lads are lucky," the young lieutenant in command of the launch said calmly. "We're having trouble with our engines and had to moor behind one of the wrecks in the harbour to effect temporary repairs. We wouldn't be here, else." He gave a tight smile.

"Our misfortune is your fortune, eh?"

"Yes indeed, Captain," Tulloch agreed.

"Where are we headed?"

"Bardia," the lieutenant replied. "Unless Rommel's got there before us."

"The speed that man travels," Tulloch said. "He'll be waiting for us with tea and sandwiches."

The lieutenant smiled again, although his gaze never strayed from the sea, searching for mines and any hunting enemy craft, surface or submarine.

"Maybe so, lieutenant," he said. He snapped an order to the helmsman, and the launch altered course slightly to avoid the stern of a sunken ship that thrust from the safe channel.

"We lost a lot of ships in these waters, keeping Tobruk supplied. I never thought we'd hand the place to Rommel."

Four Platoon crowded on the launch as it headed steadily east, throwing up an arrow-straight wake astern. Tulloch watched the North African coast gliding past to starboard, a yellow-brown smear shimmering under the sun, with the sounds of conflict gradually fading behind them.

"This is easier than marching, sir," Drysdale said.

"The boys will be glad of the rest."

A young seaman brought mugs of strong tea and thick bully beef sandwiches to everybody.

"Get that dahn yer," he said in a broad London accent. "Somebody needs to look arter you Pongos!"

Four Platoon responded gratefully. For the old sweats, the Dunkirk veterans, it was the second time the Navy had rescued them.

"I could get used to this," Elliot said, lying on deck with his hands folded behind his head. He waved a filthy hand to the seaman.

"Carry on, my man. Feed the horses, will you? And ensure my Rolls is ready for my afternoon spin around the estate."

The seaman gave a mock bow.

"Certainly, my Lord, and I'll have the maids all warmed up for you and waiting in the master's bedroom."

"Just the job," Elliot agreed.

They both heard the aircraft and looked up to see a flight of three Italian Fiat CR42 Falco fighters cruising above the coast.

"Get your guns ready, Pongos," the seaman advised. "The Eyeties don't like us much along this coast."

Elliot rose to his feet, sandwich in one hand and rifle in the other.

"Thanks, mate. You'd better get down below and leave the fighting to us."

"Stand by!" Tulloch ordered.

Four Platoon lined the rail with their rifles ready. Innes balanced the Bren, peering narrow-eyed into the blue abyss above.

"I've only got a magazine and a half," he said.

"Let's hope that's enough," Tulloch said.

The ratings on the Oerlikon shifted their aim to follow the Italians, steel helmets pushed back, and capable hands waiting to fire.

"Get ready to repel the aircraft," Tulloch warned, and Four Platoon crouched or stood on the deck, rifles raised. Tulloch hoped the aircraft would ignore the launch, but instead, they circled above, coming lower.

"Ready, lads," Tulloch said, watching the single-engined fighters. With a top speed of 267 miles per hour, they carried eight machine guns and two 220-pound bombs. Although British Hurricanes or Spitfires outmatched them, a flight of three such planes should be more than sufficient to damage or destroy an overloaded motor launch.

At that moment, the launch's engine coughed, stuttered and died.

Chapter Twelve

"Well, that's a bugger," Innes said calmly as the launch began to drift, powerless, on the tide.

"Just a bit," Sergeant Drysdale agreed.

"Don't fire," the lieutenant in charge of the launch ordered. "They may not know who we are." His orders came clearly from the bridge.

"Midshipman, break out the emergency flag."

"Aye, aye, sir," the youthful midshipman replied. A moment later, he hoisted the Italian flag.

"What the hell?" Hogg asked. "I'm no' fighting under the Eyetie flag!"

"Keep quiet!" Drysdale snarled.

"Wave to the nice aircraft."

"What?" Hogg glared at the sergeant. "I'll wave my bloody bayonet at them!"

"You'll wave your paw when I tell you, you bloody disgrace!" Drysdale said.

"Come on, lads! Everybody wave at the aircraft. Pretend it's your favourite auntie coming to visit!"

With the Italian flag flapping above a launch that did not attempt to flee or fight, the Fiat Falcos circled twice before flapping their wings and continuing their flight to the west.

"Thank God for that," Drysdale said.

"Amen," Tulloch agreed as the launch's commander shouted at the engineers to "get the bloody boat on the move before bloody Mussolini comes to the bloody party for a slice of the sergeant's auntie's bloody cake."

The launch floated a few miles off the North African coast while the engineers laboured to fix the engines and Four Platoon lay on the deck.

"This is like one of those luxury cruises for useless rich buggers," Hogg said.

"Keep a watch out for mines," Sergeant Drysdale reminded him curtly.

"Yes, Sergeant," Hogg rose and moved two paces to the rail.

"And watch for aircraft!" Drysdale added, "And submarines."

The lieutenant and midshipman scanned the horizon for shipping while the petty officer and Oerlikon crew searched the sky. Four Platoon either watched the waves or lay on deck, recovering from the past few days or preparing for whatever was to come.

Tulloch started as the engineers began to hammer down below, with the noise carrying across the near-silent sea.

"If there's a submarine nearby," the lieutenant said, "the hammering will sound like a dinner bell. Fresh meat inviting a torpedo."

"Do you carry any depth charges?" Tulloch asked.

"Not even one," the lieutenant replied.

Tulloch nodded.

"Let's hope there are no U-boats."

The hammering continued, with some men flinching at each blow and the launch drifting slowly with the tide. The lieutenant glanced at the coast.

"Unless we fix that engine soon, we'll be aground, and I don't know who controls this section of the coast."

Tulloch scanned the land through his binoculars.

"With the situation so fluid, it could be anybody," he said. "There are British and enemy units all over the place. I can see two columns of dust that might be columns heading east."

"Sir!" The petty officer called from the deck. "We can see something in the water, three points off the port bow and three cables' length ahead. It may be a periscope."

The lieutenant, midshipman and Tulloch swung their binoculars to the left. Tulloch felt the tension rise in the launch.

"I see it," the lieutenant confirmed. "It's not a periscope."

"It's a man," the midshipman said quietly.

"Do you have a boat to bring him in?" Tulloch asked.

"No," the lieutenant replied shortly.

"Has he seen us?" the midshipman asked. "He's not trying to swim this way."

"He's dead," Tulloch told him.

As the work on the engine continued, the body floated towards them, stripped of all clothes and dignity as it bobbed on the surface. The men watched in silence. Tulloch wondered what had happened.

"He might be British, Italian or German," the midshipman said. "Some poor sailorman from a lost ship."

The corpse came closer, with one arm pointing upward like a submarine's periscope.

"He's trying to come aboard," Kennedy said.

"Somebody fetch a boathook!" the petty officer ordered. "At least we can give the lad a decent burial."

Three men lined the rail, waiting to hook the body and drag it on board, but before they could reach across, a quirk of current swept him away. He floated past, seeming to grin at the launch as he continued to point upward at an uncaring sky.

"Poor bugger," Cattanach said. "Nobody will know who he is or what happened to him."

At that moment, the engine roared to life, and men cheered, immediately forgetting the mini-drama of the unknown corpse.

"That's better," the lieutenant said. "Half speed ahead!"

Four Platoon joined the crew in raising a cheer as the launch moved forward, creating a wake that bounced the corpse on the waves. Tulloch saw the body spin and turn to stare at them through hollow eye sockets and then slide beneath the waves. He saw Cattanach watching, and then the sea was empty.

"We'll be in Bardia in no time," the lieutenant said comfortably, "if the engine holds out."

THE LAUNCH PULLED UP AT A BOMB-BATTERED QUAY WHERE Royal Naval seamen sweltered as they unloaded a freighter. A mixed crew manned a Bofors anti-aircraft gun while more waited with an Oerlikon, wary of air attack. Few even glanced at the launch; they had seen ships and boats enter and leave the harbour, and one more vessel carrying tired, khaki-clad men was hardly a novelty.

"Here we are, lads," Tulloch said, ushering Four Platoon ashore. "Thank you for the lift, Lieutenant."

"My pleasure, Lieutenant. Always glad to help the junior service."

Eighteen miles west of the Egyptian border, Bardia was hot and congested with British and Allied military refugees licking their wounds and searching for their parent units. Vehicles filled the narrow streets: fifteen hundred-weight and three-ton trucks carrying exhausted men, carriers with red-capped military police, and staff cars with red-tabbed staff officers. Ambulances threaded through the crowds, sometimes with the Military Police ensuring they had passage and creating order out of chaos.

"Where do we go now?" Kennedy asked, looking around the hectic town.

"We find somebody who knows what he's doing and see

where the Lothians are," Tulloch replied. "Whoever and wherever that somebody might be."

"Sir!" The Military Police corporal looked like he had stepped onto an Aldershot parade ground, with his uniform immaculate, knife-edge creases in his trousers, and his red cap pulled low over his forehead.

"Yes, Corporal," Tulloch replied.

"Did you arrive on that motor launch, sir?" The corporal nodded to the launch.

"We did," Tulloch agreed. He saw the corporal run a disapproving eye over the battered uniforms of Four Platoon.

"Standing orders that all new arrivals must report to Major Bryce, sir. He's in the building displaying the flag." The corporal lifted a hand to indicate a large white building a hundred yards from the quay.

"Thank you, Corporal," Tulloch replied.

"I'll take you, sir," the corporal said as if he doubted Tulloch's ability to navigate across the road.

"Thank you, Corporal," Tulloch said. "I'm sure we'll find our way."

Tulloch left Kennedy in charge of Four Platoon as he entered the building. A small crowd of officers milled in a hallway, with a pair of stalwart MPs directing them to one of three rooms.

"I'm looking for Major Bryce," Tulloch told a flint-eyed sergeant.

"He's in the office at the end, sir," the sergeant said.

"Who are you?" Major Bryce wore the red tabs of a staff officer and the smug face of a man who seldom ventured close to the enemy. The papers on his desk were arranged in tidy piles, with three pens in a neat row and his blotting paper squared in front of him.

"Lieutenant Tulloch, sir, Lothian Rifles. I've brought the remains of Four Platoon, C Company back from Gazala via Tobruk."

"Lothian Rifles?" The major consulted the clipboard that

hung on the wall behind him. "Ah, yes, you lot are still attached to 50 Div. The rest of the Lothians are at Mersa Matruh under General Gott's XIII Corps."

"Did the Lothians get out safely, sir?" Tulloch asked. "We saw many units going in the bag."

Major Bryce frowned as he replaced the clipboard. "Of course, they got out safely. They wouldn't be with Gott otherwise."

"How many, sir?"

"How the devil should I know?" the major barked. "Go and join them. You can count the numbers when you get there."

"We'll need transport, sir," Tulloch said. "And my men haven't eaten or slept properly for days."

"See Captain Gibbs about transport," Major Bryce said offhand. "He's on the southern outskirts of this fly-ridden hole. There's a canteen tent somewhere. Get some food and water there." He scribbled something in the margin of a sheet of paper and looked up as a wounded captain arrived outside with a battered half company of Durhams. "Dismissed, Lieutenant. Who are you, Captain?"

"Come on, lads," Tulloch said to his men. "We have a Captain Gibbs to find. The Lothians are at Mersa Matruh."

GENERAL HOLMES'S X CORPS HAD BASED THEMSELVES AT Mersa Matruh. Newly arrived from peaceful Palestine, they were unfamiliar with the conditions in the Western Desert and faced a triumphant Rommel, fresh from his victory at Gazala and intent on pushing the British eastward to the Nile Delta.

Four Platoon clambered off the trucks, straightened themselves up and looked around. Infantry, artillery, and supporting units moved around in seeming chaos, with MPs trying to install order and harassed officers hurrying with messages and orders.

The Lothians were camped on the outskirts, diminished in numbers but still defiant. Before he arrived, Tulloch heard the pipers playing *Flowers of Edinburgh* and saw Lieutenant Erskine sitting on an ammunition box, cleaning a Bren gun.

"You got back then." Erskine did not get up. "The old man is in the tent in the middle."

"Thanks, Erskine," Tulloch said. "Look after the men, Sergeant."

"Yes, sir," Drysdale replied. He did not hide his satisfaction at being back with the battalion. Tulloch knew that Drysdale had been born into the Lothians and knew no other home.

"Glad you got here," Colonel Hume greeted Tulloch. "We lost a lot of men escaping from the Box. How many men did you bring back?"

"Twenty-seven, sir. Three wounded. How many are left in the battalion?"

"Just under five hundred with your platoon," Hume said. "We've lost over two hundred men in the last fortnight, including Major Brownlow." He shook his head, looking old and grey with responsibility. "We're making a stand here at Mersa Matruh. Did you hear that Tobruk has fallen?"

"We were there, sir," Tulloch told him quietly.

"What was it like?"

"Grim, sir," Tulloch replied. "Worse than Dunkirk. I've never seen so many demoralised men."

Hume grunted. "Demoralisation seems to be spreading in the army," he said. "I don't think it's everywhere yet. Our lads are shaken and disappointed with the retreats and defeats, but the fighting spirit remains. However, many men view Rommel as a superman who cannot be defeated."

"That's what I've been hearing, sir," Tulloch agreed.

"I wonder if people said something similar about Napoleon or Montrose," Hume said with a tired smile. "They had a string of victories until they met a better general."

"They did, sir," Tulloch agreed. "Let's hope Neil Ritchie is that general. Maybe Mersa Matruh will be Rommel's Waterloo."

"Did you not hear the news?" Hume asked quickly. "No, you've been a bit busy. Auchinleck has removed Ritchie from command and taken over the 8th Army himself."

"The Auck?" Tulloch said. "Let's hope he's the man. What's the plan now, sir?" Tulloch asked.

"We either stop Rommel here," Hume said, "or we delay him while General Norrie strengthens the line at El Alamein. That's our next fall-back line if we can't hold him."

Tulloch nodded. He knew Norrie as a brave armoured commander. "Who do we have, sir?"

"Fifty Div, who are still reorganising after their rapid gallop from Gazala, and 10th Indian Div, who are good."

Tulloch nodded again. "The men are good material, sir. The Durhams fought well at Gazala."

Hume read Tulloch's thoughts. "The men are as good as any, but are the senior officers sufficiently competent to defeat Rommel?" There was no humour in his smile. "Only time and battle will tell, Tulloch. Auchinleck is trying to install more mobility and wants to keep the Eighth Army intact as a force in being, win or lose."

Tulloch grunted. "I see, sir."

"The Auck has decided that Rommel's mobile forces run rings around our static defences. Mersa Matruh is to be a mobile battle, so he is sending transport to us, making every infantry unit at the front fully mobile."

"That's good, sir," Tulloch said.

Hume grinned again. "I hope he thinks we have time to retrain. He's ordered us not to get cut off."

"Has he told Rommel not to cut us off, sir?"

"I doubt it," Hume replied. "You'd best get back to your platoon, Tulloch. I am glad you made it back."

"Thank you, sir."

"Oh, and Tulloch," Hume said. "Drop in at the mail office on your way. There are some letters for your platoon."

"Yes, sir. Thank you, sir."

Another defensive position, with little time to prepare and manned by soldiers who have been recently defeated by the same general who will attack again. Our only advantage is that Rommel has longer supply lines, except he captured tons of our stores in Tobruk.

Chapter Thirteen

MERSA MATRUH, JUNE 1942

The mail office was a small tent in the centre of the camp, with a near-permanent queue of hopeful soldiers outside. Captain Kilner and Lieutenant Rutlane arrived at the tent when Tulloch arrived.

"The enemy will be cock-a-hoop after Gazala and Tobruk," Rutlane said mournfully. "They'll run right through us."

"Only if we allow them," Captain Kilner replied. "Remember March 1918, when the Huns pushed us right back? We held them then and defeated them."

"That was a different war," Rutlane said. "And they didn't have Rommel to lead them."

Tulloch stepped away without joining the conversation. He felt vaguely disturbed, for British officers did not indulge in defeatist talk, yet he had experienced a great deal recently.

"Mail, Sergeant!" Tulloch extracted three letters bearing his name and handed the rest to Drysdale.

"I'll see to it, sir," Drysdale said.

Two of Tulloch's letters were in his mother's writing, and the third was from Amanda. He opened his mother's first, scanned them to ensure everything was all right at home, and then held Amanda's letter closely, deciding to keep it until later. He would get his men comfortable before reading her words.

Tulloch settled his platoon back into C Company, posted sentries and checked the Allies' position. Mersa Matruh was a small town on the Egyptian coast over a hundred miles from the Libyan border with a rail connection to Alexandria. The British had built up the town's defences two years previously in preparation for the Italian invasion of Egypt. In 1941, they added more wire and mines before Operation Crusader, which was the push to relieve Tobruk.

Tulloch nodded. Mersa Matruh seemed more secure than Tobruk, and every day that Rommel delayed gave the Allies more chance to strengthen the defences. This town may be Rommel's full stop. Perhaps the Allies could build up and push the Axis back to Benghazi or even further.

Tulloch shook his head. He was only a lieutenant in a British infantry regiment with no power to alter the course of the war. He could only do his duty and encourage the men he commanded to do theirs. Tulloch touched the letter in his pocket. If he were fortunate, he would survive the war, although, with so much death around, survival seemed less likely every day.

Four Platoon clustered around Sergeant Drysdale when he handed out the mail. Every man hoped for a letter from home, from parents, siblings, wives or girls. It was a tenuous link that reminded them that life was not all about killing and fighting, but little things still mattered. They wanted to hear about rationed meat, silly disputes with neighbours, and how the new baby or puppy was settling in. The everyday trivial matters that reminded them there was another world waiting for them.

"See that woman of mine?" Gordon said, holding up a sheet of paper. "She says she'll give me anything if I return home with a medal."

"What's she like? Have you got a photae?" Elliot asked, stepping closer. "You know what that means, don't you? She wants to boast about her man."

"I know," Gordon replied, "and I'm not showing you her picture, Shuggie!"

Tulloch moved on. *It's time to read Amanda's letter.*

Amanda wrote short letters that packed a lot of information into a few words. Tulloch leaned against the tent pole, unaware he was smiling as he read. Some phrases leapt out. "I miss you," from Amanda, meant as much as an entire paragraph from anybody else. "I am looking forward to meeting you again" was tantamount to a declaration of undying love. "We are not too far away," was Amanda telling him she was still working in Cairo.

Tulloch refolded the letter and placed it inside his tunic, knowing he would reread it later. Too restless to settle and with Four Platoon safe with Drysdale and Kennedy, Tulloch walked around the Lothians' position, ensuring the sentries were in position and alert.

"It's quiet, Tulloch," Muirhead joined him. "No aircraft, ours or theirs, and no sound of artillery."

"We have a wee breathing space," Tulloch said.

They completed their tour of the Lothians' position, halted on a small hump and peered to the west. Tulloch did not know how often he had searched for attacking Axis troops over the past few weeks.

"Mersa Matruh is the final barrier to Rommel before our defences at El Alamein," Muirhead said. "What do you reckon, Tulloch?"

"I reckon we'll have to stop Rommel," Tulloch replied.

Muirhead spread a map on the ground, comparing the printed information with the physical geography laid out before them. Mersa Matruh dominated the ten-mile-wide coastal plain that stretched southward to a steep ridge. Beyond the ridge, another plain poured south to the Sidi Hamaza escarpment.

"The position is fairly strong," Tulloch said. "If we can hold the ridges, we can split the enemy advance."

"And hopefully use our armour to strike at his flanks," Muirhead agreed. "If Rommel gives us time to prepare and plays the game according to Auchinleck's plan."

Tulloch studied the map again. A track known as the Mingar Quaim ran to the east of the Sidi Hamaza escarpment, while beyond was eighty miles of bleak desert that ended at the impassable Qattara Depression. "There is still a lot of space for Rommel to manoeuvre in," Tulloch said. "That's one of his main strengths."

"Forget the south," Muirhead said. "We can only fight our own battle at Mersa. We have minefields around the town on the west and south but nothing on the east, and we have an airfield to the south, which Rommel will undoubtedly target."

"He will," Tulloch agreed. He pored over the map. "He'll want the airfield, the harbour and the coastal road, the Via Balbia, to Alexandria." He traced the road with his finger. "He's frighteningly close now."

Muirhead grunted. "He hammered our armour at Gazala," he said. "He might want to finish the job here, and after capturing Tobruk in one day, he'll try to take Mersa Matruh as quickly as possible. Any delay we cause him gives our lads time to build up the defences at Alamein."

"Maybe so," Tulloch said, thinking they continued to look over their shoulder at the next defensive site. "But despite our losses, we still have quality infantry. Rommel might want to destroy the infantry next, and then the gate to the Delta, the Suez Canal, and the Middle East oilfields will be wide open."

"We have General William Holmes's X Corps to defend the line," Muirhead said. "The 10th Indian Division is in the town, and we are with the 50th Division on the east, protecting the rear. Thirteen Corps is stationed above the second escarpment, waiting. The Auck said that when Rommel assaults either corps, the other is to attack the German's flank." He glanced at Tulloch. "You said something similar a moment ago."

"Who is in Thirteen Corps?" Tulloch asked.

"5th Indian Infantry Division, 2nd New Zealand Division and 1st Armoured Division," Muirhead replied. "It sounds impressive, but the 5th Indian is only one brigade strong, and the 2nd New Zealand is fresh from garrisoning Syria and lacks battle experience. The armour lost a great deal of equipment at Gazala but now have 159 tanks, including sixty new American Grants with 75-mm guns."

"I was not over-impressed with the Grant tanks," Tulloch said, "but at least they have decent firepower."

Muirhead grinned. "Now we've made the general's decisions for them, we'd better get back where we belong. Let's hope for better luck this round."

Tulloch returned to Four Platoon. They looked tired after their journey from Gazala, but after being fed, rested and obtaining more ammunition, they took their place with the battalion.

"Here we go again," Innes said.

"Once more into the breeches," Elliot replied. "Or out of the breeches."

"You're a skirt-chasing bugger, aren't you, Shug?" Gordon said without malice.

"Aye, Gordae, how's your lassie coming on? The one wanting a hero?"

Gordon grinned. "She's waiting for me, Shug, ready, waiting and willing."

"Only if you get her a shiny wee medal," Elliot taunted.

"I'll get her one," Gordon said. "Archie Gordon, MM. That sounds good!"

Hogg checked his rifle, sighted along the barrel and grunted. "Maybe this time we'll go forward, not back."

"Maybe," Atkins said. "That depends on Rommel and whichever general we have in charge of us this week."

"The Auk's in charge now," Innes told him.

"Is he any better than Ritchie or Cunningham?" Atkins asked.

"I'll tell you in a few days," Innes said. "If we're in Alex, then he wasnae. If we're pushing for Benghazi, then he was."

Tulloch listened to his platoon's cynical, sensible comments. Higher command might not have shared their plans with the men, but the ordinary British soldier knew the difference between a good officer and a poor one and treated them accordingly.

"What now, sir?" Innes asked Tulloch.

"Now we dig in and wait, Innes," Tulloch replied.

"Just the job, sir," Innes said. "It's a fine evening."

They watched the glorious sunset together, both thinking of the sun setting behind the Pentlands, Edinburgh's guardian hills, although they did not share their thoughts.

ON THE EVENING OF THE 25TH OF JUNE, THE LOTHIANS HEARD engines outside their wire.

"Shall I give them a burst, sir?" Innes asked, hopefully.

"No," Tulloch shook his head. "It could be some of our Long Range Desert Group boys coming back. Hold your fire, and don't give our position away."

Innes nodded and hugged the Bren closer to his cheek. Despite Tulloch's advice, Four Platoon worked their rifle bolts and peered into the fast-gathering gloom. The engines muttered for half an hour, but when Muirhead sent a Very flare up, the vehicles drove away, with dust concealing their identity.

They learned the following day that the vehicles had been German, and British armoured car patrols advanced cautiously, searching for evidence of a German attack. They saw thick black smoke rising in the west and learned the RAF had destroyed an Axis fuel column.

"That should slow down Rommel's attack," Muirhead murmured.

"Every day is a bonus," Tulloch said. "But I am concerned

about the huge gap to the south of us. As far as I am aware, we only have a narrow minefield there and a couple of small columns of a hundred men and a few guns on patrol. They won't have the firepower to slow anything. I'm unsure what their purpose is."

"I am unsure what our purpose is," Muirhead replied with a wry grin. "Brigadier Whyte has ordered us to fight Rommel, slow him and damage him as much as possible, yet ensure he doesn't trap us. We have to keep the army in being yet fight the enemy. I suppose the orders emanate from Auchinleck, but they are unclear."

Order, counter-order, disorder, Tulloch thought. "We'll hold off Rommel as best we can," he said.

"That's all we can do," Muirhead agreed.

With Colonel Hume pacing the positions, giving advice and orders, the Lothians deepened their trenches, added more sandbags and erected range markers and booby traps in the barbed wire. They also learned to call the dugouts "doovers" and built up a supply of ammunition. They saw columns of dust to the south and west, wrote letters home, conversed with the neighbouring Durhams and Northumbrian artillery and watched the aircraft trails in the sky. The Lothians' regular patrols, mainly led by Erskine, occasionally skirmished with the enemy, destroying a couple of halftracks without incurring any casualties. The men waited, some nonchalant, others hiding their anxiety. They looked westward, knowing the Germans were there.

Delayed by the loss of his supplies, Rommel's attack did not start until the afternoon of the 26th of June. Tulloch and the Lothians heard the engines from the south and the sound of gunfire, intermittent at first and increasing slowly.

"Rommel's started the ball rolling," Muirhead commented.

Tulloch stood on a slight ridge behind the Lothians' position and scanned the land to the south.

"Lots of dust," he reported. "Too much for a simple feint. I'd say Rommel has pushed his 21st Panzer Division between the two escarpments, maybe with the 90th Light as well."

"Our skinny minefield and wee mobile groups won't be able to cope with a force like that," Muirhead said. "Rommel has put his strongest force against our weakest point."

"He's a good soldier," Tulloch approved reluctantly. "I wish I knew what was happening."

"All will be revealed in the fullness of time," Muirhead replied.

Messages came into the battalion HQ, confirming Tulloch's assessment. While the 21th Panzers cleared the way across the northern section of the plain, the 15th Panzer Division and XX Motorised Corps pushed into the plain to the south. The British 22nd Armoured Brigade met the southern push and stopped the advance in a confused battle of swirling sand, burning tanks, and hammering guns.

"Rommel will be heading this way next," Muirhead warned as the news filtered through. "50 Div is isolated here."

Partly because of the loss of their fuel convoy, the 21th Panzer and 90th Light Division advance halted as night fell. Aware the enemy would attack them next, the Lothians made what provisions they could, strengthening their defences by deepening the trenches and adding more sandbags to the anti-tank gun emplacements. As always, Tulloch checked his men, seeing resignation in many faces as they prepared for the inevitable German attack and the resulting withdrawal.

"Where are we going next, sir?" Elliot asked. "Alamein? Alex? Jerusalem, Delhi?"

"We'll hold on here," Tulloch no longer believed his reassurances.

"Yes, sir," Elliot said. "I hope it's Alex, sir. The women there are said to be something special."

"How would you know, Shuggie?" Hogg asked. "You're all talk and no action, you."

"Get some sleep, lads," Tulloch advised and walked on, sharing his men's feelings.

Four Platoon waited, with men stretched out to sleep in slit trenches and dugouts as the desert cold bit into tense bodies. Cattanach slept like a baby, instantly unconscious, while Gordon mumbled and twitched as old memories haunted his dreams. One youngster sobbed until Corporal Borthwick, flint-eyed and unemotional, pressed a hip flask into his hand.

"Drink this, Wullie. It'll help you sleep."

Stand-to sounded at half past five, with the liquid notes of the bugles drifting across the desert. Tulloch took his place behind the thin strands of wire, scanning the land to the south where Rommel's men lurked.

"They'll come today," Muirhead said softly.

How often have I heard these words recently? "Yes, sir," Tulloch agreed.

Chapter Fourteen

The German attack began with a short and heavy bombardment, followed by an intense assault on the 9th Battalion of the Durham Light Infantry.

"Ready, lads!" Tulloch shouted as the smoke of the bombardment drifted away. He stood in his trench, rifle in hand, peering to the west and south. The German shells had passed over the Lothians' position to concentrate on the 9th Durhams.

"Fire into the German flanks," Hume ordered. "Give the Durhams a hand!"

Innes aimed his Bren at the distant shapes, dimly seen through the screen of sand, and fired magazine after magazine.

"The Germans have a screen of armoured cars and half-tracks," Tulloch commented. "We're not doing much damage."

"I wish I had my Boys!" Smith said, looking hard at Tulloch, who ignored the implied criticism.

Outnumbered, outgunned and outmanoeuvred, the 9th Durhams fought to the last round before they succumbed. Tulloch saw the battered remnants withdraw, with most of their positions shattered. Dead and wounded men lay amidst the shell holes.

With their tails up after they disposed of the 9th Durhams, the 90th Light Division headed towards the Lothians. The 50th Division's artillery found them and fired salvo after salvo of twenty-five-pounder shells that stopped the German advance and forced them back. Burning half-tracks, wrecked vehicles, and dead men lay scattered over the sand.

"Thank God for the gunners," Muirhead said as Mungo Macquarie led a team of medical orderlies to tend the wounded, British and German.

Colonel Hume appeared, walking around his battalion, strengthening the defences with rolls of barbed wire he had borrowed from the Durhams. The men licked their wounds as the smoke and dust cleared, sipped at their water bottles and prayed to survive the day.

"Every little helps," Hume said, passing two new Bren gun barrels onto Innes. "You might need these, Innes."

"Thank you, sir," Innes lifted the barrels as if they were gold bars. "These things get warped when they overheat."

"I find the period before a battle worse than the fighting," Muirhead said. "Sometimes it's a relief when the actual fighting begins."

"You could be right," Tulloch said.

The men dug the trenches even deeper, filled more sandbags, and watched as Colonel Hume persuaded the divisional artillery to position an extra couple of anti-tank guns to overlook their position. They watched the sky for enemy aircraft and listened to reports from other areas of the battlefield.

The 2nd New Zealand Division held off the 21st Panzers in a fierce fight that proved they were a quality unit, although as the battle wore on, they were in danger of being surrounded.

"Auchinleck has issued orders to the corps commanders," Muirhead passed on reports from regimental headquarters. "We have to retreat if Rommel threatens to cut us off rather than risk being captured or destroyed."

Tulloch raised his eyebrows. "I'd rather sit tight and fight it out," he said.

"Rommel's running rings around us," Muirhead said.

As the Lothians waited, firing the occasional shot at too-inquisitive parties of Germans, Rommel pushed the 90th Light Division northward to the coast. They sidestepped the Lothians, pushed the Durhams aside, and that evening reached the sea, trapping X Corps behind them. Muirhead moved to Battalion HQ, hoping for information.

"What's happening?" Tulloch asked. "The Germans seem to be ignoring us."

"Gott's retreating," Muirhead reported. "The New Zealanders are isolated, but so are the German 90th Light, with the 21st Panzers about fifteen miles away and engaged by the Kiwis. The Germans are as divided as we are, with our 1st Armoured Division holding their 15th Panzers and XX Motorised."

"It's all a bit of a mess," Tulloch said. "Can't Gott cut off the 90th Light and destroy them? Fifty Div and 10th Indian would leap at the chance." He closed his mouth, realising he was complaining without purpose.

"Gott does not seem to agree," Muirhead replied, unable to keep the bitterness from his voice. "We could turn the tables on Rommel."

The bogeyman of Rommel has our generals jumping at shadows.

"What's Gott's intention?" Tulloch asked.

Muirhead shrugged. "Fall back, delay Rommel a bit and fall back again," he suggested. "I don't know what he's thinking."

On the evening of the 27th of June, Auchinleck ordered the Eighth Army to withdraw to Fuka in Egypt, closer to the Allies' last-gasp position of El Alamein. Well to the south of the Lothians, the 2nd New Zealand Division broke out through the 21st Panzer Division. However, General Holmes in Mersa Matruh did not get Auchinleck's message until the following morning.

"Message from the brigadier," Colonel Hume informed his officers at an impromptu conference. "We are to counterattack to the south and disrupt the German attack."

"That's more like it," Muirhead said. "When do we leave?"

"We're raiding with two companies, one six-pounder anti-tank gun, two three-inch mortars, and a truck-mounted Vickers. We've had to borrow a six-pounder from the Durhams." Hume said. "Muirhead and Kilner, take your companies."

"Yes, sir," Muirhead replied as Erskine looked disappointed.

"Leave at 02.00 hours tomorrow morning," Hume ordered.

Captain Kilner, the officer commanding B Company, nodded. "What's the target, sir?"

"Stay together, cause some mayhem, and damage the enemy. General Auchinleck demands that we incur as few casualties as possible." Hume lowered his voice. "As if you normally try suicide missions."

"Yes, sir," Muirhead agreed.

As they left the Lothians' position, Tulloch saw Erskine watching, wondered why the colonel had not used his undoubted expertise in patrolling and pushed the thought away. Colonel Hume would have his reasons. The raiding force moved out under a sky of brilliant stars, with the men determined to hit hard at anything that got in their way. Tulloch rode in the three-tonner that held half Four Platoon with a rifle at his side and his heart pounding.

Hume led the column due south, moving in desert formation with Lieutenant Kennedy as navigator. Tulloch was unsure if Kennedy would ever make a good officer, but he had proved an excellent desert navigator. Colonel Hume had given him a set of coordinates and ordered him to guide the raiders there. Now, they followed Kennedy's directions, trusting in his skill.

Hood was too experienced a soldier to ask questions as they drove on, with the dust already thick around the convoy. Under the glittering stars, the desert seemed empty and cold.

They drove until midnight, with the monotonous growl of

the vehicles accompanying the spreading dust. Hume halted them in the lee of a low ridge, with tyre tracks disfiguring the desert on the far side.

"Now we wait," Hume said. "No talking. Tulloch, send out scouts to the north and east. Kilner, do the same on the west and south. Let me know immediately if they see something."

Tulloch had never heard the colonel sound so grim. He sent Sergeant Drysdale five hundred yards to the west and Corporal Borthwick the same distance south, organised his men and checked his rifle.

The raiding party waited in silence, holding their weapons, watching the desert and hoping for success. Tulloch lay beside Four Platoon, feeling their tension and desire to win. He knew these men intimately, closer than brothers, although he had never had siblings. His seniority in rank undoubtedly created an invisible yet tangible barrier, but years of combat and hardship also formed an equally palpable comradeship.

"What are we waiting for, sir?" Innes whispered.

"Anything that comes," Tulloch replied. "Keep quiet."

A soft wind disturbed the desert surface, blowing loose sand over the Lothians. Within twenty minutes, they lay under a yellow-brown covering, protecting their weapons, breathing softly.

A light band on the eastern horizon signified the imminent onset of dawn, and nearly simultaneously, one of Kilner's scouting parties returned.

"Convoy approaching, sir," the sergeant reported. "It's coming fast."

"Probably Italian then," Colonel Hume said. "The Germans don't like to operate at night. Bring the other scouts closer, inform them what's happening and stand by."

The Lothians waited, silent except for suddenly harsh breathing and the quiet snick of men pulling back the bolts of their rifles.

Tulloch heard the grumble of engines in the distance, gradually growing louder as though a Western counterpart to the rising dawn in the East. The Lothians shifted slightly in anticipation, and then Kilner saw a light in the southwest.

The men strained their eyes, peering into the darkness until they saw the faint gleam of shaded headlights dim through the dark.

"Here they come, boys," Hume spoke in a low tone that somehow carried to every man. "You know the drill."

Hume's training had prepared every man for his part. They watched as the tiny light grew perceptibly larger, still dim yet nearly recognisable as a vehicle's hooded headlights.

The dawn burst in fiery orange that reflected from the vast plain of the Western desert. The sun's rays reflected from the windscreen of the leading truck, revealing the two armoured cars and single halftrack that comprised the convoy's escort. The Lothians held their fire, waiting as Hume had trained them.

The first armoured car was third in the column, with the second at the tail and the halftrack in the centre, all part-concealed by dust. Hume waited until the convoy was level with the Lothians and gave a single sharp blast on his whistle.

The crew of the six-pounder reacted first. They had their gun trained on the leading armoured car and fired immediately after the whistle sounded. The gun's bark shattered the half-light, and the shot crashed into the armoured car. The gunners had selected solid shot that pierced the armour and killed or wounded half the crew before tearing an exit hole in the far side of the vehicle.

The infantry fired, with the Vickers concentrating on the halftrack and the Bren and riflemen targeting the soft-bodied vehicles. The mortars joined in, landing their bombs at the rear of the column where the second armoured car searched for the ambushers.

Innes fired in short, aimed bursts, hitting the cab of each vehicle in a methodical procession down the column. The crews baled out, throwing open the passenger doors and escaping into the desert. The German infantry escort evacuated the halftrack and ran towards the ambush, firing MP40 submachine guns in a brave attempt to defend the convoy. The Lothians shot them down, leaving them sprawled on the desert sand.

Jinking to avoid the mortar blasts, the second armoured car still fired at the ambushers, but the gunners had reloaded the six-pounder, altered their aim and fired. The first shot screamed above the car's turret to soar somewhere into the desert. The car fired back, and then a mortar bomb exploded at its side. The car shook, and the six-pounder smashed a shot into the hull.

By that time, the surviving trucks had scattered, and the Vickers searched them out individually. The Italians had abandoned a dozen trucks, and three were on fire as the Lothians completed their work of destruction, with small groups of men standing in abject surrender.

"Cease fire," Hume ordered. "B Company, search the trucks for documents and set them alight except for one. Gather the prisoners. C Company, secure the perimeter."

Muirhead sent Tulloch's platoon to watch the south and east and Kennedy's to the north and west. Tulloch dug his men in, with the veterans scraping out shallow dips without orders and the replacements, no longer inexperienced, copying them. Every scrap of cover mattered when under fire.

With Hume giving orders, B Company completed its search of the convoy in fifteen frantic minutes. Hume loaded the prisoners, primarily Italian drivers, onto the single truck the Lothians retained and gathered the raiding party around him.

"Rommel may have split our army," Hume said in a tone of cold fury, "but that does not mean the enemy are better soldiers than us." He glared around officers and men. "I don't want any more defeatist talk in this battalion. We are the Lothian Rifles. Understood?" He jerked a thumb to the smoking remains of the Axis convoy.

Tulloch felt the force of Hume's anger. "Understood, sir."

"Gin ye daur!" Hume said. "Get on the buses."

The raiding party returned to their vehicles and headed back to Mersa Matruh. They saw two flights of aircraft, one British and the other enemy, but both were too intent on other business to bother about an obscure convoy.

"Sir!" the signals officer ran to greet Hume the moment the convoy returned. "There are urgent messages for you."

Hume jumped to the ground. "I'll read them in my doover. Bring them to me with a mug of tea."

When Hume strode to his dugout, Tulloch ensured Four Platoon was fed, and they topped up their water bottles.

"Get some rest," Tulloch advised. "I suspect we might be busy later."

Muirhead looked worried when he walked across, pipe in mouth.

"I think the situation has deteriorated since we were on patrol," Muirhead said. "The old man looks very agitated."

Both looked up when heavy machine gun fire sounded from the north.

"Something's happening," Tulloch said.

"That's artillery now," Muirhead replied as they heard a series of explosions. "What the devil is happening up there? Is Rommel attacking again?"

"We'll soon know," Tulloch said. "Here comes the colonel."

"Gather the officers," Hume snapped. "Quickly!" He climbed onto the back of a carrier. "Gentlemen. We patrolled to distract the Germans from Gott's division, but we needn't have bothered. It seems General Gott has already withdrawn from the battlefield, leaving 50 Div alone."

The officers looked at each other without comment.

Hume continued. "Now it is our turn to leave Mersa Matruh, gentlemen. Generals Auchinleck and Holmes have discussed the present situation, and the idea is to split into columns and break out to the south."

"Another breakout, sir?" Kilner asked.

"Another breakout," Hume confirmed. "We head south for a while and then drive eastward to El Alamein."

Tulloch felt a thrill run through him. He knew that El Alamein was the final stop, the last possible defensive position to halt the Axis advance. If Rommel got past the British lines at Alamein, Alexandria and the Delta would be at his mercy.

We haven't been able to stop Rommel so far. Let's hope we can pull something out of the bag at Alamein. If not, we've lost Africa and maybe the Middle East.

Chapter Fifteen

MERSA MATRUH, JUNE 1942

"The Lothians are staying intact," Hume said. "We fight as a unit, and I have no intention of allowing Rommel the satisfaction of capturing, destroying, or dividing us." He raised his voice slightly. "We represent the people of Midlothian, gentlemen, and we won't let them down."

"Gin ye daur!" Kilner said quietly but with feeling.

"I don't know what the other columns intend," Hume said, "but we'll go hell-for-leather and shoot anything and everything in our path." He jammed his pipe between his teeth. "We'll stick together, gentlemen, and arrive in Alamein as the Lothian Rifles, not as a scattered rabble of refugees."

Tulloch felt the officers' mood lift.

"After that, it's up to the generals," Hume said.

"Our intelligence informed me that the Afrika Korps has shifted away eastward, so only the German 90th Light Division and the Italians are around Matruh," Hume said. "We've fought and bested them before, and we'll do it again. That's all, gentlemen. Go and prepare your men."

"When are we leaving, sir?" Captain Muirhead asked.

"After dark," Hume replied. "We won't be alone. The Northumbrians are also on the move." He gave a bitter grin. "The desert will be busy tonight."

The Lothians heard motor engines from the 50th Division as the officers prepared the men to leave. Fortunately, the battalion had transport, so nobody was reduced to marching.

"On the buses, off the buses, go here, go there," Elliot grumbled.

"I had enough moonlight flits as a bairn," Hogg replied. "Escaping the rent man. I never thought I'd do it as a soldier."

"Who said you were a soldier?" Sergeant Drysdale asked. "Get on the bloody bus, Hogg, or I'll help you up with the toe of my boot."

"I'm going," Hogg said, hoisting himself onto a three-ton truck.

As the men boarded the trucks, the Vickers and Bren gunner teams checked their weapons, and the mechanics ensured every vehicle was roadworthy. Hardie, recently appointed as Intelligence Officer and a temporary replacement for the dead Major Brownlow, sat in the leading carrier as navigator. Tulloch was in the middle of the column with Four Platoon. Hood sat in the driving seat, calmly staring out of the window.

Twenty minutes before midnight, Colonel Hume gave the order to move, and the Lothians began their breakout.

"Keep alert, lads," Tulloch told Four Platoon. "Listen for the enemy, and if we meet them, fire like buggery."

Four Platoon responded with various noises. Hogg stamped his feet, Innes tapped his Bren, and Cattanach looked as quiet and determined as ever.

Hood gunned his engine, and the Lothians moved out, heading south into the desert night to break through an unknown number of enemy units who could be anywhere, in any strength and travelling in any direction.

The Lothians' convoy moved slowly and in two columns, following Hardie's carrier. The men were silent, many trying to sleep, others staring at their boots or allowing their thoughts to wash over them. Every man kept his personal weapon close at hand, knowing they might need it any minute.

Tulloch saw star shells and flares rise into the sky to the east and west and heard intermittent gunfire, with one prolonged bout of machine-gun fire and a couple of explosions that lit up the sky to the east.

"Somebody's run into trouble, sir," Hood said.

"Let's hope the Northumbrians give as good as they get," Tulloch replied.

"I'm sure they will, sir," Hood said. "The Geordies are a tough bunch."

After two hours, Hardie called a halt to check his position by compass bearing and the stars, allowing the men five minutes to ease cramped limbs. The stars were brilliant, with the air sharp and invigorating. The firing in the south had ended, leaving only a hissing wind to disturb the hush of the desert.

"I like it here," Cattanach said unexpectedly, looking around him. "I like the desert."

"You like this desolation?" Elliot sounded astonished.

"Aye," Cattanach replied. "I'd like to come back here after the war." He gazed up at the stars. "Look at that sky. Is that not brilliant?"

"It's just bloody stars," Elliot said.

"I like the sense of space," Cattanach said.

"Have you been drinking?" Elliot asked. "There's nothing here."

Tulloch had never heard Cattanach speak so much. He was notoriously the quietest man in the platoon and possibly the company.

"It's the nothing that I like," Cattanach said. He lit a cigarette and inhaled slowly before expelling the smoke in a steady stream. "I grew up with eight of us in one room, in a common stair in a tenement with ten houses, on a street with a hundred other tenements all crowded."

Tulloch lingered, knowing it was unusual for men to discuss their past.

"I never left Leith until I joined the army," Cattanach said quietly. "I never saw so much space."

"We've got space in the Borders," Elliot said. "And better soil."

"I like the desert." Cattanach lifted a handful of the dry, stony sand. "I like the freedom."

"Freedom? There's no freedom in the bloody army," Elliot said.

"There's freedom in the desert," Cattanach replied. "I don't want to return to narrow streets and damp, crowded rooms."

"Right, lads," Hume shouted from the head of the column. "Back on the buses."

The men boarded the trucks, and the column drove on, accompanied by the usual thick cloud of dust. Tulloch stared ahead, now seeing little more than the rear of the truck in front, partially obscured by dust and sand.

If I survive this war, I'll never complain about travelling in Scotland again. There can be little more uncomfortable than driving in a desert. He grunted as the truck jolted over a sand-hidden rock, grabbed the dashboard for support and stared outside at the monotonous desert.

"Italians!" Tulloch heard the warning as if through a dream and realised he was half-dozing in the cab. *When did I last sleep?*

Hogg shouted again. "They're all around us!"

"Look alert, Four Platoon!" Tulloch roared, hoping the men could hear him above the engine's roar. He wound down the window for greater clarity, coughed in the inrush of dust, and realised what had happened.

In the dark of the night, the column had driven straight into an Italian camp. The Italian infantry had bedded down in the open, without sentries or a barrier, and now the Lothians were driving between neat rows of tents. Confused Italian soldiers emerged to stare at the strange vehicles invading their domain.

"Fire!" Tulloch's order echoed the length of the column. "Fire into the tents!"

"Rummel them up!" Elliot shouted, aiming his Lee-Enfield at the dimly white shapes of the tents.

Every vehicle in the column contributed to the mayhem, with Bren guns and rifles hammering at the surprised Italians.

"It hardly seems fair, shooting them while they're asleep!" Cattanach said.

"They'd shoot you," Sergeant Drysdale reminded.

Four Platoon fired with professional detachment and no ill feeling, killing and wounding men, knowing each enemy death was a minuscule step towards winning the war.

Tulloch fired his Lee-Enfield, aiming at the larger tents where he presumed the officers slept. He emptied his magazine and reloaded, allowing Hood to follow the vehicle in front.

The column drove through, firing to left and right, with only a desultory reply from the surprised Italians. Tulloch did not know how many casualties they inflicted, but they left the camp reeling and motored on into the desert.

A single bullet crashed against the back of Tulloch's truck.

"Whatever happens now," Hood said, "we've done some damage, sir."

"We have," Tulloch agreed.

After another hour, they stopped to refuel, and Hardie checked the maps. The men discussed the assault on the Italian camp and wondered what lay ahead.

"Daylight brings the *Luftwaffe* and the *Regia Aeronautica*," Tulloch said. The desert stretched all around them, empty but no longer hostile—a place of escape and security compared to the horrors of the front line.

"We'll be vulnerable in this open land," Rutlane said.

"Nobody will know who we are," Muirhead said. "From the air, we could be anybody." He glanced at Erskine, who stood calmly smoking an Egyptian cigarette. "What do you say, Erskine?"

"Whatever you think, old boy," Erskine replied calmly. He seemed disinterested.

"We'll reorder the column," Hume decided. "We'll change the leading platoon and the rearguard every hour."

When Colonel Hume gave the order, Hardie checked the stars, made a few calculations, and ordered them east into the threatening dawn.

With the sun rising in their faces, the Lothians growled on. They stopped twice as vehicles slammed into soft sand, and men dug them out and used sand channels to continue, and once more because Erskine's truck was out of formation, and Erskine was fast asleep in the back of the truck. Rutlane had taken charge of the company and was inexperienced in desert driving.

Hume snarled at Erskine to retake command of D Company, and they moved on into the heat of the morning, with Muirhead's C Company in the van and Tulloch in the vehicle immediately behind Hardie.

"There's a column ahead, sir," Hood warned. "I can see the dust."

"Ours or theirs?" Tulloch asked.

"Not sure, sir," Hood replied.

"Drive carefully, Hood," Tulloch advised. He peered forward, cursing the dust that concealed the identity of everything until they were close.

"Yes, sir. The last vehicle ahead is a British three-tonner, sir," Hood said.

"I don't care about the vehicle's make," Tulloch snapped. "I care about the driver and passengers." With the rival armies using captured enemy vehicles, recognition was nearly impossible.

"Yes, sir," Hood replied.

Tulloch wanted to drop back, but Hume's orders were to remain in formation to ensure nobody straggled and became lost in the desert. They drove in silence for a while, following Hardie's lead until somebody opened the flap of the vehicle in front. The man wore an olive-green uniform that had faded to the colour of sand. He stared at Tulloch's truck.

"He's a German!" Hood murmured.

"What the devil?" Tulloch said.

The German must have shouted a similar warning to his comrades, for his truck veered off the road.

Hardie also realised the situation and signalled to slow down, but slowing an entire battalion while on the move was easier said than performed.

The German convoy was smaller than the British and did not wait to dispute the road. Instead, it scattered across the desert, weaving to the left and right to disrupt any British marksmen.

"Fire at them!" Tulloch ordered.

Four Platoon responded immediately, with Hogg ready with his rifle and Innes only a second behind. The other platoons also fired when they understood the position. The Germans returned fire until the Lothians' carriers moved out, with the Vickers tearing into the soft-bodied enemy vehicles. A running battle erupted across the desert for a few moments, with neither side sure of the other's strength and men more intent on survival than destroying the enemy.

Tulloch heard a metallic ping as a bullet crashed into the side door of his truck, and another screamed overhead, and then the skirmish was over. Two German vehicles burned furiously, and another was wrecked, with its crew standing with their hands above their heads.

"Take care of these prisoners, Kilner," Colonel Hume ordered. "Dr Macquarie, tend to any wounded men; Kennedy, remove any documents. We'll be back on the move in ten minutes."

Tulloch wondered if the rising smoke would attract enemy aircraft as he checked his men, found no casualties, and herded them back onboard the trucks. "That's a little revenge, lads."

"It's like scoring a goal in the 89th minute when we are six-nothing down to the Hibees," Hogg said, reloading his rifle.

"We'll win the second leg," Innes said, examining his Bren gun. "This barrel is about finished, sir. I've only two replacements left, so I'll need more soon."

Tulloch nodded. The constant fighting and retreating were wearing out the men and equipment. "I'll see what I can do when we reach base, Innes."

"When will that be, sir?" Innes asked.

Tulloch forced a grin. "You'll know as soon as I do," he said.

The sun was at its zenith, beating down on them, and the usual quota of flies appeared from nowhere to torment the men. Under the merciless eyes of Provost Sergeant Crosier, they loaded the prisoners onto a fifteen-hundredweight truck, and Hardie checked their position on the map.

Tulloch heard the abrupt snarl of an NCO.

"Enough of that, Hogg!"

Tulloch saw Corporal Russell of D Company berating Hogg until Sergeant Drysdale separated them. He decided not to interfere, knowing Drysdale could deal with any infraction of discipline.

"Back on board, men!" Hume ordered.

The column reformed and moved on through the usual cloud of dust, with men discussing the skirmish or sitting in accepting silence. Some tried to sleep, others grumbled or spoke of life after the war. The trucks lurched and swayed, then entered an area of soft sand. After half an hour, they stopped, with sand clogging the wheels.

"Debus!" Hume ordered wearily, and the men disembarked. Some reached for shovels to dig the vehicles out, and others grabbed the now-familiar sand channels.

"Watch the sky for aircraft," the officers ordered and set up the Bren gunners as anti-aircraft protection. Waiting as static targets while men laboured with shovels was frustrating and nerve-wracking.

"This situation is ridiculous," Muirhead said as the NCOs supervised the sweating soldiers. "British, Italian and German convoys are all racing eastward, all mixed up, and nobody knows what's happening. What a blasted shambles."

"This whole war is a blasted shambles," Erskine said. "It has been from the first day. The only decent general we had was O'Connor. Now we have these commando fellows and the SAS; can't we send some into O'Connor's prison camp and free him?"

Kennedy nodded. "We'll have to do something," he agreed. "At present, the men are calling Rommel unbeatable."

"He's not," Muirhead said flatly. "Man to man, we're as good as the Germans. Their tanks are better than ours, and Rommel uses them better; that's all."

"Kipling wrote that only the Fuzzy-Wuzzies didn't care a damn about facing a British regiment," Kennedy said. "It doesn't seem right that less than fifty years later, the Germans are pushing us back time after time."

"It's not right," Muirhead sounded confident. "We're not as bad as we seem. Things will change; you'll see."

"We're free!" Sergeant Paterson shouted, sliding the sand channel under the rear wheels.

"Don't board the trucks yet," Hume ordered. "Drive on!"

The trucks lurched forward, kicking up loose sand as the men either marched at their side or helped by pushing the vehicles, with NCOs giving gratuitous advice and lending an occasional hand.

The column staggered on, with the sky thankfully clear of prowling aircraft and no betraying dust visible.

"Those Germans couldn't have contacted their headquarters, or the Luftwaffe would be searching for us," Muirhead said.

"Maybe we damaged their communications truck," Tulloch suggested.

"Or they are as disorganised as we are," Muirhead said. "We seem to all be heading east, British, Italian and German."

"Maybe we should join forces," Tulloch said ironically. "Get things properly organised."

Muirhead grinned. "I'll suggest that to Rommel next time we meet."

After half a mile, the ground became firmer, and Hume ordered the men to board the trucks. Thankfully, the men piled back into their transport and continued eastward, hoping not to meet enemy tanks or aircraft. They stopped twice more when vehicles bogged in soft sand, and the Lothians were hot and frustrated as the sun began to sink behind them.

"Dust ahead!" the ominous warning came from the head of the column.

Chapter Sixteen

"Take a carrier and see what's happening ahead, Tulloch," Hume ordered. He motioned for the trucks to scatter, ready to fight or flee as Tulloch jumped into the closest carrier and ordered the driver to push forward.

"Take it canny, Townsend," Tulloch warned. He nodded to the Bren gunner, a man he did not know. "Keep alert."

"I will, sir."

They moved in the usual haze of dust, with Tulloch peering forward through his binoculars.

"Armoured cars," Tulloch said. "They look British, but that means nothing out in the Blue. Do we have a Boys on board?"

"Yes, sir," the Bren gunner, a lanky youth with acne, replied. He lifted the Boys from beside Tulloch's feet and loaded it. "I've never fired one before."

"Now might be your chance," Tulloch said dryly. "Mind for the kick. It's brutal."

"Yes, sir." The youth handled the Boys clumsily, pulling it hard into his shoulder.

The dust cloud came closer and stopped. Two British scout

cars motored towards them. The youth aimed his Boys, taking a deep breath.

A man poked his head out of the car. "Identify yourselves!" The order was sharp, clear and undoubtedly British, with a strong Yorkshire accent.

"Lothian Rifles!" Tulloch replied. "Who are you?"

"Yeomanry," the officer replied briefly. "Where are you from?"

"Mersa Matruh," Tulloch replied. "Have many got out?"

"Some," the officer said, glancing over the scattered Lothians. "Not everybody. The Durhams lost too many men. You have to report to these coordinates," he handed over a slip of paper. "Glad you could join us, Lothians."

"Glad to be here," Tulloch replied and returned to Colonel Hume.

Hume glanced at the assembly coordinates. "Take us there, Hardie, but stop a couple of miles short."

Hardie nodded. "Yes, sir."

They moved again, glad to have contacted another British unit, yet still unsure what the future held. After an hour, Colonel Hume held up his hand.

"Debus!" Hume ordered when Hardie eased to a stop. The men left the trucks to stand bemused under the desert sun. They looked at one another as the dust gradually settled. They were travel-stained veterans who had faced and fought the enemy, men in tattered, faded uniforms, but all held their personal weapons.

Hume stood on the bonnet of a fifteen-hundredweight truck and motioned his men closer. The Lothians clustered around the colonel, with each company behind its officers.

"The Lothians have survived another battle," Hume said, "and we've acquitted ourselves well once again. Smarten yourselves up, and pipers, play the *Flowers o' Edinburgh*. We'll arrive like soldiers, not tramps!"

The men obeyed, and the always helpful NCOs ensured that

all buttons were fastened and the men wore their uniforms correctly.

Tulloch remembered the Black Watch's return from Crete when a piper played the remnants of the regiment into Alexandria and wondered if Hume had the same idea. It was a gesture of defiance as much as regimental pride, the Lothians telling the world they were not defeated, whatever the situation.

The Bren gun carriers led the Lothians in, with a piper standing in each, as though they had returned from a victory rather than struggling from yet another defeat. Each vehicle was a precise distance from the next, and the men sat at attention.

Other units watched the Lothians arrive, and although some had renewed hope, Tulloch could sense the frustration. A few men gave the thumbs-up, others stood in silence, and some cheered. The Lothians passed them all, with the men as immobile as the sentries at Edinburgh Castle.

"Gin ye daur," Sergeant Drysdale mouthed. "Gin ye daur."

Only Captain Erskine looked vaguely bored, while Lieutenant Rutlane seemed to view the proceedings with his upper lip slightly curled.

A red-capped Military Police corporal directed traffic, and a harassed staff officer ushered the Lothians to their allocated position and arranged food, water and supplies.

"We were fortunate," Muirhead said as C Company settled into its new home. "Other units suffered a lot more than us. The 29th Indian Infantry is gone. The 21st Panzer Division smashed them, and the 8th Durhams lost an entire company in an ambush."

"Mersa Matruh has fallen as well," Kennedy seemed keen to broadcast bad news.

"On the 29th of June," Muirhead agreed. "The whole thing was a shambles, as we thought. The German 90th Light Division and the Italian 133rd Armoured Littorio Division captured the town. The Littorio did well. They repelled a breakout attempt by our 10th Indian Division, while the 27th Brescia and 102nd

Motorised Trento divisions bombarded our positions. The garrison surrendered to the 7th Bersaglieri Regiment." He shook his head sorrowfully. "We lost another six thousand men and more on the retreat here."

"Snafu," Kennedy said. "Situation Normal, All Fouled Up. Rommel won again."

"Rommel, Rommel, Rommel," Tulloch said. "It's always blasted Rommel."

As the Lothians settled in and counted their casualties and losses, Tulloch assessed the battle at Matruh.

"We were totally disorganised," he said. "But we did delay the enemy for a while."

"We're losing too many good men," Muirhead said. "And I blame our indecisive generals. Most of X Corps have been sent further east and renamed Delta Force. I think we're the only X Corps unit that's at Alamein. Thank God the 2nd New Zealand Division is also here."

"Things look even worse than they did in 1940," Kennedy said. "With the *Luftwaffe* and the *Regia Aeronautica* at Mersa Matruh, Alexandria is vulnerable. The Royal Navy has moved its Mediterranean fleet further away."

"Admiral Cunningham won't be pleased at that," Tulloch said.

"The Yanks think we're finished," Kennedy said. "One of their leading intelligence wallahs said the Germans will defeat us within the week."

"That was good of him," Tulloch could not keep the bitterness from his voice. "Did he predict the Japanese attack on Pearl Harbour as well? And Hitler's declaration of war on the USA?"

Kennedy shrugged. "I heard that the people in Egypt are panicking. Hundreds of civilians are fleeing to Palestine, half the Egyptians in Cairo and Alex are kicking at the doors of the British consulates to get a visa. The officials in Cairo are burning all the classified documents they can find." He gave a wry smile. "Somebody said it was like Ash Wednesday."

Tulloch filled his pipe and listened to the conversation. He created his own filling by opening his army-issue Victory V cigarettes and using the tobacco.

Muirhead grunted. "I heard we're preparing to flood the Nile Delta," he said, "and creating defences along the Suez Canal and at Alex. Some of the brass hats are talking about a scorched earth policy, and others are preparing to withdraw to Jerusalem."

Kennedy shook his head as Tulloch lit his pipe. "That's a foul concoction, Tulloch. Remind me never to borrow your tobacco. I wonder what the Germans are planning next?"

"We'll know when they arrive," Muirhead said.

Tulloch thought of the stifled frustration that affected the British army. They were becoming nearly philosophical about constant defeat, which was an attitude Tulloch had never experienced.

"If Rommel has sufficient fuel, he'll drive right through our next position," Kennedy said.

Muirhead glanced at Tulloch and raised his eyebrows.

"Let's hope that doesn't happen," Tulloch said.

"It will," Kennedy predicted. "We're not good enough to stop him."

"Yes, we are," Tulloch said quietly. "It's time you stopped that sort of talk, Kennedy. You might discourage the men."

Kennedy shrugged. "They're already discouraged."

Tulloch fought his rising anger. He kept his voice low. "Enough, Kennedy. If I hear you talking like that in front of my platoon, I'll shoot you myself." He held Kennedy's gaze until his fellow lieutenant looked away.

Muirhead touched Tulloch's shoulder. "Easy, Douglas. We're all a bit on edge just now."

Tulloch nodded. "Aye," he said.

Chapter Seventeen

EL ALAMEIN JULY 1942

Tulloch thought El Alamein was little more than a fly-infested railway station hard by the Mediterranean. He glanced at the peeling paint on the walls and the railway tracks that stretched eastward to Alexandria and westward towards Axis-held Libya. From Alamein, the desert stretched ten miles south to the Ruweisat Ridge.

"Drive south, Hood," Tulloch ordered. He had borrowed a universal carrier, with Hood as the driver and Kennedy and Muirhead as his companions. The Bren lay at the side, although Tulloch hoped they would not need it.

Hood drove carefully, with the expected dust cloud covering them as they passed units of British and Allied soldiers preparing defences against Rommel's inevitable attack.

"Stop at that ridge," Muirhead ordered.

The Ruweisat Ridge was low but significant in a flat landscape and a fine observation spot. Tulloch and Muirhead examined it through their binoculars.

"This ridge will be key," Tulloch said. "If we can hold it, we'll see what Rommel is up to."

"He'll outflank it and take us from the rear," Kennedy said. "That's what he did at Gazala."

"The Auck is defending a line of Boxes between Alamein and the Qattara Depression, twenty miles south of here, with this Ruweisat Ridge the only decent feature," Tulloch said. "Rommel can either make a wide detour south of the Depression and waste fuel he can't afford, or hammer through or between the defensive Boxes and waste men he also can't afford."

"The Boxes are not as strong as we had at Gazala," Kennedy pointed out. "Only the one near Alamein is anything like complete. Rommel can roam at will between them."

"The more he roams, the more fuel he will use," Tulloch said. "And in the meantime, General Norrie is creating more Boxes of the kind that failed to stop Rommel at Gazala." He kept his voice low so Innes and Hood could not hear his discontent.

"Three Boxes," Kennedy murmured. "One at Alamein, one at Bab el Qattara, about eighteen miles further south with neither mines nor wire, while the last, the Naq Abu Dweiss, beside the Depression, has hardly a dent on the ground." He scratched his head, waving a hand uselessly at the circling flies. "If we couldn't stop Rommel with prepared positions at Gazala, how can we stop him without them here?"

"We inflicted losses on him at Gazala, too," Tulloch pointed out, "and he's at the end of a long supply line that the RAF and the Long Range Desert Group harass daily. Rather than concentrate on our weaknesses, maybe we should think of problems the enemy has."

"Auchinleck isn't thinking of Rommel's problems," Kennedy pointed out. "He's building defences at Cairo and Alex and flooding half the Delta. He expects Rommel to beat us again."

"He's only taking precautions," Tulloch said, clutching at every straw he could.

"Have you heard about Mussolini?" Muirhead changed the subject.

"What about him?" Tulloch responded wearily. "What's he done now?"

"I heard he's going to Libya and planning a victory parade through Cairo," Muirhead said.

Tulloch grunted. "That's a bit premature. Did Mussolini not plan that back in '40, before O'Connor smashed his army?"

"The Italians captured O'Connor," Kennedy reminded.

Muirhead forced a smile. "Cheer up, gentlemen. Mussolini hasn't got to Cairo yet, and as you said, the enemy has their own problems."

"We don't have a chance," Kennedy said. Jamming his cap on his head, he slumped away, with a cloud of flies following.

"Hume should transfer that man," Muirhead said quietly. "He's a poison dwarf, spreading his defeatist talk around the battalion. It's men like him that lower morale and lose us battles." He glanced at Tulloch. "Shooting him is not allowed, Douglas."

Tulloch grunted in reply. He knew that Kennedy was not alone. He had never known morale to be so low. After Dunkirk, the survivors had been defiant, willing to fight Hitler's Panzers with pikes and homemade bombs. However, the recent reverses and the capitulation of Tobruk had left the 8th Army confused, wondering what they had to do to win.

"Let's get back to the men, sir," Tulloch said. "We've seen enough here."

———

WHILE THE LOTHIANS DUG DEFENSIVE TRENCHES AND created sandbagged dugouts, Auchinleck prepared for another battle with Rommel.

"The Auk is making changes at the front," Muirhead said.

Tulloch glanced along the line. "As long as he sends reinforcements here, we're rather lonely on our own."

Muirhead laughed without humour. "He has. He's sent XXX

Corps, the 1st South African and the 5th and 10th Indian Divisions to hold the right of the line and XIII Corps, that's the 4th Indian and 2nd New Zealand, to hold the left."

Tulloch shook his head. "The South Africans handed Tobruk to Rommel on a plate. I hope they do better this time."

"The South Africans will be operating beside us," Muirhead told him. "We'll have to ensure the Jocks don't cause trouble by mentioning the capitulation at Tobruk."

Tulloch nodded. Scottish infantry was amongst the best in the world, but they could also be inflammatory when they thought their allies were not pulling their weight. Tulloch could imagine Hogg and Smith taunting the South Africans about their colleagues' actions at Tobruk. "I'll remind them," he said. "Who is filling the gaps between the Boxes?"

"The 1st Armoured Division," Muirhead said, "or what's left of it, together with the 7th Armoured. They're the mobile reserve. I presume Auchinleck intends the Boxes to slow Rommel, who will move through the gaps, allowing our armour to attack their flanks."

"Similar tactics to Gazala then," Tulloch said.

"Similar tactics," Muirhead agreed.

"With similar results," Kennedy said. "If we survive, I'll see you all in Alex or Jerusalem." He paused for a significant moment. "Or in a prisoner-of-war camp."

"The enemy will be as tired as we are," Tulloch reminded. "They've also fought hard battles; they have a long supply line and fewer reinforcements. They'll be short of water and ammunition."

"But they have Rommel," Kennedy said, walking away before Tulloch retorted.

Erskine sauntered across with his hands in his pockets and an Egyptian cigarette in his mouth. "That was a message from higher command," he said casually. "RAF reconnaissance reports the enemy is approaching. We'll have another crack at them, gentlemen!"

Tulloch stamped his feet on the ground, unsure how he felt but keen to have another round with Rommel. "Gin ye daur, Rommel," he said softly. "Gin ye daur."

———

THE LOTHIANS SAW THE DUST AT EIGHT IN THE MORNING, AN ominous yellow-grey cloud rising from the west.

"Here they come, lads," Tulloch warned. He saw Four Platoon's faces, grimly resigned, tired but defiant.

The men settled into their positions, with the anti-tank guns ready for the expected assault and the Bren gunners and riflemen licking dry, sand-smeared lips. All were Gazala and Mersa Matruh veterans; some had experience that extended to Dunkirk and the Northwest Frontier. They knew what to expect.

"Who are we facing? The 90th Light? The 21st Panzer or the Littorio Division?" Smith asked. Tulloch had indented for a new Boys, which Smith had cleaned lovingly and now held hopefully.

"Who cares?" Hood replied. "They're all the same when you shoot them."

"Come on, you bastards," Hogg murmured. "Hoggie of the Gorgie Boys is waiting for you."

The pipers began to play, with the distinctive sounds of the Lowland Pipes floating above the hiss of the desert wind and the distant engine rumble.

The dust cloud approached and stopped while the defiant pipes continued to taunt the enemy. The forward listening posts reported that the enemy was the 90th Light Infantry and requested permission to return inside the defensive Box.

"In you come," Muirhead agreed.

The men scrambled back, with Muirhead counting them one by one. Busy engineers replaced the wire and the few mines. The men continued to wait, hoping their artillery would discourage any attack. Mercifully, the sky was clear of aircraft, achingly blue as it stretched to infinity.

"It's a grand day," Innes said. "I could be walking in Princes Street Gardens with Jillian today."

"Is that your girl?" Hogg asked.

"Aye. We'll get wed when this nonsense is over," Innes smoothed a hand along the barrel of his Bren.

Silence returned. The dust cleared, allowing the officers time to study the enemy.

"Where is their armoured support?" Erskine asked. "They have half-tracks and a few armoured cars but no tanks."

"Thank God for small mercies," Tulloch replied. He glanced at Smith, knowing he was eager to try his new Boys.

The sound of aircraft engines made everybody look up.

"Ours or theirs?" Muirhead asked.

"Probably one or the other," Erskine replied.

The aircraft flew past, high above, and a few moments later, the Lothians heard bombing from the south.

"The RAF are with us, then," Erskine said.

"I heard the Americans have some heavy bombers here, too," Muirhead said.

"That can only be good," Tulloch agreed.

The Germans hovered outside the Allied defences, a constant menace yet without attacking or firing. The Lothians remained alert, eating at their posts, grumbling, pestered by flies, and waiting as the tension mounted.

"When will they come?" Elliot asked.

"When they're ready," Innes told him. "Relax, Shug. The longer they take, the better, as far as I'm concerned."

When Erskine asked Hume's permission to take out a fighting patrol, the colonel shook his head. "Sorry, Erskine. Orders from above say we've to conserve our strength."

The day eased into night, with the Lothians still waiting for the inevitable enemy attack.

"The bastards are toying with us," Elliot said.

"Nah," Hogg replied. "They're scared to face the Lothians. They know what will happen to them."

"They never come at night," Smith said. "We'll be fine until daylight."

The attack came at three in the morning when men were at their lowest.

"Here they come, lads!" Tulloch said.

"It's the first of July," Muirhead murmured, "the anniversary of the Battle of the Somme." He grinned, showing white teeth in a humourless face. "Let's send them back."

The 90th Light advanced through the British minefields, as steady and professional as German infantry always were. The South African artillery had been waiting and opened fire when the Germans came in range, hammering them with twenty-five-pounder shells. The explosions blossomed through the night, each one revealing a tiny vignette of the battle, with brief images of men and vehicles advancing, shouting, and dying in the furnace of battle.

"That's more like it, South Africans!" Muirhead approved.

"Just the job!" Smith agreed.

"Over there!" Drysdale shouted. "On your left flank, One section!"

A star shell revealed a platoon of the 90th pushed close to the Lothians' position until the Bren and rifles of One Section halted them. The Vickers machine guns hammered at the enemy, sending a cone of bullets towards them, with resulting screams and shouts.

"They're persistent buggers, aren't they?" Muirhead said.

Tulloch nodded. "They're getting no change from us!" He looked for Kennedy, who was in a trench behind his platoon. "Keep them back, Four Platoon!"

The dawn rose suddenly, surprising Tulloch, who had not realised how much time had passed. The sun blazed in the eyes of the German soldiers, aiding the defenders.

"They're falling back," Muirhead said. "Cease fire, men. Conserve your ammunition."

All that day, the 90th probed the Allied defence, with the

Lothians repulsing the infantry and the South African artillery hitting the halftracks and armoured cars.

"They're not pressing their attacks," Muirhead said.

"Maybe they're testing us or looking for a weak spot," Tulloch suggested.

"We should counterattack now when they are disorganised," Erskine said.

"We have to preserve the integrity of the 8th Army," Kilner told him primly. "Or something like that."

"News from the south," Muirhead said. "The 18th Indian Infantry Brigade is holding the 21st Panzer Division, and the 1st Armoured Division is driving back the 15th Panzer Division south of Deir el Shein."

"Maybe this is Rommel's high tide mark," Tulloch said. "He's met his match in the Auk!"

"They're coming again," Muirhead warned. "Back to the coal face, gentlemen!"

Tulloch slid into his trench with words of encouragement for his men. Four Platoon waited until the 90th Light came in range and opened up, with the anti-tank guns targeting the halftracks.

"Come on, lads!" Smith protested. "Let one of the halftracks get within range of my elephant gun!" He held his Boys hopefully.

The Germans probed without committing a full-scale attack. When their infantry came close, the South Africans and Lothians repelled them with small arms and Vickers machine guns, and when they moved further away, South African artillery punished them with shell fire. By late afternoon, the Germans had withdrawn from the Alamein Box and headed south to push eastward, deeper into Egypt. The South African artillery followed them until the 90th Light Infantry dug into defensive positions.

"We've repulsed them, men!" Tulloch said. "Any casualties?"

"None in Four Platoon, sir," Drysdale replied.

Intent on their battle with the 90th Light, the Lothians

ignored the fighting further south. By the evening, they heard that the 21st Panzer Division had pushed back the 18th Indian Infantry Brigade after a brutal, bloody struggle.

"The 18th did well," Tulloch said.

"They held back an entire Panzer division," Muirhead agreed. "And gained Auchinleck some time to strengthen the Ruweisat Ridge defences." He nodded to the south. "Rommel lost eighteen tanks today, and we helped the South Africans push away the 90th Light."

"Tomorrow is another day," Tulloch said. "We'll see what it brings." He glanced at his platoon. "I'd better feed and water the men."

The Lothians remained on alert the next day, listening to firing from the south and the occasional reports from headquarters.

"The 90th Light has joined the Afrika Korps, and they're attacking our positions at the Ruweisat Ridge," Muirhead informed Tulloch. "As we thought they would."

The battle at Ruweisat Ridge continued all day, with British armour and British and Indian artillery fighting the 15th and 21st Panzer Divisions. The British blunted the German attacks and pushed them back, with the RAF making repeated bombing runs in support. By night, the Germans withdrew, battered but not yet defeated.

"They're leaving us alone up here," Kennedy said.

"Rommel is concentrating on the Ruweisat Ridge," Muirhead told him. "Keep strengthening our defences, Kennedy, in case they try again."

Chapter Eighteen

EL ALAMEIN, EGYPT, JULY 1942

While the Lothians remained virtually undisturbed, they listened to the radio reports from the other parts of the battlefield.

German and Italian forces pushed at the Ruweisat Ridge, with the Allies holding them, gradually reducing the enemy armour and wearing down the weary men. The RAF, flying from Egyptian airfields and with fewer problems with fuel, gained domination of the sky. Far to the south, the New Zealand 2nd Division, including elements of the Indian 5th Division and 7th Motor Brigade, pushed out of the Qattara Box and attacked the enemy flank, nearly wiping out all the tanks of the Italian Ariete Division.

"What do you think, sir?" Tulloch asked. "Has the Auk stopped Rommel's advance?"

"It seems so," Muirhead said.

"Why are we sitting doing nothing?" Erskine asked. "We can hit their flanks and damage them!"

"Orders from above," Muirhead reminded.

"I've asked the colonel repeatedly for permission to take a strike force out," Erskine said.

"The colonel is also under orders from above," Muirhead told him.

Erskine grunted and chain-smoked his Egyptian cigarettes. "It's a waste of a bloody good opportunity," he said.

The New Zealanders pushed forward the next day until the Italian Brescia Division blasted them with intensive artillery fire. The New Zealanders and XIII Corps attack faltered and stopped, so both sides glared at each other while the blood of the dead and wounded soaked into the desert sand.

With his attack blunted, his men exhausted, and the RAF and British columns destroying many of his supply columns, Rommel temporarily halted his offensive.

"Stalemate," Kilner said.

"Maybe," Tulloch replied. "Or perhaps we've stopped Rommel dead. He's facing the same problems as we did when we invaded Libya: lack of supplies and his men and equipment worn out."

"Rommel will sort them out, and then he'll attack and push right through us," Kennedy said.

"He will if we all had your attitude, Kennedy," Tulloch said as Muirhead and Erskine stopped to listen. "I've had about enough of your constant complaining."

"I'm only representing facts, Tulloch. We've had it."

"No, we've not," Captain Muirhead said quietly. "I've warned you before, Kennedy. I hope you don't let the men hear you talking like that."

Kennedy lifted his chin. "The men aren't stupid. They know what's happening."

"Keep your opinions to yourself, Kennedy," Muirhead warned. "We don't want the men's morale undermined."

As the Axis armies reached the limit of their supply lines, tried to replace their losses, and consolidated their gains, the Allies benefitted from their shorter communication and supply lines. Auchinleck reinforced the Alamein line with the 9th Australian Division in the north and the 5th Indian Brigade on the Ruweisat Ridge. When the untested 161st Indian Infantry Brigade joined the 5th Indian Division, Tulloch knew that Auchinleck's El Alamein position grew stronger daily.

The Lothians were not involved when General Ramsden attacked the Axis positions at Tel el Eisa and Tel el Makh Khad. Tulloch sat in his dugout, listening as the wind carried the occasional sound of battle and watching the distant flashes on the horizon.

"Somebody's pounding the enemy," Erskine said as they heard the rumble of artillery and saw the resulting explosions.

"Good," Tulloch said. He waited for Kennedy to give a negative assessment and was relieved when the lieutenant kept silent.

"I hate doing nothing," Erskine grated.

"Our chance will come," Muirhead said. "Have patience, Erskine."

Later that day, the Lothians heard that following an intense bombardment, the Australian 26th Brigade attacked the Italian 60th Infantry Division and captured 1,500 prisoners and the German Signals Intercept Company 621.

"Well done, the Aussies," Muirhead said. "That 621 Company read all our radio communications."

Erskine grinned. "That would confuse them," he said.

"The Aussies always do well." Tulloch began to fill his pipe. "No wonder Rommel could anticipate our moves if he heard all our signals. Hardly a desert fox, then."

Muirhead lifted a lazy eyebrow, saying nothing.

News continued to filter in through the battalion's intelligence officer. The South Africans, under a cloud since the German capture of Tobruk, pushed the Axis out of Tel el Makh Khad and ably supported the Australians.

"I feel as if we're only observers here," Tulloch said.

"We've done our bit," Kennedy said as Erskine grunted, puffing at his Egyptian cigarettes.

The Lothian officers frequently found reasons to pass the HQ dugout, trying to glean information about the battle that raged on the extended front. The news passed from man to man across and down the ranks until every member of the Lothians knew as much as the officers did.

German and Italian attacks met fierce Australian and British artillery and withdrew, leaving smoking wrecks and casualties as a memory of their failure. The Allied counterattacks continued, with Australian infantry and British tanks capturing the west of Tel el Eisa and fighting off enemy retaliation. The Allies followed this success with a vigorous raid on Axis positions on Deir el Abyad, which captured 1,000 Italians before the enemy forced them back at the Miteirya Ridge.

"Maybe Rommel has shot his bolt," Lieutenant Hardie said. "He's reached the end of the line."

"Maybe," Tulloch agreed. "This entire desert war is like a game. One side attacks and pushes back the enemy until the supply lines are stretched. The other side retreats until the first side reaches the end of the supply line, then the second side attacks until their supply line is strained, and the whole damned stupid game starts again. Even Rommel can't seem to manage his supplies."

"The Royal Navy, RAF and LRDG have something to do with that," Hardie said. "We'd be in a much worse situation without them."

Tulloch nodded. "I won't argue with that," he said.

The intermittent but fierce fighting continued all along the line, with the 21st Panzer Division losing 600 men in an abortive attack on the Australians and Auchinleck's counterattacks achieving partial success before the enemy halted them.

"They'll come here next," Tulloch said quietly. "We've probed, and Rommel's probed, and both sides know the other's weakness. The Germans are aware the Australians will knock them back, and we lack the Aussies' anti-tank firepower."

Muirhead nodded. "I agree, Tulloch. Get your men ready."

"Yes, sir," Tulloch knew Four Platoon was as ready as possible.

Positioned alongside the Lothians, the Royal Durban Light Infantry were equally ill-equipped with anti-tank guns. They waited expectantly for Rommel's attack.

Private Oldham regaled the platoon with his rendering of *Lili Marlene* until Elliot joined in with a more obscene version.

"You cannae sing, Shuggie!" Hogg told him. "Your voice is like a bloody crow."

"You see if you can do better!" Elliot retaliated, and the two began to argue until Corporal Borthwick snarled them to silence.

Tulloch saw the distant flashes of artillery to the west. "Down boys! Hitler's sending his hate!"

The Lothians lay or crouched in their dugouts and trenches as the Germans began their assault with a powerful artillery barrage. The shellfire caused casualties and cut the Lothians' and South Africans' phone lines, so they could not order artillery support. The Germans followed the barrage with screaming Stuka dive bombers, and then the 21st Panzer Division attacked.

"Here they come!" Tulloch shouted as he emerged from his dugout, shook the sand from his uniform and lifted his rifle. "Let's send them back!"

The Lothians' and South African anti-tank guns waited until the Panzers were eight hundred yards away and opened fire, with the six-pounders sending their shells screaming across the desert.

The Lothians remained in their dugouts, firing on the few occasions the German infantry appeared. The artillery and tanks mostly engaged in a long-range duel, with the infantry mainly passive observers under the arc of the guns.

"The tanks are getting closer," Muirhead said worriedly. "If Rommel takes this Box, he will cut off the Australians, and the Auk will order the 8th Army back to the Nile Delta."

"The closer they get, the better targets they make," Tulloch tried to sound optimistic, ducking as a shell exploded ten yards away.

All day, the Allied artillery and German tanks disputed the perimeter of the El Alamein Box. The Germans inched closer, gaining territory at the expense of tanks and lives. The Allies called up more support, so the British 7th Medium Regiment and the 9th Australian Field Artillery joined in, with the 79th British Anti-Tank Regiment also supporting the South Africans and Lothians.

In the evening, with the German tanks silhouetted against the setting sun, the fighting eased off.

"I only fired three shots," Hogg grumbled as the Germans withdrew and the smoke and dust died away. "The bastards never came close."

"You can get them next time, Hoggie," Innes consoled him. "I'm sure Hitler has more men waiting to invade Egypt."

"Why do they want it? It's all flies and stour," Hogg replied. "I dunno why we're fighting for a bloody desert."

With the German withdrawal from the Alamein Box, a wary hush descended on the battlefield. Both sides counted their casualties and prepared for the next round.

As Rommel dug in to wait for reinforcements, Auchinleck decided to attack the Axis positions on the Ruweisat Ridge.

"What's Auchinleck's idea?" Kennedy asked.

"The Auk is targeting the Italians," Tulloch said. "Italian equipment is not the same quality as the Germans'. If Auchinleck breaks the Italians, Rommel won't be able to hold on with only his Germans."

Auchinleck sent the New Zealanders and 2nd Armoured Brigade to attack the ridge. They made steady initial progress, but some Italians dug stubbornly in and, together with uncleared minefields, delayed the New Zealand supports. Having bypassed the pockets of resistance, the forward troops became isolated, stuck without heavy weapons. When the British armoured brigades remained trapped behind the minefields, the 8th Panzer

Regiment counterattacked and forced the most forward New Zealand infantry to surrender.

"Auchinleck's push on the Ruweisat Ridge failed then," Muirhead said grimly.

"So far," Tulloch said, still hoping for good news.

As the New Zealanders struggled, the 5th Indian Brigade attacked on the east. They captured part of the Ruweisat Ridge, with British tanks and artillery giving crucial support. Simultaneously, the British 22nd Armoured Brigade, backed by artillery, repelled a push by the German 90th Light Division.

Auchinleck's duel with Rommel swayed back and forth, with first one side and then the other launching limited attacks that sometimes gained local success. Despite their bravery and casualties, neither side could gain overall victory. Rommel lost many precious tanks without penetrating the British line but blunted every Allied counterattack. The New Zealanders had taken the brunt of the Allied casualties, with several instances when they achieved their objectives, but British tanks could not support them. The armour's failure was not due to a lack of courage. In one attempt, the British 23rd Armoured Brigade lost eighty-seven tanks, including forty utterly destroyed.

Tulloch remembered the Yeomanry's mad charge at the German 88-mm battery at Gazala and understood why the armour took so many casualties.

"Our armoured tactics are wrong," he said.

"What do you suggest?" Muirhead asked quietly.

"I don't know," Tulloch admitted. He began to fill his pipe with tobacco from Victory-V cigarettes.

"Nor do I," Muirhead said. "Even our best attacks had mixed fortunes. The generals seem to plan them hastily, and there is poor cooperation between our infantry and armour."

"You sound like Kennedy," Tulloch said.

"I sound like a man with experience. The Lothians were hardly involved in the battle," Muirhead said as the fighting eased to a halt, with both armies having made little progress. He scanned the surroundings through his binoculars. "The fighting seems to have stopped for now."

"That's maybe no bad thing," Tulloch replied. "We didn't cover ourselves in glory."

"We stopped Rommel," Muirhead reminded.

"We outnumbered him in men and tanks," Tulloch said. "We threw away the lives of hundreds of good men by inadequate planning and poor tactics. As far as I see it, both armies fought a fine defensive battle but failed in offence." He drew on his pipe and ejected foul-smelling smoke. "Rommel's still vulnerable at the end of long lines of communication, but he'll get stronger."

"Now it's you that sounds like Kennedy," Muirhead said, grinning sourly. "What's the date? The first of August. The Auk ordered all offensives to end yesterday. We must prepare for another defensive battle."

"I hope we do better than we did at Gazala," Tulloch said.

"So do I. We'll need new tactics if we are to win." Muirhead looked up as Erskine sauntered to them, hands in his pockets and a cigarette between his teeth. "What do you think, Erskine?"

Erskine removed his cigarette. "We've been fighting this war for nearly three years now, Muirhead, and I don't think we're any nearer victory now than we were after Dunkirk."

"Hitler hasn't won yet," Tulloch searched for a gleam of hope. "And we are no longer alone. We have the Russians and the Americans on our side now. Hitler may have overreached himself, attacking Russia and declaring war against America while still fighting us. Russia is soaking up the bulk of Hitler's army and much of the Luftwaffe, while the Royal Navy has taken care of most of his surface fleet."

"The U-boats are a menace, though," Erskine reminded.

"The Royal Navy will take care of them in time," Tulloch said.

"I hope the good Lord grants us sufficient time," Muirhead replied.

"Amen to that," Tulloch said quietly.

Chapter Nineteen

EL ALAMEIN AND CAIRO, AUGUST 1942

"Are you quite comfortable, gentlemen?" Colonel Hume stepped behind them.

The officers stood to attention. "Sorry, sir. I didn't see you there," Muirhead said.

Hume nodded. "We're going out of the line soon. Get your men prepared." He sniffed. "That's terrible tobacco you're smoking, Douglas. I'd invest in something better if I were you."

"Yes, sir," Tulloch agreed. "Where are we going?"

"Mareopolis," Hume told them, "southwest of Alexandria." He stepped back. "The rest of the 50th Division retired to refit there after Gazala. Now it's our turn."

"Fifty Div had a bad time," Muirhead said. "They needed a rest."

In the two months since arriving in the Gazala line, the 50th Division had been fighting and retreating nearly continually, suffering over nine thousand casualties. It had also lost much of its transport, supporting equipment, and artillery. The fighting had reduced the infantry battalions to half their normal strength, all requiring rest and retraining while reinforcements filled the gaps.

"We're leaving at oh five hundred hours tomorrow," Hume said and walked away.

———————

"WE'VE FARED BETTER THAN MOST," MUIRHEAD SAID AS THEY surveyed the campsite at Mareopolis. The Lothians were on a patch of hot, soft sand ten yards above sea level, a breeding ground for flies and scorpions. They put up their tents in long, neat lines, set up the battalion cookhouse and hospital, and welcomed the trickle of reinforcements that arrived. The men began to relax, although they kept a lookout for any raiding enemy aircraft and trained for the next bout with the Axis powers.

After a week, Colonel Hume called his officers together.

"Sit down, gentlemen." Hume looked worried as his officers sat on the soft sand, wondering what fate had in store for them next. "We've never had any problem with desertions before in the Lothians," Hume said. "We have the usual quota of men absent without leave, overstaying their leave, getting drunk and failing to return to base on time, picked up by the police for brawling, that sort of thing, but never desertions."

The officers glanced at one another, with Tulloch mentally counting the men in Four Platoon. He had seen them all that morning with the usual grumbles, but nobody was missing. Muirhead lit his pipe while Erskine leaned back, chain-smoking Egyptian cigarettes and looking bored.

"I am open to comments, gentlemen," Hume said.

"Maybe the pressure of the past few months was too much, sir," Muirhead suggested. "We've been pretty hectic with battle after battle, and the men don't like retreating. That always lowers morale."

"Maybe," Hume said. "Maybe." He mused for a moment. "I

think there's something more behind it. We had nine men desert since we returned from the front, and six came from your D Company, Erskine."

"Yes, sir." Erskine removed the cigarette from his mouth to reply. "I can't think why, sir. My company hasn't had it any worse than any other."

"Find out why, Erskine, and sort it," Hume said. "I have the Military Police scouring Alex for the men. I want them returned to the Lothians so we can deal with them internally rather than sending them to the Glasshouse."

Tulloch nodded. He had heard about the brutal treatment the redcaps meted out to inmates in the Glasshouse prison and did not want any of the Lothians' men incarcerated there. After enduring battle and fear in the desert, they deserved better than the horror of a military prison.

"I agree, sir," Erskine drawled. "Men incarcerated in the Glasshouse are no good to anybody, and we need all the bodies we can find to fill the ranks." He took a long draw of his cigarette and released a thin column of smoke. "I'll have a word with my company and dissuade any more from deserting. After all," he said, "where would they go in Egypt?"

"Where indeed?" Hume treated Erskine with a stern look.

"Speak to your men, gentlemen," Hume addressed everybody. "Tell them that deserters let the regiment down and themselves down, and remind them that men who run face imprisonment or worse." He paused to allow his words to sink in. "That's all, gentlemen. Dismissed."

As Tulloch returned to Four Platoon, he passed a small crowd of men gathered around the library truck. He saw Innes among the hopeful readers, and Cattenach slide a Penguin book into his battledress pocket.

"What's the book, Cattenach?" Tulloch asked.

"*Peril at End House*, sir," Cattenach replied, seemingly surprised to be asked. "It's one of Agatha Christie's."

"Excellent choice," Tulloch approved. "Nothing like a good mystery to take your mind away from the war for a while."

"Yes, sir," Cattenach agreed.

Tulloch walked on, relieved that his platoon seemed content. He heard gasping as he neared Four Platoon's tents. He frowned as he saw the perspiring man running in circles with his full kit on his back and both hands holding his rifle above his head. Provost Sergeant Crosier and a provost corporal screamed at the running man in a constant, near-maniacal bellow.

"Get those knees higher, Hogg, and keep your arms straight! You've hardly started, you bastard! Move! Run! Keep those knees up! Up!"

With sweat running down his face and soaking into the fabric of his uniform, Hogg ran around the Lothians' camp, pursued by the two screeching provost NCOs.

"Sergeant," Tulloch said quietly, and Sergeant Crosier doubled to him, slamming to immaculate attention. "Hogg's in my platoon. I didn't authorise any disciplinary action. What's he supposed to have done?"

Crosier was tall, wiry and basilisk-eyed with a heavy, jowly face. "He disobeyed a lawful order, sir, and verbally abused a superior."

Tulloch saw the corporal shouting at Hogg as he completed a circuit of the Lothians' position. Tulloch saw a groove in the sand and knew it was not Hogg's first circuit. Corporal Russell sat on the roof of a fifteen-hundredweight truck, drinking from his water bottle.

"Which superior was that, Sergeant Crosier?" Tulloch asked mildly.

"Corporal Russell, sir, from D Company."

Tulloch nodded. "Thank you, Sergeant," Tulloch said. "How long do you intend to discipline my man?"

"Ten laps, sir. He's done three so far."

Tulloch knew Hogg was as tough a soldier as any in the battalion, but ten laps in the blistering heat, wearing full kit, would drain him. Tulloch also knew that the army depended on strict discipline, and allowing a man to abuse his superior set a dangerous precedent. "All right, Sergeant. Don't kill him."

"He'll live, sir," Crosier promised and dropped his voice. "He's safe with me, sir. I know their limits."

Tulloch nodded, saw Hogg pound past, red-faced and perspiring, and gave him an encouraging nod. "Carry on, Sergeant," he said. "I want him fit and well when you're finished with him."

Russell took another swig of his bottle.

"Enjoying the view, Corporal?" Tulloch asked. "I think the pioneers need a hand in digging latrines. You've just volunteered." He felt satisfaction at the dismay on Russell's face. "Now, Corporal! Double!"

"Yes, sir!" Russell gave a hurried salute and hurried away. Tulloch saw Hogg give the corporal's retreating back a baleful glare and pound on, wearing a deep groove in the sand.

When he returned to Four Company, Tulloch sought out Sergeant Drysdale. "I see Hogg's in trouble, Sergeant."

"Yes, sir. Hogg's got a mouth on him and argued with Corporal Russell in D Company."

"Keep them apart, Sergeant," Tulloch said. "Send Hogg to the other side of the camp or put him on guard duty or fatigues. I don't want Russell or Sergeant Crosier to get their claws into him again."

"I'll do that, sir," Drysdale replied and hesitated. "Hogg can be trouble, sir."

"I know that, Sergeant," Tulloch said. "But he's our trouble, and we can deal with him without calling on the provost branch."

"Yes, sir," Drysdale agreed.

Tulloch watched Hogg for a moment, wondering what he was thinking, and turned away to attend to his administrative duties. The army thrived on paperwork and issued hundreds of forms, each specifically numbered and designed to irritate the patience of serving officers.

———

"TULLOCH," COLONEL HUME THRUST HIS HEAD INTO THE TENT and stepped inside. "We don't know how long we're out of the line, so I want everybody to have some leave before we return. It might improve morale."

"And end the desertions, sir?"

"Hopefully," Hume said. "Work out a rota for your men and include yourself."

"Me, sir?" Leave was not something Tulloch had contemplated with Rommel's army so close to Alexandria.

"You, sir." Hume mustered a smile. "You have five days, Douglas, but prepare to be recalled if the situation deteriorates."

———

AMANDA SAT ON THE BOTTOM STEP OF THE GREAT PYRAMID OF Giza with her cap pushed forward to shade her face and a few stray strands of hair flopping over her left ear. Her tanned face highlighted the serious grey of her eyes and the new worry lines at the corner of her mouth. "What was it like at Gazala?"

Tulloch pondered for a moment before he replied. "Grim," he said. "Retreating and fighting and retreating again. It was like a repeat of France. We know that man-for-man, we are as good as they are, but still, they defeat us. The men are utterly frustrated, with morale beginning to slide, sickness rising, and men deserting."

"Desertion?" Amanda repeated. "That's unusual in the Lothians."

"That makes it worrying," Tulloch told her. "We're normally a pretty contented battalion, so the colonel is unhappy."

"He will be," Amanda replied. "How long are you away from the front?"

"I was going to ask if you knew," Tulloch replied. "You work in intelligence."

"I don't work in that side of things," Amanda said.

They sat in silence for a while, satisfied with each other's company without needing to speak. A string of camels passed, and the Arab driver looked at the two Britons hopefully. When Tulloch shook his head, the Arab ambled away, long-striding and unhurried.

"I am not entirely sure what you do," Tulloch said at last.

"I analyse documents," Amanda replied carefully, watching the camels.

"What sort of documents?" Tulloch asked.

"Whatever sort the brass hats give me to analyse," Amanda said. "I'm sorry, Douglas, I can't tell you anymore."

Tulloch nodded. "I understand." His smile was twisted. "You can tell me after the war."

Amanda nodded, looking at him sideways. "That will be soon, I hope."

They were quiet again, sitting side by side, not quite touching.

"How do you feel about the higher command?" Amanda asked.

Tulloch had not expected the question. He opened his mouth to reply, wondered if Amanda was asking as a friend or in her role in Intelligence, and gave a muted reply. "I am sure they do their best," he said cautiously.

"How do your fellow officers feel about them?"

"The same as me," Tulloch replied. "Many are frustrated at the course of the campaign so far."

"That's not surprising," Amanda said quietly. "How do they feel about General Auchinleck?" She faced him with her eyes level and eyebrows raised. "How do you feel about the Auk?"

Tulloch pondered his reply. "I don't know if he's as good as O'Connor or, more importantly, as good as Rommel."

Amanda's eyes softened as she smiled. "Maybe Rommel is not quite as good as his reputation suggests," she said.

"He's played merry hell with us," Tulloch reminded. "More than once, and he captured Tobruk and Mersa too easily."

"He had certain advantages you don't know about," Amanda responded, her smile broadening.

"Better tanks, you mean?" Tulloch asked. "We met some of them."

"More than that," Amanda lowered her voice, although nobody was within a quarter of a mile. "Rommel knew our dispositions and our generals' intentions even before the battles began."

"How the hell did he know that? Is there a German spy in our HQ?" Tulloch could not help his sudden flare of anger. He thought of the dead and wounded British and Allied soldiers left in the hot desert sand.

"The Axis powers don't need a spy," Amanda said. "They have better than that. We tell our American allies our plans, you see."

"Do we?" Tulloch asked.

"We do," Amanda confirmed. "We keep them informed, and Bonner Fellers, the American military attaché in Egypt, sent reports of our intentions to the US State Department. Unfortunately, the Italian Intelligence Service cracked the American code months ago. The Italians read Fellers' reports and handed them to Rommel, meaning the German general has known exactly what we planned."

Tulloch was quiet as he digested the information. "No wonder he could counter our moves," he said, shaking his head. "No bloody wonder! Rommel is not quite as foxy as his reputation suggests, and the Italians have proved to be a more formidable enemy than the press would have the public believe."

"The Italians are good soldiers, but often badly led, with poor equipment and fighting in a cause few believe in," Amanda revealed more of her knowledge. "The press does the Italians a grave injustice when it decries them." She sighed. "Enough war talk, Douglas. Let's talk about something more cheerful, shall we? What are your plans when the war ends?"

Tulloch thought for a moment. "I haven't thought that far ahead," he admitted.

"Well, think now," Amanda shuffled closer on the rough stone of the pyramid. "Will you stay in the army? Or will you leave? Where will you go if you leave, and what will you do?"

"The world will be very different after the war, I think," Tulloch said.

"I think it will," Amanda agreed. "However long it lasts, people will not want to return to the same bad housing and poverty they had before. The government, or somebody, will have to make better provision for everybody."

"I doubt there will be enough money for that," Tulloch said.

"In that case," Amanda said, "what are we fighting for?" Her eyes were disconcertingly level. "Either we're fighting for a better world or we're throwing away countless lives for nothing."

Tulloch nodded. "We're certainly throwing away too many lives. I hope the result is worth it."

"What about us?" Amanda asked suddenly.

"What about us?" Tulloch countered.

"Will there be an us after the war?" She remained within touching distance, yet the few inches felt as limitless as the Sahara. Or as close as a single movement.

Tulloch made an easy decision. "Yes," he said. "Yes, there will be an us after the war. If you want an us."

The Sahara disappeared from Tulloch's consciousness as Amanda closed the final few inches. He felt a sudden thrill as her hip touched his. She leaned across and kissed him lightly.

"Good," Amanda said. "I'd like that." She opened her mouth to voice the question in her eyes but withdrew without asking.

Tulloch read the query and understood Amanda's concern, yet he could not reassure her. Not with Rommel building up for another, and perhaps final, assault on Alexandria and a breakthrough to Suez and the oil wells of the Middle East. He could not raise Amanda's hopes because he knew Colonel Hume's patience had ended. Hume was past the point of retreating and would fight to the last bullet and the last man, whatever the general in charge ordered.

Tulloch could not promise Amanda a relationship when he did not expect to live after the next battle. He looked to the west, where the sun set in a blood-red sky, and wondered if she could ever understand that his hesitation was for her sake.

───────

"YOU CANNAE DO THAT, HOGGIE," INNES'S URGENT TONES alerted Tulloch as he walked past on his way to the makeshift officers' mess.

"Aye, I can," Hogg grated.

Tulloch halted, wondering what the problem was. The men spoke inside their tent, with their voices carrying, although the white canvas prevented them from seeing outside.

"I'm going to kill him," Hogg continued. "Bloody corporal."

Tulloch had heard similar threats against NCOs throughout his career. Usually, it was a young recruit complaining about being assigned extra guard duty or fatigues. Tulloch would ignore the rant, knowing a corporal with years of service could handle the misdirected rage of a youth. Hogg, however, was different. He was an experienced soldier, an old sweat who had killed men in battle and who had worked under a dozen different NCOs. Hogg was known for his unpredictability, so his comrades walked warily around him. When Hogg declared he would kill a corporal, Tulloch knew he was being serious.

Tulloch lingered, stuffing tobacco into his pipe to cover himself as he listened.

"He's no' that bad," Innes said. "If you keep out of his way, you'll be fine."

"If he keeps out of my way, he'll be fine," Hogg countered.

Tulloch heard the distinctive sound of somebody drawing a bayonet.

"It only takes two inches to kill a man," Hogg said. "One inch in the right place."

"They'll hang you," Innes tried to reason with Hogg. "That evil bastard, Sergeant Crosier, will arrest you, and a court martial will sentence you to hang."

"Maybe," Hogg replied. "I could run."

"Where?"

"I could join these lads from D Company. Crosier hasnae caught them. They'll be halfway to Scotland by now and sitting pretty while we fight Rommel."

"How will you know where to go?" Innes asked.

Hogg swore. "Madame Clara's," he replied. "That's where everybody goes when they're on the trot."

Tulloch lit his pipe, saw Cattanach and Gordon approach, and walked on, worried. He could guess that Hogg referred to Corporal Russell, but the mention of desertion was also unsettling. *What and where is Madame Clara's?*

Tulloch swore silently and strode to Sergeant Drysdale. "Sergeant!"

"Yes, sir?"

"What's happened in my absence?"

Drysdale frowned. "We've been bleeding the replacements into the battalion, sir. The colonel detailed Sergeant Paterson and me to drill them and introduce them to our ways."

"Ah," Tulloch nodded, hiding his anger. "I detailed you to ensure Hogg didn't fall foul of Corporal Russell of D Company."

"Yes, sir," Drysdale said no more. He was too experienced as an NCO to make excuses.

"I take it you were too busy with training the recruits."

"Yes, sir," Drysdale said.

Tulloch nodded. "Very well. Carry on, Sergeant." He walked

on, paced around the camp to think, called on Lieutenant Kennedy for an update on the platoon, and entered his tent.

Hood came to attention when Tulloch stepped in. As expected, the tent was pristine, with everything in order.

"Hood," Tulloch said. "I think you would prefer to be back with your mates rather than acting as my batman."

"Have I done anything wrong, sir?" Hood looked confused.

"Not a thing," Tulloch told him. "I'd give you a glowing reference."

"Thank you, sir," Hood remained at attention. "Then why, sir?"

"You are a good soldier, Hood, and happier with your colleagues. I need a man like you to help the new people learn the ropes."

Hood's face remained impassive, but he was no fool and knew Tulloch was hiding the truth. "Yes, sir."

"Report to Sergeant Drysdale, Hood, and tell him your new role."

"Yes, sir," Hood saluted and left the tent.

Tulloch gave Hood five minutes and strode into the desert sun, feeling like a fraud or a headmaster rather than a platoon commander.

"Sergeant Drysdale!" Tulloch shouted.

"Yes, sir?" Drysdale marched up, looking slightly perplexed.

"I have rather a delicate job for you."

"What's that, sir?" Drysdale asked.

"I need a new batman, and I want you to detail a man for the job."

Drysdale looked relieved, as though he had expected Tulloch to rebuke him. "As you wish, sir. Cattanach is a good man, sober and attentive."

"I am sure he is," Tulloch said. "I want you to detail Hogg without letting him know I chose him."

"Hogg, sir?" Drysdale looked surprised. "Begging your pardon, sir, but Hogg is a good soldier in a duffy but rough around the edges. I don't think he'd be the best choice as a batman. Remember, he has also got into a lot of trouble recently, falling foul of the Provost Sergeant."

"I know," Tulloch said. "I think a few months, or even a few weeks, as my batman would quieten him down a little, Sergeant."

"If you say so, sir," Drysdale said doubtfully.

"I'll give it a shot anyway," Tulloch said. "Where is he now?"

"He's getting ready to go on fatigues, sir, whitewashing stones to mark out the parade ground three hours a day for the next week."

Tulloch nodded. "He'll be glad to be out of that. When his whitewashing time is up today, send him to me, Sergeant."

"I will, sir," Drysdale replied.

"Thank you, Sergeant. Now, find me Elliot."

"Elliot's on the rifle range, sir."

Elliot looked concerned when Tulloch called him over. He stood at attention, sweat trickling down his thin face and his rifle at his side.

"Stand easy, Elliot, you're not in trouble."

Elliot relaxed slightly.

"You have a reputation for being a lady's man, Elliot. Is that not correct?"

"I like women, sir," Elliot replied cautiously. "And they like me. I've got three sisters, see, and I ken how to talk to them."

Tulloch allowed Elliot to talk for a while. "Have you heard of an establishment called Madame Clara's, Elliot?"

Elliot grinned. "Everybody knows Madame Clara's, sir. It's right in the middle of the red light district in Alex. Were you thinking of paying a visit?"

"Not in the way you imagine, Elliot," Tulloch told him. "Where is it?" He listened as Elliot gave him directions.

"Describe it to me. In detail," Tulloch demanded and took mental notes. "Thank you, Elliot. Report back to the range now." He walked away with his mind busy. Desertion could be a cancer that ate into the fabric of the battalion. Hogg's chance remark allowed him to ease the situation.

Chapter Twenty

MAREOPOLIS, AUGUST 1942

"Well, Hogg," Tulloch said. "You are my batman now. Have Hood and Sergeant Drysdale instructed you in your duties?"

"Yes, sir," Hogg stood at attention with his ugly, flat face expressionless.

"Good," Tulloch said. "As my batman, you are in a privileged position. You don't attend so many parades and are less likely to fall foul of the Provost Sergeant."

"Yes, sir," Hogg replied.

"You don't like him much, do you, Hogg?"

"Sergeant Crosier is all right, sir," Hogg's reply surprised Tulloch. "He's just a loud-mouthed polisman." He shrugged. "They're all the same."

"Oh? So why have you been getting into trouble recently?"

"It's no' Sergeant Crosier, sir, it's Corporal Russell."

Tulloch did not admit he knew about Russell. *Play the daft laddie and see if Hogg bites.* "What's Corporal Russell done to irritate you, Hogg?"

Hogg narrowed his eyes suspiciously, instinctively aware that Tulloch was fishing. "We don't like each other, sir."

"I can't think why not, Hogg," Tulloch said. "I've always found Corporal Russell a pleasant enough fellow."

"Maybe so, sir, but you're an officer," Hogg said. "Folk act differently with officers than with the men. I knew Rab Russell before the war, you see, sir."

"Did you, Hogg?" Tulloch knew that before the war, Hogg had been a member of an Edinburgh street gang in the Hungry Thirties, when half of Scotland seemed to be unemployed and poverty haunted the nation. "Russell's a Glasgow man, isn't he?"

"Yes, sir," Hogg relaxed a little.

"How do you know him?"

Hogg looked wary again. "We did things together, sir," he said.

"You're not on trial, Hogg," Tulloch said, smiling. "I want to know why you two don't get on, that's all."

"Rab Russell was a Billy Boy, sir. He was one of Billy Fullerton's razor men. You must have heard of Billy Fullerton. King Billy?"

"I know he was a gang leader in Glasgow," Tulloch said. "That's about all."

"You must have heard the song, sir." Hogg cleared his throat and chanted in a surprisingly clear voice.

"Hello, hello! We are the Billy Boys;
Hurrah! Hello! You know us by the noise;
We're up to here; we never fear - we all are Billy's
     sons,
We are the Glasgow Billy Boys.

We belong to Glasgow, we're Orange, and we're
  true,
Scotland is our country, our colours white and
  blue.
We're Protestants and proud of it. We're known
  near and far,
Glasgow Billy Boys, they call us."

"I have heard the song," Tulloch admitted, still smiling.

"That was the Billy Boys' anthem, sir. King Billy – Billy Fullerton – wrote it and created the gang to fight the Catholics in Glasgow," Hogg explained.

"How were you involved, Hogg?"

"Well, sir, some of us Gorgie boys used to accompany the Billy Boys when they went on the Orange Marches in Ulster, celebrating the Battle of the Boyne. That was when King William defeated James's Catholic army in 1690, sir."

"I see," Tulloch had never known the taciturn Hogg to speak so much.

"Rab Russell didnae like Edinburgh lads coming with his boys, and we fell out. That's one reason, sir."

Tulloch could understand the territorial dispute between hungry, frustrated and disenchanted teenagers who desperately sought somewhere to belong. "And the other?"

Hogg looked uneasy again. "Politics, sir."

"Politics?" Tulloch encouraged.

"Yes, sir. The Tories paid the Billy Boys to attack Trades Union and Communist meetings in Glasgow, and Russell was one of the keenest to join in. He was one of Mosley's men, sir, a fascist, and I am more of a communist."

"Russell is a fascist?" Tulloch did not hide his surprise.

"He was a Blackshirt, sir. He marched with Mosley's fascists," Hogg said.

Tulloch lifted his chin. "Did he indeed? Thank you for the information, Hogg." He pondered for a moment. "I have one order for you, Hogg. Keep out of Russell's way. Don't antagonise him in any way. Do you understand?"

"Yes, sir," Hogg said. "What if he antagonises me, sir?"

"He's a corporal, Hogg. He's superior in rank."

Hogg gave his short and succinct opinion of Corporal Russell.

"That's enough, Hogg," Tulloch said. "You're my batman now. You have too many responsibilities to worry about a corporal in another company."

"Yes, sir."

Tulloch played his trump card. "When you are under my orders, Hogg, Corporal Russell has no authority over you. If he tries to cause trouble, refer him to me."

Before Hogg gave a defiant reply, Tulloch continued. "I heard that Sergeant Drysdale has you on fatigues this week."

"Yes, sir," Hogg replied.

"You can consider yourself off them, Hogg. Your duties to me are more important than whitewashing stones. Dismissed!"

That's one platoon problem solved, and now I'll speak to the colonel about the deserters.

———

"IT's ALL CHANGE IN THE HIGHER COMMAND," COLONEL Hume addressed the Lothians' officers. "You may have heard Churchill dropped into Cairo *en route* to Moscow to meet Stalin."

The officers grunted or nodded. Churchill's stopover in Cairo had caused quite a buzz in Egypt, especially as Sir Alan Brooke accompanied him. Brooke was the Chief of the General Staff and was reputed to be the only man capable of curtailing some of Churchill's more hare-brained schemes. He was also a skilled strategist and the man on whom much of the Western war effort turned.

"After the recent encounters in the desert, Churchill and

Brooke have decided to replace Auchinleck with Gott as commander of the Eighth Army," Hume said.

Tulloch glanced at Muirhead, who raised his eyebrows. In Tulloch's opinion, Gott was hardly a brilliant general, while the Auk had succeeded in stopping Rommel at Alamein. He said nothing as Hume continued.

"General Sir Harold Alexander will be Commander-in-Chief of Middle East Command. Churchill and Brooke decided to have Persia and Iraq as a distinct command and offered the post to Auchinleck, who turned it down."

Muirhead shook his head as they returned to C Company. "We're stirring the pot but using the same ingredients."

"Maybe," Tulloch said.

"And if we use the same ingredients, we'll come up with the same cake, except maybe with a different flavour." Muirhead shrugged. "You look a little preoccupied, Tulloch."

"I might know where the deserters are," Tulloch said.

Muirhead looked at him sideways. "Have you told the old man?"

"Not yet."

"Tell him," Muirhead said. "We can't afford to lose men, and every desertion lowers morale a little more."

Tulloch nodded. "I was going to ask you first."

"You've asked me, and I've told you what to do," Muirhead said. "The colonel will send you to bring them back."

———

COLONEL HUME'S FACE DARKENED AS HE LISTENED TO Tulloch's report. "An overheard conversation is a fragile hook on which to hang one's coat, Tulloch," he said.

"It might be correct, sir," Tulloch said.

Hume pondered for a moment. "Do you know where Madame Clara's is?"

"One of my men told me, sir," Tulloch admitted. "It's in the centre of the red-light district in Alex. Apparently, it's well known."

"All right, Tulloch," Hume came to a decision. "Take a patrol there and see if you can find any of our men. I'll tell the MPs to keep out of our way but be ready for trouble."

"Yes, sir," Tulloch said. "I'll take a dozen of Four Platoon, sir. I know them best."

"Take Sergeant Crosier and his men as well," Hume said. "They have more experience in these matters."

Tulloch requisitioned a three-ton truck and a fifteen hundredweight for the journey to Alexandria. He had Hood drive, with Elliot guiding them through the streets, giving precise directions and a running commentary on every woman they passed.

"We can see for ourselves, Shuggie," Hood told him. "We don't need your help."

Tulloch kept Four Platoon and the Provost's men separate and noticed the prevalence of redcaps in the streets.

"Is it far, Elliot?" Tulloch asked.

Elliot screwed up his face. "About a mile as the crow flies, sir, but longer by road. We'll have to walk the last bit. The streets are too narrow for the trucks."

As they drove, the area became progressively poorer, with dilapidated flat-roofed houses and dark alleys where men lounged, watching the British trucks growl past. Elliot directed them to a parking space beside a grove of sad-looking palm trees, and Tulloch stepped outside, with Sergeant Drysdale chivvying the men to disembark.

"Right, lads," Tulloch said. "We're going to hunt for deserters in Madame Clara's establishment. Elliot will guide us there, and Sergeant Drysdale and Crosier will direct operations." Tulloch knew the two sergeants were experienced in such matters. He looked over his men, all Four Platoon veterans. He would have liked to have Hogg with him if things got rough, but he decided to keep Hogg and Sergeant Crosier well apart. The others,

Innes, Smith, Cattanach and the rest, were dependable in any situation.

"Lead on, Elliot," Tulloch ordered.

Sergeant Crosier left a provost corporal to guard the trucks and trotted at the rear of Four Platoon, with Elliot leading them through a succession of streets, each one narrower and more disreputable than the last.

After ten minutes, Elliot stopped in a courtyard with a single palm tree, overlooked by tall buildings with shuttered windows behind battered verandas. A lone round-headed door, green-painted and iron-studded, stood in a shadowed corner.

"Is that Madame Clara's?" Tulloch asked.

"Yes, sir," Elliot replied.

"I would have thought there would be a name above the door," Tulloch said. "Is there a back door? Another entrance?"

"I don't know of one, sir," Elliot replied.

"Sir," Sergeant Drysdale said. "Shall we go in? The longer we're here, the more time they have to escape."

"What do you suggest, Sergeant?"

"Maybe you'd best let Crosier and I take over here, sir," Drysdale said tactfully.

"Carry on, Sergeant," Tulloch stepped back.

The sergeants conferred for a minute, and Drysdale waited outside with eight men while Crosier, a provost corporal, and the remaining eight of Four Platoon charged inside. Tulloch had expected the raiding party to move in quietly, but they ran in shouting, with Crosier in the lead.

"It's Provost Sergeant Crosier here! You're all under arrest! Come quietly, you bastards!"

Less than two minutes after Crosier led in his men, Madame Clara's door burst open, and half a dozen men ran out in various stages of undress. Sergeant Drysdale waited for them.

"Fixed bayonets, lads. I want this over quickly and without anybody being hurt."

The deserters ran into a semi-circle of pointing bayonets,

with the unsympathetic faces of Four Platoon's veterans behind them. The deserters stopped, cursing. One man showed fight until Drysdale felled him with a single punch. Two turned back as a crowd of women and civilian men stared from the doorway. Crosier and the provost corporal stood with their arms folded and the remaining men of Four Platoon behind them.

Tulloch stepped forward when a middle-aged woman emerged from the building. She had dyed red hair and carried a large club, which she brandished threateningly.

"Who are you to disturb my house?"

Sergeant Crosier forestalled her by putting a black-haired hand on the woman's shoulder.

"You've been harbouring possible deserters," Crosier told the woman in a voice that could cut through ice. "Any more of that, and we'll close you down for good. Now get back inside with your guards." He nodded to two large men who lurked in the doorway. "Or I'll put them both in handcuffs."

Tulloch watched as Madame Clara and the guards hurriedly returned through the door, followed by the other civilians.

"Time to go, boys," Tulloch ordered.

The deserters glared at him, with one tousle-haired man stepping forward with his fists clenched. Innes lifted his bayonet half an inch to the man's chest.

"I wouldnae, chum."

Tulloch kept an eye on the man as Sergeant Drysdale supervised them through the streets to the waiting trucks. A few local men watched without comment, although Drysdale and Crosier kept a wary eye on them.

"Right, lads, get these deserters on board the fifteen hundredweight. Sergeant Crosier will look after them."

Four Platoon ushered the six men towards the truck, with Crosier and a provost corporal last on board.

"Where do you think you're going?" A tall Military Police lieutenant stepped from the shelter of the palm trees.

Chapter Twenty-One

"Back to our battalion with our prisoners," Tulloch faced the policeman.

"They are deserters," the lieutenant said. "The Military Police take care of deserters."

Tulloch felt a subtle change in the mood of Four Platoon as their sympathies shifted against the MPs. "They were AWOL," he said. "Absent Without Leave rather than deserters, and we'll deal with the matter internally."

Half a dozen Military Police formed up behind their officer.

"Madame Clara's is a well-known haunt of deserters," the lieutenant claimed.

"These men are in our custody," Tulloch kept his temper. He could feel Four Platoon preparing to defend the regiment. Few people liked the Redcaps, and after nearly three years of war, the Lothian veterans would fight anybody at the toss of a coin.

"Get our lads on the wagon, Four Platoon!" Sergeant Drysdale ordered. "Sergeant Crosier will look after them!"

As Four Platoon obeyed, Tulloch and the Military Police lieutenant glared at each other, neither willing to back down.

"I heard there were some genuine deserters at Madame Clara's," Tulloch suggested. "They might still be there if you hurry, Lieutenant. It would be a pity to waste your night." He glanced over his shoulder as Four Platoon formed up behind him, two lines of hard-eyed veterans, still with long bayonets fixed to their rifles. He was glad he had left Hogg behind, or there might be murder in Alexandria's streets.

"Get on board, lads," Tulloch ordered. "These gentlemen have work to do." He waited until Four Platoon were on the truck and climbed into the cab.

"Move forward slowly, Hood," he ordered.

"The polis might not move, sir," Hood replied.

"They will," Tulloch said with more conviction than he felt. "Drive on."

The lieutenant stepped aside at the last moment, with his Redcaps reluctantly following. The Lothians' trucks passed them, accompanied by a succession of jeers and catcalls from the men inside, instantly roared to silence by Sergeant Drysdale. Tulloch felt the baleful glares of the Military Police and resolved to keep his men in the camp for the next week in case of any reprisals.

Thank goodness that's finished, Tulloch told himself. *Now, we must find out why the men deserted and cure the disease.*

"DID YOU HEAR THE NEWS?" MUIRHEAD ASKED THE following morning as they perused the orders of the day.

"Which news?" Tulloch replied warily. "Good or bad?"

"Is it ever good?" Muirhead asked with a crooked smile. "The Germans have shot down General Gott's aircraft and killed him, together with a couple of RAF fitters and thirteen wounded men travelling to hospital."

Tulloch shook his head. "No, I hadn't heard that," he said. His mind was too busy with the deserters to think about

General Gott's death.

"We are an army without a leader," Muirhead said. "I wonder who'll be next to take command."

Tulloch shook his head. "I have no idea," he said. "I never saw Gott. I know he was a competent commander but war-weary. I hope we get somebody who knows how to defeat Rommel."

Muirhead shrugged. "I can't think who," he said. "We need a man with desert experience and new ideas. As far as I can see, we've used up everybody in the pot unless they bring back the Auk or Ritchie."

"Maybe," Tulloch said. "Or promote somebody from a more junior rank."

"We're in a bloody mess," Muirhead gave a twisted grin. "Colonel Hume is adamant he won't lead the Lothians in another retreat, whatever higher command orders; the enemy is defeating, capturing or killing all our generals, and half our men are deserting."

"Not half," Tulloch said. "Only a disaffected few."

"A few is a few too many," Muirhead said. "And Erskine is leaving the battalion."

"I didn't know that," Tulloch said. "Where's he going?"

"He's joining the SAS," Muirhead told him. They looked up as Colonel Hume arrived.

"Tulloch," Hume said quietly. "I want a word with you."

─────────

TULLOCH STOOD IN FRONT OF HUME'S DESK WITH THE CANVAS of the tent rustling in the growing wind.

"I've had a complaint about you, Tulloch. I heard you had a confrontation with the Military Police," Hume said.

"Yes, sir," Tulloch agreed, waiting for Hume's anger.

"What happened?" Hume asked.

200

Tulloch explained the recent encounter.

Hume grunted. "Was that it? Hardly worth mentioning. Consider yourself reprimanded. Where are the men you brought back?"

"Sergeant Crosier is looking after them, sir. He'll bring them before you later."

"If Sergeant Crosier has them, they'll wish they were in the Glasshouse," Hume said. "I'll find out why they deserted before I award any sentence."

"May I speak to them, sir?" Tulloch asked.

Hume considered for a moment. "Do you know any of them, Tulloch?"

"No, sir," Tulloch admitted.

"You can interview them after my award," Hume told him. "You'll have plenty of time unless our new army commander sends us back into the Blue."

"Do we have a new commander yet, sir?" Tulloch asked.

"Not to my knowledge," Hume replied. He leaned back in his chair, smiling slightly as he looked at Tulloch. "You've been with the battalion for some years now, haven't you, Tulloch?"

"Yes, sir," Tulloch agreed. "I joined in 'thirty-seven, just before we went to the Northwest Frontier."

"All that seems a long time ago now," Hume said. "We'll see a different world after the war."

"Yes, sir," Tulloch agreed.

"You'll have heard Captain Erskine is leaving us," Hume continued.

"Yes, sir," Tulloch said. "He's joining the SAS, I believe."

Hume nodded. "It's a role that suits his peculiar talents, swanning around the desert causing trouble to everybody. He'll be happier there than tied to regimental discipline."

"I am sure he'll do very well," Tulloch said diplomatically.

"That leaves me a company commander short," Hume said. "I've recommended you for promotion a couple of times,

Tulloch. You're a decent enough soldier, and you have experience in battle. The War Office have finally seen sense and agreed to my recommendation. Congratulations, Captain."

"Thank you, sir," Tulloch accepted Hume's proffered hand. He had come to this interview expecting at least a biting reprimand for squaring up to the Military Police and was leaving with promotion and command of a company.

"It's a bit of a poisoned chalice I am handing you, Tulloch," Hume said. "Erskine was a good man in a fight, but there's something wrong in D Company with desertions and mutterings. I want you to sort things out."

"Yes, sir," Tulloch said as he tried to take in the magnitude of his promotion. Commanding a company was a far larger task than commanding a platoon. He would have less personal contact with the men and more responsibility.

"D Company took a bit of a hammering in the Gazala battle and the subsequent withdrawal," Hume continued. "They lost an entire platoon, ambushed and captured in a wadi, and what with that and the losses and desertions, I have merged Six and Seven Platoons into a single unit, Six Platoon, under Lieutenant Rutlane."

Tulloch nodded, hoping that Rutlane had improved with experience. "Yes, sir. Does that mean I have a platoon-strength company?"

"No. You don't know the men, so I am transferring Sergeant Drysdale and Four Platoon from C Company to D to ease the transition and augment the numbers."

"Thank you, sir. That will help. Drysdale is a good man."

"I've had my eye on him for some time," Hume said. "He'll make a good CSM one day."

"Even an RSM, sir," Tulloch suggested.

Hume nodded. "In time. I'm transferring Lieutenant McGill from the Motor Pool to command Four Platoon. He's young but enthusiastic." Hume held out his hand. "Good luck, Captain Tulloch."

"Thank you, sir," Tulloch shook the colonel's hand.

I am a captain with my own company, Tulloch thought as he left the colonel's tent. *The most troublesome company in the battalion, with desertions and disputes between the men. My lads might find it hard to adjust.*

Chapter Twenty-Two

F our Platoon accepted the change of companies with equanimity. The Lothian Rifles was a family regiment, with most men from the same part of Lowland Scotland and friendships across platoon and company barriers common.

"You've got a promotion, sir," Hogg lacked Hood's smoothness as a batman but had managed to stay out of trouble with Corporal Russell. "That's good."

"Thank you, Hogg," Tulloch replied.

"Yes, sir," Hogg said. "A captain's batman is better than a mere lieutenant's."

"I am glad you think so," Tulloch said. *Trust an old sweat to find an advantage in any situation.*

Tulloch called D Company together to get to know them and allow them to view him. Most of the men looked sullen, with only a few hopeful. Tulloch decided to make his speech short and sweet.

"My name is Captain Douglas Tulloch. Some of you may know me. I am the new commander of D Company in place of Captain Erskine, who has gone elsewhere."

The men did not react.

"We'll get to know each other in time," Tulloch said. He knew his introductory speech was weak and wondered how he would compare to the debonair Captain Erskine with his intimate knowledge of unarmed combat. "In the meantime, carry on as normal."

As the men dispersed, Tulloch called the two platoon commanders to him. Lieutenants McGill and Rutlane approached, with McGill looking apprehensive and Rutlane as sullen as the men. Tulloch had spoken to McGill a few times and thought him quiet, almost subdued, while he classified Rutlane in the same category as Kennedy.

"Gentlemen," Tulloch led his lieutenants away from the men. "I am concerned with the desertions from this company. What is wrong here?"

McGill, as new to the company as Tulloch, said nothing while Rutlane frowned.

"Nothing is wrong, sir, except some disaffected men."

"I'll work it out in time," Tulloch told them. "As from today, I'll depend on you two to keep morale up in your platoons. Men with high morale don't desert."

"Yes, sir," McGill replied.

"Both of you," Tulloch stared into Rutlane's eyes.

"Yes, sir," Rutlane said.

"Now send me the NCOs," Tulloch ordered.

Each platoon had a sergeant and two corporals. Tulloch thought Sergeant Davidson a little subdued and Corporal Russell too pugnacious, which might explain why their platoon was unsettled.

"You men are responsible for the day-to-day organisation of the men," Tulloch said. "We have had eight incidents of desertion in the Lothians, six from D Company. I don't want any more."

Davidson looked upset, Russell angry, as Tulloch decided on a softly-softly approach until he knew his men better.

"I am sure we can sort things out between us," Tulloch said. "Now the company is altered, we'll learn to work together. We'll have a company exercise this afternoon and a parade tomorrow morning."

When Davidson continued to look worried, Tulloch wondered if he was the right man for the job.

"I want everybody on parade for a route march at 13.00 hours, no packs but rifles, bayonets, ammunition and water bottles. Dismissed."

Six Platoon looked disgruntled and thin on the ground as they stood beside Four Platoon. They had lost men in the recent actions, while the would-be deserters were under Sergeant Crosier's command for the next fortnight and not on parade.

"We've all had a bad time recently," Tulloch told them. "Let's ensure the future is better, Germans and Italians permitting."

Six Platoon did not react. Tulloch thought the men looked sullen or nervous, some untidy and others with old or dirty uniforms. He grunted. *I have a lot of work to do.*

"Come on, lads!"

Tulloch led them at a steady marching pace for the first two miles before glancing over his shoulder.

Four Platoon were marching well, with Six Platoon already beginning to straggle. Corporal Russell was at the rear, screaming at a young soldier limping thirty yards behind the others.

"Halt!" Tulloch ordered and marched back. "What's the trouble here?"

"Private Pringle is lagging, sir," Russell reported.

"I see that," Tulloch replied. "What's the matter, Pringle?"

"My feet hurt, sir," Pringle said nervously.

Tulloch saw Lieutenant Rutlane watching from a distance. "Let's see them."

"Sir?" Pringle looked astonished.

"Take your boots off, Pringle, and show me your feet."

"He's malingering, sir!" Russell said. "There's nothing the matter with him."

Pringle winced as he removed his boots, which were worn through in three places, revealing threadbare stockings and badly blistered feet.

"When did you last get new boots, Pringle?" Tulloch asked, crouching at Pringle's side.

"I don't know, sir."

"New stockings?"

"Never, sir," Pringle looked guilty.

"Right," Tulloch stood up. "Six Platoon! Remove your boots!"

The men obeyed, some grumbling. Tulloch walked along the platoon, examining each man's footwear.

"This is a blasted disgrace!" Tulloch said at the end of his inspection. "How can men be expected to march and fight with defective boots and worn-out stockings?" He stepped back, genuinely angry. "Back to camp, everybody. Lieutenant Rutlane, report to me when we arrive."

Tulloch ordered D Company to parade with full kit that afternoon and thoroughly inspected each man. Although the weapons were immaculate, he found a host of discrepancies in the uniforms and boots. Tulloch ordered a complete uniform for each man, which sent the quartermaster into a frenzy.

When he finished ordering new uniforms, Tulloch transferred Davidson to the motor pool, promoted an old sweat named Harris to corporal to balance Russell, and recruited Sergeant Paterson in Davidson's place.

"New broom time, Tulloch?" Muirhead asked when he heard of the changes.

"Exactly so," Tulloch replied.

"Why is that?"

"Erskine was a fine fighting man," Tulloch replied, "but less fine as a company commander. He neglected the men's wellbeing."

"Is that why so many deserted?" Muirhead asked.

"I'd say so," Tulloch said. "It might have contributed anyway. I'll know more when Sergeant Crosier releases the deserters."

Muirhead began to fill his pipe. "Free advice as a fellow company commander, Tulloch. Don't be too easy on the men at first. See what they're made of, and then ease up. Get to know them, as you did with Four Platoon, and make friends with the NCOs," he grinned, "and the platoon commanders. McGill has potential, although I am unsure about Rutlane."

"So am I," Tulloch admitted.

Tulloch took Muirhead's advice. He drove D Company hard in training yet ensured their kit arrived, and they were regularly fed and watered. When the provost branch returned the deserters, Tulloch asked them why they had gone AWOL.

The men stood sullenly mute.

"All right," Tulloch said. "You won't or can't tell me. That's past and forgotten now, and D Company has changed. I am glad to have you back. Dismissed." He watched them return to their tents, wondered if he should have sent them to the Glasshouse and shrugged. He'd find out soon enough.

"Sir!" Hogg saluted, glowering at Tulloch under the rim of his balmoral. "Colonel Hume has called a meeting of the officers."

"When, Hogg?" Tulloch asked.

"In ten minutes, sir," Hogg replied.

Muirhead made space for Tulloch at his side, with the African sun beating down on them.

"Any idea what this is all about?" Tulloch asked.

"None at all," Muirhead replied. "Here's the Old Man."

Hume stepped onto the back of the universal carrier and surveyed his officers.

"Quiet now, gentlemen." Hume wore a curious smile as he waited for the officers to settle down. "We have yet another new commander of the Eighth Army," he said. "A general by the name of Bernard Montgomery."

The officers looked at each other, with the old hands nodding at the name. Tulloch felt a sudden lurch.

"Some of you may remember him from France," Hume said. "He fought a successful rearguard action with his division."

Tulloch nodded. He remembered Montgomery as the most efficient and professional of soldiers who did not suffer fools gladly. He glanced at Muirhead, who raised his eyebrows, saying nothing.

"When I hear more, I will keep you posted, gentlemen," Hume said. "In the meantime, keep training your men. That's all."

The officers left amidst a hum of conversation, not all positive.

"Montgomery has no experience in the desert," Lieutenant Kennedy said. "He hasn't even got his knees brown yet. Why has Churchill saddled us with a man who hasn't commanded a unit in action since the Germans kicked us out at Dunkirk?"

"He was probably the best divisional commander in France," Tulloch said.

"Commanding a division in Europe is different to commanding an army in Africa," Kennedy retorted.

"It is," Tulloch replied. "But so far, the desert-worthy generals haven't won many laurels. Let's see what Montgomery does before we dismiss him."

Kennedy grunted. "We'd be better off sticking with the devil we know," he said. "The Auk stopped Rommel at El Alamein."

"None of Auchinleck's counterattacks worked," Tulloch reminded dryly. "Although I agree he stopped Rommel's advance." He considered for a moment. "The RAF did sterling work delaying the German columns, while South African and New Zealand artillery, together with the 1st Armoured Division, halted them. I grant you that the Auk took the initiative from Rommel."

Kennedy looked away. "Auchinleck did his best and stopped Rommel."

"He did better than most," Tulloch agreed. He said no more, but inwardly, he thought that after three years of war, suffering and sacrifice, the British Army had not won a single battle against the Germans or Japanese.

Please, God, let Bernard Montgomery turn the tide. He's working on the side of the angels against the forces of darkness; guide him to victory, Lord, if it be your will.

Tulloch stopped. He was not overly religious but thought the Allies needed divine aid if Good was to triumph over Evil in this war.

Chapter Twenty-Three

MAREOPOLIS, AUGUST 1942

The deserters stood in a row before Tulloch. With their hair shorn and uniforms immaculate, they looked like a different group of men from the scruffy tearaways he had arrested at Madame Clara's.

"Right, men," Tulloch addressed them sternly, "desertion is one of the most serious crimes in the army. I could have had you court-martialled, and that would mean the Glasshouse, at least." He allowed the words to sink in. "What the hell were you thinking of?"

The men stared ahead, wordless.

"Where did you think you would go? There are no ships to Britain except under convoy, and you could not remain at Madame Clara's forever."

The men still did not speak.

Tulloch paced along the line, looking at each face in turn. He stopped at the man who had been most truculent during the arrest. "Well, Adamson. What do you have to say for yourself?"

Adamson remained at attention but had to reply to a direct question. "Nothing, sir," he said.

"Why did you try to desert?" Tulloch persisted.

Adamson's eyes swivelled right and left, seeking help from his companions. Tulloch did not let him off the hook.

"Why did you try to desert?"

"Why not, sir?" Adamson replied. "Rommel defeats us whenever we fight. Hitler has won the war, so there's no point in fighting." He continued, gaining confidence as Tulloch did not blast him into silence. "The officers don't care about us and talk of inevitable defeat, so why bother?"

Tulloch allowed Adamson to have his say while most other deserters looked uncomfortable. Only one man, Private Pickering, nodded in agreement.

"I am the Company Commander now, Adamson, and I care about all the men under my command." Tulloch stepped back, talking quietly. "I believe we will defeat Rommel and win this war. I do not know what happened in D Company before I took command, but I know what will happen in the future. We will fight, and we will win." Tulloch wondered if his words were having any effect. Except for Adamson, the men were expressionless.

"We have a new army commander now, men, General Montgomery, and we will all pull together under him. The past is gone; we learn from our mistakes and move on. All of us."

The men remained static. Tulloch was unsure if he had expected shouts of derision or an outbreak of *God Save the King*. Knowing his men, it would more likely be *The Ball of Kirriemuir*.

Tulloch walked the length of the line again, studying each face. "I expect better from you men in the future," he said. "If any of you try to desert again, I will shoot you myself. But I don't think you will."

Some of the men shifted slightly.

"Welcome back to D Company," Tulloch said. "Dismiss." He watched them turn smartly and march away and wondered if he had been too lenient. *Only time will tell.*

TULLOCH LOOKED UP FROM THE PILE OF FORMS ON HIS DESK. "Good morning to you, Muirhead. Have you come to help me with this muck?"

"Not a chance," Muirhead said. "This new chap Montgomery is already making waves. He's not meant to take command until the 15th of August, but he's told everybody, including General Alexander, his chief, that he's assuming command of 8th Army on the 13th."

Tulloch grinned. "That sounds like the Montgomery I had as an instructor in Baluchistan many years ago."

"He took one look at the Auk's headquarters and changed everything," Muirhead continued, nearly laughing. "Auchinleck had all the staff living in the open in the middle of the desert inside a sort of wire cage. Monty swept all that away and moved his HQ near the sea and nearer the RAF HQ so he could liaise better."

"That makes sense," Tulloch said. "The more cooperation with the RAF, the better."

"There is more," Muirhead said.

"What?" Tulloch was already beginning to like Montgomery's style.

Muirhead opened a camp chair and sat down. "A couple of days ago, the Auk sent us orders instructing us where we'll withdraw if Rommel breaks through."

"I saw them," Tulloch admitted. "If Rommel pierces the Alamein line, we're returning to the Delta and further up the Nile into the Sudan, Sinai, or even the Holy Land. Anywhere as long as we keep the 8th Army as a force." He paused for a moment. "I heard the Auk has issued orders that we will – will, not may – withdraw if Rommel attacks and we have to prepare for a German attack from the Caucasus."

Muirhead produced his pipe. "Well, you can forget that now.

Monty has said there will be no withdrawal. None. We stand and fight or die at Alamein."

Tulloch took a deep breath. "Colonel Hume will agree with that."

Muirhead began to fill his pipe. "I heard Alexander's orders to Montgomery were clear: Monty has to destroy Rommel and his army."

"As simple as that?" Tulloch asked.

"As simple as that," Muirhead confirmed.

Over the next few days, General Montgomery issued orders that proved his resolve. He told 8th Army that the old systems of fighting in small brigade units and Jock Columns had ended. The army would fight in divisions.

"That's good," Muirhead approved. "Rommel loves when we are in bits and pieces. He can destroy us in detail, outnumbering us at the point of contact, although overall, we have more men and tanks."

Tulloch agreed. "Maybe Monty is the answer," he said cautiously.

"Maybe he is," Muirhead agreed.

While Tulloch continued to train his company and merge both platoons into a cohesive whole, Montgomery shifted newly arrived divisions from the Delta closer to the Alamein line. Egypt was busy, with the staff officers burdened with writing orders that altered the entire strategy of the previous army commander. Convoys of trucks carried ammunition, fuel, and supplies from the Delta closer to the fighting line, while Montgomery removed senior officers he considered unfit for duty.

"He's weeding out the weak links," Muirhead said. "You'd better be careful, Tulloch, or you'll be next."

Tulloch grinned. "If you saw the mess I was making of D Company, you would not joke about it."

"Who's joking?" Muirhead said with the first genuine smile Tulloch had seen for weeks.

News eased from Montgomery's headquarters and slowly filtered down to Tulloch's level.

"Monty expects Rommel to attack soon," Muirhead said. "He's been inspecting the southern flank of the defences."

Tulloch nodded. "It will be an interesting encounter between the experienced Desert Fox and a new broom who hasn't fought since France in 1940."

"It might not be significant, but Monty spent hours at the Alam Halfa Ridge and the Ruweisat Ridge," Muirhead said.

"We know the Ruweisat Ridge well," Muirhead reminded. "Where is Alam Halfa?"

Tulloch dragged a map from under the pile of documents on his desk. "Here," he stabbed a finger down. "About five miles behind the lines and southeast of the Ruweisat Ridge."

Muirhead looked and grunted. "I presume Monty knows what he's doing."

"I hope so," Tulloch said. "Dear God, I hope so."

TULLOCH STOOD IN FRONT OF HUME'S DESK, WONDERING WHY the colonel had summoned him.

"Tulloch," Colonel Hume looked troubled. "You'll remember Colonel Clark. You worked for him a couple of years ago."

"Yes, sir," Tulloch said. "He's something to do with military intelligence." *He's also Amanda's father, so I must keep on his good side.*

"Colonel Clark has requested to see you," Hume said.

"Why, sir?" Tulloch was immediately wary. He did not wish to become involved in intelligence work again.

"I do not know," Hume said. "Be careful, Tulloch. Men like Clark are dangerous."

"I'll be careful, sir," Tulloch promised. "When does he want to see me?"

"Did you see the jeep parked outside my tent, Tulloch?" Hume asked.

"Yes, sir."

"The driver has orders to take you to Colonel Clark."

"My own chauffeur?" Tulloch said. "I didn't know I was so important."

"That's what worries me, Tulloch," Hume said. "Be very careful."

Tulloch nodded, immediately wary. "I will, sir."

"Captain Tulloch? In you come, sir!" the jeep driver was in his late thirties with a deeply tanned face and an Ulster accent. "Settle down now, and we'll have you with the colonel in two flicks of Hitler's forked tail."

It was Tulloch's first trip in a jeep, and he enjoyed the ride. He was impressed by the vehicle's manoeuvrability and ability to drive over rough terrain.

"Where is Colonel Clark?" Tulloch asked.

"Monty's headquarters, sir," the driver replied, steering around a burned-out fifteen-hundredweight truck. "We have to be careful in this area, sir. We call it Stuka Alley because of all the German air raids."

Tulloch scanned the azure blue of the sky, mercifully free of any aircraft, hostile or friendly. He saw the submachine gun behind the driver's seat.

"Is that a Thompson?"

"Yes, sir. A Tommy gun," the driver said. "A Chicago type-writer, if you prefer."

Tulloch lifted it. "It's heavier than I expected," he said.

"Around ten pounds weight, sir," the driver steered around another wrecked vehicle. "I carry one in case the Germans raid this far. Colonel Clark would be a valuable capture for them."

"I suppose he would," Tulloch agreed.

The driver increased his speed. "Nearly there, sir!"

Tulloch had little time to look around Montgomery's head-quarters before the driver pulled up at a large caravan with a pair of stalwart Redcaps standing guard outside.

The tallest MP, a skull-faced corporal, blocked Tulloch's entrance with practised politeness.

"May I have your name, sir?" His gaze seemed to bore inside Tulloch's head.

"Captain Tulloch, Lothian Rifles, Corporal," Tulloch replied. "I am expected."

"Right you are, sir," the corporal replied, opening the caravan door.

Tulloch stepped inside, unsure what to expect.

"Come in, Captain!" the voice sounded from the left, and Tulloch saw Clark waiting for him.

———

"We have a small task for you, Tulloch." Colonel Clark looked as eccentric as ever. A pair of battered cord trousers covered his lower half, with a faded khaki shirt hanging loosely above. The colonel was obviously a fisherman, as he had half a dozen fishing flies around the battered bush hat that hung on a corner of his chair.

"Yes, sir," Tulloch said.

"You sound wary," Clark smiled, with his eyes dancing.

"Just a bit, sir," Tulloch agreed. "What do you want me to do?"

"I want you to help the enemy," Clark said as his smile increased. Tulloch could see little of Amanda in her father's plump face and sparkling eyes.

"Why should I do that, sir?"

Clark laughed. "You've been in action, Tulloch, and you've done some work for the intelligence services as well."

"I have, sir," Tulloch was even more guarded.

"All I want you to do is take a carrier for a drive, hit a mine and abandon it near the enemy." Clark's smile did not falter, as if he regularly asked such things. *Perhaps he does,* Tulloch thought.

"Why, sir?" Tulloch asked.

"We want to give a certain document to Rommel." The laughter died from Clark's eyes to reveal the steel beneath. Tulloch saw a little more of Amanda.

"I see," Tulloch said. "The carrier will carry this document; the enemy will find it and give it to Rommel."

"Precisely," Clark said.

"Yes, sir. Would the SAS not be better for that sort of thing, sir? They specialise in cloak and dagger stuff in the desert."

"That's why I don't want to use them," Clark said. "If Rommel hears that his men retrieved the document from an SAS vehicle, he will wonder why it was near his front line rather than deep in the desert where they normally operate. On the other hand, a careless infantryman is much more likely to carry such a document on a routine patrol."

"I see, sir," Tulloch said.

"It's a dangerous operation," Clark said, "and I can't order you to carry it out. I need a volunteer. Are you willing?"

Tulloch nodded. "Yes, sir." If he refused, he would brand himself as a coward, while agreeing might help his case with Amanda.

"I hoped you would volunteer," Clark said, dropping the jovial act. "I'll have the document delivered to you, Tulloch. Take care of it until you set out on patrol. I don't want it getting burned or damaged before Rommel sees it."

"I'll take care of it, sir," Tulloch said. "When do you want it delivered?"

"I'll let you know," Clark said. "It will be soon after we give you the document." He stood up and extended his hand. "I'll give you another package as well."

"Yes, sir," Tulloch said. "Do you want that delivered as well?"

"Just leave it in the universal carrier," Clark told him. His handshake was firm and surprisingly strong.

Chapter Twenty-Four

"Rifle range today," Tulloch said cheerfully. "Lieutenant Rutlane's Six Platoon against Lieutenant McGill's Four Platoon." He saw the men's faces drop slightly. "I've been to the NAAFI tent and bought a crate of beer for the successful platoon." The men's expressions altered to mild interest. "Ten rounds at a static target each, followed by ten at a mobile target. We leave in ten minutes."

Tulloch watched as the platoons competed against each other. He saw Hogg and Corporal Russell exchanging glowers in mutual dislike, and Rutlane and McGill engaged in seemingly amiable conversation before they took charge of their respective platoons. Tulloch acted as judge and referee, although the result was never in doubt as he had kept Four Platoon at regular practice.

Four Platoon won that competition, so to soothe any wounded pride, Tulloch had another competition for unarmed combat. Captain Erskine had been an expert in such things, and Tulloch expected his Six Platoon to be equally proficient.

Tulloch watched as Six Platoon emerged victorious, with

Hogg, Innes, and, surprisingly, Cattanach the only members of Four Platoon to win their encounters.

Tulloch had Sergeant Drysdale perfect their bayonet drill while Sergeant Paterson proved an expert in throwing grenades. Tulloch watched his company gradually improve and begin to gel, with even Adamson slightly less surly, although he noted Hogg and Russell continued to avoid each other.

"Well, gentlemen," Tulloch said to McGill and Rutlane. "We're ready to pit D Company against Captain Kilner's E Company."

"If you think so, sir," McGill said.

"Kilner's a veteran of the Great War," Rutlane said. "He'll smash us."

"No, he won't," Tulloch said softly. He noticed Adamson and Hogg passing a few yards away and raised his voice slightly. "I have faith in my men. They'll do us proud." If Tulloch knew British soldiers, his words would spread across D Company within an hour. He also knew nothing pulled men together quicker than having a mutual opponent.

From company training, Tulloch pushed for regimental training, with the Lothians involved in a field exercise with a veteran battalion of the Durham Light Infantry. The night exercise followed a traditional army practice of one battalion guarding a fixed spot with a marker flag and the other attempting to infiltrate the defence. The objective was to grab or retain the flag.

The Lothians were well-versed in defensive warfare but less experienced in offence, so Colonel Hume offered them as the attacking force.

"We need the practice," he said.

"We'll be waiting," the Durhams' colonel responded grimly.

Hume split the Lothians into three units, with a noisy diversionary attack on the west flank.

"They'll know that it's a diversion," Hume said. "And expect an attack on the opposite flank."

The officers nodded.

"So we'll give him an attack on the north flank," Hume said, smiling. "We'll press it home and keep them occupied while our third attack goes on from the south, silent and straight to the flag."

Tulloch smiled. Hume had learned his craft on India's Northwest Frontier and was an expert in guile and deception.

"Muirhead, take C Company for the south attack. Tulloch, take D Company for the west flank diversion, and I will do the same on the north flank." Hume gave more detailed instructions as the officers took notes.

D Company listened as Tulloch instructed them in their part in the exercise.

"We are acting as a diversion," Tulloch told them. "But I want a little more than that. The opposition will know we are a diversion, so let's rummel them up, as Shuggie Elliot would say." He noted Elliot's pleasure at an officer knowing his nickname.

"How?" Rutlane asked.

"Your Six Platoon will put in a mock attack at ten at night," Tulloch told him. "They'll expect you, so when you make contact, act like you're in company strength. McGill's Four Platoon will keep low and silent, crawling from the south and taking the opposition in the flank."

The men nodded.

"When the Durhams react, as they will, Six Platoon will push forward," Tulloch said. "The bigger diversion we create, the better chance C Company has to succeed."

The exercise was Tulloch's first opportunity to show his skill as a Company Commander, and he could not have picked a more redoubtable opponent. The Durhams were a tough, wily battalion of veterans.

Tulloch thought Rutlane's Six Platoon was half-hearted in its attack, lacking effort as they made noise and pushed toward the Durhams. He listened for a few moments before he joined them.

"Come on, lads! You can do better than that!"

The men responded without enthusiasm. "What's the point,

sir?" a short, stocky private asked. "It's only an exercise, and they'll beat us anyway. We always get beat."

"The point is to ensure the Germans don't defeat us again," Tulloch restrained his impulse to blast the man. "Now, get forward and make a noise!" He saw a shadowy figure behind him. "You too, Corporal Russell. Lead your men!"

With Tulloch urging Six Platoon on, the noise level increased, although they made little progress against the dug-in Durhams.

"We're getting nowhere," Rutlane said.

"You're diverting the opposition," Tulloch told him. He hoped McGill's platoon was having more success.

"We may as well give up now," Rutlane said.

"Push forward!" Tulloch ordered. He raised his voice. "Come on, Six Platoon!"

The men followed, firing blank ammunition, throwing flash-bang grenades, and making as much noise as possible. Tulloch saw the Durhams slowly withdrawing before them.

"Careful, lads!" Tulloch shouted.

Six Platoon ran forward for the Durhams to rise from hidden trenches on either side.

"You're dead, Lothians!" a cheerful Durham captain called. "The game's over for you!"

Tulloch prepared to fight. "Not yet," he said. "Come on, Six Platoon!" He realised he was alone as Rutlane raised his hands in surrender, and most of his men followed. Only Corporal Russell and the truculent Adamson hesitated.

The Durham captain laughed. "You don't have much support, Captain."

Tulloch nodded. "Neither do I," he agreed.

At that moment, McGill led Four Platoon into the defender's flank, with Sergeant Drysdale giving urgent orders.

"Come on, Four Platoon!" McGill shouted.

"Rummel them up!" Elliot roared as Hogg moved in with his bayonet fixed. Tulloch saw him eye Corporal Russell.

"Take off your bayonet, Hogg! This is an exercise, not a real battle!"

The Lothians and Durhams stared at each other, both ready to fight, until a tall major of a Yorkshire regiment intervened.

"Well done, both units," the Yorkshireman said. "The exercise is over now, so no need for fisticuffs."

"Who won?" Tulloch and the Durham captain asked together.

"Nobody," the Yorkshire major replied. "It was a draw."

Maybe nobody won, Tulloch told himself, *but I learned a lot about Six Platoon. Perhaps that was the real object of the exercise. I understand more about the desertions now.*

"Yes, Tulloch?" Colonel Hume asked.

"I want to transfer Rutlane, sir," Tulloch said. "I don't believe he has the right spirit to command a platoon."

"Where do you wish to transfer him?" Hume asked.

"Anywhere but D Company," Tulloch replied.

"Motor Pool?" Hume asked.

"Right out of the battalion, sir," Tulloch said. "He's no fighting spirit, and I suspect he lowers Six Platoon's morale. He was too quick to surrender during the exercise."

Hume scribbled a note. "I had my doubts about Rutlane when he arrived," he admitted. "I can't make any promises, but I'll transfer him as soon as I find a replacement."

"Thank you, sir," Tulloch said. "I'd rather operate without a lieutenant than have Rutlane, sir."

"Leave it with me, Tulloch," Hume said.

As Tulloch returned to D Company, he saw a small group of men standing beside two dusty jeeps.

"Are you Tulloch?" the tallest man in the group asked. He wore a British officer's uniform with no badges of rank, and the men at his back looked sturdy and capable. Like their leader, they wore neither regimental insignia nor indication of rank. A long, bulky package wrapped in canvas lay across the back seat of the second jeep.

"I am Captain Tulloch. Who are you?" Tulloch was not accustomed to strange men accosting him, in or out of uniform.

"General Clark sent me," the man did not give his name.

That explained the lack of insignia. "You should have something for me," Tulloch said, unsure if he should call the man sir.

"I have two things for you," the man replied. "I have this," he handed over a sealed envelope. "And I have this," he jerked a thumb over his shoulder at the canvas-wrapped package.

"General Clark mentioned a package," Tulloch said. "He didn't mention it was so large."

"Colonel Hume assures me it would add plausibility to your mission," the man told him. He raised his voice and gave a sharp command. "Show Captain Tulloch!"

The other men stepped into the second jeep and peeled back the top half of the canvas cover. Tulloch stared at a recent corpse wearing the uniform and insignia of a lieutenant in the Lothians. Tulloch did not recognise the dead man.

"A touch of realism," the man said calmly. "You can put the document in his tunic or elsewhere in the carrier. We've given the dead fellow everything he needs, from personal possessions to letters from his sweetheart."

"My lads won't be happy accompanying a corpse," Tulloch said.

"They'll do as they're damned well told," the man replied.

"They imperil their lives every day," Tulloch reminded acidly. "Doing as they're damned well told."

The man's smile did not reach his eyes. "Then they won't object to driving a corpse towards the enemy."

"Are you coming with us?" Tulloch asked.

"Not me, old boy," the man replied. "I've done my job in delivering chummy here," he jerked a thumb at the wrapped corpse, "and the envelope in your hand. Both of which you will take care of."

Tulloch slid the envelope into his inside pocket. "If you've done your job, then you can disappear." He turned away. "Put the body in my carrier. My men have a hard enough life fighting the enemy without handling anonymous corpses."

"That's not my job," the man replied.

"It is now," Tulloch said. "Who the hell are you, anyway?" He strode away. When he turned around, the three men had vanished, and the corpse, still in its cover, was in the back of his carrier.

Chapter Twenty-Five

"**M**onty's at it again," Muirhead said, smiling. "He's passed the word that he will not tolerate bellyaching in the army."

"Bellyaching?" Tulloch asked.

Muirhead smiled. "I had to ask as well," he admitted. "Montgomery said that before he arrived, subordinate officers had often queried orders from their superior officers, giving unsound reasons for not doing as they were told. Monty says that his orders are not open for discussion but are a basis for action."

"So querying orders is bellyaching," Tulloch said. "Our new army commander is certainly putting his foot down."

"He expects Rommel to attack," Muirhead said. "He's reiterated his orders that Eighth Army will stand and fight. No more looking over our shoulders. No more withdrawals."

Tulloch nodded. "That's what I heard," he said.

"We're in a supporting role this time," Muirhead told him. "Monty has planned a different type of battle with our armour dug in behind a screen of six-pounder anti-tank guns."

"Rommel might do his usual trick and bypass our defences," Tulloch said.

"That's the simplicity and beauty of Montgomery's plan," Muirhead said. "By not loosing our armour, he's keeping them as a threat with minimal losses. If Rommel runs on to attack Cairo and Alex, he'll find Monty with 400 tanks on his tail."

"All we have to do is invite Rommel in and hold our ground," Tulloch said.

Muirhead watched Tulloch through narrowed eyes. "I heard you spoke to Colonel Clark from Intelligence."

"I did," Tulloch agreed.

"Don't tell me what your orders are," Muirhead said. "I don't want to know."

"That's for the best," Tulloch agreed. "I can tell you I am taking a patrol into no-man's land."

"Good luck, Douglas," Muirhead said quietly.

Tulloch chose Hogg and Hood to accompany him. "We're going towards the enemy lines," Tulloch told them. "We're leaving the carrier as a free gift for Rommel and returning on foot."

"Why are we leaving the carrier, sir?" Hogg asked. "Is it rigged with explosives?"

"Not quite," Tulloch said. "You get the idea, though."

Hogg and Hood glanced at each other. Hood grinned, and Hogg stamped his feet.

They understood.

"Are we going to fool Rommel, sir?" Hood asked.

"We are," Tulloch wondered if Higher Command understood anything about Scottish soldiers. Few of the other ranks had enjoyed the extensive education of their officers, but their natural wit and common sense allowed them to recognise what was happening.

"Just the job," Hood said, satisfied with the answer.

"It's a waste of a good carrier, abandoning it to Fritz," Hogg said. "They things cost a lot of money. I could get a decent return from a scrappy for this much metal."

"We can't just abandon a usable vehicle," Hood patted the armoured side of the carrier. "Rommel's no fool."

"We're going to hit a mine," Tulloch said blandly.

"Then we'll be deid," Hogg said. "A carrier's too heavy to set off an anti-personnel mine, and an anti-tank mine will blow us to bits."

"Not if we do it properly," Tulloch said. "We're going to abandon the carrier and then blow off a track, leaving this fellow," he patted the unfortunate corpse, "to fool the enemy."

"The bus will be crowded, sir, what with him," Hood indicated the corpse, "and us. Who is he anyway? He's not one of our officers."

"He is now," Tulloch said. "And that's enough questions, lads."

Hogg shrugged. "All right, sir," he said. "At least he's better company than Corporal Russell." He patted the corpse's shoulder. "You sit there like a good officer, sir, and we'll deliver you to nice Uncle Rommel."

Tulloch realised that veterans such as Hogg and Hood had seen too many corpses for one more to concern them.

"Get some sleep if you can, eat, and bring a full water bottle." Tulloch knew he didn't need to tell his veterans the basics.

Colonel Hume looked concerned as Tulloch prepared the carrier in the late evening, keeping a canvas cover over the dead officer.

"Don't get yourself killed, Tulloch," Hume advised. "We're getting short of experienced officers."

"I'll try not to, sir." Tulloch put half a dozen grenades in the front of the carrier.

"I'll give you two hours and have Sergeant Drysdale fire green and red Very Lights every hour and half-hour to guide you back," Hume continued.

"Thank you, sir," Tulloch said.

Hume fiddled with his empty pipe for a moment. "Best of British, Douglas."

"You too, sir," Tulloch said. He watched Hume stomp away, becoming aware of the weight of responsibility a battalion colonel carried, with the life of every man in the unit in his hands.

They set off an hour after dark, with the wind raising a delicate tracery of dust and a three-quarters moon looking wan and yellow high above.

Once again, tired engineers opened a lane through the defensive wire and the minefield.

"The challenge is Victory," the engineer sergeant reminded wearily, "and the reply is Cigarettes." His smile was bleak. "Plural, remember cigarettes with an S and not a singular cigarette. One fag is no good to anybody."

"We'll remember," Tulloch said.

The ground was flat, featureless, and grim, with memories of Rommel's previous attempt to break through the El Alamein line. Although the engineers of both sides had rescued most damaged vehicles for salvage, several burnt-out wrecks remained as a reminder of savage encounters.

Tulloch ordered Hood to drive slowly to raise a minimum of dust. He navigated toward the German lines, using a rough map previous patrols and RAF observers had created.

Three hundred yards outside the British minefield, Tulloch removed the canvas from the corpse and threw it into the desert.

"There you go, my silent friend," he said. "Your last mission." He opened the packet Colonel Clark had given him, tossed away the covering, and glanced at the document. *It's a map of our positions and minefields,* Tulloch saw. *I presume it gives Rommel false information.*

The wind increased as they drove, whipping up the sand to sting their hands and faces and rattling from the carrier's side.

"I can't see much in this muck, sir," Hood said.

"Steer by the compass," Tulloch ordered. "We have to get closer to the German lines."

"Yes, sir," Hood replied. He kept his head down and eyes slitted to protect himself from the flying dust. The carrier growled on, with Hogg holding the unfamiliar Bren gun and Tulloch staring ahead. He tried to judge where they were by his watch and compass, for the sandstorm hid the stars. If he stopped too far from the German lines, a British patrol might pick up the carrier, while if he ventured too close, the enemy might genuinely attack them. If the Germans destroyed the carrier, they might also spoil the map and ruin the entire operation. Tulloch grunted; *if the Germans attack, they could kill us all, never mind the blasted map!*

"Sir!" Hogg grated. "I can hear something. An engine, but it's hard to say what with this bloody wind."

"Slow down, Hood," Tulloch said quietly.

Hood slowed, with the engine noise reduced to a purr. Tulloch strained to hear above the hiss of the wind and the patter of sand against the carrier's sides.

"Over that way, sir," Hogg jerked his head to the south. "I think there are two engines."

"Cut the engine," Tulloch ordered.

Hood obeyed and reached for his rifle, peering into the sand-laden dark. Tulloch could hear the sound now, a low growl under the wind's higher whine.

"Keep quiet and hope they don't come this way," Tulloch ordered.

Hogg pulled his helmet over his forehead and readied the Bren gun as Hood worked the bolt of his rifle. They stared into the night, with Tulloch feeling very vulnerable. The universal, or Bren gun, carrier was a practical vehicle, with its armour some protection against small arms but little use against a tank or an armoured car.

For a moment, Tulloch was tempted to abandon the carrier where they were but knew he could not. They were a long way from the German minefields, and there was no guarantee that the enemy would find the vehicle or the map. Besides, he told himself, the unseen vehicles could be British, Australian, or New Zealanders.

"They've cut their engines, too," Hogg whispered, pulling the Bren closer to his cheek.

"They heard us," Tulloch said. "Stay put. I'm going to look."

"Be careful, sir," Hood cautioned.

Sliding out of the vehicle, Tulloch padded across the desert towards where he had heard the engine sounds. He knew he should have remained with the carrier but had to know who else was out here.

Tulloch walked for five minutes, continually turning to ensure he could see the carrier, although it was only a vague shape in the dark. He held his pistol, peering into the night without hearing anything other than the wind. Somebody coughed nearby.

Tulloch crouched, pointing his revolver, peering through the dust-laden haze. He could see nobody.

The wind increased, hurling sand against Tulloch's face. He lifted his scarf to cover his mouth and walked forward slowly, one step at a time.

He saw the shape against the smearing dust—a lone man, walking as cautiously as he was, peering into the murk. *Friend or enemy?* Tulloch could not tell. British, German, and Italian uniforms looked similar in the dark.

That man is doing the same as me, wondering who is sharing the desert night.

Tulloch crouched again, moving slowly as he watched the other man through the whirling sand. He extended his revolver, ready to fire if the man proved hostile. The wind dropped suddenly, creating a gap in the sand that allowed the moon to shine through. The other man was young, with a thin, anxious face marred by a single straight scar down his left cheek.

Is that a duelling scar or a war wound? Either way, he is a German officer.

The young German caught sight of Tulloch and pointed his Luger. "Sieg!" he called, hopefully. "Sieg!"

That must be their password. Tulloch aimed his revolver but did not fire. *A shot would attract the German vehicle, which might be more powerful than our carrier. I can't risk losing the map and my men.*

Tulloch saw the same sequence of thoughts passing through the German officer's head as he stared through the dark.

We both have the same dilemma, Tulloch thought. *I am a British officer. My duty is to fight and kill the enemy, but would I jeopardise my mission by fighting here?*

The wind rose again, concealing the German. Tulloch returned to his crouch, then lay on the sand, knowing he would be nearly invisible in the dark.

I have seen my enemy, and he looks just like me.

Neither of us is willing to chance an encounter with a superior force, Tulloch realised. *We both have a mission to fulfil.* He spoke quietly, hoping the German officer would understand.

"Kamerad!"

Nobody replied.

"Kamerad!" Tulloch tried again with one of the few German words he knew.

"Kamerad!" the reply floated through the dark.

Tulloch stepped forward, still holding his revolver. He saw the German do the same, Luger in hand. They stopped simultaneously, thirty yards apart. The German lifted his Luger and placed it in his holster. Tulloch did the same with his revolver, and they stepped closer, both wary.

The German was older than Tulloch had thought, perhaps in his mid-twenties, with an open face. He held out his hand in friendship. Tulloch took it, meeting the man's gaze.

"Here," Tulloch fished out a packet of Victory V cigarettes from his tunic pocket. "They're terrible but better than nothing."

The German looked startled. "*Danke*," he said, holding up the cigarette packet.

They stood together for a few moments in awkward silence, aware that they could shoot at each other the following day.

"We'd best be off," Tulloch said and smiled as the German replied in his own language. "Good luck, Fritz."

"*Viel Glück*, Tommy," the German replied.

They shook hands again, smiled, and walked away. Tulloch heard the German's footsteps thudding on the hard ground and moved faster. For a moment, he thought he had lost his way, but the carrier loomed through the dark with the distinctive shape of British helmets.

"Right, lads," Tulloch said as he hauled himself on board. "They're German. Start the engine, Hood, and push forward."

"Was it a tank, sir?" Hogg asked.

"I never found out," Tulloch said. "Move a bit faster, Hood. Put some distance between them and us."

Hood pushed forward as the wind died away, with Tulloch peering forward. After five minutes, Tulloch slowed them down.

"We must be nearing the edge of the German minefield," he said. "Be careful."

They heard the sudden chatter of a machine gun to the north, and then a flare soared upwards to explode in white fury high above. Tulloch suddenly felt naked as the harsh light exposed the carrier standing on the level plain.

"They'll see us," Hood said.

"They'd have to be blind not to!" Hogg replied. "I wish that sandstorm had continued a bit longer."

Tulloch saw the flash of artillery and heard the bark a second later. "It's time we were out, boys. Abandon the bus!" He placed the grenades onto the nearside track as the first shells exploded, none closer than fifty yards.

"Get out!" Tulloch ordered as Hood hesitated. He pulled the pin of the top grenade and threw himself onto the sand outside. "Run, men!"

The second German salvo was closer than the first, with one shell landing only a few yards from the carrier. Tulloch threw Hood and Hogg to the ground as the grenades exploded, spreading lethal fragments above their heads.

That should convince the Germans that the map is genuine.

"Run!" Tulloch ordered, "before they send out a patrol to find us."

"Where to, sir?" Hood asked.

"Back to the Lothians," Tulloch replied. "As fast as we can."

They loped across the desert, with shells exploding behind them. Whenever a star shell lit up the sky, they dropped to the ground, with Hogg hugging the Bren as if it was his sweetheart. When they heard a machine gun stammer behind them, Hood grunted.

"Fritz is firing at shadows," he said.

"Good," Tulloch replied. "The more ammunition he wastes tonight, the less he'll have when we face him again."

"Sir!" Hogg said. "I can hear another engine."

Chapter Twenty-Six

"Keep still," Tulloch ordered. He heard Hogg prepare the Bren gun.

A German halftrack grumbled into view, with an officer standing beside the driver and half a dozen men sitting in the back.

"What the hell do we do now?" Hood asked.

"We show ourselves before they see us," Tulloch said. He expected the incredulous looks from his men. "Stand up." *The Germans can't miss us on this open plain now the sandstorm has passed, and the moon is out.*

"Sling your Bren, Hogg," Tulloch said. "Don't make it obvious. Take off your helmets quickly! Bury them in the sand."

In the dark and without the distinctive British helmets, all three were virtually indistinguishable from German soldiers. Tulloch was very grateful that Hume did not insist on his men wearing shorts, with the Lothians favouring longer trousers at night.

The halftrack came closer, with the officer studying the patrol through his binoculars and the men in the body of the halftrack training weapons on them. Tulloch lifted a hand in acknowledgement.

"Sieg!" he shouted the password he had learned earlier that night.

"Rommel!" the German officer replied.

Tulloch waved them away with urgent gestures that nobody could mistake. The German officer raised a hand and drove away, with his dust slowly creeping over the Lothians.

"What did you say to him, sir?" Hood asked.

"I gave them the German password," Tulloch said.

"You telt them to go away," Hogg said curiously.

"There are so many small scouting patrols going about between the two armies," Tulloch explained. "He would think we are on a mission for Rommel."

"We fooled them again, eh?" Hogg said.

"We did," Tulloch replied. "Now get your helmets on, and let's get back to the battalion. We won't be so lucky a second time."

"Where is the battalion, sir?" Hood asked.

Tulloch checked his watch. *Nearly the half hour.* "Watch for red and green Very lights," he said. "That's our marker."

The flares soared upwards, precisely on time, as Tulloch expected from Sergeant Drysdale.

"That's our mark, lads," Tulloch said. "Head for the lights."

COLONEL HUME GREETED TULLOCH WITH A WORRIED NOD. "All right, Tulloch?"

"Yes, sir," Tulloch replied. "We delivered the package without firing a shot. Oh, and tonight's German password is Sieg, with the counter as Rommel."

Hume smiled. "I'll pass that on to Intelligence," he said. "How on earth do you know that?"

"A friendly German told me," Tulloch said.

"You'll have to tell me sometime," Hume replied. "I'll notify Colonel Clark. You and your men better get some rest. We expect an important visitor soon."

Shortly after noon, Hume gathered the battalion together, officers and men in a horseshoe formation.

"What's happening?" Kilner asked.

"We're waiting for somebody important," Tulloch told him.

"Some brasshat with a big mouth and limited experience," Kilner said.

"No doubt," Tulloch agreed.

A staff car rolled into the open side of the horseshoe with the Lothians watching through cynical, bitter eyes.

When the doors opened, an officer of medium height stepped out. He was slender, almost thin, and was wearing a new desert shirt and slacks. He had a pointed face, high cheekbones, and a long, sharp nose. Wearing an Australian bush hat, he waved the car away and waited for the buzz of recognition to die down before speaking.

"That's Montgomery!" Muirhead said as Tulloch saw Colonel Hume's smug expression.

"That's the first army commander I've ever seen," Lieutenant Hardie said.

"Me too," Tulloch agreed.

"And me," Kilner said. "And I've been in the army since 1915."

Everybody fell silent when Montgomery began to speak in a crisp, clear voice.

"I want to introduce myself to you. I am Bernard Montgomery, and I will lead you to victory over the enemy. I have confidence in you. I know you have had some bad fortune in the past and have withdrawn before the enemy's advance. Those days are past. You have lived and fought in an atmosphere of doubt, of looking back to select the next place to which to withdraw. You have experienced a loss of confidence in our ability to defeat Rommel, and you have heard of desperate defence measures by reserves in preparing positions in Cairo and the Delta."

Montgomery halted for a moment and looked around his audience. The Lothians, battered veterans of three years of war, studied him. Tulloch could feel Montgomery's presence from where he stood. He had never known the battalion so quiet.

"All that must cease," Montgomery said in his crisp, sharp voice. "The defence of Egypt lies here at Alamein and on the Ruweisat Ridge. What is the use of digging trenches in the Delta? It is quite useless; if we lose this position, we lose Egypt. Here, we will stand and fight; there will be no further withdrawal. I have ordered that all plans and instructions dealing with further withdrawals are to be burned. We will stand and fight *here*."

The Lothians broke into a spontaneous cheer, the first that Tulloch had ever heard from a British regiment in response to an address from a senior officer. But Montgomery was not yet finished.

"I want to impress on everyone that the bad times are over. Fresh divisions from the UK are arriving in Egypt, together with ample reinforcements for our present divisions. We have 300 to 400 new Sherman tanks coming. Our mandate from the Prime Minister is to destroy the Axis forces in North Africa. I have seen it, written on half a sheet of notepaper. And it will be done beyond any possibility of doubt.

I understand that Rommel is expected to attack at any moment. Excellent. Let him attack. Meanwhile, we will start to plan a great offensive; it will be the beginning of a campaign which will hit Rommel and his Army for six right out of Africa."

Montgomery stopped to look around at the battalion. For a second, he looked directly at Tulloch and then away again. In that instant, Tulloch knew the army had found its general.

Tulloch felt no doubt at all.

General Bernard Montgomery would meet Rommel in battle and defeat him. Tulloch did not remember who started the cheering; he only knew he was shouting as fervently as the youngest and most impressionable recruit, and Muirhead was at his side. Even Captain Kilner, grizzled and scarred by decades in uniform, was cheering the small, sharp-nosed general.

After a brief word with Colonel Hume, General Montgomery returned to his staff car and drove away with his Australian hat prominently on display.

"Dismiss!" Hume ordered.

The Lothians dispersed, with their morale higher than it had been for months and the men marching with a new purpose.

"So that's our new Army Commander," Muirhead said as he walked beside Tulloch. "He's a funny wee chap, isn't he?"

Tulloch nodded. "We've met him before, in France."

"I remember," Muirhead said. "He commanded the 3rd Division and brought it back intact."

Tulloch walked through his company, catching snatches of conversation from the men.

"We'll hit Rommel for six, will we?" Corporal Russell said. "Montgomery's never faced Rommel before, and he thinks he'll beat him. It's no' a cricket game."

Corporal Borthwick shook his head. "I don't agree with you, Rab. Monty seems to know what he's doing. He's already cleared out a lot of dead wood in the army."

"Aye, maybe aye, maybe och aye," Russell replied. "We'll see what he's like when he meets a squadron of Panzers and a flight of Stukas. Rommel will learn him, I'm telling you."

"Monty's the lad for me," Hogg said with satisfaction. "No retreat. We'll stand here and stop the Germans."

Innes shook his head. "The thing about generals who say no retreat," he said, "is that it's us, the PBI, who stand and fight while they're at the back shouting words of encouragement."

"I liked Monty," Hood said. "I think he'll be all right."

Tulloch walked on, Muirhead smiling faintly at his side. Scottish soldiers were naturally cynical, having mainly grown up in the hard years of the Thirties when jobs were elusive and poverty a fact of life. For some, the army was a refuge from hardship and desperately bad housing, and they had no reason to respect higher authority.

"Mixed reactions from the men," Muirhead said.

"Many generals can talk a good fight," Tulloch said. "Once Monty wins a battle, men will have more faith. When he defeats Rommel, the men will follow him anywhere."

Muirhead was silent for a few moments. "Rommel is a good soldier," he said at last, "but not unbeatable. As your girl told you, he had the advantage of knowing our plans and dispositions in advance. He also had the advantage of creating battle groups and the Afrika Korps, a mini-army including mobile infantry, tanks, and self-propelled artillery."

Tulloch nodded. "It was an advantage he created himself, and that proves he's a good soldier."

Muirhead continued. "The German army is different from ours, with no static brigade or divisional formations, so it's easier to alter, even during a battle. That gives Rommel's Afrika Korps much more flexibility than we have, with our armoured cavalry regiments, ponderous staff system and infantry-based divisions. We have poor coordination between our infantry and armoured divisions and fight as we have for the past hundred years."

Tulloch nodded. He watched Sergeant Drysdale supervise a squad of replacements, training them to be soldiers in the Lothians. *Thank God for the NCOs.*

"Poor coordination seems to be one of our faults," Tulloch said. "Our Boxes could not support each other at Gazala, and our army and air force seem to be fighting separate wars."

"I think Monty will solve both these problems," Muirhead said.

"Time will tell," Tulloch replied. The war had been a series of disappointments punctuated by intense bravery and sickening disasters, of which Dunkirk and the fall of Singapore and Tobruk had only been the worst. "If Monty's words prove to be only rhetoric..." he left the sentence unfinished.

The Lothians watched with unfeigned interest as Montgomery continued to reorganise 8th Army. He cancelled all orders to prepare for a retreat, commanded the engineers to lay new minefields, and brought more anti-tank guns to the front. As the Lothians nodded approval, Montgomery created an interwoven system of defences that included infantry, artillery, and armour and ordered the tanks to dig themselves in.

"Who gives the order to let loose the armour?" one eager cavalryman asked.

Montgomery favoured him with a cold stare. "The armour will sit hull down and fight it out with the enemy," he replied. "Let Rommel's army expose themselves, not our men."

Whatever Montgomery did, his message was always clear: 8th Army would not withdraw from its positions. It would remain where it was, stand and fight.

"That's clear enough," Tulloch said. "With Montgomery in command, there are no mixed messages, no confusion of order and counter order." Despite the inherent cynicism of the British soldier, he could feel the Lothians' morale rising by the day.

Montgomery toured the front, strengthened the rocky Ruweisat Ridge with deeper minefields, blasted out positions for the 5th Indian Division, which garrisoned the bleak ridge and positioned a brigade of Valentine tanks at the rear. To the south, Montgomery placed a New Zealand division, bolstered by a brigade from the 44th Division, fresh from digging holes in the Delta.

Muirhead shook his head, smiling. "Montgomery has stirred things up. He's got half the army moving to the front, plump staff majors doing route marches in preparation for a fight and columns marching and driving hither and yon."

"Where are we headed?" men asked their officers, who asked Colonel Hume the same question.

"The Alam Halfa Ridge," Hume said. "We're attached to 50 Div, but temporarily to 44 Div."

"Isn't that behind the main position?" Kilner asked.

"It is," Hume agreed. "We're fighting under the command of a General Horrocks, fresh out from Blighty. He's a tankie, and Monty chose him personally."

"Let's hope he doesn't try any of the tally-ho tactics," Tulloch said. "If our armour does a crazy charge, the German tanks will form a screen with their 88s and knock them out one by one. Our tanks seem only to know how to attack."

"Is that not bellyaching?" Muirhead asked gently.

Tulloch smiled. "Point taken," he conceded.

"Did you hear Montgomery has hung a picture of Rommel in his caravan?" Muirhead asked. "Monty wants to get inside Rommel's head."

"He covers every angle," Tulloch replied.

The Lothians moved the next day, their column of soft-bodied trucks joining the dozens of others that motored across the desert.

"The whole bloody place is alive," Hogg commented.

Tulloch agreed. It seemed as if somebody had reached down and stirred Egypt with a giant stick, causing men and vehicles to drive north, south, and westward.

As they neared the Alam Halfa Ridge, the Lothians passed engineers working furiously with bulldozers and explosives, creating secure positions for the British armour on the slopes. In front of the tanks, gunners manoeuvred six-pounder anti-tank guns into position and worked out their fields of fire.

"Montgomery has issued a Special Message to the officers and men of Eighth Army."

Hume addressed the Lothians. "He reiterates his previous words to the Lothians and says no withdrawal and no surrender."

"No surrender," Hogg mouthed. "The same as the siege of Londonderry."

"Montgomery tells us to destroy once and for all the enemy forces now in Egypt, to go into battle with stout hearts and ends with a plea to God to give us the victory."

As the Lothians broke up, Hogg shouted, "No surrender!"

Both sides continued to build up their forces, with Rommel boasting around 230 Mark III and Mark IV Panzers, superior to the undergunned Valentines, Matildas, Stuarts, and outmoded Grants of the British. Many German tanks carried long-barrelled 50-mm or 75-mm guns. Including the Italian armour, Rommel's tanks outnumbered Montgomery's by 500 to 478.

While they waited for Rommel's attack, the British units exercised, preparing for every possible scenario. For the first time in the campaign, the armour, infantry, artillery, and RAF acted in unison.

When Tulloch viewed a plan of the British defences, he compared them mentally with the map he had left in the carrier. The actual minefields were deeper and in slightly different positions, half the gun positions were absent from the planted map, and some descriptions of ground conditions were inaccurate.

"The enemy will come tonight," Kilner said. "I can feel it."

Tulloch lifted his head. Kilner was a veteran of the First World War, and he trusted his judgement. "Now we'll see how good Montgomery is."

Kilner nodded, sucking on his empty pipe. "Aye," he said. "Aye."

Chapter Twenty-Seven

ALAM HALFA, AUGUST AND SEPTEMBER 1942

The moon was full that night, shining bright above the desert and the waiting Allied forces. Hogg was the first Lothian to hear the growl of distant engines.

"Far away from us, sir," Hogg said.

"Which direction, Hogg?"

"To the south, sir," Hogg replied.

They heard the aircraft shortly afterwards, and news filtered through slowly. An RAF reconnaissance aircraft found the long enemy convoys and called up reinforcements. The Royal Navy supplied Fairey Albacores, who dropped flares for RAF Wellington bombers and Royal Artillery to hammer the advancing vehicles.

"That's interservice cooperation," Tulloch said. "Montgomery's already made his mark."

"Oh, there's more," Muirhead said blandly. "The enemy drove straight into a minefield and lost a dozen vehicles." He glanced at Tulloch. "They seem to have believed the minefields were less extensive than they are."

"I wonder why," Tulloch said.

The German and Italian armour ploughed into the British minefields, slowed down and sat in frustration as the Desert Air Force, the RAF, flew sortie after sortie to hammer at them. Simultaneously, British artillery fired repeated salvos, causing casualties and setting trucks and tanks ablaze.

News continued to come in, punctuated by the occasional burst of gunfire carried on the wind.

"The Germans tried to raid, and the Australians skelped their arses," Muirhead said cheerfully. "Another raid wiped out a West Yorkshire company, but the Essex lads pushed them back. The South Africans and New Zealanders countered and took scores of Italian prisoners."

The officers listened, passing the information to their men.

"7th Armoured Division is playing merry hell with Rommel's men," Muirhead reported. "They're going in, hitting and retiring before the German 88s or tanks can retaliate. According to German radio messages, we've killed the commander of the Afrika Korps. Our tanks are concentrating on their soft-skinned vehicles, leaving the artillery to deal with the Panzers."

Tulloch absorbed the information, hoping Rommel had lost tanks as well as trucks. Rommel pushed his army slowly on, and the following day, an unfortunate sandstorm grounded the Desert Air Force and allowed the Panzers to escape from the minefield.

"We can't see much in this muck," Tulloch peered into the sandstorm, focussing his binoculars. "All I can see is a yellow-brown curtain."

"I can hear something, sir," Hogg said.

"All I hear is the wind," Tulloch told him.

"It's no' that, sir," Hogg said. "I can hear engines, sir, and that squealing clanking sound that tanks make."

Tulloch grunted. He had experienced Hogg's powerful hearing before. "Rommel's men have fought across nearly 1400 miles of Africa. They won't stop when they're only 70 miles from Alex."

Hogg indicated the waiting British tanks and artillery. "They won't get any further," he said grimly.

The wind dropped, releasing countless billions of grains of sand and revealing the Afrika Korps' advance beneath their curtain of dust.

"Here they come," Tulloch stood amidst his company, watching through binoculars. The dust clouds grew closer, with the RAF still absent and the British waiting on Alam Halfa Ridge.

When the Germans stopped, the dust cleared, revealing rank after rank of German tanks, Panzer Mark III and Mark IV, with their long barrels pointing to the Allied positions and their crews confident after an unbroken series of victories over British generals.

"Bloody hell," somebody breathed. "There's millions of the buggers."

"Plenty targets for the gunners, then," Sergeant Drysdale said.

"Our intelligence says we're facing the 15th and 21st Panzer Divisions," Muirhead said quietly. "We have the 22nd Armoured Brigade and British and New Zealand artillery."

Tulloch inspected the British armour. The light tanks were hull down, while the Grants, with their main armament mounted in their hulls, were more exposed. In previous battles, the sight of German armour would have prodded British tanks into an immediate counterattack. Now, they sat tight. The Germans moved again, creeping forward with the dust rising around them.

He heard the first salvo of shots from the longer-range German tanks and saw the explosions and resulting columns of stones, smoke, and dirt along the ridge. A few shells exploded among the Lothians without causing casualties.

"That's the devil of a gun these German tanks are carrying," Muirhead said as the German 75-mm guns began to knock out the exposed Grants, setting them on fire as the survivors scrambled out.

The British waited, unable to fire, until the Germans came into range. Then, the entire 22nd Armoured Brigade and Allied artillery opened fire. The City of London Yeomanry fired first as the Scots Greys moved from their reserve positions to replace the burning Grants.

"Just the job!" McGill said as the British fire exploded around the German armour. Within a few minutes, smoke was pouring from two German tanks, and others were scattering from the barrage. The Rifle Brigade's six-pounders waited until the enemy armour was close before they fired.

"Monty has lured Rommel into a trap," Muirhead said with satisfaction. "Come into my parlour, said the spider to the fly."

"Some flies," Rutlane said. "The Panzers are more like wasps, dangerous insects with a powerful sting! Watch out!"

One squadron of German tanks altered their attack, firing directly at the Lothians' positions.

"Get to your men!" Hume ordered, and the officers ran to their companies and platoons before diving for cover.

The shelling intensified, with German shells landing among the trenches and dugouts. Unable to retaliate, the Lothians lay in the bottom of their trenches, swearing, silent, or praying as the shells burst all around them.

"No!"

Tulloch heard the man scream. He looked up as a private from Six Platoon rose from his trench, holding his helmet on with both hands.

"That man!" Tulloch recognised Preston, one of the erstwhile deserters. "Stop!"

Preston looked at him through wide, unfocused eyes, screaming hysterically.

"Get down!" Tulloch ordered, hoping the voice of authority would crack through Preston's fear. He knew Preston was no coward and had performed well at Gazala, but every man had his breaking point.

Swearing, Tulloch rolled from his trench and crawled towards the screaming man, stopping when a shell exploded a few yards away, showering him with dust and stones. He threw himself at Preston, bringing him down in a rugby tackle.

"Keep down, you blasted idiot!" Tulloch grated. "You're safer in the trench!" He saw a man running towards him and realised it was Macquarie with his medical bag.

"Into a trench!" Macquarie sounded calm despite the shells exploding all around. "Quickly!"

"Here, sir!" Adamson lifted his head from a dugout five yards away. "There's space in here!"

They bundled Preston inside the dugout, squeezed in, and kept down as another salvo of shells burst on the surface.

"This lad's had enough," Macquarie said as he thrust a hypodermic syringe into Preston's arm. "That will keep him quiet. Shell shock. I'll send him to the hospital in Alex."

The shelling eased off five minutes later as the Germans concentrated on the British armour. Only then did Tulloch realise he had not seen Rutlane during the bombardment.

The Lothians remained in their trenches, with the bolder spirits watching, impotent to help in this contest between armour. When it became evident that the British tanks would not leave their positions for a suicidal charge, the Germans withdrew and moved around the side of the ridge.

"They're trying to outflank us," Muirhead said.

"Watch!" Tulloch said. "If I recall correctly, their map says the ground is level ahead, while ours says there is soft sand."

Muirhead grinned. "I wonder how you know that."

The British anti-tank guns were waiting, hammering the sides of the moving tanks, causing casualties, especially when the soft sand bogged the Germans down.

When evening closed in, the Germans withdrew, leaving twenty-two tanks destroyed or badly damaged, with twenty-one British also out of action.

"We won that round," Tulloch said.

"Only because Rommel made a right haggis of things with his

Panzers," Muirhead said. "He misjudged the depth of our mine-fields in the south, and when they eventually extracted themselves, our tanks and artillery fought them gun to gun, with the gunners causing mayhem when the Germans ran into the soft sand."

Tulloch nodded, glad his expedition to place the doctored map had been useful.

"This fellow Montgomery has stopped Rommel cold," Muirhead said.

"This fellow Montgomery has," Tulloch agreed.

That night, the RAF began bombing again, with Albacores locating concentrations of German tanks and reconnaissance units and Blenheims dropping their bombs. A combination of flares and burning trucks lit up the aircraft's targets.

While the tanks had fought their duel at Alam Halfa, the Italian Bologna Infantry Division, supported by a regiment of German infantry, attacked the New Zealanders, Indians, and South Africans on Ruweisat Ridge. The result was in doubt for a while until a powerful Allied counterattack recaptured any lost ground.

When darkness fell, the Royal Navy and RAF continued the army's attack, bombing the supply convoys that trundled over the harsh desert miles.

"Rommel won't be feeling too confident now," Muirhead said as they watched the distant flashes in the night. "He'll be worried about his fuel. The Royal Navy has already played the cat and banjo with his petrol tankers."

"What do we do?" McGill asked.

"We sit tight," Tulloch replied. "And repel the enemy if their infantry attack."

The Lothians slept fitfully, waiting for an attack that did not happen. The following dawn, the 15th Panzer Division tried a flank attack on the 22nd Armoured Brigade while the 21st Panzer Division sat immobile.

Smith lifted his Boys, eager to become involved, but Tulloch ordered him back to his trench. "A Boys is not much good against a Mark IV Panzer, Smith."

"I could try, sir," Smith offered.

"If you see any halftracks or soft-skinned vehicles," Tulloch relented slightly, "you can fire at them. Leave the tanks for the gunners."

"Yes, sir," Smith agreed reluctantly.

As the 15th Panzers attacked, the 8th Armoured Brigade threw itself at the German flank. The Germans recoiled and returned to their original positions, followed by Allied shelling.

"I feel like an observer," McGill said.

"That's all we've been so far," Tulloch agreed.

The RAF continued their work, strafing and bombing the Axis vehicles, causing casualties and disconcerting the German higher command as they realised Montgomery was a different kind of general.

By late morning on September the 2nd, the Allies could see that Rommel's offensive had stalled. The combination of Allied artillery, hull-down tanks, and the RAF had stopped his armour while the New Zealand, British, and Indian infantry stubbornly held their positions. Unlike in earlier actions, the Axis could not tempt the British armour into suicide charges across open ground.

"He's shot his bolt," Muirhead said. "Rommel will withdraw soon."

As the Axis began to recoil, Montgomery unleashed the 4th Armoured Brigade's armoured cars on their supply lines while the RAF, 7th Armoured Division, and 2nd New Zealand Division attacked Rommel's flanks.

"When do we get a crack at them?" Hogg asked plaintively.

"We'll get our chance, never fear," Tulloch replied. "There is plenty of space in Africa for another battle."

On the night of September 3rd, the New Zealanders assaulted the Italians and Germans. British Valentines lost themselves in the dark, ended up in a minefield, and lost twelve tanks.

Meanwhile, the Germans and Italians repulsed the New Zealanders with heavy losses. The Lothians sat tight, listening to the sounds of distant battle, seeing the flashes across the desert, and wondering if the Germans would attack them next.

Before the furore of the New Zealand attack died away, Rommel withdrew his battered army. He had sent them into Montgomery's trap, had failed to break through, and experienced his first battlefield defeat.

"We never got to fire a shot," Hogg grumbled, rubbing a cloth over the barrel of his rifle.

"You're still alive," Drysdale told him. "Every day you stay alive in a war is a bonus. Shut your mouth and count your blessings."

Tulloch moved on to where Muirhead and Colonel Hume examined the battlefield through their binoculars.

"Hogg's correct," Tulloch said. "Montgomery defeated Rommel in a straight fight, and the Lothians were hardly involved."

Muirhead looked southward. "We were here," he said, "and your patrol was more than useful." He looked sideways at Tulloch.

Colonel Hume puffed smoke into the air. "It feels strange, doesn't it," he said.

"What does, sir?" Tulloch asked.

"Winning a battle without a single Lothian loss." Hume removed the pipe from his mouth. "I'd prefer that to sharing in glory. Take a fifteen hundredweight and see what you can salvage out there, gentlemen. We could always use some new jerrycans."

"Yes, sir."

Lieutenant Kennedy at the motor pool was reluctant to release one of his precious trucks but relented before superior rank.

"Bring it back undamaged, please, sir."

"If we can," Muirhead replied. "No promises. There might be a few stray Germans out there looking for revenge."

They picked up Captain Macquarie on their way down the ridge and roamed across the battlefield, where German tanks and vehicles lay in smouldering ruin. While Macquarie checked the casualties to see if any were still alive, Tulloch and Muirhead searched for anything salvageable. They picked up some jerry cans and a Luger before they found the abandoned German halftrack.

Tulloch stopped, feeling something slide in his stomach. "I'm going to look at this vehicle," he said, disembarking from the truck.

Under a carpet of questing flies, two men lay dead in the back of the halftrack, one decapitated and the other twisted and blackened, with his face contorted in death. An officer slumped in the cab with his body punctured by shrapnel and his mouth and eyes open. The explosion that killed him had ripped his tunic open, and a packet of Victory Vee cigarettes had slid onto his lap, with one cigarette landing at his side. Tulloch looked at the man's face, with the duelling scar vivid across his tanned cheek.

"He must have been looting the British dead," Muirhead said, pointing to the cigarette packet.

"No," Tulloch said. "I don't think so." Reaching forward, he closed the officer's eyes. "Godspeed, Fritz," he said.

"That's very humane of you," Macquarie sounded puzzled, yet there was a light behind his tired eyes.

"He was our enemy," Tulloch said, "yet in most ways, he was no different from us. Only the German regime is evil."

Macquarie touched Tulloch's shoulder. "Welcome to the real world, Douglas," he said quietly. "I can't do anything for these men except ensure they have a decent burial. Drive on, Hood."

"Yes, sir," Hood restarted the engine, and they pushed on across the battle-scarred ground, as the stink of cordite, smoke, raw blood, and scorched human flesh polluted the clean desert air.

Chapter Twenty-Eight

With the smoke from Alam Halfa hardly cleared, Montgomery's Eighth Army began preparing for the next encounter.

"We won the defensive battle," Muirhead said soberly, "but our counter-offensives were less successful. It's one thing to sit tight and hammer at the enemy when they are in the open, but another to winkle and push him out of a defensive position."

"We learned that in the last war," Kilner said, smoothing a hand over his neat, grey moustache. "Our worst losses always came in the major pushes. It wasn't until Haig mastered the art of attacking in 1918 that we won."

Tulloch listened, remembering the stories of the horrendous losses of the Somme, Arras and Passchendaele.

"Monty prevented our armour from their tally-ho hunting tactics," Muirhead said, "and he co-ordinated the Air Force, the Fleet Air Arm and the Army. Let's see how he is in an offensive battle when our armour advances against Rommel's hull-down Panzers and dug-in 88s."

Kilner traced a picture in the sand with his finger. "I am not sure Monty is confident about an offensive battle," he said. "He could have attacked Rommel's army as he withdrew and pushed him right back to Libya. As it stands, Rommel has gained some ground on our southern flank, controls our minefields and holds some ridges from where he overlooks our 13 Corps."

"Let's see what happens next," Tulloch suggested.

After three more days on Alam Halfa Ridge, orders came for the Lothians to leave the front and withdraw behind the lines to train for the next battle.

"Here we go again," Innes said, checking his Bren.

"Bugger this for a game of soldiers," Hogg gave his usual comment.

"Less of that, Hogg," Russell snarled at him. "I'll have no defeatist talk!"

Hogg turned with his mouth open to retaliate, and Tulloch shouted him over. "Hogg! Get my baggage into the fifteen hundredweight." Things had been too busy for Tulloch to think about the dispute between Hogg and Russell. He resolved to soothe troubled waters over the next few days. In the meantime, he had D Company move southeast, away from the front.

The desert was still congested, with military traffic moving in every direction while aircraft patrolled the skies.

"I recognise the signs," Kilner said as they followed their guide into a large camp where rows of neat white tents waited under the sun. "This campaign is reaching a turning point." He looked around. "Maybe it's already reached it."

"What turning point?" Tulloch asked.

"I saw it in April 1918," Kilner said, "when the German March offensive reached its zenith, and we stopped them and slowly pushed them back." He watched his company debus from their trucks. "General Haig gave his famous Backs to the Wall speech, and we fought with rifles, bayonets, boots and finger-nails." He lifted his head and listened to his lieutenants super-vising his men, but his eyes were a quarter of a century and thousands of miles away.

"That was a different war, Alex," Tulloch said.

"Aye," Kilner agreed. "A different war against the same enemy. We should have finished them off then rather than allow them to rebuild."

"Aye," Tulloch agreed. "We would have saved ourselves a lot of trouble."

They settled their companies in, ensured they had sufficient food and water, posted sentries and entered the tent that acted as an officers' mess.

Muirhead lifted a hand in acknowledgement from the cane chair on which he sat. "Join us, Tulloch," he said as Kilner sat beside him. "Tell us what you think of this war."

"It's a continuation of the last," Kilner said. "I was just saying that to Douglas here."

"I think it's a different kind of war," Muirhead said. "Wider spread and more vicious."

"Every war is vicious," Kilner sat with his back bowed and his head down. "Nothing in this war is worse than Ypres or the Somme."

"What do you think, Douglas?" Muirhead asked.

"The actual fighting is as ugly as ever," Tulloch said. "Nobody dies well in battle, and nobody ever has. That won't change. I think we're fighting a great evil here," Tulloch stuffed tobacco into the bowl of his pipe. "I don't know about you, but I believe everything is created for a purpose. We don't know for sure what the purpose is, and probably never will, but I believe the British Empire had three reasons for its existence."

"What were they?" Muirhead asked with mild interest.

"We existed to defeat the evil of Bonaparte, end the evil of the slave trade, and fight the evil of German militarism and fascism. We achieved the first two, and we're in the process of ending the third," Tulloch said. "It all sounds so simple, doesn't it?"

Muirhead ignored Tulloch's question. "What then?" he asked.

"If the Empire has three reasons for existence, what will happen when the reasons no longer exist?"

"Then the Empire will disintegrate," Tulloch said, lighting his pipe. "It will have fulfilled its purpose. Great Britain has worn herself out policing the world, trying to end slavery and piracy, trying to impose civilisation on people who are not yet ready to be civilised and defending what we claim is our territory. It's time to hand the torch to somebody else."

Muirhead nodded. "America, perhaps. They share many of our ideas. And then what?"

Tulloch shrugged, thinking of the dead of all sides that littered the desert. "The next evil is already building, and then will come another, but we will no longer be the mainstay against them."

"Do you think the Americans are ready to accept our mantle?"

"Possibly," Tulloch said and grinned cynically. "It will be their turn to be misunderstood, reviled and ridiculed, even as they strive to maintain a balance in the world and instal democracy and decency."

"And commercial gain and the class system," Kilner said, equally cynical.

"Those too," Tulloch agreed. "I never claimed perfection for anybody."

Kilner nodded. "You did not, Douglas. Nobody, no regime and no system of government is perfect or ever will be." He sighed. "I'm old enough to remember the promises made during the last lot, stuff about building a land fit for heroes and all that rot. Most of my regulars only signed up because they could not get another job." He sighed again, suddenly looking like an old man despite his upright stance and springy step. "I hope we do better after we win this blasted war."

"I hope so, too," Tulloch said.

"I wonder when Monty will decide on the next push," Muirhead puffed at his pipe.

"As soon as he is ready," Tulloch replied. "And we'd better win this one. I am not exaggerating when I say the future of the world is at stake."

Kilner gave the smile of an older man to an enthusiastic youngster. "Very melodramatic, Douglas. We'll win this war. We always come out on top in the wars we have to win."

———

"Kit inspection!" Tulloch called. "D Company! Kit inspection in ten minutes! I want everybody's kit laid out on the sand! Jildi!"

NCOs and men grumbled, swearing at this unwelcome and unwanted intrusion into their day.

"As if it wasnae bad enough fighting the Germans and the bloody flies without the officers making things worse!" a private from Six Platoon growled. "Old Erskine never done anything like this!"

"Old Erskine couldnae care less about our kit," Adamson replied. "Or anything else."

Tulloch ignored the grousing. He knew that Sergeant Drysdale would have Four Platoon up to scratch with all their equipment and uniforms checked, but he was less sure about Lieutenant Rutlane and Sergeant Paterson's Six Platoon.

Tulloch checked each man's kit, taking notes of any deficiencies or losses.

"Your boots need to be replaced, Gordon. Oldham, indent for a new shirt. MacInnes, your bayonet is rusty, and your rifle's a disgrace!"

Tulloch walked the length of both platoons, noting the men's demeanour and equipment. Cattanach was as quiet and efficient as always, with his equipment spotless and his uniform as clean as the conditions permitted.

"All right, Cattanach?"

"Yes, sir," Cattanach replied.

"Have you ever considered a promotion, Cattanach?"

For the first time in Tulloch's experience, Cattanach exhibited nervousness. "No, sir," he replied quickly.

"As you wish," Tulloch nodded and walked on. A reluctant NCO was worse than none, and maybe Cattanach was too quiet to control the sometimes volatile Four Platoon.

"Corporal Russell," Tulloch stopped beside the corporal.

"Sir!" Russell stood at attention with his chin up.

Tulloch opened Russell's kitbag and emptied the contents on the ground. Amongst the usual assortment of spare clothing was a pamphlet advertising one of Oswald Mosley's fascist party meetings in Glasgow.

Tulloch glanced at the pamphlet without comment. He continued his inspection and spoke to his company.

"Not bad at all, children. Those of you who need new equipment, see the Quartermaster; he has the necessary forms. I intend to inspect everybody once a month from now on." He did not add a threat, but he was sure the men understood. "Corporal Russell, report to my tent in half an hour."

When Russell entered his tent, Tulloch asked a direct question.

"Are you a fascist, Russell?"

"I was a member of the British Fascist Party, sir," Russell replied.

"Does that not impede your loyalty when we fight fascist Italy and Germany?" Tulloch held Russell's gaze.

"No, sir," Russell replied immediately. "I am loyal to the King and the Protestant succession."

"How do you feel about shooting fellow fascists?" Tulloch asked.

"They're the king's enemies," Russell said, "and that makes them my enemies."

"How do you feel about Private Hogg of Four Platoon?"

Russell hesitated before he replied. "We don't get along, sir."

"Why not?"

Again, Russell hesitated. "We knew each other before the war, sir."

"I noticed you've had him on charges," Tulloch said. "I hope there was a military reason for them, and you are not harbouring some years-old grudge."

"I am not, sir," Russell said.

Tulloch nodded. "If I find anything different," he said quietly. "I'll break you, Russell. Your corporal's stripes are hanging by a thread at present. I'm watching you and everything you do."

"I've not done anything wrong, sir," Russell protested.

"Keep it that way," Tulloch said shortly. "Dismissed, Corporal."

When Russell left, Tulloch wondered if he had been too hard on the man. He pondered for a moment and called in Sergeant Paterson to ask why Six Platoon still did not have its full quota of kit. He would speak to Rutlane later.

"WE'RE MOVING AGAIN!" THE WORDS SPREAD THROUGH THE battalion. "Further behind the lines."

The Lothians headed south and east to three different camps, with British armour and artillery passing them and Allied infantry marching in endless columns. Eventually, they halted somewhere in the south, with the Qattara Depression only a few miles away and the feeling of enormous space pulling at the men.

"Are you all right, Cattanach?" Tulloch found the private staring southward.

"I love this place, sir," Cattanach said. "I can understand why the Arabs have their philosophy of fatalism. Just accept the desert's judgement."

Tulloch nodded. "You may be right, Cattanach. The desert is a strange place, uniquely evocative, inspiring, yet frightening."

"I don't find it frightening, sir," Cattanach said.

"So I see," Tulloch murmured and continued his inspection of D Company.

Colonel Hume spent hours on the telephone or radio absorbing orders from above and distributing them to his men. D Company grumbled, marched, and camped as Tulloch trained them, trying to fuse both platoons into a single unit. He was satisfied that McGill was a competent officer if lacking in personality, while Rutlane fell beneath his standards.

"You'll have to keep him a bit longer," Hume said with a wry smile. "Officer replacements are hard to find, and he is now an experienced man."

"Yes, sir," Tulloch was not prepared to meekly accept the Colonel's decision. "Are there no young second lieutenants available?"

"No," Hume said. "Try to train him up, Tulloch."

"I will, sir."

Tulloch pushed his lieutenants as hard as he could, teaching them battle tactics and the basics of command. He supervised their platoons, checking everything they did until Muirhead took him aside.

"You'll ruin these lads' confidence," Muirhead said. "Let them make mistakes. That's how we learn. All of us." He grinned. "I know you're new to commanding a company, Douglas, but you must learn to delegate authority. If anything goes badly wrong, the Jocks will soon let you know. Scottish soldiers are not backwards in coming forward when their officers don't come to scratch."

Tulloch nodded and tried to relax as the days eased into weeks and Montgomery's build-up for the Allied attack continued.

"It will soon be time," Muirhead said as they watched a column of new American-built Shermans rumbling past. "These tanks look just the job to face Rommel's Panzers, don't they? Well done, and thank you, Cousin Jonathan."

Tulloch nodded, still thinking of his platoon commanders.

"It's time our tankies faced the Germans on even terms. We've lost far too many good men because of inferior equipment."

That following day, Montgomery ordered the Lothians to move again.

"There's trouble in the wind," Muirhead said. "And that bodes ill for Uncle Rommel and his merry men."

Tulloch nodded. He saw the steel behind Muirhead's smile.

Chapter Twenty-Nine

"What are these?" Hogg asked as they passed a line of trucks covered in canvas tarpaulins with long poles thrusting from the front.

"What do they look like?" Sergeant Drysdale asked.

"Nothing," the unimaginative Hogg replied. "Trucks covered in tarpaulins."

Innes, more inventive and perhaps more intelligent, looked closely. "They're all broken-down or damaged trucks," he said. "No good to anybody."

"Even dead trucks are good for something," Drysdale said, "especially if people don't know they're broken or what they are. Think, lads."

The battalion motored past, kicking up dust that settled on the long line of canvas-covered wrecks.

"Think what you'd see if you were a Luftwaffe pilot," Drysdale hinted.

"From above," Innes said. "These broken vehicles might look like tanks."

Hogg shrugged. "Why would they think that?" He stared at the trucks briefly and shrugged, dismissing the camouflaged vehicles as unimportant.

"A German spotter plane will see rank after rank of what he thinks are tanks and report his observation to higher command," Innes explained. "Eventually, Rommel will hear about them, think Montgomery has hundreds of tanks in the south, and plan his moves accordingly."

"Just the job," Drysdale said. "You might make a half-decent corporal in a few years, Innes, with a lot of work."

Hogg wrestled with the idea of camouflaged trucks. "That's bloody daft," he gave his considered opinion. "The fellae in the plane must be a daftie to think they lorries are tanks."

"That's the idea," Innes said.

"It's bloody daft," Hogg repeated and sat back, satisfied he had made his point and won the argument.

"He's a tricky fellow, is our Monty," Drysdale said, equally satisfied as the Lothians' convoy moved slowly north to their final campground before the Allies launched their long-awaited assault.

"THIS, GENTLEMEN, IS WHERE WE WILL FIGHT AND DEFEAT Rommel and send the Axis army spinning out of Egypt." The smiling intelligence major introduced the Lothians' officers to a sand model of Montgomery's proposed El Alamein battlefield, with the features carefully modelled.

Tulloch viewed the sand model as the major described what every unit of Montgomery's army would do and how the enemy would react. After a few moments, Muirhead lifted a hand.

"This is all very interesting, sir, but you haven't mentioned where we fit in."

The major grinned. "For the purpose of the next exercise, Captain, the Lothians are the German 90th Light Infantry."

"My boys won't like that," Tulloch thought of Hogg's reaction at being told he was a German.

Colonel Hume smiled. "The 51st Div will like it even less when we repulse them," he said.

With the idea in their head, the battalion joined the 51st Highland Division in a training area where they fought the battle in practice. They held the German line and showed the inexperienced Highlanders some of the tricks of the trade. They advanced over similar ground against mock defences that intelligence patrols and RAF reconnaissance flights had identified. After a fortnight's hard training, the Lothians and the Highlanders knew the contours of the area where the 51st would fight.

"If we're not fighting, sir," Muirhead asked as the officers assembled after a long night exercise, "what will we be doing?"

"We're not taking part in the initial assault," Hume told the officers. "Yet we have an important part to play."

The officers listened, taking notes, glad to be involved in any capacity.

"We are temporarily attached to the 51st Highland Division," Hume said, "while the powers-that-be decide where best to put us. As you know, 51 Div. are to make the initial assault and break-through on Rommel's defences, along with the 9th Australian, the New Zealanders and the 1st South Africans. I tried to persuade General Wimberley, the Highlanders' divisional commander, to bring us into their fold, but he refused. He wants an all-Highland show, and we are Lowlanders and therefore anathema to their pure Teuchter blood." Hume waited for the self-deprecating laughter.

"However, General Wimberley graciously consented to us helping in the preliminaries, probably because we have much experience in the desert. The Highland Division is on the front line, with four thousand yards of desert in front of them, and then there are the German minefields and the Germans themselves. There are no wadis, ridges or undulations, only flat, featureless desert."

The officers nodded. Tulloch pictured a raw infantry division, thousands of men unused to the desert or battle, preparing to advance against veteran troops in prepared positions commanded by the best general the enemy had produced.

"Monty has decided to attack at night," Colonel Hume continued. "Which is very sensible of him. Together with the 5th Seaforths, our task is to mark the position of the 51st start line, or the men will be milling around, falling over each other and marching in the wrong direction. They have no landmarks to guide them, remember."

The officers nodded, remembering how confused they were when they first encountered desert navigation.

"When we have laid white tape for the start line a thousand yards in front of the division's position, we will tape routes for four of the nine battalions while 5th Seaforths tape the rest."

Tulloch knew they could not lay the tape too soon before the advance. A sharp-eyed German patrol could find it, and the British would lose any surprise. On the other hand, if they began taping the night of the attack, a delay would hamper the advancing Highlanders, who would have to move after the sun rose. A daylight attack against strongly held Axis positions would be virtual suicide.

"It's all about timing," Colonel Hume told them, holding his smoking pipe in his hand. "Our part in this battle is neither glamorous nor glorious, but it is vital." He nodded to Tulloch. "I'm giving the tape laying task to D Company. C Company will act as a screen out in the desert to ensure no nosey Germans intervene, and Kilner is in reserve with B Company."

Tulloch glanced at Kilner and Muirhead, who nodded to him.

"Muirhead," Hume said. "If the enemy comes, I don't want any returning to their lines. Rommel cannot learn what we are doing here."

Muirhead lifted a finger. "Yes, sir. My boys will do their job."

"Good," Hume said. "Kilner, be ready to help Muirhead."

"Yes, sir," the laconic Kilner said.

"Tulloch, your men must ignore everything else and accurately lay the cables and tapes. Precision is everything," Hume held Tulloch's gaze for a long moment. "Are there any questions?"

"No, sir," the officers replied in unison.

"Good. I knew I could rely on you. The success of the entire operation depends on your work." Hume's smile could not disguise the strain he was under. "Good luck, gentlemen."

WITH MUIRHEAD'S C COMPANY FIVE HUNDRED YARDS further out in no man's land, Tulloch led D Company to ascertain the beginning and end of the Start Line. In a flat plain with no natural features, he sent Lieutenants McGill, Rutlane, and Sergeant Drysdale to fixed points behind the British lines and had them march slowly on compass bearings until their courses combined.

"This is the first Start Line, gentlemen," Tulloch decided and placed a metal stake in the ground. "This is the southernmost point from where the Highland Division's offensive will begin."

A burst of machine gun fire interrupted them, and they froze, searching for the source. When nothing came close, they continued, talking in subdued whispers.

They walked along the 51st Division's front and ascertained the other end of the Start Line, and Sergeant Drysdale supervised Innes and Smith in unrolling a drum of signal cable between the two points. A scimitar moon provided light, augmented by a host of stars, the natural beauty contrasting with the ugliness that would unfold on this nondescript patch of the Western Desert.

"That's a good start," Tulloch said. He heard another outbreak of firing and saw muzzle flares a few hundred yards out in the desert. The steady thump of a Bren punctuated the irregular crack of rifles and crazed chatter of a German MG 34.

"C Company is having a duffy," Hogg said, staring over the

desert. They saw the muzzle flares of rifles and heard the crump of a grenade.

"They can take care of themselves," Tulloch said. "We have a job to do here."

D Company laboured in the moonlit night, throwing an occasional anxious glance to the westward where the firefight continued, punctuated by an occasional barked order and a single pitiful scream. They froze as a Very Light soared upwards from No man's land, bright above D Company. The working party tried to make themselves invisible against the stark background.

"That could be a recall signal for the German patrol, sir," Drysdale said quietly.

"Maybe," Tulloch checked his men. They lay on the ground or stood still. McGill was placing a picket in the harsh ground, keeping his face down so the Very Light did not reflect from his white skin. Hogg was glaring toward the German lines as if the force of his dislike could alter the course of the war. Cattanach was holding a picket, waiting for the order to continue. Russell was crouching down, staring at the ground.

Where's Rutlane?

Tulloch ran his gaze over the men, naming them one by one, until he saw Rutlane lying with his face to the ground. He took a deep breath. *He's doing nothing wrong. It's a sensible precaution in the circumstances.*

When the Very Light faded and dropped, Tulloch gave a quiet order. "Back to work, men!"

The Bren fired again, with its regular beat a reminder of a desperate struggle only a few hundred yards away. Stray bullets whined overhead, with one cutting a furrow in the sand near Tulloch's feet.

A hoarse voice sounded from the west, a man shouting in German. The firing continued, died away and erupted again.

"C Company's having a real duffy," Hogg sounded jealous.

"Get on with your work, Hogg!" Sergeant Drysdale snarled.

267

Trying to ignore the nearby skirmish, D Company continued their work, attaching metal pickets to the signal cable every fifty yards. One man swore when the cable looped around his thumb, drawing blood.

"That'll fester," Drysdale said. "Cover it up before the flies get in."

When Corporal Borthwick drove in the last picket, the firing died away, and the men of D Company stared westward, wondering what had happened.

"Somebody's coming, sir," Hogg warned.

Tulloch saw the men emerge from the west a moment later as a corporal led a three-man patrol back. "Captain Tulloch? I'm looking for Captain Tulloch!"

"That's me, Corporal," Tulloch stepped forward.

"Captain Muirhead sends his compliments, sir, and he wants to know how long you will be."

"Tell Captain Muirhead we've completed our task for tonight."

"Thank you, sir," the corporal saluted, disappearing into the dark.

Muirhead appeared ten minutes later with his company marching in extended order.

"All right, Tulloch?"

"All right, Muirhead," Tulloch replied. "Did you meet some trouble?"

"A German patrol," Muirhead said grimly. "They won't be reporting to Uncle Rommel." He paused for a second. "None of them."

Tulloch noted the stern satisfaction of C Company as they returned. He knew they would never talk about their actions that night. The stretcher-bearers carried one dead man and two wounded back, one seriously injured.

"Thank you for the cover, Muirhead," Tulloch said.

On the second night, Colonel Hume had B Company as the screen and C Company in reserve as Tulloch's men ran cables from the start lines back to the regiments that would be advancing. The work was nerve-wracking because it had to be as accurate as the initial Start Line, and Tulloch paced each route before he was satisfied.

D Company sat on the desert gravel when they finished, with few of them realising their part in making history. They had done their duty and only wanted a quiet fag, a brew and a few hours' kip.

"That was a quieter night," Kilner said as he ushered B Company back to the British positions just as dawn broke. "No German patrols to interrupt us. Are we all ready for the push?"

"As ready as we can be," Tulloch found he was shaking with nervous strain. He filled his pipe with trembling fingers and drew on the tobacco. "We'll put in the finishing touches a couple of hours before the assault begins."

"No, we won't," Colonel Hume contradicted. "Each regiment in 51 Div will fix tape to their cables this evening so they learn the routes. We've done our part, Tulloch."

"Yes, sir," Tulloch did not argue. After two consecutive nights working in No man's land, he only wanted to sleep. Montgomery and Rommel could have all the guts and glory as long as they left him alone.

Chapter Thirty

EL ALAMEIN LINE, EGYPT, OCTOBER 1942

The two armies held their breaths, aware that another major battle was imminent. Men checked their weapons, wrote letters home and prayed to be spared from death or mutilation as they guarded a front that extended from the Mediterranean Sea in the north to the Qattara Depression, forty miles in the south.

"We attack and push them back, then they counter and push us back," Tulloch repeated his mantra. "When either of us reaches the limit of our supply lines, the attack falters. This time, Rommel's attack has run out of steam, and now it's our turn."

"Yes, sir," McGill agreed.

"The same old story, except this time, we have Montgomery," Tulloch said. He looked across the defences of minefields, barbed wire and booby traps, where burned-out tanks and soft-bodied vehicles marked previous encounters. "This time, we can't afford to stop. We must win."

"What are we facing, sir?" McGill asked.

"Our Intelligence reports Rommel has around 430,000 anti-tank mines and 15,000 anti-personnel mines, laid in two main belts with lesser fields to force our armour into killing fields or dead ends."

McGill nodded. "Rommel's more concerned with our tanks than our infantry then, sir."

"This open desert is perfect for armoured warfare," Tulloch said. "The tanks can manoeuvre like ships at sea."

"Yes, sir," McGill agreed again. "How wide are the enemy minefields?"

Tulloch had the figures at the front of his mind. "We estimate six thousand yards, with the inner belt around a mile deep, with German and Italian armour, artillery and infantry waiting behind."

"Has anybody ever defeated Rommel, sir?"

"Auchinleck fought him to a draw at El Alamein a few months ago, but the Auk's counterattacks made no headway. Monty stopped his advance at Alam Halfa and frustrated his advance," Tulloch said. "Nobody has ever defeated Rommel in an offensive battle." He paused. "Yet."

McGill took a deep breath. "Do you think we'll beat him this time, sir?"

Tulloch looked westward, where the enemy waited behind their minefields and barbed wire. "Yes," he replied. "We'll beat him this time."

"Lieutenant Rutlane doesn't believe so, sir," McGill said.

"What do you believe, McGill?" Tulloch asked.

McGill was quiet for a moment. "I think Monty will smash Rommel, sir," he said.

"Good man," Tulloch replied. "Now go to your platoon and ensure our men are ready for whatever tomorrow brings."

Tulloch wrote to Amanda that afternoon.

"23rd October 1942.

My Dear Amanda,

We are waiting for the battle to begin. I cannot give the name and place, but it may be the largest and most crucial battle

271

of my war so far. With Monty opposed to Rommel, the two desert gladiators and their armies are prepared for battle.

The Battalion is ready to fight, fully recovered from the previous actions, and better trained than ever before. My company—and even writing *my company* seems strange—is quiet, with the men fully aware of what may occur.

If I survive these next few days, Amanda, I have something to ask you. We have not spent much time together, but you have become central to my life. I am sure you know what I intend to ask!

Until we meet, take care of yourself and always remember that I am thinking of you when we go forward.

I am always your loving

Douglas."

Tulloch reread the letter, hoping he had conveyed his message to prepare Amanda for his intentions without putting too much pressure on her. He smiled, decided she would understand, folded the notepaper into an envelope and carefully wrote her address across the front. He considered writing SWALK across the back, shook his head because Amanda would not appreciate the gesture and placed the letter with the mail.

"Is that to your girl?" Muirhead asked.

"It is," Tulloch said.

Muirhead smiled. "I wrote to Barbara as well. I kept it bright and cheerful, although I can't see beyond the next twenty-four hours."

"I am the same," Tulloch said. "She'll understand."

"Women do, don't they?" Muirhead replied. "Have you heard Wimberley's orders for the Highland Division?"

"I have not," Tulloch replied.

"He has given written orders saying there will be no surrender for unwounded men. I quote his standing orders: 'Any troops of the Highland Division cut off will continue to fight.'"

"St Valery haunts the 51st," Tulloch said. The original 51st Highland Division had fought in France in 1940, and after a stubborn withdrawal, a German Panzer Division had forced the survivors to surrender at St Valery. A rising star named Erwin Rommel led the Germans that black day. The War Office renumbered the 9th Scottish Division as the 51st and trained them for battle. Unblooded and eager, they waited for their first action in the war, again facing Rommel.

"Aye, well," Muirhead said. "El Alamein is no St Valery, and the 51st will not be surrendering this battle."

Colonel Hume stepped behind them. "Check your watches, gentlemen. Zero hour is set for 21:40 tonight."

Tulloch and Muirhead looked at each other, with Tulloch feeling a familiar tightening in his stomach.

"We're in reserve," Hume reminded. "All we have to do is sit and wait for orders." He removed his empty pipe from his pocket and thrust it between his teeth. "Monty's reattached us to 50 Div, so if they go into action, so do we."

"I don't like being an observer when other men go into danger, sir," Tulloch said.

"We obey orders," Hume replied with a wry smile. "Anything else is bellyaching." He stepped away. "Our turn will come, Tulloch."

The day passed slowly and quietly, with the Lothians behind the 51st Division waiting for transport to take them to the Northumbrians. The line was mainly silent, with just an occasional burst of machine gun fire to remind Tulloch of the tens of thousands of men waiting to kill each other.

As the afternoon eased into a warm evening, the hands of Tulloch's watch crept slowly onwards, with every second increasing the tension. At nine-forty that evening, a single gun fired one round. The lines had been quiet until then, with an occasional Very light brightening the sky and the chatter of heavy machine guns as nervous men fired at shadows. Then silence, hanging heavy over the heads of waiting men. When somebody coughed, his comrades started and berated him. Somebody gave a nervous giggle.

"The world is waiting," McGill said, lighting a cigarette. He puffed out smoke and misquoted Shakespeare.

"And gentlemen in Scotland now abed,
Shall think themselves accursed they were not
    here,
And hold their manhoods cheap while any speaks
That fought with us upon Egyptian sands."

That single artillery round signalled the start of the battle. As McGill finished his quote, the British artillery opened fire, with the heaviest bombardment of the African war so far. Tulloch took a deep breath, turned in his trench, and looked back towards the British lines. The entire horizon turned pink amidst a silence he could have cut into chunks, and then the noise arrived.

The entire force of the Eighth Army's artillery fired with a sound so deafening that nobody could talk or think. The earth beneath the Lothians' feet shook, so men looked at each other in wonder. The noise was louder than anything Tulloch had heard before as over eight hundred guns fired in discordant unison, with the shells arcing over the Allied infantry as they checked their watches and waited for the orders to send them off.

"Monty is saying good evening," Drysdale mouthed.

"God help the poor buggers under that lot!" Innes replied.

Hogg lifted his rifle as if he wanted to advance with the Highlanders until Corporal Borthwick put a restraining hand on his arm.

"Steady Hoggie," he mouthed.

"I'm steady," Hogg replied.

The guns eased slightly, with the shells passing overhead in a constant whine and exploding on the enemy positions in white and red flashes that illuminated the rising smoke and dust. Each muzzle flare illuminated the surrounding area, allowing the observers to witness the stark images of the artillery, the sweating, toiling gunners, and the discarded empty green ammunition boxes.

The Highlanders left their positions and moved forward, rank after rank of khaki-clad men advancing with levelled bayonets.

After a few moments, Tulloch heard the murderous clatter of the machine guns, Allied and Axis, and then the hair-raising wail of Highland bagpipes.

"That's the 51st Division going in," Muirhead said.

Tulloch watched as the Highlanders advanced to battle. They marched behind the skirling pipes, lines of steel-helmeted men from Dornoch and Dundee, Gairloch and Glasgow, Auchiltibuie and Aberdeen. They carried their rifles at the high port, moonlight reflecting from the long eighteen-inch bayonets and their boots thumping hollowly on the hard, dry sand.

The regiments sounded like a roll call of honour and bravery: the Cameron Highlanders, the Seaforth Highlanders, the Black Watch, the Gordon Highlanders, the Argyll and Sutherland Highlanders. Tulloch remembered his youth when he admired the old picture of the Sutherland Highlanders—the Thin Red Line—facing the Russian cavalry at Balaclava and how he had wanted to join that regiment. Now they were marching past him, marching to a different enemy and rather than General Colin Campbell in command, they had Major-General Wimberley and Lieutenant-General Bernard Montgomery.

"God be with you, lads," Tulloch murmured as the Highlanders marched into the night, facing the Axis guns. "*Slàinte na Gaidheal*; here's to the Highlanders!"

The Lothians watched and listened, with some praying and many thanking their God that they were not advancing.

"When are we going forward, sir?" Innes asked.

"When Monty sends us," Tulloch replied as 51 Div marched forward into the hell of a creeping barrage, minefields, barbed wire and enemy tanks. "When Monty sends us."

Chapter Thirty-One

The Lothians waited as reports came in from the battlefield. The veteran Australians in the north made steady progress, with the unblooded Highlanders not far behind. They pushed forward into the Axis massive minefield, struggling to clear a path for the armour.

"When are the tanks forcing through?" McGill asked.

"They seem reluctant to face the anti-tank mines and the German 88s," Tulloch replied.

The British artillery barrage continued, with the gunners so deafened by the sound of their guns they could not hear the noise they made. The gunners fired for an hour, red-eyed with fatigue, sand coated over their sweat, then stopped for ten minutes to allow their gun barrels to cool. In that interval, an officer inspected the gun for faults and signalled when the bombardment was to recommence.

The Highlanders took casualties as the enemy fired artillery, mortars, machine guns and rifles. Piper Duncan McIntyre died leading his company of the 5th Black Watch, killed by a mortar bomb, still playing the pipes.

"The ghosts of the old warriors will honour them," Tulloch said softly when the reports came in.

The 7th Argylls lost men to booby traps and anti-personnel mines in the first part of the advance and to artillery in the second. They continued to their objective, finding that not all Italians fought honourably as some feigned surrender and then threw grenades. The Argylls resorted to their bayonets and cleared the way over a carpet of enemy dead and prisoners. Sergeant Bauld captured enemy machine-gun nests while Major Lindsay Macdougall of Lunga used a megaphone so his men could hear him through the hellish din of battle.

As the advance progressed, the Lothians moved south of the Ruweisat Ridge to rejoin the 50th Division, with the men grousing.

"Why can't we go in with the 51st?" Hogg asked.

"Because we're attached to the 50th," Sergeant Drysdale replied. "Now shut your mouth and get on the bus."

D Company filed on board, unsure what was happening as they drove south, away from the main battle.

"Don't they like us anymore?" Smith asked.

"The longer we're out of the battle, the more chance we have to survive," Elliot reminded them.

"There is that," Smith agreed and closed his mouth as the truck moved off, sucking dust into its interior.

As they drove into Fifty Division's camp, Tulloch watched the familiar landscape roll past.

"What now, sir?" Hood asked as he pulled up the handbrake.

"Now we wait," Muirhead said.

"Yes, sir," Hood said and closed his eyes. He was asleep in seconds, much to Tulloch's envy.

The reports continued to reach the Lothians as the 1st Armoured Division edged into the open to face the 15th Panzer Division in circling, murderous combat. In the south, the New Zealanders were methodically eradicating the enemy strongpoints.

"Montgomery calls that his crumbling attack," Kilner told them. "Eating away at the enemy piece by piece."

"We're winning," Muirhead said, "but very slowly and at great cost."

"We're winning," Tulloch repeated. "How many men have said that when facing Rommel."

"We're losing men," Muirhead said. "The Australians and Highlanders in particular." He sighed. "This is turning into a war of attrition, like the last war."

"We won that one," Tulloch reminded.

"At terrible cost," Muirhead said. "I don't think we ever recovered from that Pyrrhic victory."

Tulloch did not argue. He remembered the horrific number of names inscribed on war memorials in every town and village in Scotland and the widows and mothers who still grieved for their menfolk.

"Aye," he said, and they both understood the significance of that single word.

Time passed slowly for the Lothians as they listened to the thunder of artillery and the machine guns' murderous chatter. The officers read the situation reports with worried eyes as the men saw the stream of ambulances pass them and wondered when their turn would come. Hogg cleaned his rifle, sharpened his bayonet, and growled to himself. Cattanach read *Sherlock Holmes*, and Hood slept away his time off duty.

"Bloody tanks are scared to fight," some wounded infantrymen reported. "We're doing all the work."

Remembering the incredible bravery of the British armour in earlier battles, Tulloch doubted the accuracy of the reports. He kept his company posted about events on the front line and wrote to Amanda and his parents. When the mail arrived, Tulloch had two letters, both from his mother. He hid his disappointment and did his duty, ensuring Hogg and Russell did not clash, and continued to train D Company.

"The advance has stalled temporarily," Kilner reported.

"We've pushed Rommel back, inflicted casualties and damaged him, but without making a decisive breakthrough."

"Monty hasn't finished yet," Muirhead replied. "He's retaining the initiative and keeping Rommel on the hop. I hope he's following a plan and not just probing in the hope of breaking through."

"Here's the colonel now," Tulloch said. "He looks tense."

"We're moving, gentlemen," Colonel Hume told the officers. "We've sat in reserve long enough, and now Fifty Div is going into action."

The officers nodded as the anticipation heightened. "Including us, sir?" Tulloch asked.

"Including us, Tulloch," the colonel confirmed. "You can tell your batman to stop glowering at me whenever I pass. He'll get his fill of fighting."

"I'll tell him, sir," Tulloch said.

"General Montgomery has named it Operation Supercharge," Hume said. "We're going to smash through the enemy line in the north," his grin was slightly twisted. "It's about thirty miles from where we are now."

AT DUSK ON THE 28ᵀᴴ OF OCTOBER, THE LOTHIANS ASSEMBLED, with the news spreading of their imminent departure for the battle. They were quiet, remembering their previous actions and aware of the horrors ahead. As a company commander, Tulloch found himself more detached from the men than usual and strove to gauge the mood of his company while trying to avoid favouritism for Four Platoon.

"They're ready for it, sir," McGill reported. "They trust you."

"I think they'll fight, sir," Rutlane said. "I haven't heard anybody talking about desertions."

Tulloch called D Company together and told them as much as he knew of the current situation.

"Feed the men," Colonel Hume ordered quietly. "Section by section."

Tulloch tried to listen as the men gathered, hearing the usual mixture of grumbles and advice.

"You watch my back, Hoggie, and I'll watch yours," Innes said.

"I always watch your back," Hogg grunted, examining his bayonet.

"If I get kilt, Smithie," Hood said, "take my kit, and I'll do the same for you."

"You're no' getting my kit, Craw," Smith replied.

That was the first time Tulloch had heard Hood's nickname and surmised it came from the Hoodie Crow. He was surprised the mainly town-bred Lothians had picked an essentially country name for one of their own. After serving with the battalion for years, the men could still surprise him.

"Make sure you carry your full quota of ammunition," Tulloch shouted. "Two grenades each and a spare mag for the Brens." He watched the NCOs checking the men, ensuring they carried all their equipment.

At one the following morning, Colonel Hume gave the order to embus as a long convoy of trucks rolled up for 50 Div.

"Here we go again, sir," Hogg said.

"All aboard, who's going aboard!" Sergeant Drysdale shouted. "That means everybody, Elliot, including you!"

"I'm coming," Elliot said. "Dinnae rush me, Sergeant."

"I'll do more than rush you, Elliot, you idle bugger! Get fell in!"

The convoy drove slowly from the centre to the northern end of the Alamein line. Used to night driving with dimmed headlights, Tulloch was surprised that lights marked the route.

"The Luftwaffe will love that," Tulloch said. "We may as well send them a postcard telling them where we are."

"Since Monty came over, the RAF seems to be in the ascendancy," Muirhead said. "Monty has got the Desert Air Force and the army working together. Before Monty, we fought separate wars. Now we work together, and the RAF gives us close support."

Tulloch grunted cynically. "Maybe aye and maybe no," he said, "but I still don't think we should advertise where we are to the Luftwaffe."

The convoy reached the coast at three in the morning and eased into the camp. They were two hundred yards from the railway line, with the surf crashing silver in the distance.

"What happens now?" McGill asked.

"Now we wait for orders," Tulloch replied. "And you ensure Four Platoon is fed and watered. Put out sentries in case Rommel tries a seaborne raid."

"Yes, sir," McGill said.

They slept on the soft sand and waited all the next day, with the men taking turns bathing in the sea, although most were too tense to enjoy the water. Tulloch watched the healthy bodies, nut-brown except for the white areas that shorts had covered, and thought how innocent and vulnerable they looked.

"Not knowing what will happen next is worse than fighting," Muirhead strolled over to Tulloch, his feet sinking ankle-deep in the sand.

"It's as bad," Tulloch agreed.

"This would make a wonderful beach for donkey rides and candy floss in peacetime," Muirhead remarked.

"I'll pass your suggestion on to the Egyptian government," Tulloch said.

Muirhead laughed. "How do you find D Company?"

"Subdued." Tulloch knew that was the real point of Muirhead's casual visit.

"Will they fight?" Muirhead's eyes were suddenly incisive.

Tulloch was silent for a moment. "I hope they do," he said. "Four Platoon will."

"And Six Platoon?" Muirhead retained his penetrating gaze.

"Ask me in a few days," Tulloch replied.

Muirhead nodded. "Aye. We'll know a lot in a few days. Here's your batman coming now, Tulloch, with his usual happy smile."

Hogg approached Tulloch, scowling. "There's a message from the colonel for you, sir. You've to report to Brigade HQ." He glanced at Muirhead. "All the company commanders, Mr Muirhead, sir, so your batman will tell you soon."

"Thank you, Hogg," Tulloch said as Muirhead gave Hogg a searching nod. "Maybe we'll know now, Muirhead."

"Maybe," Muirhead said softly.

————

COLONEL HUME CLENCHED HIS PIPE FIRMLY BETWEEN HIS teeth as General Freyberg addressed the Lothians and Highland Division officers. Lieutenant General Bernard Freyberg, VC, DSO and bars, was a veteran of Gallipoli and France in the First World War and Greece and Crete in the present war. Now, Freyberg commanded the New Zealand Expeditionary Force and was the officer commanding Operation Supercharge.

"Good morning, gentlemen," General Freyberg greeted them with a pleasant smile. He touched his neat moustache and pointed to a map of the battlefield that stood on the easel behind him. "This is the situation as it stands. We have given the enemy such a heavy battering for the past seven days that they are reeling. We have inflicted severe losses on their infantry, armour and artillery and pushed for miles through their defences."

The officers nodded as Freyberg confirmed what they already guessed.

"General Montgomery thinks that one more heavy assault, Operation Supercharge, will break through and finish the battle." Freyberg shifted his pointer to the west.

Tulloch studied the map, wondering if the neat arrows and lines resembled the reality on the ground. Everything was tidy in the intelligence department, far removed from the blood, guts, and fear in the Blue.

"The attack will consist of a brigade from the 51st Highland Div, the Lothians' battalion, a brigade of the Durham Light Infantry and a battalion of Maoris." Freyberg waited for comments before he continued. "In the North African campaign, we and the enemy have used the armour to hammer a gap and followed up with supporting infantry. Montgomery is working in reverse, with the infantry making the initial assault."

Tulloch remembered the wounded men's comments about the armour and wondered if Montgomery had played to his strengths or merely concealed his weaknesses.

General Freyberg continued. "As soon as the infantry punch a hole in Rommel's defences, the 8th and 9th Armoured Brigade, the 1st Armoured Division and X Corps will pass through and cry havoc in the Axis rear. The enemy will either surrender or run."

"The Germans won't surrender," Rutlane murmured as Muirhead glanced at Tulloch.

"I agree with Rutlane," Muirhead said. "The Germans are not likely to surrender en masse or panic and run."

Freyberg stood back. "That's the basic outline, gentlemen. Your battalion commanders will be given more detailed instructions later. For now, remember you will be involved in making history."

"I don't want to make history," Rutlane said as he returned to Six Platoon. "I only want to survive."

"Try to do both," McGill recommended. "And thank God we have Monty in charge and not Ritchie."

The preparations for a major assault continued. The food and water rations increased, much to the men's delight. Used to living on two pints of water a day, they found that four pints were an unexpected luxury, while a delivery of tinned pineapples was nearly unheard of in the desert.

"The last meal of condemned men," McGill said with a wry smile.

"Don't look a gift horse in the mouth," Tulloch advised. "Ensure the men eat to keep their strength up."

As the Lothians enjoyed the army's pampering, further treats arrived, including fresh kit for men who had lost theirs during the last few months. More ammunition arrived, spare barrels for the Bren guns, and an unlimited supply of grenades. There was even a box of anti-tank grenades. The men were more interested in the Thompson submachine guns, which the NCOs tested, and some immediately claimed for themselves.

Drysdale returned to Four Platoon with his Tommy gun. "It's heavy, but it increases the platoon's firepower," he claimed and spent the next two hours on the range, trying out his new toy.

Macquarie toured the men, treating desert sores and Gyppy Tummy as he ensured maximum fitness for the ordeal ahead. The RSM spoke to the NCOs and zeroed every weapon, frowning at the Thompson guns, which he treated with the suspicion of an old soldier of any innovation. In the meantime, Tulloch fretted over his men, hoping his two platoons could merge into a single unit when they went into action.

He took them on route marches, parades and exercises, attempting to fuse them, but they still appeared as two separate entities.

"Give it time," Kilner, old and vastly experienced, advised. "Six Platoon is not used to you yet."

"We might not have much time," Tulloch said, "and I don't want to go into action with a disunified company."

"Action will pull them together," Kilner said. "I've seen it before."

In the afternoon of the 30th of October, Colonel Hume sent Muirhead's C Company ahead with the advance parties of the DLI, Highlanders and Maoris. The men left cheerfully, the trucks kicking up dust that settled on the rest of the battalion. Tulloch watched with some envy at the ease with which Muirhead managed his men.

"Whatever is happening," Kilner said, "it's going to be big. Bigger than Gazala or anything we did under O'Connor."

Tulloch nodded. "Montgomery has altered the war," he said. "We're more organised now."

"Are you glad to be part of it?" Kilner asked.

"Glad and apprehensive," Tulloch admitted.

Kilner looked over his B Company. "Aye," he said. "Both. These big pushes always create big casualty lists."

"Exactly so," Tulloch agreed.

Once again, Freyberg called all company commanders and above into his tent and skimmed a wooden pointer over his neat plan of the impending Supercharge battle.

"Thirteen field artillery regiments will support the infantry," he said, "together with three medium artillery regiments. We will attack on a four-thousand-yard front, with our objective the Rahman Track." Freyberg cracked his pointer onto the plan. "The track extends southwards from the sea to the Qattara Depression. You'll know it by the line of telegraph poles unless the artillery knocks them down."

When Freyberg stopped, hoping the officers would laugh at his attempt at humour, the silence reminded him that there was nothing humorous about a battle.

"Our immediate enemy is the German 90th Light Division, who we know well."

Again, nobody smiled or laughed. The Lothians remembered the skill and professionalism of the 90th Light Division.

"We will advance behind a creeping barrage which will keep the enemy under cover until we reach them, making our job much easier. Be careful not to advance too far into the barrage. That advice goes particularly for the less experienced officers and those who command men unused to battle."

The veteran officers nodded acknowledgement while the less experienced took hurried notes.

Freyberg continued. "The barrage will lift twenty-two times to allow the infantry to catch up. By that time, we will be halfway into the advance, and at this point," Freyberg pointed to a figure seven on the map, "the figure seven indicates a line of seven enemy tanks or 88s. When we reach these guns, we will shift our attack northward, and the covering barrage will begin again."

"Will the barrage concentrate on the guns, sir?" Kilner asked.

"It will do," Freyberg assured them.

Tulloch looked at Muirhead, who raised his eyebrows.

"This is the real thing," Muirhead said quietly as they left the meeting. "Higher Command is bleeding us information piece by piece, but Monty is determined to win this battle. Where the Auk gave half-hearted attacks, Monty is pushing everything into his offensive."

"We haven't been involved in a major offensive since O'Connor's attacks or Keren last year," Tulloch said. "I hope we haven't forgotten what to do."

Muirhead's smile lacked humour. "I think this attack will be like nothing we've been in before," he said. "Montgomery has a professional ruthlessness I've never seen before." He took a deep breath. "8th Army has a new confidence as well. The next few days, weeks and months will be interesting."

Chapter Thirty-Two

On the night of the 30th of October, the Lothians moved again, a long convoy of trucks snaking towards the front. The men sat in contemplative silence as the vehicles lurched over the rutted surface, now fully aware they were going into battle. Many smoked the army issue cigarettes, others stared into space or tried to sleep. A few scribbled a final note to dimly remembered loved ones in far-off Scotland. Cattanach and Hogg slept, with Hogg's hands curled around his rifle.

It was not a peaceful night as the convoy passed through artillery positions, with the guns firing almost continually.

"What's happening, sir? Why are the guns firing?" Hood asked.

"The Aussies are putting in an attack," Tulloch said. "The artillery is supporting them."

"It'll be our turn soon, sir," Hood sounded serious.

"Very soon," Tulloch agreed.

Hood grunted and watched the muzzle flare as a nearby

battery of heavy guns fired a salvo. The gunners had stripped to the waist despite the chill of the desert night.

As the road became congested, the Lothians halted between two busy artillery batteries, with the truck engines idling and the men watching the gunners at work.

"We're moving again," Colonel Hume shouted above the head-splitting cracks of the artillery. "Leave the trucks behind, men. We're marching from this point."

"Just what I need, a night march across a freezing bloody desert," Elliot grumbled.

"You need the exercise, Elliot," Sergeant Drysdale said. "You're getting fat."

"It's all this rich food, Sergeant," Elliot replied. "I had pineapples twice this last three years."

"Come on, D Company," Tulloch encouraged.

The men marched on through the dark, with efficient Military Policemen guiding them and the flash and bark of the guns a constant companion.

After another stumbling ninety minutes, they arrived at their destination. A Highland NCO in a dark green kilt directed them.

"Here you are, Lothians," he said, waving his right arm. Bandages swathed his left arm. "Our old position. We even dug slit trenches for you." He grinned. "Make yourselves comfortable!"

Tulloch looked around. The Lothians were only one unit in an area crowded with an army preparing for another push. Trucks waited in serried ranks, some under camouflaged covers, others in the open. There were guns, from twenty-five-pounders firing forward to six-pounder anti-tank guns limbered for an advance. Tanks of various types looked as ugly and evil as ever as they pointed their barrels towards the west. Everywhere between, uniformed men marched or walked, from harassed staff officers with clipboards to signallers with rolls of wire and immaculate Military Policemen striving to keep order.

"Right, platoon commanders," Tulloch ordered. "Get your men settled in." He had to shout above the noise of artillery, engines and men's voices.

D Company found themselves trenches and dugouts, erected tents, grumbled, ate their rations and watched the rapid build-up around them.

"Monty doesn't do things by half," McGill said.

Tulloch nodded. There was hardly space for another man in the assembly area. A lone German aircraft flew over and dropped a single bomb, which landed square on the HQ truck of the 8th Durhams, blowing it up and killing the adjutant.

"Rommel's no' deid yet," Hogg said.

"No, he's not," Innes replied. "But he only sent one plane. A few months ago, he'd have sent half the Luftwaffe and bombed us to hell."

Hogg grunted, unwilling to admit Innes was correct yet equally unable to find an adequate response. "Aye, right," he said at last.

Colonel Hume gathered the officers together. "This is it, gentlemen." He stood with his helmet slanted to the back of his head and his thumbs thrust into his belt. "We're going forward on the night of November the First with a Highland brigade on our left and the Durhams on our right. The Cheshires' Vickers guns are in support, and we'll advance under the arc of the guns." He allowed his gaze to encompass every man there. "It will be an old-fashioned slogging match, gentlemen, and this time, we are right in the forefront."

Tulloch felt the tension in the atmosphere. The officers wanted the Lothians to shine but worried about the inevitable casualties. A career-minded few may have hoped for glory and personal advancement.

"The artillery will initially fire two thousand yards ahead, and as we reach the barrage, it will creep forward. You'll see horizontal tracer to the right and left; that's our Bofors guns marking our flanks. Whatever you do, keep within the tracer."

Tulloch nodded. He would have to warn the flanking platoon. He hoped Rutlane could recognise tracer.

The battalions' supporting tanks arrived that afternoon, a squadron of Valentines from a regiment of cheerful English Yeomanry. They parked close to the Lothians and invited officers and men to inspect the tanks and speak to the crews.

"Come on, Jocks, don't be shy!" One red-faced tank commander said. "Did you forget your skirts today?"

Tulloch stopped Hogg from responding with his usual targeted aggression. "They can't help being English, Hogg, but they're on our side this time. Be nice."

The Lothians wandered around the tanks, familiarising themselves with their shape so they would recognise them in the smoke and confusion of battle. The crews showed each man the location of the bell push at the back in case they needed to talk to the tank commanders, shook hands, and wished them luck.

"We'll see you later, boys," the Yeomanry colonel said, and Tulloch remembered the Yeomanry's suicidal charge against the German 88s at Gazala.

"Take care, Tankies," Tulloch replied. "Don't be too rash."

When he was sure every man in D Company had seen the Valentines, Tulloch accompanied his lieutenants to the Start Line. Unlike on the opening day of the El Alamein battle, huge oil drums marked where the Lothians would begin their advance.

"Here we go again," McGill said, tapping the nearest oil drum with the toe of his boot.

Tulloch nodded. His previous offensive battles had been against the Italians. This time the German 90th Light Division would be dug in, ready and waiting, an experienced and formidable opponent.

"The intelligence officers will tape out our route to the Start Line after dark," Tulloch told his lieutenants. "We won't get lost."

"No, sir," McGill agreed.

Rutlane gave a nervous smile and shuffled his boots in the

sand. Tulloch wondered how he would act when under fire as they returned to the battalion's position.

They heard the Stukas an instant before the aircraft screamed out of the sun, targeting an artillery position three hundred yards away. Three Stukas dived, dropped their bombs and climbed away, with British anti-aircraft fire following them as they headed west.

"Rommel's not finished yet," Tulloch said.

One of the British field guns lay on its side with a dead gunner underneath and another, shocked, staring at his leg, missing from the knee downwards.

"Every casualty is a personal tragedy for some family," Tulloch said. He watched as an ambulance roared up and a pair of medical orderlies carried away the wounded man.

"The brass has postponed the attack for twenty-four hours," Kilner reported when they arrived at battalion HQ. "We'll just have to sit it out here until General Freyberg orders us forward."

"I'll speak to the neighbours," Tulloch said. "The Aussies know the area better than we do."

"We're lucky to have them," Kilner said. "I fought beside them in the last war. Some ignorant officers thought them rough and ready. I found them superb soldiers who never gave up."

"I remember them from O'Connor's advance," Tulloch said quietly. "Tough men who held Tobruk for months against everything Rommel threw at them."

"That's the lads," Kilner said quietly. "Thank the Lord they're on our side." He looked up. "Here comes the colonel."

Hume gathered his officers to discuss the forthcoming advance.

"We'll attack on a two-company front, gentlemen. C and D Companies will lead until we reach the first objective, codename Penicuik, when Kilner's B Company will move to the right of Muirhead's C Company and Tulloch's D Company will drop into a supporting role."

Tulloch rechecked the map, reminding himself that Penicuik

was only a reference on the map, 3,500 yards west of the Start Line.

"When we reach Penicuik," Hume said, "we halt for half an hour, as does the barrage. Then it's forward again, five thousand yards to the next objective. Remember not to cross the tracer boundaries, and remember we have the Yeomanry's Valentines, plus anti-tank guns and heavy machine guns in support."

The officers nodded, grateful for the armour while aware the German tanks outclassed the Valentines.

"The engineers will closely follow us," Hume continued, "clearing paths in the minefield for the tanks. The sappers can't operate on the whole four-thousand-yard front, so they will create lanes, which the tanks will follow until they are clear of the mines, whereupon they will spread out and engage and destroy the enemy's armour."

Tulloch nodded. Of all the actions he had fought, Supercharge was the best organised.

The Lothians spent another uncomfortable night in the busy assembly area, trying to sleep amidst the clanking rumble of tanks and hum of truck engines. Tulloch toured D Company, spoke to his lieutenants and NCOs and answered the men's questions as best he could before retiring to his tent.

Once again, Tulloch wrote a letter to Amanda, telling her his thoughts, though not his fears. He lay awake for a while, then closed his eyes and tried to sleep, knowing that tomorrow would be challenging. He ran over the operation in his mind, memorising the various steps.

My first action as a Company Commander and it's a big one. We must burst through the enemy lines this time. We have top-quality troops on either flank, and the artillery will support us well. I only hope Six Platoon will behave. I wish I had more faith in Lieutenant Rutlane.

The following day, a convoy of trucks carried the Lothians to join the Durhams in a concentration area near Tel el Eisa railway station.

"Another Godless place in the middle of nowhere," McGill said.

"It's hardly Godless," Muirhead said quietly. "Tel el Eisa means the Little Hill of Jesus. Is that not ironical?" His mouth twisted in a cynical smile. "An army mustering at a place named after Jesus."

———

"SORRY, LADS. WE HAVE TO GATHER ALL PERSONAL PAPERS AND letters," Tulloch said to D Company. "If any of us are killed or captured, Monty wants to ensure the enemy doesn't get any valuable intelligence."

"He won't get any intelligence at all from Hoggie!" Elliot said. "We've been trying for years!" He moved away quickly as Hogg stepped towards him to inflict instant revenge.

"We'll put our possessions into sandbags that the Quartermaster will hold, and we'll pick them up after the battle," Tulloch instructed D Company.

"The QM will likely go through them and take what he fancies," an anonymous voice sounded from the back of the company.

When the men looked doubtful, Tulloch removed his letters, including his latest from Amanda and the last two from his mother. "I'll go first." He held them up to show the men, tied them with a strip of linen, wrote his name on top and dropped them in a sandbag. He watched them fall with mixed feelings, wondering if he would be alive to retrieve them and what he would experience before then. "Come on, lads! Let's be having you!"

Most of the men had a few letters to drop into the bag, with the solitary soldiers, orphans and misfits pretending to join in or turning away with a laugh or a sneer. Adamson watched from a distance and shook his head when Tulloch approached him.

"I've none, sir," Adamson said openly.

Tulloch nodded and moved on. *Adamson is an interesting man. He helped with the Preston affair at Alam Halfa, and he's not given a whisper of trouble since we dragged the deserters back from Alex. I'll watch him.*

With the sandbags filled, sealed and handed to the Quartermaster, a pouch-eyed, overweight rogue who battalion rumour insisted had been a banker sacked for embezzlement, the Lothians readied themselves for the next stage.

D Company was subdued as Tulloch inspected them, ensuring each man had his quota of ammunition, spare Bren ammunition or mortar bomb, hand grenades, anti-tank grenades, water bottle and other equipment. He also gave words of encouragement where he thought they would help.

"You're looking good, Innes. Careful with the Bren now."

"Adamson, fire low; remember, you're not attacking the moon, just the enemy."

"Hogg, it's the Germans and Italians you're fighting. The Durhams and New Zealanders are on our side. So are the Highlanders."

Dressed in khaki drill shorts and pullovers, the men were quiet as Tulloch gave them a final inspection. He ensured each section had an anti-tank grenade, and every man carried an extra bandolier of ammunition, an entrenching tool and either a pick or shovel. Tulloch expected the comments about being paid less than navvies or miners.

"The lads are ready, sir," McGill, twenty-one years old with innocent brown eyes, reported.

Tulloch nodded. "Are you ready?"

"Yes, sir," McGill replied.

D Company joined the battalion at seven in the evening and marched to the Start Line. Tulloch recognised the walk, a slow desert stride, kicking up dust, with their shoulders aching from the rifle sling and the rifle bolt bumping against the hip and thigh, a persistent, nagging irritation that would develop into a bruise. The men were constantly tired, always wary, seeming to plod, some walking splay-footed but always watching for enemy aircraft and mines.

It was five miles to the F.U.P. – the Forming Up Position - at the Start Line, with the night sultry, bringing sweat to add to the dust that covered the men. They passed Tel el Eisa station in the first few minutes, plodding along the Diamond Track as trucks roared past carrying stores and ammunition. A minefield spread on the right of the track, still bearing evidence of a previous advance. The bodies of men slowly rotted on the barbed wire, stinking of death and corruption.

The veterans observed the dead bodies without any interest as the replacements stared, swallowed and looked away.

"Welcome to sunny Egypt," Hood grunted. "Home to pyramids, Gyppy Tummy, flies, heat, desert wastes and decomposing bodies."

Hogg grinned sourly. "When I get home, I'm never leaving Edinburgh again. I've had my share of sunny foreign climes."

When they passed the minefield, the Lothians looked to their right, where a New Zealand artillery battery was firing non-stop to support an Australian attack.

Two and a half hours after setting off, the battalion reached the FUP. Behind them, the battalion's carriers, ambulances and transport arrived with anti-tank guns and the Yeomanry's Matilda tanks.

"Remember what we're doing," Tulloch reminded D Company. "We're clearing a gap in the enemy's line so the sappers can clear the minefields for the vehicles."

The men of D Company nodded, grunted or looked blank. Oldham began to sing *Lily Marlene* in a low voice. Innes checked his Bren gun, tapping his spare barrel and magazines.

"All right, lads?" Tulloch asked.

"Yes, sir," Corporal Borthwick replied. "What happens when we break the German lines?"

"Once the sappers clear the mines, the armour will pass

through us and fan out behind the enemy, causing panic and creating mayhem."

"Unless the Germans destroy them all again," Rutlane said quietly.

Tulloch ignored Rutlane's comment, hoping the men had not heard.

The officers checked their compasses and peered westward into the ominous dark. Tulloch spoke to Muirhead to ensure their respective companies did not become entangled in the advance.

"My first advance as a Company Commander," Tulloch said.

"The responsibility is heavier for a Company Commander than a Platoon Commander," Muirhead told him, "but nothing you can't handle. Keep your men in hand, ensure nobody advances too fast and gets killed by friendly artillery, and have men in reserve for casualties."

"I've posted three men from each platoon as a reserve under Corporal Russell," Tulloch said. "It's all I can spare."

"Aye," Muirhead nodded. "We're a bit light on numbers after the last show." He grunted. "The last two shows."

The men lay down to try and snatch a few minutes of sleep, but only Cattanach and one or two others succeeded.

"Hogg!" Tulloch called.

"Sir?" Hogg asked, standing at attention.

"I want you to count our paces. We are advancing three and a half thousand yards to the first objective. That's three and a half thousand paces across the desert to a position they call Penicuik." Tulloch saw the dismay on Hogg's face. "It's a vital task, Hogg."

"Yes, sir," Hogg said, lifting his chin. "I won't let you down."

"I know that," Tulloch replied. "I'll be moving around to check on the men, Hogg. Whatever happens, you must march in a straight line, following the compass bearing. Do you understand?"

"Yes, sir," Hogg said. "If any Germans come, sir, can I fight them?"

"Yes, Hogg," Tulloch replied. "As long as you don't lose count."

Hogg looked more cheerful. "I won't, sir," he said. "Although I'd never walk three hundred steps to get to Penicuik, let alone three thousand."

A battalion runner trotted across the sand, halting in a cloud of dust. "Captain Tulloch, sir."

"Yes?" The runner was from Headquarters Company, and Tulloch did not know his name.

"The battalion mortars have still not arrived, sir and Colonel Hume says to tell you that the German 90th Light is on the north side of our line of advance and the 164th Infantry to the south, backed by the Italian Trieste Infantry Division."

"Thank you, Runner," Tulloch said, and the man ran into the dark, carrying his message to the other company commanders. Intelligence reports had already informed Tulloch that the 15th Panzer and Littorio Divisions waited in reserve behind the enemy front line.

"Is there any good news?" Muirhead asked as he strolled over to D Company.

"Yes, indeed," Tulloch said. "Rommel hasn't laid any anti-personnel mines in front of us. Only anti-tank."

"That's a blessing," Muirhead said. "I abhor these schu-mines. Evil things."

Schu mines were wooden, so mine detectors, intended to hunt for metal, often missed them. The wooden box held 200 grams of TNT that would easily take a man's leg off.

Shortly before midnight, Colonel Hume toured the battalion, accompanied by three men carrying thermos flasks with a mixture of rum and hot cocoa.

"The condemned man's last request," McGill said as his platoon gathered for a warming drink.

"It won't do any good," Rutlane sighed. "We'll never penetrate the German lines." He looked away when he caught Tulloch's warning glare.

"Just the job!" Innes said, lowering the flask and wiping a hand across his mouth. He grinned at Hogg. "How about you, Hoggie? Don't you want some?"

"No' me," Hogg replied. "I've got to count to three and a half thousand. If I had a drink, I might lose count and lead youse all the wrong way."

"That's all right, Hoggie," Smith said, reaching for the thermos. "Nobody will take any notice of you anyway."

"You can bugger off," Hogg told him without malice.

"Get the men ready," Colonel Hume said tersely. "Five minutes!"

"Right, lads," Tulloch ordered. "On your feet. Fix bayonets, and get ready; we're going to kick Rommel out of Africa!"

Chapter Thirty-Three

OPERATION SUPERCHARGE, EL ALAMEIN, OCTOBER AND NOVEMBER 1942

Tulloch sent McGill to scout the first fifty yards, snip any Allied wire, and then return. The men stamped their feet on the sand to keep warm, fixed bayonets with a series of sinister snicks and mumbled in low tones. Oldham sang the opening stanzas of *Lily Marlene.*

"Underneath the lantern,

By the barrack gate,

Darling, I remember

The way you used to wait."

His voice tailed off to a whisper as he peered into the dark ahead.

"Sing away, Oldie," Gordon encouraged. "You might frighten the Germans into surrender with your screeching."

"You can bugger off, Gordon," Oldham responded.

Somebody laughed, high-pitched and nervous. Tulloch saw Rutlane picking imaginary threads from his tunic.

"All right, Rutlane?" Tulloch asked.

"Yes, sir." Rutlane turned wide eyes on him, blinking.

"Good man. Keep steady now, lead your men, and we'll get through this."

"Yes, sir," Rutlane gave a nervous grin.

McGill returned. "All done, sir," he reported quietly. "We have a passage."

Tulloch checked that his revolver was loaded, although he knew he had thumbed in the cartridges ten minutes earlier.

The sappers have marked our path through the British minefield, and then we fan out. I know what we're doing.

"Remember to count, Hogg."

"Yes, sir," Hogg replied. "I won't forget."

The battalion waited, subdued and thoughtful, yet Tulloch sensed the tense excitement. He nodded to Rutlane. "All right, Lieutenant?"

"All right, sir," Rutlane replied with a fixed, twisted smile that fooled nobody.

"Right, men," Colonel Hume ordered. "Off we go."

Tulloch checked his watch. 12:55: the absolute dead of night. They followed the marked path through the Allied minefield, still moving quietly, careful not to overstep the tape. The men shuffled in the dark, following the path, heads down and shoulders slumped.

"One, two, three," Hogg began in a slow, monotone that Tulloch knew would irritate him after a while.

"Good man, Hogg," Tulloch said.

"Four, five, six..."

Although they expected it, the sound of the British barrage made everybody start. The artillery boomed behind them, rank after rank of Allied guns pouring shells at the German and Italian lines. Three hundred twenty-five pounders firing at once, hammering at the enemy positions, guns and trenches.

"Jesus!" Somebody blasphemed.

"Aye," Innes said. "He's on our side, this war."

Tulloch checked his watch. It was 13:05. The artillery was dead on time, as it usually was. *Thank God for the Gunners.*

"Eight hundred and one, eight hundred and two," Hogg continued.

The twenty-five-pounder shells passed overhead with a sound like a whiplash, while the heavier rounds sounded like a passing train. The noise made speech impossible, disturbed thought and dehumanised the men, so they felt like automatons, rifle-carrying machines carried on the waves of sound.

"One thousand and three, one thousand and four," Hogg continued his chant.

The men grew used to the sound of passing shells, accepting it as part of the advance, part of this surreal existence fate had ordained for them. Some twisted their heads to see the muzzle flashes from the Allied lines; others peered forward to where the shells exploded on the Axis positions. Most looked downward at the dust their boots kicked up.

The intelligence reports had specified targets for most Allied guns. Others aimed in the enemy's general direction, forcing them to stay under cover until the Allied infantry was nearly on them.

Tulloch heard the Lowland pipes of the Lothians competing with the high wail of the Highland pipes to their left. On the right, one of the Durham officers blew a hunting horn and beyond that, Tulloch heard the ferocious yells of the Maoris, the native warriors of New Zealand.

"One thousand two hundred and twenty-two, one thousand two hundred and twenty-three," Hogg continued.

That's a good chunk of the way and the enemy hasn't replied yet. Please, God, we don't have many casualties in this action.

When Hogg reached one thousand three hundred, half a dozen Very lights soared up from the Axis positions, and guns began to probe for the advancing troops. German and Italian machine guns gave their murderous rattle, and Tulloch saw men fall in the Lothian ranks.

Behind the infantry, the engineers were busy sweeping the ground for mines. The infantry knew they were safe from the heavy anti-tank mines, but everybody dreaded the anti-personnel mines.

"Space for the pipers!" The Lothian pipers had to roar to be heard above the hellish noise. They pushed forward to their proper place at the forefront of the advance and swaggered forward, pipes playing to taunt the enemy and encourage the men.

"*Flowers o' Edinburgh*, lads!" the pipe-corporal yelled.

"Right, Wullie!" the pipers replied, and the regimental march sounded through the screams of shells, wounded men, and the vicious chatter of machine guns. The Bofors fired on either flank, the tracer bullets helping keep the infantry on track.

"Here's a length of barbed wire, sir!" Corporal Borthwick shouted.

A single strand of barbed wire stretched at waist level across the ground, north and south, as far as Tulloch could see.

"What's that?" Rutlane asked. "It must be some German trick, a booby trap to blow us all up."

"It marks the end of their minefield," Tulloch said. "We've gone through it." He raised his voice. "Careful now, boys! The enemy will have dugouts and trenches here!"

"Now the sappers will clear a passage for the tanks," McGill said with satisfaction.

A machine gun opened up on the right flank, firing on fixed lines. Men fell, Lothians and Durhams. Stretcher-bearers ran to help, carrying the wounded back to Captain Macquarie at the battalion first aid post. Mortar shells landed without warning, causing casualties. Tulloch saw gaps in C Company to his left. He heard desultory shooting and the crump of a grenade.

"Come oot o' there, you!" Corporal Russell grabbed a reluctant Italian from a slit trench and dragged him to the surface. "Sir! What will I do with this fellow?"

The Italian was in shock from the bombardment, shaking and with his mouth drooping open.

"Send him to the rear," Tulloch saw Private O'Hara walking

back holding a bleeding arm. "Tell O'Hara there to look after him."

The Lothians continued the advance, collecting a few prisoners, Italian and German, passing dugouts and trenches destroyed by the bombardment and the occasional dead and wounded enemy soldier. Every few moments, the bombardment stopped, and Tulloch checked his men and listened to Hogg's constant counting.

"How far ahead is Penicuik, sir?" Hogg asked.

"Never mind, just count!"

"Yes, sir."

A machine gun rattled ahead, firing regular five-second bursts. A man screamed, another shouted something incoherent, and a Bren fired, one short burst and then a longer, three-second burst. A grenade exploded, and then silence. The advance continued with the Lowland pipes wailing encouragement. More enemy soldiers emerged from dugouts, mouths open in shock, uniforms torn, arms raised in surrender.

"It's all right, lads," Drysdale said to the prisoners. "Your war is over now." The Italians seemed glad to surrender, the Germans more dignified in defeat. Both nationalities were stunned by the ferocity of the bombardment.

A barrage of smoke shells landed from the British artillery, signifying that the barrage was about to lift.

The Lothians marched on into the dust and smoke. Tulloch coughed at the stink of high explosive and looked up as more German Very Lights splashed high above.

Another machine gun opened fire in front. Its chatter evil, murderous. Two men from C Company fell, and others threw themselves to the ground. Tulloch saw the distinctive German helmet fifty yards to his left and saw the Spandau swinging towards D Company.

"Machine gun!" Tulloch roared. He saw Private Gordon running towards the gun, firing his rifle from the hip and yelling, "Come on, you Nazi bastards!"

The Spandau clattered again, and Gordon fell, with his rifle dropping at his side, to land bayonet first in the sand. The momentary diversion allowed Sergeant Drysdale to approach on the opposite side. He threw a grenade that landed outside the German trench and followed up with a burst from his Thompson machine gun. The German machine gunner fell forward, and Drysdale threw another grenade into the nest, finishing any survivors with his Thompson. He looked up, his teeth bared and eyes wild in a sand-smeared face.

"Press on," Tulloch ordered, nodding to Drysdale. *That's a Military Medal for you, my friend.*

"Poor old Gordae," Hood muttered. "His girl wanted him to come home a hero with a medal."

"Press on!" Tulloch ordered again. He wondered how many men had died hoping to impress their women.

The bombardment began again, plastering the ground a hundred and twenty yards in front of the infantry.

"Two thousand three hundred and one," Hogg chanted, "two thousand three hundred and two..."

"Good lad, Hogg!" Tulloch encouraged.

"Two thousand three hundred and three..."

"The guns are getting too far ahead!" Colonel Hume said. "Pick the pace up!"

The Lothians marched faster. General Freyberg had ordained that the advancing troops were never to lag more than a hundred yards behind the barrage once they crossed the halfway point. They had passed that point, and Tulloch reckoned that the closest shell bursts were a hundred and fifty yards away.

"I cannae count that fast!" Hogg complained as the Lothians increased their speed.

"Do your best!" Tulloch shouted. He heard the explosion before he saw the flash as one of the pipers yelled and fell, holding his legs.

"Mines!" the pipe corporal shouted.

"Ware mines!" Tulloch repeated the warning. "Leave the casualties for the stretcher-bearers!"

Macquarie and his boys will be busy today. So will the padre.

Tulloch saw Cattanach speak briefly to the wounded piper, lift his pipes and begin to play.

Our Private Cattanach is a lad o' pairts.

The pipe music continued, spurring the men on. When Cattanach played the *Barren Rocks of Aden*, Tulloch thought it was quite fitting for the Lothians' surroundings. He pushed away the wild thought, jumped over a shattered dugout, saw a wounded German in the bottom looking up desperately through a blood-smeared face, and carried on with D Company behind him.

As the barrage seemed to linger, the Lothians neared the bursting shells. Tulloch knew that twenty-five-pounder shells typically exploded forward, sending the splinters away from men behind them, making it safer to creep closer.

"Keep moving, D Company!"

"Two thousand two hundred and thirty," Hogg nearly shouted. "Where the hell is Penicuik?"

"Near the Pentland Hills," Corporal Borthwick replied, laughing at his attempted humour. Hogg responded with two stark words.

The guns fired another volley of smoke, and the barrage lifted momentarily. Tulloch tried to remember how often this had happened. Freyberg had said the barrage would lift twenty-two times to allow the infantry to catch up. Was that the twelfth time now? Or the thirteenth?

"Sir!" Hogg shouted. "There's something ahead. I think it's enemy guns, sir."

"Thank you, Hogg." Tulloch peered into the line of exploding shells and subsequent curtain of dust and smoke. "What's your count?"

"Two thousand five hundred, sir," Hogg replied.

"Dead on target, Hogg." Tulloch approved. The British

artillery had hit the line of enemy guns hard, destroying five of them and strewing enemy dead around like broken dolls. The crews had abandoned the remaining two, leaving them dark and forlorn against the desert sand.

"Consolidate!" Colonel Hume ordered. "Company commanders, bring your men together!"

The Lothians gathered, checking the ranks for casualties. D Company had lost two men. Tulloch had not seen them fall.

"Swing northward," Hume ordered. "Don't get too far ahead."

Tulloch heard the Highland pipes on their left and the blast of the hunting horn from the Durhams. Although the temperature was barely above zero, he felt sweat on his face and running down his back.

"Still with us, lads?" Tulloch checked his men. Rutlane stood at the head of his men, looking pale, while McGill smiled nervously.

"Still here, sir," McGill said, forcing a smile.

"Me too," Rutlane looked as if he were about to faint.

"Stick it, Rutlane," Tulloch encouraged. "You're doing well."

The barrage began again, hammering the ground less than a hundred yards from the Lothians. The men moved forward, passing broken trenches and bewildered enemy soldiers emerging from dugouts with their hands in the air.

"Captain Muirhead!" Hume shouted. "Organise a section to send the prisoners back to base!"

"Yes, sir," Muirhead called out a corporal's name and strode on.

"That's us, sir!" Hogg shouted. "We should be at Penicuik now!"

McGill passed the news on to his platoon. "That's the first objective reached, boys! We're at Penicuik!"

"Penicuik be buggered," a voice replied from the dark. "My ma lives in Penicuik, and she'd have a hairy fit if it was in a mess like this!"

Colonel Hume called a halt as the bombardment turned to eye-nipping smoke again. The stench of high explosives filled the air. One young private was on all fours, retching onto the sand. Beside him, the top half of a German lay, with the man shredded from the waist down. The wounded man made whining noises, begging for his mother and plucking at what remained of his lower half.

"Stretcher bearer!" Tulloch shouted although he knew the German could not live with such appalling injuries. He looked around for any features that might distinguish Penicuik from any other point on the map. He saw none in the gloom, drifting dust and smoke.

"Kilner!" Colonel Hume snapped, "Move your company to the right of Muirhead's C Company. We will halt here for half an hour to consolidate and allow the sappers to catch up."

The officers nodded, mentally and emotionally drained.

"Then it's forward again, five thousand yards to the next objective."

Chapter Thirty-Four

OPERATION SUPERCHARGE, EL ALAMEIN
NOVEMBER 1942

Colonel Hume called for the signallers to bring up the 18
Set and radioed the Lothians' position back to base.
Tracer bullets and enemy shells flashed through the
night, with each explosion revealing a tiny vignette of the battlefield, images frozen in time in Tulloch's mind. Tulloch knew this
advance would be seared into his memory as indelibly as his first
actions on the Northwest Frontier or the retreat through
Belgium and France in 1940. He hoped he survived to describe it
to Amanda or his parents, although he knew, within himself, that
he could never reveal the truth with all its horrors.

Tulloch checked his men and thought of the unruffled staff
officers with their maps and plans, moving little arrows from
place to place. It was all so easy for chairbound warriors but
different in the Blue.

"Where are the tanks?" Elliot shouted. "The tanks should be
supporting us!"

"They can't come until the sappers have cleared a route,"
Corporal Borthwick explained calmly. "They'll be there."

"I cannae hear them," Elliot said.

Oldham lit a cigarette, holding it in his cupped hand as he crouched on the ground, coughing and rubbing his eyes. Hood was at his side, reloading his rifle.

"I got another of them," Hood said quietly. "Some German fellae popping out of a trench."

"They got Gordae, though," Connington said. "He telt me he was going for a gong for his wumman, and he charged a machine gun. They diced him."

"The sergeant sorted them oot," Hood said.

"Aye. The sarge did that."

Tulloch listened to the men's desultory, fragmented conversation as they recounted incidents of the first stage of the advance. He sought out his lieutenants. McGill was putting a bandage on a wounded man's arm, and Rutlane was trying to light a cigarette with trembling hands.

"Here," Tulloch struck a match. "Draw deeply, Rutlane. It will help calm your nerves."

"I'm not afraid," Rutlane said, with his mouth twisted into a mockery of a smile.

"Of course, you're not," Tulloch told him, hiding his fear behind an equally false grin.

Battle makes liars of us all.

Colonel Hume glanced up from the radio, his eyes steady. "The tanks are only a few hundred yards behind us, boys," he said. "We're moving north when the barrage starts again."

Tulloch looked behind him. The Lothians had left the anti-tank minefield well behind and were in an area of flat, stony gravel. The bombardment started again, pounding the ground in front, with each explosion throwing up a column of smoke and small stones.

"Where are the tanks?" Elliot repeated.

"They're on their way," Borthwick reassured him.

"I can hear them!" Hogg said, jerking a thumb over his shoulder. "Listen!"

All of Four Platoon and some men of Six Platoon quietened to listen. They disregarded the enemy shelling and machine guns, even the sound of Highland and Lowland pipes and the shouts from the Maoris and Durhams as they strained to hear the British armour.

"I hear them," Oldham said.

"So can I," Hood agreed.

Somebody laughed, and then the colonel blew his whistle. The Lothians advanced again, following the creeping barrage and heartened by the knowledge that the British armour was close behind.

Tulloch's D Company had taken the first reserve position, as Kilner's B Company replaced them in front. The men remained tense, knowing the enemy was still dangerous and could launch a counteroffensive anytime.

They breathed in fine sand and the stink of cordite, mingled with raw blood, roasted human flesh and the sickly stench of death. They stepped over abandoned trenches, moving carefully in case the enemy had planted booby traps or lay, feigning death, ready to shoot a passing British soldier in the back.

"Dinnae take any chances," Elliot said, firing his rifle into every seemingly empty dugout they passed.

"Save your ammunition, Elliot," Sergeant Drysdale grated. "Dead men can't shoot you."

"Live men bloody can," Elliot responded.

A salvo of mortars landed on B Company, tumbling men to the ground.

"That would have been us if we were still in front!" Rutlane said.

"Keep moving!" Tulloch ordered. "Leave the wounded for the stretcher-bearers." He hardened his heart to the moans and screams as they passed the injured, with the stretcher-bearers doing their best. Colonel Hume spoke on the radio, requesting the artillery to seek out the enemy mortars, and then two machine gun nests opened fire at once.

Three men of C Company fell, and another two of B Company.

"They've got us in a crossfire!" somebody shouted.

"Come on, boys!" Kilner shouted and ran forward with his men following. The German machine guns rattled, bringing down Kilner and half a dozen men. The rest threw themselves to the ground, searching for any cover. Kilner regained his feet, limping. The Lothians' advance halted.

"Mortars!" Hume shouted. "Kill these Spandau nests!"

The Lothian mortar platoon set up their two and three-inch mortars, and the bombs soon dropped around the machine gun nests. As they did, the Axis defenders searched for the mortars with short, probing bursts.

One bomb landed just behind the Spandau nest on the left flank, sending up a great column of dust and smoke.

"Nearly!" Hood shouted.

"Where's the bloody tanks!" Elliot asked. "Where's our support?"

"Here they come, Shuggy!" Hood said, jerking a thumb behind him.

The first of the Matildas creaked through the Lothians, with the tank commander's head and shoulders thrust above the turret.

"There's a couple of machine-gun nests ahead!" Tulloch told them. "We'd be obliged if you could deal with them for us. Watch for the dropping mortars."

"Our pleasure!" the leading tank commander replied, withdrawing into his steel cocoon. He drove on, with the infantry parting before him, wishing him luck and banging on the side of the vehicle.

Tulloch watched as the Matilda approached the machine gun nest on the left. The Germans were brave men, firing at the tank, with their bullets rebounding from the armour. The Matilda ran straight into the trench, flattening it on top of the men inside, then turned around and drove at the second machine-gun nest.

After witnessing the fate of their comrades, the men in the second nest rose with their hands in the air.

"Just the job, Tankies!" Elliot shouted.

The advance continued as the Lothians hurried to catch up on the creeping barrage, now nearly five hundred yards ahead. Shells exploded amongst the men, with shrapnel spreading around. Private Atkins gave a small grunt and looked down at his battledress. He touched a piece of sharp metal that thrust from his chest, gave a twisted smile and crumpled to the sand.

The Lothians marched on over ground pitted with shell holes, with dazed Italian and German soldiers rising with raised hands to surrender. Others, dead and wounded, lay amidst the wreckage of their dugouts. Tulloch noted the replacement soldiers staring at the prisoners as if they were from a different species.

"They're only men like us!" Tulloch said. "Move on! Let the walking wounded escort the prisoners back."

"The artillery has been very effective, sir," McGill said.

"The guns have made it much easier for us," Tulloch agreed.

"Keep moving!" Colonel Hume ordered. "Keep the momentum!" He called for the signaller. "Tell General Freyberg where we are. He won't see us in the smoke."

"The 18 Set isn't working, sir!" the signaller reported to Hume. "Either some dust got inside, or the shrapnel bust it."

The colonel swore. "Are you sure?"

"I've tried everything I know, sir," the signaller reported.

"Discard the wireless," Hume ordered. "You're a rifleman now."

"Yes, sir."

"Right, Rifleman, run back to brigade HQ and tell them where we are." Hume gave the coordinates.

"Yes, sir," the signalman replied, running to the rear.

"Push on!" Hume ordered.

A Spandau fired from the flank, accompanied by a shower of stick grenades and German voices shouting in defiance. Innes dropped to the ground, aimed and fired short bursts from his Bren. Hogg joined him, firing and working the bolt of his rifle like a man possessed.

"Keep them occupied!" Corporal Russell shouted, moving to the left with his section.

"The Spandau's firing high!" Drysdale said. "Look at the tracer!"

Tulloch saw that Drysdale was correct, with the tracer bullets rising two feet above the Lothians' heads.

"Bugger them, then," Hogg shouted, rose to a crouch and ran forward, jinking from side to side. Innes continued to fire the Bren, taking care to avoid Hogg and keeping the Germans' attention.

"They're mine, Hogg!" Russell ran in with his bayonet levelled, a yard ahead of Hogg.

"That'll be bloody right, you fascist bastard!"

The Germans in the trench looked up, belatedly realising they were firing high. One tried to lower the Spandau; another scrabbled for a Schmeisser MP40 submachine gun. Russell thrust his bayonet into the stomach of the Spandau man while Hogg stabbed the second in the throat.

A third German lunged at Russell, but Hogg was quicker, slicing around with his bayonet to slash the man across the face. The German fell, screaming, and Hogg finished him with a thrust to the chest.

The Lothians encountered more of the enemy now, some resisting, others dazed by the bombardment and unsure where they were, and some with broken minds. When the enemy fired from dugouts or sangars, the Lothians cleared them with bayonets and grenades. When the enemy surrendered, the Lothians sent them back, usually under the escort of the walking wounded.

B Company passed a damaged German tank, and the limping

Kilner ordered one of his lieutenants to fire a Very pistol into the petrol tank.

"Blow the bastard up," Kilner demanded. "Show the Huns they're losing the war."

The lieutenant fired his Very pistol, and the fuel exploded in a great whoosh, with orange flames rising high.

"Just the job!" McGill said.

The pipers, Lowland and Highland, continued to play through the smoke, dust and confusion.

"I dinnae like the pipes," Elliot complained. "They let Rommel know where we are."

"That's the idea," Sergeant Drysdale said. "The enemy will hear the pipes coming closer and closer, and they'll know how long they have to live. Puts the wind up them, see?"

The Lothians moved on, hurrying to catch up with the still-rolling barrage and quickly dealing with any resistance. Three hours after the advance started, the shelling ended. The sudden silence was deafening, leaving Tulloch feeling strangely lonely, although thousands of British and New Zealand soldiers surrounded him. The smoke and dust sunk to the ground and gradually cleared, except for the knee-high mist the men's boots kicked up.

"Keep moving, men!" Hume said. "We're not at our second objective yet. Don't bunch!"

"Come on, D Company!" Tulloch shouted and led his men, with Cattanach and the other pipers in the van. They heard the Highland pipes to their left and the strange blast of the Durhams' hunting horn to their right, a reminder the advance continued. Above them, the moon and stars became visible in the clearing sky.

Even when the bombardment stopped, the night restricted visibility to around forty yards. The Lothians shot anything that moved, taking casualties from mortars, machine guns and the occasional stubborn enemy infantrymen who refused to abandon their trenches. The men only gave quarter to the enemy after they surrendered and were disarmed, for they had experience of Italian and occasionally German soldiers who claimed to surrender and shot their captors in the back.

"Don't neglect the trenches," Tulloch ordered. "Even if they look empty, toss a grenade in them or winkle the defenders out with a bayonet."

"Sergeant Drysdale didnae like me doing that, sir," Elliot complained.

"Well, I'm ordering you to do it," Tulloch snapped.

The veterans nodded, accepting Tulloch's experience, while the replacements, fresh from the training ground, looked shocked. Tulloch knew a few hours of real battle would end their naïve idealism.

"Look!" Hogg said. "Can you see that?" He lifted his head. "There's something ahead!"

"Panzers!" Rutlane shouted. He pointed to the west.

"Jesus!" Adamson blasphemed. "There's more than one of the bastards!"

Tulloch saw the German tanks loom from the dust ahead. He counted three, four and then five Mark IIIs directly before the Lothians.

"Runner!" Colonel Hume stood beside Tulloch. "Where's the runners?" He looked forward, where Kilner's B Company had taken to the ground, desperately rolling into shell craters or hacking out slit trenches as protection against the Panzers.

"I'll go, sir!" Hood volunteered.

"Get back quickly, man, and get us armoured support and artillery," Hume ordered.

"Yes, sir," Hood said.

"Tell HQ we have five Mark III Panzers on this map reference!" Hume scribbled the coordinates on a pad of paper, ripped off the top sheet and handed it to Hood. "Run, man!"

The Lothians threw themselves into whatever cover they could, some dropping into abandoned enemy trenches, others into shell craters. A few scrabbled at the ground with entrenching tools to make themselves as deep holes as possible.

Smith lifted his Boys, the only anti-tank weapon D Company possessed except for anti-tank grenades. "I'll try this, sir!"

The Panzers were waiting a few hundred yards in front of the Lothians, like cats stalking mice. The barrels of their main armament swung from side to side, searching for victims.

"That's our marker!" Tulloch shouted. "Intelligence got it wrong; they're dug-in tanks, not guns. We're in the right place, boys!"

"Why don't they fire?" McGill asked.

"They can't see us in the dark," Tulloch realised. "We are small, and the dust and smoke screen us."

"Why don't they come forward?" McGill asked, showing his inexperience.

"They're dug in and probably under orders to sit tight," Tulloch said, "like our armour at Alam Halfa."

"Come on, Two Section," Sergeant Drysdale shouted, running forward in a weaving crouch. He approached the closest tank, threw a 74 Anti-tank Grenade against the side, and withdrew. The infantry called the 74 Grenade a Sticky Bomb. It was a simple device: a glass ball holding high explosives with a handle so a soldier could throw the weapon. A woollen jacket coated with adhesive allowed the grenade to stick to the enemy tank.

You're a brave man, Drysdale, Tulloch thought.

The 74 Grenade exploded inward, rocking the first of the dug-in tanks and immediately killing the crew. Drysdale gave a low chuckle.

"Gin ye daur, you bastards!"

The tanks to the right swivelled their gun barrels while their machine guns opened fire, searching for the Lothians.

Hood ran past Tulloch, gasping and jinking to avoid the Germans' bullets. "Where's the colonel, sir? I have a message for the colonel."

"Over there," Tulloch pointed to the left, where Hume had jumped into a dugout.

"Thank you, sir!" Hood scrambled into the dugout as one of the Panzers sprayed the area with its machine gun. Columns of sand and gravel rose waist-high as bullets whined and screamed around.

A moment later, Colonel Hume lifted his voice. "Keep your heads down, Lothians! The artillery will hammer this area in three minutes! Three minutes!"

The tanks continued to fire, raising fountains of dust as their bullets crashed into sandbags and burrowed into the ground. The minutes passed slowly, each one seeming like an hour and then Tulloch saw the flashes from the rear.

"Here comes the bombardment!"

Tulloch heard the whistle of passing shells and then the murderous crash as they landed on and around the German tanks. The Lothians lay flat, praying, silent or swearing as the shells landed, for everybody knew how easy it was for an artillery shell to fall short.

The bombardment lasted for five minutes that seemed to last an eternity, and when it stopped, the German tanks were burning wrecks or blackened, twisted metal. Shell craters disfigured the ground, and one wounded man called piteously for help. A pair of Medical Orderlies ran to him, carrying a stretcher.

"Right, Lothians!" Colonel Hume emerged from his dugout. "E Company take over from C Company, and we move forward to our final position."

The men emerged cautiously, padding forward on the shell-pocked ground. Tulloch counted his men. He had two short.

"One dead sir, McKinlay of Six Platoon, and Connington of Four Platoon wounded. A shell splinter from our artillery got him." Sergeant Drysdale reported.

Tam McKinlay, a quiet, sober man from Gilmerton, and Connington, a miner from Loanhead. I hope Connington's wound is not serious.

The Lothians moved northward, fewer in numbers but still

following the pipes. They passed more dugouts where the enemy showed sporadic resistance. Grenades and bayonets cleared the way.

"Halt!" Colonel Hume shouted. "We've reached our objective."

They had reached the Rahman Tack, the road through the desert where the passage of scores of vehicles had rutted and grooved the sand. A couple of burned-out wrecks spiralled smoke to show where the Allied artillery or the RAF had destroyed them.

"Consolidate the position!" Hume ordered. He fired three flares from his Very Pistol, red, green and then green again, to signal to HQ that the Lothians had reached their final objective.

"Dig in, D Company!" Tulloch shouted. "Dig in before the Germans counterattack!"

D Company obeyed, with men hacking at the ground with their entrenching tools where it was soft or using their picks where there was rock beneath the surface. The miners had the advantage here, being experienced with this sort of work, while men from Edinburgh offices or Penicuik mills were less skilled if equally keen.

"Platoon commanders! Set up Bren positions!" Tulloch ordered. "Where are the mortars? I want them to cover our front. Get the Boys anti-tank rifles in the centre of each platoon!" He paced the front of his company, nearly unaware of the occasional burst of machine gun fire or dropping enemy mortar bombs.

The men tunnelled like khaki-clad moles, burrowing into the ground with the colliers throwing up sand with professional skill, creating a barrier between the trenches and any advancing enemy. The rest attempted to emulate them, wielding their picks like weapons as they dug deeper into the ground.

"Bugger this for a game of soldiers!" Hogg grunted and raised his voice. "Over here, sir! I've made us a grand wee hole."

Colonel Hume had his Number One HQ Company filling

sandbags and distributing them. "Get back to General Freyberg, signallers," Hume ordered. "See if you can bag an 18 Set. Take ours with you in case they can fix it."

"Here come our tanks!" Elliot sounded pleased as he looked behind him.

The men glanced over their shoulders as half a dozen Matilda tanks rolled up behind the battalion, with the tank commanders peering out from the turrets. Somebody cheered.

"Go on Tankies! Give Rommel hell!"

The mood of the Lothians lifted at the thought of armoured support. Men began to feel that the worst was behind them, and they had survived. Some of the young replacements waved at the Matildas.

"Look ahead," Hogg sobered the mood. "More tanks."

The German Panzers growled out of the smoke and dusk in the west, squat, ugly, efficient shapes heading slowly toward the Lothians.

"This time, they're mobile," Tulloch said. "And we can't call up artillery in case we destroy the Matildas."

The two armoured forces squared off, with the larger and better-armed German tanks having all the advantages and the Lothian Rifles stuck in the middle.

"We've reached the crisis of the battle," McGill said quietly. "If the Panzers win here, they could push us right back to the Start Line."

"Or beyond," Rutlane said.

"Or beyond," McGill agreed.

Chapter Thirty-Five

OPERATION SUPERCHARGE, EL ALAMEIN

NOVEMBER 1942

The Lothians stared as the German tanks growled towards them, monsters whose armour was impervious to the Boys anti-tank gun and whose machine guns would cut down any man sufficiently close to lob a Sticky Bomb.

Smith aimed the Boys, aware his actions were nearly futile but determined to try a shot at the Panzers.

"Here we are, lads!" A Northumbrian voice shouted, and a two-pounder anti-tank gun arrived behind the Lothians' position. "Our colonel thought you might like some support!"

"The Geordies are always welcome," Tulloch replied as the three-man gun crew quickly set up the two-pounder.

"Somebody has to show you Jocks how to fight," the gun captain replied, adding a belated "sir" to show there was no disrespect intended.

The Matildas opened fire first, six tanks blasting out their shells over the heads of the Lothians. They exploded among the

German tanks in smoke and fury but not much else. The solid shot of the armour-piercing shells ricochetted from the German armour with as little effect as a boy throwing stones against a wall, although the HE did blow the tracks from one tank.

"Bloody hell!" Elliot said.

The Germans fired back, their 50 and 75-mm shells far more effective than their Allied opponents. One Matilda burst into flame, and a second slewed to one side, with two of the crew escaping into a slaughter of German bullets.

"Bastards," Smith said. He fired his Boys rifle with more venom than success and saw the shot clatter from the nearest Panzer. "I didn't even scratch the bloody paintwork!"

The Durhams' two-pounder fired round after round, hitting one tank without stopping its relentless progress.

The Matildas moved forward, trying to avoid the Lothians' slit trenches as they advanced against their more powerful enemy. The Panzers concentrated into a rough Vee formation, firing in a regular, unhurried barrage that accounted for two more Matildas within three minutes. German solid shot bounced among the Lothians' positions, ploughing through the sand barriers while their HE shells exploded among the helpless infantrymen.

"We're being murdered!" Elliot said, crouching at the bottom of his trench with a hand holding his helmet in place.

"Anybody got a Sticky Bomb?" Drysdale shouted. "Pass it over to me!"

Once clear of the Lothians' trenches, the Matildas moved faster, jinking to avoid the German shells.

"What are they going to do?" McGill asked.

"I don't know," Tulloch replied.

The Germans hit another Matilda, with flames licking up the side. Two men emerged, one ablaze. Captain Macquarie ran to him with a blanket and tried to douse the fire as a German machine gun tore up the ground all around.

"Here comes the infantry!" Hogg shouted.

German infantry advanced to support their armour, moving with the fast professionalism that had characterised them since the beginning of the war.

"Target the infantry!" Colonel Hume shouted. "Ignore the tanks!"

Another Matilda burst into flames while one tried to ram a Panzer, rocking the enemy tank as it crashed into the side. Both vehicles slewed away.

"Brave men, these Tankies!" McGill commented soberly.

"Look after your platoon, McGill!" Tulloch shouted, firing his rifle at the rapidly advancing infantry.

The Lothians met the German infantry with Bren and rifle fire, desert veterans fighting desert veterans in the middle of the battling armour. Innes fired his Bren in short, disciplined bursts while Hogg worked his rifle faster than Tulloch had ever imagined.

Tulloch knew that McGill was a competent platoon commander, while Drysdale was the best platoon sergeant he knew, so Four Platoon was in good hands. He was not so sure about Six Platoon and remained close to Rutlane. Mitchell, Six Platoon's left flank Bren gunner, fired long bursts that would nearly empty the magazine.

"Short, aimed bursts, man!" Sergeant Paterson ordered. "You'll overheat the barrel!"

Sergeant Paterson was a broad-chested, stocky, blond-haired man. Although Tulloch had brought him into Six Platoon, he was unsure if he had made the correct choice. Now, watching the sergeant, Tulloch gained more faith in his abilities.

The Germans came in directly from the front, using the smoke from burning Matildas as cover. The British Brens sprayed the smoke, forcing the attackers into the open for the riflemen to pick off. The Lothians' mortars fired non-stop, pounding the German rear, searching for their officers and disrupting their communications.

"Keep firing, Six Platoon!" Tulloch shouted. He fired his Lee-

Enfield whenever he saw a target and watched over Rutlane, encouraging him with his presence.

"We're holding them, sir," a long-faced private said. Tulloch recognised him as one of the deserters.

"We are, Thom," Tulloch agreed. He saw Mitchell swearing as his gun jammed and stepped toward him, crouching low.

"What's the matter, Mitchell?"

"The bugger's jammed, sir," Mitchell was wide-eyed, with his hair tousled.

"Let's see," Tulloch took the Bren, grunting as he grabbed the barrel. "Your barrel's overheated like the sergeant warned. Do you have a spare?"

Mitchell gaped until his neighbour grabbed a spare barrel from the bottom of the trench. "Here, sir."

"Fit the bloody thing, Mitchell, and kill Germans! That's your job!"

"Yes, sir," Mitchell looked relieved as he removed the old barrel and dropped it on the ground. In the few moments it had taken to replace the barrel, the Germans had advanced twenty yards, with one party sliding into an abandoned trench only thirty yards away.

"Sergeant Paterson!" Tulloch shouted. "Grenades!"

Paterson needed no second urging. He threw three grenades, one after the other, so two were in the air when the first landed. They exploded in a triple crash, spreading deadly splinters the length of the trench.

One of the occupants screamed, long and loud, with the sound slowly diminishing to a terrible whimper. Another scrambled out for Adamson to shoot him.

"They're retiring!" Hood said. "Send them back, boys!"

The Lothians continued firing as the Germans withdrew in good order, section by section, with each group covering the next.

As the infantry contested the trenches, the tanks fought their personal battles, allowing the infantry to fight around them. One by one, the Matildas faced the more powerful Panzers, and one by one, they died.

"What the hell are these Tankies doing?" McGill asked. "They haven't got a chance."

"It's another suicide charge from our cavalry," Tulloch said.

Tulloch heard the whoosh of a passing shell and saw the explosion on the flank of the central Panzer.

"Where did that come from?" McGill asked.

Tulloch glanced over his shoulder. A line of Sherman tanks had pushed through the cleared path in the minefield and now spread out behind the Lothians and Durhams. With their thick armour and more powerful guns, they matched the German Panzers and began to fire across the intervening space.

"The Matildas were keeping the Germans occupied until the Shermans arrived," Tulloch told McGill. "They were the sacrificial bait."

McGill shook his head. "The poor buggers," he said. "The incredibly brave, poor men."

"Get your heads down, lads!" Tulloch roared.

Four Platoon obeyed at once, with Six Platoon, not yet used to their company commander, a fraction slower to react.

The Shermans formed a half-moon behind the Lothians and Durhams, firing non-stop at the Panzers and their rapidly retreating infantry support.

"Sir!" the signaller jinked past the Shermans and burning Matildas as if they did not matter. "Colonel Hume, sir! A lad from the Royal Signals was at HQ, and he fixed the radio!" He slid into Hume's trench. "It was a faulty valve, sir, and he replaced it."

"Good man," Hume said. "Did you not notice the tanks?"

"Yes, sir," the signaller replied. "They didn't fire at me. I have a message from General Freyberg, sir. He says to congratulate you on reaching your objective, and could you ensure the way is clear for the tanks to break through."

"Thank you, signaller," Hume replied. "If you could radio the general to tell them the tanks are already here, and we'll do our best."

"Yes, sir!"

The Shermans moved forward a little, fired at the Germans, shifted sideways and fired again. Tulloch had never seen so many heavy tanks firing simultaneously, with their shots crashing into the Panzers. Unused to facing tanks as powerful as themselves, the Germans were surprised by the Shermans' attack.

When the Shermans destroyed four of their number, the Panzers began a slow withdrawal, still fighting. The Shermans remained static, with one already burning fiercely and emitting thick black smoke.

"What now?" Muirhead looked weary as he emerged from his dugout. Flies clustered on the blood that had dried on his cheekbone.

"Now we edge forward," Hume replied. "We watch for mine-fields and clear the way for the tanks."

"C and D Companies take the lead," Hume ordered. "B and E Companies in support!"

The Lothians abandoned their recently scraped trenches, stepping cautiously past the burning and shattered tanks. A section of sappers joined them with their mine detectors. Oldham began to sing:

"Underneath the lantern,
By the barrack gate
Darling, I remember
The way you used to wait."

"Why are you so bloody happy?" Elliot asked caustically.

"We've won the battle," Oldham said. "The Germans are on the retreat, and we've got a score of Shermans backing us."

Elliot grunted. "We've no' won yet, Oldie."

"Near enough, Shuggie," Oldham replied and began to sing again.

They passed the tanks and their unfortunate occupants, walking through the acrid, stinking smoke with its smell of burning human flesh, and moved on, step by laboured step, towards the retreating enemy. Tulloch was between the pipers, with Cattanach on his right and the pipe corporal on his left. An occasional shell landed, mainly without any result other than further disturbing the already pitted and scarred ground.

The Sherman tanks growled and squeaked behind them. Monsters of steel, with their sloped armour and 75-millimetre guns, they seemed invulnerable as they trundled along.

"We're pushing the Germans back, sir," Hogg said.

"We are, Hogg," Tulloch agreed.

"Captain Tulloch, sir!" The runner nearly pulled at Tulloch's sleeve, eager to impart information. "Colonel Hume wants you to take a section ahead and scout that ridge, sir."

Tulloch peered ahead. Dawn was not far off, with the stars paling between the billowing smoke. He could see a rise ahead, a surprising undulation in the flat landscape, and the fact that it was visible proved that daylight was approaching.

"Give my regards to the Colonel and tell him I'll report my findings to him."

As the runner returned, Hume gave the order to halt and dig in. The Lothians obeyed, quickly hacking at the ground to create shelter. Any higher ground in this landscape was an important vantage point. If the enemy decided to make a stand, they would undoubtedly choose the ridge.

"Sergeant Drysdale, I want you, Innes, Hogg and Hood. We're going to recce that ridge in front." In times like these, Tulloch wanted his trusted veterans to accompany him.

"Yes, sir," Drysdale replied.

Leaving all surplus gear behind, Tulloch led the five-man patrol forward. They moved slowly and quietly across the now gravelly sand, with the sound of battle seeming distant on either side. Tulloch had the strange thought that, at that moment, he was probably the most forward soldier of the 8th Army, except for the SAS and the men of the Long-Range Desert Group. He glanced over his shoulder, and in the flickering flames of the burning tanks, he saw sections of Montgomery's army. The fire-light reflected from the armour of the tanks and the soldiers' steel helmets; it showed the occasional white face and gleamed from naked bayonets.

We are more visible than I realised.

When they approached, the ridge seemed higher, and Tulloch signalled for his patrol to go down. They crawled over the harsh gravel, inching towards the rise. The men moved in extended order, keeping space between them in case an enemy machine gun opened fire.

"Sir!" Hogg whispered the word and pointed to his nose.

Tulloch sniffed. Hogg was correct; he could smell tobacco. There were men smoking close by. Signalling for the others to remain where they were, Tulloch crawled forward, inching to the base of the ridge. He heard a snatch of conversation, a few words in German, and a subdued cough.

Tulloch lay still, allowing his eyes to become accustomed to the paling dark away from the torches of burning tanks. He heard faint movement, subdued conversation, and the rustle of cloth and metal striking metal—enough to tell him the enemy occupied the ridge. A shift in the cloud allowed moonlight to ghost down, reflecting on something in small patches.

Tulloch frowned, unsure what he was observing. He tried to work it out.

The wind shifted again, with the moonshine momentarily stronger.

It's a gun barrel, partly covered by camouflage netting. An 88!

Tulloch began to return, slowly moving backwards to his men. Where there was one 88, there would be more, waiting for the Allied tanks to attack.

"Back, men. The Germans have garrisoned the ridge."

"Sir," Drysdale whispered. "If the Germans have guns on the ridge, they might have more elsewhere. Rommel might have copied Monty's tactics at Alam Halfa and laid a trap for our armour."

Tulloch nodded. "You could be right, Sergeant. We'll have a decko."

The ground to the south of the ridge was featureless under the waning moon, level, and stony—perfect tank country. However, as Tulloch's men probed with their bayonets, they quickly found anti-tank mines.

"The ground's thick with them, sir," Hood said.

"They've left a narrow corridor at the base of the ridge, sir," Drysdale pointed out. "A killing ground one tank broad."

"That will be to allow their own vehicles access," Tulloch replied. "We'd better report to the colonel."

Colonel Hume listened to Tulloch's report and passed the information to HQ.

"General Montgomery wants us to break through this morning," Freyberg replied to Hume. "Push the tanks forward!"

Hume looked older when he relayed the message to his officers.

"The 88s will slaughter the tanks," Tulloch said. "We could take the guns in flank."

"I told Freyberg that," Hume replied. "They want the tanks to bypass the ridge."

Tulloch took a deep breath. "I've seen too many burning tanks for one day," he replied.

"So have we all," Colonel Hume looked infinitely weary. "We'll pick up the pieces later, gentlemen, as always."

Tulloch nodded. That was the way of the world.

The Allies fired a three-minute stonk—an intensive artillery barrage—at the ridge, and then the Shermans rolled forward, with each tank firing as they advanced.

"Can't we get more artillery on the ridge?" McGill asked.

"We've only pushed a few guns through the minefield here," Hume replied. "Most are needed elsewhere. The Durhams and the Maoris have hit trouble."

Tulloch heard the rumble of artillery in the north.

For the first few moments, the Shermans' advance was

successful. They skirted the ridge, keeping to the narrow track, and then the 88s fired. Silhouetted against the rising sun, the Shermans were an easy target, and the first three immediately burst into flames. Tulloch did not see anybody escape.

"The Germans are slaughtering us!" Rutlane's voice shook. "They've been luring us into a trap all the time."

Tulloch saw one shell hit the sloping armour of the fourth tank and ricochet off, turning over in the air as it whirled into the desert. Overtaking the fourth tank, the fifth drove wide and managed a hundred yards before it hit a mine. The explosion blew off a track, and the tank lay there with the crew baling out in rushed panic. The 88s ignored the damaged tank to concentrate on the others in the long column.

"Support the tanks!" Colonel Hume ordered. "Mortars! Fire on the ridge. Bren gunners, aim for the muzzle flares!"

The Lothians' two and three-inch mortars fired continually at the 88s while a Durham Vickers gun probed the ridge without reducing the Germans' rate of fire.

"They must be well dug in!" Tulloch said.

With shells exploding around them, the Shermans halted and hastily withdrew through the Lothians to harbour further from the 88s.

"That's a bugger," Muirhead said. "We won't move until we take these 88s out of action."

Tulloch nodded. "With our artillery busy in the north, it'll be up to us." He looked up at the ridge and felt cold dread clutch at him.

Chapter Thirty-Six

OPERATION SUPERCHARGE, EL ALAMEIN

NOVEMBER 1942

Hume was busy on the radio, talking rapidly as the Shermans retreated. When he glanced up, Tulloch had never seen him look so worried.

"General Freyberg wants us to silence the 88s," Hume said and called in his company commanders.

The sun was rising fast as the Lothians' officers assembled in the hastily prepared dugout, with the smoke from burning tanks drifting over them. Tulloch looked over the strained, tired faces, all coated with sweat-streaked dust and dirty with smoke. The men smelled of sweat, blood and high explosives, with most bearing minor wounds. Tulloch realised he had a tear in the left sleeve of his pullover, and blood had dried on his forearm. He did not recollect anything hitting him.

"The night is passing, so we'll have to attack the 88s in full daylight across open country." Hume allowed his words to sink in. "There will be casualties."

"Inevitably," Kilner said quietly.

"Tulloch," Hume continued. "You were there. Draw us a sketch map of what you saw."

Tulloch drew a rough map. "I only saw the moon reflecting on one gun barrel," he said. "But six guns fired on the Shermans."

The officers nodded. "The Germans will have infantry defending the guns," Muirhead said. "We'll have to watch for hidden machine gun nests, dugouts and trenches."

Hume made a quick plan. "Tulloch, take D Company and crest the ridge from the rear; come down on the 88s at 08.00 hours. Muirhead, you and C Company take the right flank. Kilner, you are making a diversion from the north. Bags of noise. I'll take everybody I can scrape up and go in from the front. The mortar platoon will hit them for five minutes before the attack and then switch to smoke."

"Do we have any artillery support, sir?" Kilner asked.

"I've radioed for a stonk from 07:50 until 08:00," Hume replied. "I tried to get air support, but the Desert Air Force hasn't any aircraft available. I have asked the closest Durhams to lend us their mortar platoon, though."

"That will have to do," Kilner said.

The officers were silent for a few moments, assessing the arrangements in their heads. Daylight attacks were always perilous, and with the men tired and disorganised after their exertions through the night, a morning attack against a virtually unknown German position was an unpleasant prospect.

"Gin ye daur," Hume said quietly.

"Gin ye daur," the officers echoed.

They left the dugout to return to their companies, each busy with his thoughts.

When Tulloch told his platoon leaders what was happening, McGill looked grim while Rutlane lifted his chin and breathed quickly. Tulloch thought he was controlling a panic attack.

"We'll hit them from above," Tulloch said. "We'll travel light; just personal weapons, ammunition, water bottle and field dressings. Ensure your men have spare mags for the Brens and plenty of hand grenades."

"Yes, sir," McGill said as Rutlane nodded with a sickly grin.

When the lieutenants returned to their platoons, Tulloch checked that his revolver was loaded and that he had spare ammunition.

"Are you taking a rifle as well, sir?" Hogg asked.

"Yes," Tulloch decided.

"If you don't, sir," Hogg said, "the Nazis will know you're an officer."

"That's one reason," Tulloch agreed. "A rifle also enables me to help if there is a duffy."

"Yes, sir," Hogg replied. He opened his mouth to speak but closed it again with the words unsaid.

———

TULLOCH LED D COMPANY OUT AT HALF PAST SEVEN, MOVING quickly and in extended order past the still-burning tanks. The smell of petrol and roasted human flesh was strong in the air, and Tulloch noted that even his veterans avoided looking closely at the stricken Shermans.

"Wait here," Tulloch ordered. "We'll move when the guns fire."

When the artillery began its barrage, Tulloch nodded to his platoon commanders. The guns fired quickly, hammering the area around the 88s' emplacements. More smoke and dust rose around the orange-white explosions, providing a screen for the Lothians' movements.

"Come on, D Company!" Tulloch led them at a run up the back of the ridge, sliding on the rough gravel as his men followed. The northwest side of the ridge was in deep shadow, concealing the Lothians as they scrambled and slithered their way up. Tulloch led from the front, with Four Platoon extended on his right and Six Platoon in a similar formation on his left. He glanced sideways and saw Rutlane keeping in position with Sergeant Paterson nearby.

The ridge was steeper than Tulloch expected, with a few British shells screaming over the top to explode on the north-west slopes.

"I thought the gunners were on our side," Elliot said.

"They are," Hood told him. "The bombardier knows you shagged his sister."

They ducked as a British shell exploded fifty yards away.

"I never did, Craw!" Elliot denied hotly.

"Aye, you did," Hood said. "That wee blonde one." They stepped up the slope, staring at the summit, a hard black line against the now-pale stars.

"Shiela?" Elliot sounded shocked.

"Aye, that was her name. Shiela."

"She never told me her brother was a bombardier," Elliot said, ducking as stones pattered on them from a nearby explosion.

"She told me," Hood said.

"You cannae trust anybody nowadays," Elliot shook his head.

———

THE SHELLING ROSE TO A CRESCENDO, HAMMERING THE CREST of the ridge.

Tulloch checked his watch. "Come on!" He wanted to arrive at the gun emplacements immediately after the shelling ended. He lengthened his stride and stopped at the summit. The south-east side of the ridge was a mass of exploding shells with rising dust and smoke.

"Wait!" Tulloch ordered, knowing his voice would not carry. He raised his hand. D Company halted, with the men lying on the lee side of the ridge. Tulloch motioned the platoon commanders closer.

"McGill, take Four Platoon on the right. Rutlane, take Six

Platoon on the left. Mop up everything the guns have left alive. Watch for C Company coming up the opposite side. Bayonets only! No shooting in case you hit our men!"

McGill nodded. He looked quite composed. Rutlane grinned, his eyes wild. "We won't shoot at Muirhead's men, sir." They had to shout above the noise of exploding shells.

"Watch for my signal!" Tulloch said.

He watched McGill and Rutlane return to their platoons, ducked when a shell landed close to the summit and rechecked his watch.

Time is up!

The bombardment ended as abruptly as it had started.

Tulloch raised his hand. "Now!" he shouted and rose. For a second, he was silhouetted on the skyline, with the entire eastern side of the ridge before him. He saw six 88 guns deeply entrenched in sandbagged dugouts, with smoke rising from scores of shell craters all around. The bombardment had disabled two of the guns, with one on its side among the bodies of the crew and the second on its back. The others appeared in working order, with the crews scrambling from deep dugouts to man their weapons.

"After me!" Tulloch shouted, scrambling down the slope. He glanced right and left. McGill led his Four Platoon on the right, jinking down the hill with his revolver in his hand and his men a compact line behind him. On Tulloch's left, Rutlane was shouting, pointing his pistol as he ran with Adamson at his back and the rest of Six Platoon straggling behind him. Tulloch noted that apart from Adamson, the deserters were lagging slightly.

"Gin ye daur!" Tulloch shouted.

Six Platoon reached the left-hand 88 first, with Rutlane vaulting over the thick sandbagged wall. Tulloch saw Rutlane throw himself at the foremost German, smashing his revolver into the man's face and kicking with his heavy boots.

Well done, Rutlane!

On the right, McGill's Four Platoon was a fraction slower,

arriving at their target as a compact unit with Sergeant Drysdale on the left and McGill in the centre.

Tulloch saw C Company charging up the slope in an unbroken line, with the rising sun glinting on their bayonets and Muirhead in the centre.

That was easy, Tulloch thought. An instant later, the German Spandau machine guns opened fire. One sliced into C Company, wiping out half a section before Muirhead could issue an order. The other targeted Rutlane's Six Platoon, killing two men and wounding a third.

"Cover!" Tulloch roared, knowing that advancing into concentrated machine gun fire was suicide. "Find cover!" He threw himself into a recent shell hole as the closest Spandau shifted its aim towards him. The bullets churned up the ground at the lip of the hole, throwing loose sand over him, then passed on.

Tulloch swore. The machine gunners must have deep dugouts to have survived the bombardment.

Hogg lifted his head from the sandbagged barrier of the 88, only to duck down when a burst from the Spandau ripped around him.

Tulloch swore again. The Germans had sited their machine gun nests well, with mutual support and all-around visibility, so they could defend any portion of the gun site. He lifted his head slightly to see the German artillerymen running from their dugouts to the remaining two 88s. He heard an officer give rapid orders, and both guns fired simultaneously.

"Muirhead!" Tulloch roared. "What's happening?"

"The tanks are trying the track again!" Muirhead shouted. "The 88s are firing at them!"

Tulloch grunted. The Lothians' attack had stalled, and the Germans' artillery would halt the breakthrough.

"Tulloch!" Muirhead shouted. "The Germans are mounting a counterattack! Their infantry is advancing across the plain!"

"We have to take these guns!" Tulloch shouted and raised his voice. "Sergeant Paterson!"

"Sir!" Paterson replied at once.

"How many grenades do you have?"

"Two, sir!" Paterson replied.

"Lob them at the nearest Spandau!" Tulloch shouted.

"Right, sir!"

Tulloch waited for the crump of the first grenade and raised himself from his shell hole, rifle and bayonet in hand. The second Spandau had been waiting and greeted him with a short burst that sent him tumbling back down. He felt blood running down his leg and saw a slight cut, more likely caused by a flying stone than a bullet.

The second grenade exploded, and then silence. When Tulloch cautiously raised his head, another burst of machine gun fire rattled around him. He swore loudly as a spout of sand temporarily blinded him.

"Tulloch! Are you all right? Douglas?" Muirhead sounded concerned. "Douglas?"

"I'm all right!" Tulloch replied, trying to wipe the sand from his eyes. He crouched, blinking, unable to see anything, hoping the enemy did not attempt to counterattack D Company until his vision cleared.

"It didn't work, sir!" Paterson shouted. "The grenades bounced from the dugout."

The mortar platoon was busy, landing bombs around the 88s' position. One gun fired, and then another, and Muirhead shouted again. "They're murdering the tanks! That's another gone!"

A Lothians' mortar bomb landed dangerously close to Tulloch's shell hole, nearly smothering him with a fresh shower of sand and gravel.

"Tulloch?" Muirhead shouted again.

"I'm all right. Can you send a runner to stop the mortars?" Tulloch yelled.

"I have done!" Muirhead replied. "They've got the colonel, though. I saw him fall!"

They've shot Colonel Hume!

A Spandau rattled again, although Tulloch could not see the target. Another string of mortar bombs fell, mercifully fifty yards away from Tulloch, and then silence, broken only by the regular hard crack of the 88s.

The Germans have pinned us down here and stopped our advance. I must do something, or Supercharge will fail, and Rommel will regain the initiative.

Tulloch crawled to the back of his crater and began to dig, using his bayonet to loosen the harsh gravel and his hands to shovel it away. Within a few moments, he had created a shallow depression. He had wept the worst of the sand from his eyes and could see better, although his vision remained blurred.

If I can crawl out without the Germans observing me, I might lob a grenade into the nearest machine gun nest. They are mutually supportive, so the second might get me, but Drysdale could take care of that.

Tulloch heard a hoarse yell and a chorus of cheers, and then both Spandaus rattled. The cheers ended, and a man screamed and began to moan. Tulloch guessed that either his company or Muirhead's had attempted a charge, and the Germans had driven them back.

"D Company!" Tulloch shouted. "McGill! Rutlane! Report!" He continued to slice at the gravel, slowly creating a shallow channel with a barrier between himself and the Spandaus.

"We're stuck, sir!" McGill replied at once. "The Spandaus have pinned us down."

"Me too, sir!" Rutlane's voice cracked.

"I'll need covering fire in a few moments!" Tulloch shouted and ducked as a Spandau targeted him, spraying his position. He lay prone, gasping as the bullets hammered at his makeshift barrier, chewed at the top and sent gravel and fragments of stones flying around him.

"We'll be ready, sir," McGill promised.

"The Gorgie boys are here!" Hogg roared.

"Hello! Hurrah! We are the Billy Boys!" Russell responded from Six Platoon.

Tulloch hacked out another few inches, leaving a trail of blood from his shredded fingers. He created a slight vee in his makeshift parapet and peered out. The 88s fired again, although with what effect he could not see, and the Germans in both machine gun nests looked horribly alert.

They're good soldiers, these 90th Light Infantrymen, damn them.

Tulloch scrabbled to deepen his channel and swore when his bayonet hit solid limestone. At some point in the remote past, the earth's surface had folded here, creating the geological fold of the ridge. The weather of millennia had broken the surface into loose gravel, with the original surface only eighteen inches further down. Tulloch knew he could not dig any deeper, and with the gravel shallowing ahead, he had reached his limit.

That's as far as I can go.

Tulloch took a deep breath and slowly, carefully removed a few stones from the lip of his channel to create another observation vee. He peered forward again. The situation had not changed; the Spandau nests kept the Lothians pinned down while the 88s covered the track to the west.

"What's happening, Muirhead?"

"The tanks have pulled back!" Muirhead shouted. "The German infantry are advancing over the plain, and some Panzers are on the track. Mark IV's, with portee mounted 88s."

"Right! Support me!"

Tulloch thrust his rifle through the vee, aimed at the nearest Spandau nest and fired. Without waiting to see if he had hit anybody, he leapt from his channel and charged forward, yelling, knowing he only had seconds to live.

Chapter Thirty-Seven

NOVEMBER 1942

Tulloch saw the Spandau barrel swing towards him and heard the insane chatter of the second machine gun but ran on with sixty yards to cover. Knowing his attempt was doomed, Tulloch hoped the distraction would enable McGill and Sergeant Drysdale to attack.

"Come on, boys!" the voice came from Tulloch's left. He had only covered ten yards, weaving and bobbing to put the machine gunner off his aim, when he saw Rutlane leading a charge of Six Platoon.

Rutlane's helmet bounced on the back of his head, and he thrust his revolver forward, firing until the hammer clicked on an empty chamber. Most of Six Platoon followed, with Sergeant Paterson throwing grenades one after the other.

Tulloch only had a moment to see Rutlane, and then something slammed into his leg, spinning him to the ground. He lay still, dazed, and saw McGill charge from the right, with Four

Platoon screaming and yelling behind him. The nearest Spandau fired a long burst at Six Platoon, hitting three men but miraculously missing Rutlane, who jinked like a rugby player heading for the try-line, still clicking his empty revolver.

"Come on, lads!" Tulloch saw Muirhead on the far side of the ridge, with C Company at his back, and then Kilner was also present, although Tulloch did not see from where he came.

Tulloch checked his leg, saw blood seeping from a flesh wound and stood up. The leg was painful but useable, and he limped forward. Rutlane reached the first Spandau nest and leapt inside, screaming oaths like a drunken banshee. He threw his empty revolver in the face of the closest German and grabbed at his throat as Russell headed a section of cursing men with hungry bayonets.

The German defenders tried to fight, but Six Platoon's blood was up, and they slaughtered everybody in the nest, then surged out, looking for more. McGill had led Four Platoon to the second Spandau nest and ushered out half a dozen prisoners at bayonet point.

Tulloch saw Muirhead's men take possession of the 88 batteries. The crews surrendered, walking with their hands above their heads and worried faces.

We've won! Thank God! We've taken the guns.

One group of three German infantry broke from an unseen dugout and ran to the west. Only Tulloch stood in their path, a limping officer with an empty rifle and blood running down his left leg. The Germans were panting, desperate to escape captivity.

"Halt!" Tulloch shouted the first word that came into his head. "Put your hands up!"

The first German levelled a rifle at Tulloch, evidently determined not to surrender.

"Aye, would you?" Private Adamson, bareheaded and scowling, ran forward, thrust his bayonet into the German's side, twisted and withdrew. The German screamed and crumpled, spurting blood as the other two turned on Adamson, who levelled his bayonet, snarling.

With no time to think, Tulloch stepped back and slashed with his bayonet, catching the nearest German across the arm and making him drop his rifle. The third threw his arms up in panicked surrender.

Sergeant Paterson arrived with a section, nodded to Adamson and gestured to the Germans to stand back.

"You saved my life, Adamson," Tulloch said as Sergeant Paterson ushered the prisoners away. Captain Macquarie and medical orderlies were already attending to the wounded of both sides. "Why? I stopped you deserting and handed you to the Provost Sergeant."

Adamson began to clean his bayonet, his eyes bitter in a sweat-streaked face. "Aye, sir, but you could have sent us to the Glasshouse or even had us shot for desertion." He nodded. "I'll get a medical orderly to see to your leg, sir."

"Thank you, Adamson," Tulloch said. He heard singing and saw Oldham on a stretcher singing *Lily Marlene* in English with a German prisoner carrying the upper side accompanying him in German. Hogg was crouching, holding his rifle and talking to Corporal Russell like old friends.

"Rutlane! McGill! Casualty reports!"

The platoon commanders came towards him.

"Three dead and five wounded, sir," McGill said. "I'll give a detailed report later."

"Four dead and six wounded, sir. One seriously," Rutlane reported. He looked calmer than Tulloch had ever known him.

"I saw you head that charge against the Spandau, Rutlane," Tulloch said. "I'm going to recommend you for the Military Cross."

"Thank you, sir," Rutlane said, and tears filled his eyes. He began to tremble with reaction.

"What possessed you, Rutlane?" Tulloch asked curiously. "You always seemed such a diffident, reluctant soldier until now."

Rutlane tried to hide his tears. "I had to prove myself, sir. Four Platoon is much better than mine, so I had to do something to redress the balance."

"I see," Tulloch said. "Well, you certainly did that."

"I was scared though, sir," Rutlane admitted. "Really scared."

"So were we all," Tulloch told him softly. "We all hide our fear."

———

TULLOCH GATHERED HIS THOUGHTS AS MUIRHEAD WALKED towards him, looking weary and with blood caked over his face.

"We beat them," Muirhead said, smiling.

"We did," Tulloch agreed.

To their left, the pipe major of the Argyll and Sutherland Highlanders mounted a rise and played *The Flowers of the Forest*, a lament and memorial for the dead who had sacrificed themselves to win the victory. Tulloch thought of the men from his company who had paid the ultimate price or suffered terrible wounds to break Rommel's army and knew he would never forget this moment.

"I think it was the Duke of Wellington after Waterloo who said that nothing except a battle lost can be half so melancholy as a battle won," Muirhead said softly.

"War is an obscenity, whoever wins," Tulloch said. "It's a disgusting, horrible business."

Tulloch saw Cattanach listening to the Argyll's pipe major. "Are you going to join him, Cattanach?"

"No, sir," Cattanach said. "A lone piper is more effective for a lament."

Tulloch nodded. "You know best." He listened to the notes as the piper ended the tune and tucked his pipes under his arm. The piper remained at attention for a moment and then marched away, leaving reflective silence in his wake.

"Look!" Muirhead pointed to the track below the ridge. A long line of tanks rolled along, pennants fluttering in a faint breeze as they headed inexorably west. A score of sappers were busy clearing the neighbouring minefield, and there was no sign of the enemy counterattack.

"That's a happy sight," Tulloch said.

"And look ahead," Muirhead handed over his binoculars. Away in the distance, glittering under the African sun, squadron after squadron of armoured cars roared westward to harry Rommel's retreating army. "The pursuit has begun," Muirhead said, "and to quote Monty, 'this time we will not come back!'"

"What are you gentlemen doing?" Colonel Hume appeared with a bandage like a turban around his head and his left arm in a sling. "We have a war to win! Get your men into the trucks. We're chasing the enemy out of Egypt! Benghazi next stop!"

"Glad you are alive, sir," Muirhead said.

"Move your men, Captain!" Hume repeated his order.

"Yes, sir!"

Tulloch expected the men to grouse about having to travel after fighting a battle, but they boarded the trucks without serious complaints.

"Follow the lieutenant!" Adamson shouted. "The man who charged the Spandau!" Tulloch saw Rutlane flush pink and looked away. It had taken hard work and a bloody path, but D Company had gelled at last.

"All aboard, lads!" Tulloch shouted. "Let's kick Rommel out of Egypt!"

"We'll kick the buggers right out of Africa," Hogg growled.

"The Benghazi bints are all lookers," Elliot said. "They'll be glad to see me after all these square-headed Nazis."

As they drove westward amidst long columns of Allied tanks, trucks, armoured cars and infantry, Churchill's distinctive tones sounded from the wireless, speaking about Montgomery's victory at Alamein.

"Now, this is not the end," Churchill said. "It is not even the beginning of the end. But it is, perhaps, the end of the beginning."

Tulloch peered through the thick curtain of dust that surrounded the column. He saw the sea glittering under the sun to his right, closed his eyes, and smiled. The end of the beginning would do for him.

They headed westward. After more than three years of war, they had inflicted a major defeat on a German army. There would be hard times ahead, but they had turned the corner.

Well, Amanda, how will you respond to my question?

About the Author

Born in Edinburgh, Scotland and educated at the University of Dundee, Malcolm Archibald has written in a variety of genres, from academic history to folklore, historical novels to fantasy. He won the Dundee International Book Prize with *Whales for the Wizard* in 2005 and the Society of Army Historical Research prize for Historical Military Fiction with *Blood Oath* in 2021.

Happily married for over 42 years, Malcolm has three grown children and lives outside Dundee in Scotland.

To learn more about Malcolm Archibald and discover more Next Chapter authors, visit our website at www.nextchapter.pub.

Printed in Great Britain
by Amazon